TRAPPED BY
FATE ON

RECKLESS
ROADS

NEITHER THIS, NOR THAT
Book #4

MariaLisa deMora

Edited by Hot Tree Editing

Photography: Invicta Photography

Model: Colin Ienn

Cover design: Debera Kuntz

First Published 2019

ISBN 13: 978-1-946738-23-3

DEDICATION

"Do the right thing when
no one is looking."
~Vickie Milazzo

For my friends who are straight-shooters; those who are
daring enough to tell it like it is, and have ample courage to
deal with whatever comes. The world needs more of y'all.

Contents

ACKNOWLEDGMENTS

I field a lot of questions about the somewhat awkward series title for these books, with folks wanting to understand just why NTNT exists as it does. There's no real reason, per se, more an absence of anything better to call it. Maybe it would be easier if I explained ...

When I began writing Penny and Twisted's story, back when what would eventually become Chapter Seven of *This is the Route of Twisted Pain* was all that existed of this world, there really wasn't a stated club to deal with. But when Twisted wouldn't stop talking that little story became part of a larger book, and I learned so much about him, Po'Boy, our Incoherent MC ... and their enemies.

I also learned of their allies, those friends and supporters who—even if they wore different patches—were proud to call each other brother. With the introduction of the character of Wrench, the Caddo Hobos MC came to be, and of course I already knew about the Bama Bastards, from Retro's involvement in the Rebel Wayfarers MC books.

That meant by the end of that very first full-length book, I had six diverse clubs in play, half of which featured either main characters, or potential main characters. The clubs in my books are always as prominent a character as any speaking individuals, and these were distinct in makeup, separated from each other in an assortment of ways. From officer and member personalities, or variances in protocol, bylaws, and tenets—each is an amalgamation of features from disparate real world clubs, an unequally bastardized union, as translated by someone hanging around on the outside edges.

I tried out a variety of ideas to call the series, but IMC + CoBosMC + BamaBastardsMC didn't have that catchy ring to it. At all. In frustration one night, I named the folder containing the series information "neither-this-nor-that" since that was how I thought about it.

I found I couldn't play favorites between the clubs, that would be like picking a pet book from all my babies, and I couldn't do that, either. Almost by default, that longass series moniker stuck, against every marketing instinct in my gut.

So here we are, with story number four in the series, and three main clubs are now fully represented: IMC, CoBos, and BBMC.

Retro's story takes place mainly in Alabama, which is only fair, since that's where the man is from. True to form, he's as different from Twisted and Po'Boy as Ace and Wrench are, and I fell in love with him and his inner circle of men. I hope you enjoy them, too.

Huge thanks go out to my editor, Becky Johnson, and her folks at Hot Tree Editing. I always appreciate the time and care they take with my stories. Debera Kuntz outdid herself with this cover, and I'm so pleased to be working with Christina Schellhous of Invicta Photography for the cover image.

Her image of model Colin Ienn was quite literally the inspiration for Retro's character, posted to my Facebook profile nearly four years ago by Mandi Wathey. She's a reader who requested I come up with a character to fit, sweetly asking, "Can you add him somewhere?" I did, and cast the man in Hoss' story as a brother who swoops in to save the day on his old school bike with ape hanger handlebars. He looked like such an OG, he *was* Retro.

Readers … man, you do not know the influence you can have on an author. Your encouragement can mean everything, and your emotional investment in our stories might just hand us the motivation to continue moving ahead, to keep writing. So do me a favor, the next time you read a book and love it, reach out to the author somehow and let them know. Tell 'em ML sent ya, yeah?

You never know what you might inspire.

Woofully yours,
~ML

Beginning

Jeremiah Rogers angled his body away from the other person in the room, shifted his gaze to the window, and caught sight of the reflection of his own face. Gaunt and aged in ways he hadn't been a year ago, he stared into the echo of his eyes.

Without turning, he said, "I can't offer an excuse, because there isn't one. I won't insult you by saying it never meant anything, because you know how I am. You've always known how I felt about her. She..." Here he paused, at a loss for words for so long his soon-to-be ex-wife stirred restlessly, the fabric of her jeans making a shirring noise as her legs crossed and re-crossed. The mattress groaned softly, a sound that had often been heard in this room in years past, and one that made guilt dig its hooks a little deeper into him because it had masked their lie.

Her silence drove him forwards. At this point, they'd been talking so long he was ready to just have it over with. "I knew when I took you to my bed we'd wed. Your father wouldn't have allowed anything less. I also—" He turned and saw her tear-streaked face looking at him out of the shadows. They'd been talking so long the sunset had stripped the color from the room, leaving everything in banded shades of gray and beige. He swallowed and pushed ahead, needing to have all the secrets laid bare. "I also know you didn't love me then. We've made it work all

1

these years, because neither of us wanted more." Retro shook his head. "I'm no longer content to live this way."

"What's changed?"

"You know what's changed, Wanda." She was smart, and he suspected she'd already put two-and-two together. He was done living like this, forcing himself through the days and avoiding the nights. Her lack of follow-up on her question told him he was right.

"What about our kids, Jerry? How will we tell them?"

At her words, he pulled in the deepest breath he'd taken in days, because with two sentences she'd aligned herself at his side. She knew the lay of the land. She'd always known they weren't a love match. It was one of the things that made her so bitter towards his brother Isaiah, because he'd found his love. Gone now for too many years, but Isaiah had kept his Hope's love alive in how he was raising their children. Wanda had tried to drive a rift between the brothers over it. Unsuccessfully.

"Nelda won't be surprised." Their daughter was always putting together unexpected puzzles, and from the sadness she'd borne in the past months, Jerry knew Nelda had seen how he'd been pulling away from her mother. "Boys will follow her lead." He lifted his hands and scrubbed across his face. "I never meant—"

"You're not the only one to stray, Jerry." Wanda's declaration took him by surprise and his palms were still pressed to his cheeks as he jerked and looked at her. "I haven't been happy for years."

His blood started to boil and he dropped his fists to his hips, staring down his nose at her for a moment. Then he laughed once, a humorless bark of noise meant to keep him from saying things best left unsaid, and he turned back to the window, their dimmed and blurred reflections now highlighted by a deep blackness. "Since it all happened years before you came to my bed, I wouldn't actually classify it as strayin', Wanda. Can you say they were important to you at least?" He'd had suspicions once or twice, but Wanda had been so...blameless. Every time he'd thought to bring up the idea of separating, just the look on her face would seal his lips.

"One was." She gave him that, and then he saw her reflection move, shifting to the opposite side of the bed. She slowly stood and then waited for a moment, and when he didn't turn, told the room, "I'm going to start supper."

Surreal.

He waited while she left the room, letting the door close solidly between them before he pulled out his phone. Holding it in one hand, he flipped it around and around, the sound of his fingertips across the surface a quiet rhythm of idle nervousness. From where he was standing now, it felt like he teetered on the brink, a thousand paths in front of him. It was on him to pick the right one, and he didn't have enough information. For a man who dealt in knowledge, who held truth in the highest esteem, trying to make such a decision without guidance of any kind felt like anathema.

"All right, old man. First things first." He opened the closet and took out a duffel bag. Moving quickly, efficiently, he shoved enough clothes for a few days inside and then headed to the bathroom, gathering a razor and other necessities. He planned to take up residence in the clubhouse as of tonight. A clean break felt best to him, and it wouldn't be fair to Wanda to continue to share their loveless bed, leaving the space between them cold. In his haste, he knocked over a bottle in the cabinet and jerked back even as he tried to catch it, watching as it fell to the floor, lid exploding off and clear liquid spilling across the tile. The scent of alcohol invaded the space, and he grimaced at the smell.

"Mr. Rogers, there is no real choice to be made here." Jerry stared at the doctor, not understanding. *"Her father has medical authority. Your wishes—"*

Jerry shook his head hard, hair flying back and forth. "Not my wishes. Hers. This is something we talked about because of the situation with her momma. Her father wouldn't make the decision, and she told me she didn't want to go the same way. If anything happens to me, she said, then you don't make my life end like that." He clenched his fists. "Not my wishes. I'd keep her forever, if I could. Can you tell me that she'll breathe on her own if you turn off those machines?" The doctor shook her head. "Then that's no life."

"I understand how you feel. I do. Mr. Rogers, I promise you. This is not the kind of determination a person comes to lightly, and I know that from experience." She gestured with the clipboard, drawing his attention to the motionless figure in the hospital bed. "But this isn't my decision, and unfortunately, regardless of the conversations and your recounting of her verbalized wishes, without something in writing, it isn't yours, either." She took a step backwards, the hem of her white coat wafting in the air with her movement, much as Clara's hair had waved in the wind as she rode on the back of his bike. "I'm sorry."

"Fuck." The curse burst from him as the curtains closed behind the doctor's exit. Jerry stared at Clara, trying to commit every nuance of her face to memory, just in case the other thousand memories failed him. He stepped closer, leaned his elbows on the railings of the bed, and draped his hands across her arm and shoulder. With a slow sigh, he drew restless circles on the rough fabric of the shapeless hospital gown. His speech came in a stuttering cadence, groupings of words spewing from him in an erratic fashion. "You'd hate this, baby. All of it. I know you would. Your fucking father. Everything." So much information between each of those brief statements, none of it good.

Clara's father owned the stretch of Mississippi and Louisiana where shore met the Gulf. Not the land, because that would be too easy. Her father owned the drug trade across that broad swath of two states.

She didn't know. That's the one thing her old man had demanded of Jerry when he found out they were together. He didn't want his little girl *to know her father's secrets, and Jerry understood. He hadn't told her. He also hadn't told her about his other life, so that was a double layer of guilt on him right now. "If I'd told you, would you be okay right now?"*

The painful truth was she probably would be. Clara had gotten caught up in the crossfire of one of her father's enemies, the competition trying to horn in on his territory, and she'd been hit. The bullets had spun her in a circle, blood spraying in a wide arc around her. The medical history showed she'd been "down" for sixteen minutes. Dead for more than a quarter of an hour until the CPR worked finally. It had taken two surgeries to stop the bleeding, another to take care of the bones broken by the passage of so many high-velocity slugs, and now she was here in ICU. Machines beeping all around, lights flashing, and lines charting up and down to show what was going on with her body. There was one machine that was different, though. It was the one the doctor had just explained to Jerry, the nearly flat line on the screen showed electric activity in her brain was nonexistent. Those sixteen minutes had been too long, no matter the herculean efforts of the medical personnel. Clara, his beautiful, beautiful Clara, was dead in all the ways that mattered.

He'd never hear her laugh again, never see her smile. Never feel her hands touching his face as they made love. Never experience the joy of her kisses, or the satisfaction of her pleasure. Never build a life as they'd whispered about in the safety of his bed.

Fingertips ghosting across her skin, Jerry stroked and caressed, holding on to every second with her he'd been granted. "I love you, baby. Love you so much."

Hours passed, and with an aching heart still he stood there, waiting for some change that would make this easier to bear. "God, Clara. I love you so much." Dark circles appeared on her hospital gown, salty drops pattering down in random patterns. "Everybody loves you so much. You got so many people pulling for you. Just give me a fucking sign, baby. So much love. So much."

"Retro." His club name sounded off, wrong in this setting, and he whirled to the door to see Clara's father standing there. "Say your goodbyes."

"What do you mean?" His grip tightened on the railing. "You can't kick me out. Visiting hours aren't over yet."

"They are for you. The doctor spoke to me about your adamant stance on my Clara's care." This man calling her his made him angry. His next words filled Retro's veins with ice. "You won't see her again. I can't put her at risk."

"Put her at risk?" Retro heard how his voice rose, filling the space with shouted anger and he tried to get a handle on his emotions. "It was you that put her in here like this. This is on you, old man." He turned back to the bed and stared down at the beautiful woman lying still under the sheet. "She's dead. And you did this."

"There are things at work here that you don't know." At his words Retro turned to find Petr Volkov staring at him, eyes flat and cold like a snake's. "You should let me explain."

Retro shook his head. "Don't care. Don't care about your posturing or your chess-playing. I only cared for her."

"So you're saying you do not want to know?" The man sounded astounded, as he should. Retro had developed quite the reputation for being an information hound, following stories to the ground if needed. "Then I shall tell you nothing. You've got three minutes, Retro. Use them wisely." Unflinching, the man's tone was brittle with cold. "Say your goodbyes."

"I already have." He reached out and brushed a strand of hair from Clara's cheek, tucking it behind her ear as he leaned close and kissed her lips softly, gently, reverently. She was still warm, but it was a lie. Everything in this room was a lie, because there was no real life here to prolong.

A heavy ring swung from a chain in his hand, clinking on the metal bed rail as he backed away. His promise of fidelity to her, Clara had worn the ring around her neck since the first night they'd slept together. The doctor had returned it to him earlier, and now Retro lifted it to slip the chain around his neck. "I won't forgive you for doing this to her." He turned and stared at Clara's father for a moment, then pushed past him and into the hallway. Echoes of his own footsteps chased him up the hallway, thudding faster and faster until the walls slipped past in a blur, people skittering out of his way as he raced his memories to the doors, leaving behind his heart.

Retro shook free from the grief washing through him at the years-old memory, painfully dredged up by the confrontation with Wanda. Necessary it might have been, but even now, talking circles around Clara cut him deeply. He pulled in a slow, steady breath and stooped to clean up the spill, using an old rag to soak up the pungent puddle, finishing with wide strokes. He stood, turned to the mirror, reached up to draw the chain from under his shirt. Heavy, heated from his skin, the ring twirled and swung, a lasting memento to the woman he still considered the love of his life.

Chapter One

Standing in the clubhouse, Retro watched with a beer in hand as his vice president, Rodney Brayhill, also known as Mudd, stalked towards him. The man looked pissed, which probably meant his woman had been climbing up his ass about Retro's decision to leave Wanda. And if that were the case, that meant Wanda had made a call she wasn't entitled to make, sounding an alert aimed at his brother that things had changed in his president's life.

Women, he sighed. She would have known it was a bad call, and regardless of the why of it, he'd be giving her an earful when he got home...his internal meanderings stalled out there, and he swayed in place, as if he'd been punched in the gut. He wouldn't be going home, not unless it would be to pick up Nelda or the boys for an outing. He'd made that plain to Wanda when he walked out, bag in hand, refusing her offer of a final dinner with his family.

He'd forced the issue, telling her he'd talk to the kids without her if she didn't buck up and stand beside him. They hadn't delivered quite the cohesive message he'd wanted, but it had still been better than she deserved. *Why does it hurt so fuckin' bad?*

"Before you start in on me, I had every intention of telling you when I saw you." He stared at Mudd, who'd rocked to a stop a couple of feet away. "But you been out of town working for half a month, and I didn't want it to be a text message. Plus, I didn't feel like hashing it out over the phone. So here we are, and this is me telling you, friend to friend, I've left Wanda. Kids aren't happy, but I wouldn't expect them to be." He shook his head, accepting the gesture when Mudd's hand lifted to his shoulder, squeezing tightly. "I just couldn't do it anymore, Mudd. Done? I'm so fuckin' done."

"Sorry, brother." Mudd gripped harder for a second, the hold grounding Retro in a way he needed. "Hate it came to this, but I won't be the one to ask if you're sure. I know you, and you've protected your kids from everything up to this point. You wouldn't be putting them in the line of fire if it wasn't over for you."

"Yeah, done. Just, done." He took a breath and blew it out slowly. "And now, in one of life's better little complications, my kids are upstairs, because they decided they don't wanna live with her. So I've got them parked here for a hot minute until I can figure out a better place for all of us to land. Puttin' a crimp on the brothers, but they aren't compainin'." He grinned. "*Yet.* And I know that's where we are. I've put some feelers out for a place. Ain't forever, and we all know that's truth. Regardless, my personal life doesn't impact club business. Never has, never will."

"Jesus Christ."

"Not sure Wanda even missed 'em yet, which pisses me off somethin' fierce. Settles me at the same time, because what kind of momma does that?" Retro huffed out a humorless laugh. "She's turned into a piece of work, brother."

That earned him a slow, disbelieving headshake. "Prospect," Mudd called towards the rough bar at the back of the room. "Need something with more bite than beer here. Bring me the bottle out from under the counter."

"The blue?" A disbelieving note was in the prospect's voice, and Retro smiled for a moment. It was good to question, and mostly they encouraged the trait in their prospects, few as they were. The Bama Bastards only onboarded two prospects at a time, running them through their paces for a minimum of twelve months before a vote could be offered on patching or passing, with a vote for passing only extending their trial period by a maximum of six months, thirty days at a time. After that, they were either in or out, no middle ground. Still, with the mood in the room right now, he knew exactly what Mudd would say before his VP even opened his mouth. They'd been together so long each could predict the other's reaction in most situations, and for Retro, this moment was no different.

"Yeah, the fucking blue. Yes. God *damn*, boy, you got a fuckin' death wish? Bring me the goddamn blue and two glasses." He paused, then screwed his face up as he yelled, "*Clean* glasses, you fuckin' toadstool. God, grant me patience with prospects more stupid than they need to be."

"He ain't so bad." Retro upended his beer, draining it dry. "Been keepin' me in suds all night without a word of complaint."

"And he shouldn't fuckin' complain, should he? No, he shouldn't." Mudd didn't give Retro a chance to respond, answering his own question. "Man's being given a chance to be part of the best goddamned club in fucking Alabama and he'd be stupid to complain. And if he shows his smarts and don't question the president, then he shouldn't fuckin' question me, either. I asked for something easy, giving him goddamned specific instructions, and then he had to go and ask for clarification." Mudd's voice lifted a couple of octaves, reaching a high and annoying register. "The blue? You want the blue, boss?" Voice returning to normal, he finished with a repeat of what he'd told the prospect. "Yes, the fuckin', fuckin' blue. *God*."

"You're wound tight, brother." Retro grinned at the sight of the hurrying prospect over Mudd's shoulder. With the neck of the bottle clutched tight in one hand, the man had two glasses held in his other and had lifted them up to stare at them in the light, probably verifying the cleanliness. "You put the fear of Mudd into him, though, I'll give you that."

"Tell me what the fuck is going on, and I'll un-fucking-wind." Mudd stared at him then turned away as the prospect approached with the offerings, deftly taking them from the man.

"Thought you weren't gonna give me grief over leaving Wanda?" Retro handed his empty bottle over, grinning as the prospect made a whole-hearted swipe at wiping the table fast, trying to get out of earshot before being reprimanded. "We're friends, and that gives you some leeway, but this don't sound like no grief, man."

"In Louisiana." That got Retro's full attention and he stared at Mudd as the expensive liquor was poured into the mostly clean glasses.

"What's going on in Louisiana?" He accepted the tumbler and cradled it in his hand, warming it as he waited for an answer.

"Heard IMC absorbed another riding club." Mudd settled the bottle on the table and leaned far back, hips jerking towards the edge of the seat as he kicked both feet out wide. "What do you know about that?"

Retro gave Mudd a look, deliberately raising the tension level as he took a minute to organize the multitude of details into a coherent story. He suppressed a smile, sipping at the strong scotch whisky. With things on the bubble between him and Wanda, he hadn't been keeping his fingers on the pulse of his information network quite as tightly as he normally would, but he had a pretty good idea which riding club Mudd was talking about. *Done had a little bit goin' on, but I still got it.* With a tiny smirk, he leaned back slightly, not coming close to Mudd's level of relaxation. "That'd be the Demonz Dayz, with two *Z*s." Retro rolled his eyes. "Why in the hell that crew felt the need to add that detail to their bastardized alliteration, I'll never know. Have you met their president, Romeo?" Another sip slipped past his lips and he smacked in appreciation. "This shit is fuckin' smooth, brother. Good call on the blue. So, back to Romeo." He shook his head. "Jesus fuck, why would anyone

11

want the moniker Romeo, I've no idea. Dazed is more like it, given the quality of their membership. My gut says Twisted will have his work cut out for him if he plans to keep even half of their small numbers."

"Why would he pull them in, though? That's what I don't get. Don't he have enough to deal with tryin' to keep a region with two doms in check?" Mudd sighed as he took a healthy drink, rolling the whisky around in his mouth. "Oh, hell yeah, this is the good shit."

"Incoherent and CoBos are tight, so it's not like they're livin' in a state where two clubs are battling it out." He shrugged as he laid it out for his second. "As far as pulling in the RC, why not pad the ranks just a little? I might have been more selective in which men I picked to patchover, but I know both IMC and CoBos have had a few members bail over the outed connection between Wrench and Po'Boy. From Twisted's seat, if even a few core members from DD offered enough in terms of smarts and dedication, why not? In the coming weeks, the CoBos might find an RC to do the same with, or we'll see them get more aggressive in their recruiting." He shook his head. "Have to watch that region and see how it all comes together for them."

"Just seems like a lotta work for a little bit 'o payout." Mudd yawned widely. "I know our Bastards are smaller than they are, but I still think we've got the best approach. Slow and steady, plus why would we want more than one chapter? There's just no clear benefit to what it would gain us, in my mind, at least."

Retro angled his head back, staring at the nicotine-stained ceiling tiles. "Oh, there's reasons. Broader base for income, stronger attraction for prospective members who want a larger slice of the life, more soldiers in case of a war, guaranteed safety in regions not Birmingham." He paused. "Every headache is balanced by a tick in the pro column of that list, brother. That's always the *why* when clubs go after different territories, because there's benefit in it."

"Then why haven't you ever taken the Bastards wide, boss?" Mudd tipped his head to the side, staring at Retro.

He let loose the chuckle in his throat, matching the sound with a smile. "Because I don't have those ambitions."

Mudd lifted his glass and drained it, then followed the ritual motions of pouring another three fingers of the expensive liquor before holding it out towards Retro. "Even if you don't have ambitions to be larger, I know you've taken pressure on the topic from inside and out, but you've always held firm. Why?"

Retro shook his head at the offered bottle and scanned his gaze around the room with pride. "Look around us, brother. I get what I need from the other things I do. We're small in numbers, but my God, we're far more powerful than half the clubs on the Gulf Coast. The information we field, the network we've all cultivated over the years, it all comes together and makes us an extremely valuable ally. Hell, brother, there're a dozen clubs knocking on my door any given day for a favor, a marker held, a word in someone's ear, knowledge about international movements, or a thousand other things they've thought up that we can find out for them. This means any place our men saunter in, they're the big dog. Held in respect, and that's where the very size works in our factor, because knowing how particular we are about our prospects, it's a coveted spot." He lifted his voice, yelling across the room at the man behind the bar. "Prospect, come here a minute. Bring me a beer, and get one for yourself." He sat silent while the man made his way quickly towards where he sat with Mudd. Retro reached up and took the offered beer. He angled his head at the empty seat nearby and waited until the man was seated. "Dancer, why do you want to join the Bama Bastards?"

Jim Dancer, no club name yet—that would come later once they better knew the man—stared at Retro with a dumbfounded look on his face.

Mudd laughed, and said, "Ain't no test. We were having a discussion about the club itself, and you're a good measure of what Prez here was arguing for."

Dancer flicked a glance at Mudd, then back at Retro. He took a sip from his beer and then settled more comfortably in his seat. Retro ran through what he knew about the man, matching the attitude with the info in his head. Former member of a big East Coast dominant club, his wife was from the Bessemer area, and when her parents fell ill, he'd wanted to move her home. His club wouldn't let him run a Nomad patch, so he'd dropped his center knowing what was coming, and taken his beatout. He could have been a good fit for either IMC or CoBos, but he'd picked the Bama Bastards. *My good fortune.*

"More than anything, it was the leadership that pulled me here." His tongue swiped across his top lip, and Retro saw beads of sweat still apparent. *Interesting.* The man was nervous and shouldn't be. "I heard about the club and everything I looked at said it was all true. We pull the strings on every club that is in, or borders our territory. From the outside, that looked appealing. Smaller, but still granted a place at tables folks wouldn't expect. Means it's..." He trailed off and stared at Retro.

"Say it. I think I know where you're goin', brother." Prospects were given that title if they'd earned it, and with his willingness to sit down for a frank discussion eleven months into his trial run, Dancer had more than gotten trust from Retro.

"Before Lauren's mom got bad, when we were still back in Philly, I got pulled into a beef. My MC went to war with another big club, and I couldn't go anywhere without worrying about takin' a cap. That itch never really goes away when it's bad like that. Walkin' down the street, my little girl in my arms, muscles in my back twitching on my spine, waiting for the bullet. I didn't want that. Don't want that." He shook his head. "Even before she asked to move home to care for family, I'd decided I'd pick my time to get out. Club hadn't earned my loyalty, but I gave it as long as I wore their colors. Gave it unearned, and you know what that can do to a man's head. Fuck, man, they wouldn't even pay for funerals for deaths bought in that war. Still, I gave it."

He shrugged and tipped the bottle up, pulling hard at the liquid, Adam's apple bobbing deep in his neck. "Had a chance to make a change, wanted it to be a change worth living for. Our Bastards are...respected isn't even the right word. Held in awe. BBMC won't be in a war unless it's righteous, and from how the club acts with its members, there's no way family would be hung out to dry if the worst happened. I wanted the Bastards because we stand for the best in what a club should be. This is the ideal, brother...*Prez*. And now, seeing it from the inside? It's so much more than I knew. This right here?" He lifted his bottle and pointed around the room, walls covered in pictures that spanned the gamut from current and past members, family parties, children's graduation portraits, candid images of members and old ladies, to legendary bike events the club had attended. "Every day each member is surrounded by memories of what's come before, and know they are expected to live up to that no matter what comes. History runs deep here, and it matters, man. That's why I wanted the Bama Bastards for myself. Because the club matters in ways other men won't ever know."

"Fuck, yeah," Retro muttered, one corner of his mouth curling. "Shoulda been taping that shit, would make a hella recruitment video."

"Like you'd have to recruit," Mudd drawled as he shook his head.

Retro scanned the room, pride holding his head high as he took in everything he'd made through the years. A clubhouse for a self-sustaining club that didn't owe shit to larger entities, so any war he pulled was his, and there'd be no fuckin' way family would be cut down in a goddamned drive-by.

Clara's face flashed in his mind and he held tight to her smile, how her eyes had shone for him.

"It's a goddamned good world to live in. We got everything we could want right here." He held his bottle out and waited for the matching motion from the other two men before he continued. "Here's to us, because we got this tiger by the damned tail, and we're exactly where we want to be. We're from Bama, and we are Bastards. Do *not* fuck with us."

Mudd and Dancer clicked their drinks against his and Retro drank deeply, eyes shining as he toasted his brothers.

Hours later, there was a party rolling hard and loud through the building and Retro had given up any hope of sleep until it cleared. Not that he wanted to hide away, but this still felt unfamiliar, a situation he hadn't known before, a thousand possibilities in knowing Wanda wasn't waiting for him upstairs in his room. But there wasn't anything here he wanted, not like that. Not in his bed, or his arms, because this was club, and club had always meant monogamy and restraint. He shook his head then flipped hair over his shoulder in a practiced move

Everything was still so strange, and by the time yet a third party-doll approached him with an offer, he was so frustrated with his own mind, she'd earned the rough side of his tongue. Just because he'd separated from his old lady didn't mean he was up for grabs, and the woman been firmly instructed to pass along the news that their attention was not only not welcome, but could earn them banishment. She'd blanched and backed away, lips trembling as she offered her "Sorry, Retro" mixed in with a dozen other words he didn't care to hear.

Noise from outside caught at his attention and he listened to what sounded like a half a dozen bikes pull into the clubhouse lot. Scanning the room again, he didn't note any group of brothers missing that'd be arriving late, just single numbers who couldn't make the party due to family obligations. He lifted his hand to his mouth and cut through the raucous sound with a shrill whistle that only had one meaning. Attention, and immediately from every man in the room, gazes were locked on him and hands on weapons.

"Visitors," he called out and pointed to the door. Mudd was seated on a couch and they locked eyes as several members moved towards the front of the building.

A pounding knock solidified the knot in his gut because members didn't do that, which meant whatever had come calling would be business. He walked towards the front door as Mudd levered himself upright, and was glad neither of them had continued with the hard liquor past the conversation with Dancer earlier.

The door opened before any of his men could get to it and he recognized a voice raised in laughter that eased the tension in his muscles. "I'm telling you, I do not have to knock. Retro told me more than once I've got an open invitation." That was a female voice, belonging to one tiny, red-headed dynamo.

"Woman, it's called common courtesy. Look it up." Those words weren't from anyone he could identify, but that was revealed by the next voice, one he was well familiar with as Twisted laughed and said, "Wildman, when has my Shiny Penny ever given you thought that she owned a courteous bone in her body?"

"Welcome to our friends from Incoherent," Retro shouted, and saw smiles on every face turned to the door, ready to see the new arrivals now that their identity was known. "Bring the show on inside now, wouldja? You're lettin' out the cold air and I don't wanna miss a minute of your comedy act."

A moment later, he saw his friends walking towards him, pleased when he noted the party-dolls present were quickly fading to the outskirts of the crowd. With guests, and a proper old lady in their midst, that was the appropriate response, and this action showed the measure of their respect for his club. *Everywhere I look, respect.*

Hand out, he greeted Twisted first, as was right, fists clasped between them pulling close so they could pound shoulders with their other hands. Retro reared back and stared into the man's face, trying to read his features for an idea of what brought him here, nearly five hours from home. Relaxed and easy, Twisted's expression didn't give any indication of alarm, which let Retro breathe deep, rocking back on his heels. "Brother," he said, giving a final squeeze of Twisted's hand before he greeted Wildman. A full member now, there was talk that he was being groomed for office, even if there wasn't an opening at the moment. "Wildman," he said, repeating an abbreviated version of the clasp he'd held with Twisted. The other men he didn't know by face, shaking hands and slotting each nameplate into his memory for later classification.

Finally, last in line as protocol demanded, he turned to the lone woman in the mix, her head barely coming to Twisted's shoulder. She reached up, waving every finger she owned, demanding, "Gimme some lovin', Retro." With a broad grin, Retro leaned in close and she locked her hands behind his neck as he wrapped her in his arms and carefully lifted until he could swing her feet back and forth, mindful of the precious cargo she carried.

"Penny, Penny, Penny. You are a sight for sore eyes, gal." He gave her a renewed squeeze, holding it until she pretended to wheeze. "Good to see you all," he said, setting her back on her booted feet. The support patch on the front of her vest said she'd ridden her own bike over, which further underscored the fact this was a simple social call. Twisted would never have risked her otherwise, not pregnant as she was. As if she could read his thoughts, she reached to cover the curve of her belly with the palm of one hand, the other already resting safely in her old man's grip. "Incoherent, be welcome," he called, then spoke to a prospect he knew would be standing just behind him, waiting for instructions as he'd been trained. "Buzzkill, get our guests whatever they desire. Find out from the lady what she'd prefer, too." That went against protocol, because women wouldn't typically be served from the hand of a Bastard, but when Penny went against most tenets without a second thought, he just couldn't see the sense of making her step the twenty strides to get her own water or juice. In the quiet hum of conversation surrounding them he waited a moment, then tipped his head to Twisted. "Wanna cop a squat inside or out?"

"Inside is good, like you said, you got the air on, brother. It was plenty hot on our ride up." Penny leaned sideways against Twisted as he spoke, and he dipped his chin to press a kiss against the top of her head. "Thanks much for the hospitality. I know we didn't offer any warning."

"Friends don't hafta call, you know that." Retro turned and led the way to a grouping of couches and chairs that would suit for this visit. If Twisted had come on business, they'd be in the office instead, but he'd made it plain enough this was pleasure only. "Was it a good run up? It's evening already, y'all need beds for the night?" He counted the IMC members, and made a mental note to have the prospects bunk up if needed.

"Naw, we've got enough time to jaw for a while and still make it home before too late, old man."

Penny snorted a laugh. "And I have a shield on my helmet now, so I don't mind the bugs too much."

"Begs the question why you only just wised up, woman." Retro gestured towards the available seats, taking his pick of them. He knew no one would sit until he did, because that too was protocol. "You've surely eaten your fair share of lovebugs." He referenced the dreaded swarms of flying insects that plagued the Gulf coast twice a year. "They hatch, they fuck, they splat."

"And they taste like shit," Wildman offered as he followed Twisted's lead, sitting in the final single chair, leaving the three lower-ranked IMC members to crowd together on the couch. That right there backed up the info Retro had and he hid a smile. Now, how to turn the data to his benefit, either directly or by reinforcing the seeming mysticism of his knowledge.

"Soooo." He drawled the word out long and let it hang there in the air between them, knowing Twisted and Penny would be impervious to his normal tactics. Sure enough, they sat quiet and after about seventy seconds, Wildman was the one who broke the silence.

"So, what?" Retro studied him, noting how the man attempted to curb his impatience, leaving only his question to relay how he really felt at being left hanging. "What's the Bastards been up to?"

"This and that." Retro shrugged and lifted one hand, reaching out to accept the beer from the prospect approaching from the rear. Wildman's eyes widened, then narrowed as he considered something.

"How did he do that?" one of the couch-bound IMC muttered to the member seated to his left. Twisted cleared his throat, and that single sound let Retro know these men had been coached hard about how to behave here in this clubhouse. The speaker blanched at the quiet reprimand from his national president and Retro upped the anxiety building over the small group by openly studying the three men.

"How do you feel about a change in leadership?" Twisted opened his mouth but Retro held up a hand, staying his response. "In general terms, not IMC specifically." The captive student gawped at him, mouth open like a carp on a hook. "Say, in the CoBos. Generally." The man shook his head, lips pressed to a white slash across his face. "Say in the president office of the CoBos. Specifically. Vote is comin' up fast." He gave the troublemaker relief, turning his attention to Twisted instead. "Ace made it clear last year, he won't be in the hopper going forwards. Money is on Wrench to take up the mantle."

"Money would be smart to drop on that spot of the wheel." Twisted spoke slowly as he nodded once, a shallow dip of his chin that would have been easy to miss. This clearly wasn't an easy topic for him, and Penny reflected that, her hand lifting to stroke his arm in a soothing gesture.

Retro considered his words a moment, figured he'd only get one shot at this, so asked the most critical question: "What will IMC do?" Twisted's head tipped sideways in a silent question as he stared at Retro. "Nat VP and President of friendly but separate MC should be close friends, but you're in a unique situation, as far as I know." Penny grinned and he nodded at her. "And I know a lot about a lot, and maybe more than you do about this one. You okay continuing to have this conversation here?" In other words, Retro was asking if all the people Twisted brought with him of the same mind, and trustworthy with whatever Retro might say.

"I already know what'll happen in both clubs." Twisted's mouth shifted sideways in a tight grimace. "Don't like it, but talked it through with all interested parties." That meant first he and Ace had a confab, and then Twisted had likely directed an open discussion with Po'Boy and maybe Wrench after the two long-time leaders of the two clubs had come to an agreement. "What do you think we decided? I see your brain workin' overtime behind your eyes, go on and spit it out."

"Ace steps down, gives over the president plate, Wrench takes it up and you lose your National VP to the CoBos, Po'Boy gracefully dropping his patches to head over to the other side of the line." Retro shook his head. "Not a lotta secrets in that batch of info, brother. Hate to break it to you, but some of us seen this coming from before you sent the two of them out to El Paso."

"How so, old man?" That was the second time he'd been called that in a handful of minutes and Retro found it rankled somewhat, but he shoved that to the side. *I'm not that old.*

"They've worked well together for a while now. Even our Penny girl saw it when she led us all to your rescue." That was a direct dig at Twisted, since Retro knew it still tore at the man to be reminded he'd put himself into a position of needing rescue. "Oil and water sometimes, but still, they got shit done."

Hand on Twisted's shoulder, Penny leaned forwards as she said, "More than a year in the past, and I wouldn't say they worked well on that run, Retro." She'd delivered a quiet chide, and Retro offered her a tip of his chin in respect. Her old man was hers to defend, even in small ways.

"Yeah, but they got shit done." He restated what he'd just laid out, and she nodded. "As they did in El Paso. Sometimes knowing the who is just as important as the why, and they brought us that. So you're gonna let him patch over? Easy peasy?"

"Won't be putting him through a gauntlet or a beatout. I'll let him go with deep regrets, but the rest is up to him. Have it on good authority that CoBos will not bar his entrance, which is good for him, and me since it puts off decisions I ain't ready to make yet. I don't want to combine the clubs." Twisted held up his hands, palms out. "And before you say anything, that ain't anything I've even said to Ace, so I don't wanna hear it from him later." Twisted tipped his head, giving Penny a stern glare. She made a tiny "eeep" sound and jolted, but didn't move to further interrupt her old man. He looked back at Retro. "I don't want to onboard any additional big challenges right now, but I can't stomach having my inner circle be someone else's inner circle, too."

"How's that gonna work? You've been ride or die with the man for as long as I've known you. Literally."

Twisted shrugged and put his hands around Penny's waist, lifting her from the arm of the chair and into his lap. "Same as it's been the past six months. Same as it does between you and me. A relationship worth having is worth working at, brother. Clubs are already tight. This will not change our associations one iota." He let Penny wind her fingers through his, pulling his palm flat on her belly. Retro watched as Twisted's mouth slid sideways into a small smile. Then he angled his head down and murmured, "Active tonight, little momma." Penny nodded. "Hey, buddy." Twisted crooned softly, "How you doin' in there?"

Retro watched the tender moment, throat tightening by the second. This underscored something he'd learned months ago, and the reason behind his split with Wanda, finally. "I didn't get that, you know?" He clipped his lips tight together an instant too late, seeing both Penny and Twisted's faces turning to look at him.

"The fuck you mean?" Twisted asked his question slowly, tentatively. "I saw Wanda carryin' all three of your kids. You were there, man."

Penny studied him, and he was reminded again of how intelligent she was, that trait first identified by her uncle who had crowed over her like she was the second coming. So fuckin' smart she could put a mental puzzle together faster than nearly anyone else Retro knew, and his concern grew when she frowned, a line between her brows furrowing deeply. "Leave it, Twisted," she said, earning her a glare from her old man.

"You seriously sayin' that to me?" Twisted's voice was shocked, gruff with some emotion Retro didn't even try to catalog.

"As a heart attack." Penny straightened and looked over Retro's shoulder. "Retro, could you ask your prospect to get me another juice?" She knew better than to try and order anyone around in a clubhouse. *Except her own old man*, Retro thought wryly.

"Scrub, get the lady a juice and bring back another round of beers."

That set the tone for the next thirty minutes or so, before everything fell into an uproar.

Twisted was holding forth on a story about a rally in Florida, the first since Retro'd had a member killed there, tracing back through all the security he'd required before he felt comfortable with his men going back when the prospect stationed by the door called out, "Prez." That was reserved for emergencies, otherwise those men didn't have a voice in a gathering like this. Retro held up a hand to pause Twisted and turned in his chair to find Dancer standing in the open doorway, one hand gripping the edge of the opening, straining to contain whatever had approached their clubhouse from the front lot.

"Gimme just a minute," he muttered, rising to his feet. Before he got a dozen steps towards the door, he heard a woman complaining outside and stiffened his shoulders, clipping out a brusque, "Fuck me," as he recognized the voice. Reaching out for the door, he wrenched it from the prospect's grip, opening it wide as he stepped into the breach. "Rebekka, what the *fuck* are you doing here?"

"Real nice, Jerry. Nice way to talk to your baby sister." Rebekka Rogers, youngest of the four siblings, stood just outside the clubhouse, holding to the entry like it was the only thing keeping her upright. *Probably is.* That ran through his head and then he rebuked himself for the uncharitable bent of his thoughts. Since she was old enough to leave the nest, she'd done nothing but chase trouble wherever she could find it. She only ever came home when she'd gotten in too deep somewhere and needed saving. "A 'how are you' would be nice once in a while."

"Are you crazy? Why are you here? You ain't gettin' no more money from me." She had to know that even without it being stated, but he wanted to make sure it was crystal for her. "Been there, done that, and every. Single. Time...you're still in the shit at the end of the day." With his teeth aching from the force of his clenched jaw, he stared at her. "You are a woman grown, Rebekka. At some point, you're gonna have to act like it." She blinked fast, and he saw the shine of tears in her eyes. That was new, because Rebekka didn't care enough to react to being ripped a new one. "And if you think tears are gonna work on me, you should talk to Nelda. She'd tell you it's never a good move. Go somewhere else to straighten up." He shifted and had started to close the door when he looked at her, really looked and saw something he'd never expected.

All the sass had fallen away, her expression stark and pained as she stared up into his face. He could see she was wrestling with something, so he paused and gave her a chance. "I did this." Her voice was soft, broken into shards of pain, and he saw ripples from an ugly emotion chase across her features. "I bought this. I'm sorry, Jerry. Sorrier than you could ever know. I'm just..." Her words trailed off and she turned away, giving him her back. The shirt she wore was stained in a distinct pattern across her shoulders and he lunged forwards, hand tight around her bicep to turn her to face him.

"Who marked you?" His second thought fell from his mouth without meaning to. "What did you do?" His little sister had gotten into a similar kind of shit before that put her in the hospital. Then, after she'd regained consciousness, she'd promised all of them, him, Isaiah, and their sister, Miriam, that she'd learned her lesson. It had been nearly a decade, but he supposed even a painful lesson like that one could fall away given enough time and distance. "Bekka, who took a lash to your back?" There was the sound of chairs moving across the floor inside, and he turned his head to see a determined-looking Penny parting the crowd as she headed his way. Undeterred by his deep scowl, she pushed around him and pulled Bekka into her arms.

"Get us a room, Retro." When he didn't move, she frowned at him, her severe expression belying her soft voice when she added, "Please."

Ten minutes later, he was standing in the upstairs hallway staring at a closed door, listening to his baby sister crying her eyes out, Penny's soft murmurs punctuating the sharper sounds of pain from cleaning Bekka's wounds. Twisted had propped beside him in the same position. It took a moment, but he bumped Retro's shoulder and sighed. "Gonna be a bit." He straightened and looked Retro in the face. "Let's go have a chat."

"Naw, brother. I wanna make sure she's okay." Retro didn't stir, staring fixedly at the door. She'd never cried like that before, not that he'd seen. *Not that I've seen her around much in the past couple of years.* Bekka had fallen off the map for most of the family about the time Isaiah's wife died, leaving him a single parent of a young boy and newborn girl. Their brother's problems had felt more real when measured against whatever brand of shit Bekka had been stirring at the time. *I should know what's going on.* He was the info master, after all. Why wouldn't he have thought to set an ear towards his wayward sister? He shook his head, disgusted with himself.

25

"Penny's got her. You know that's truth, Retro. Penny's got her and from the sound of it, they're bonding hard and fast." Twisted paused, and then with a sly grin asked softly, "Can we take you up on those rooms, man? I'm guessing we won't be ridin' out anytime soon. Come on, let's go back down. Then, you can order everyone around. I'm hungry and you ain't even offered me a bite to eat yet. Let's see what your prospects can rustle up."

Back in the main room of the clubhouse, Retro was surprised to see the makeup of the party had changed entirely. The club whores were totally gone, or at least out of sight, and a full dozen ole ladies were present. Then he heard a voice that shouldn't have been there and scowled, head whipping around to see Wanda trying to hold court at the bar. The only person close enough for her to talk to was Buzzkill, still manning the bar, bound by his prospect duty to the area. "God fucking hell."

"Oh, yeah. We never got to that topic earlier, did we?" He turned to stare at Twisted, who shook his head, surprise and sympathy warring for space on his expression. "The fuck is she doin' here, brother? If what we heard was truth, she shouldn't be here, and sure as fuck should *not* be sporting that." Retro followed Twisted's finger to see what he should have caught at first glance. Wanda was wearing her First Lady vest.

"Fuck. I didn't collect that when I walked out. Didn't even cross my mind then or since. I packed a bag, made her tell the kids, and then I left. I haven't seen her since, not even when I picked up the kids after they sat through a party behind a closed and locked door." He pulled in a hard breath through his nose, shoulders lifting and falling with the sigh that followed. "This is gonna get ugly."

"Ugly don't bother me none." Twisted shrugged. "Won't bother my boys, either. It's BBMC business, and I personally do *not* give a shit at fuckin' all, because all of this is waa-aaa-aay fucking overdue." Retro cut his harsh laughter off abruptly, and sliced his eyes to Twisted who shrugged again. "I *like* you, Jerry. Love you, brother. We're friends, have been a long time. She ain't never been no good for you, and anybody who had eyes could see it. Never was sure why you put up with her bullshit for so long, but that was between you and your woman."

Retro paused and stared because he didn't know what Twisted was referring to, and gave voice to that confusion with his, "What the fuck are you talking about?"

"I woulda split her tongue, if she talked out of both sides of her mouth about me the way she has you." Retro's muscles tensed as Twisted continued. "Show the world exactly how she was. My Shiny Penny? She ain't no fan of Wanda, and my woman has shared a *lot* of shit that goes down in the side meetings the ole ladies have. Penny likes a lotta people. Good people, bad people, but one she doesn't like? Your ole lady."

"Ex-ole lady." Retro swallowed the bile crawling up the back of his throat from the confirmation of his worst expectations brought to fruition, then for the second time in a single night whistled loudly, pulling all attention in the room to him, conversations quickly falling silent. He didn't mince words, because she should have known better. "Wanda, leave the vest on the bar as you leave." The order was direct and didn't open the door for questions about what he expected to happen. He wasn't concerned with embarrassing her, because as far as he was concerned, she'd already done that to herself by showing up here at all. "That's club property, and you aren't club anymore."

"Can I talk to you?" She slowly climbed to her feet, standing tall beside the stool. "Privately?"

"No." He cut it off at a single syllable and didn't give her another word, didn't release her from the death glare he directed her way. She should know he didn't play games when it came to the club. After all, they'd been together long enough.

"You wanna do this now? Here?" She rocked back on a high heel, hand coming up to cover her heart as if he'd wounded her. *Oh, yeah.* This was what he'd expected when he'd walked out, and now her quick acceptance was called into question. *I shoulda known it was too good to be true.* "Jerry, please."

"How many times you step out on me?" He held up a hand and flicked up a finger. "You said one mattered to you, so how many were there that didn't do anything except stir your betrayal?" He flicked up two more fingers. "Two? Three?" Another finger followed. "More?"

"You said you did it too." Her shout racketed around the room.

Rage and shame rolled through him. He shook his head, and his roar matched her anger, rocking the rafters because he was the one laying her betrayal out for his whole club to see, a festering wound that needed to be lanced, but knowing it was necessary didn't mean it didn't hurt. "*No.* Woman, no. Ain't fucked you in more than a year, my choice, I might add. But, I've been faithful to you from the time I put a ring on your goddamned finger."

"Your body, maybe. Your heart is another matter." She swallowed hard, tears flowing down her cheeks now. He didn't doubt she was wounded in some way, because there was an answering ache in his heart. A body didn't close the door on something they'd shared this long together without feeling pain.

"So now you've put yourself in competition with a dead woman? I didn't hide Clara. I took you to her grave before we wed, and that was long before I put a patch on your back." He shook his head. "Leave the vest on the bar, Wanda. Do yourself a favor and go now before this gets any worse for you."

"For me? How do you think your men feel seeing this go down in the clubhouse?"

"Oh, I've no doubt they feel something. Regret that I've got to put up with this here, when you and me already done this in private like it shoulda been done. Loss, because their queen has been dethroned. Fear, and that'll be the most of it, because you're showing them that even one such as you can't be trusted." He shook his head. "Embarrassment for me, but this shit cannot stand, woman. You put yourself in a corner by slipping leather on your back that you got no claim to anymore, and showing up at a place where you don't belong. And why? Why would you come here tonight? What the fuck did you hope to gain, Wanda?"

"I want you back, Jerry. I can't let you tear our family apart like this."

"You talk to the kids today? I did. And yesterday. And the day before. They told me you had a man over the next night after I left. Had a party three nights later that scared the pants off Jimmy. He's still having bad dreams. You talk to them since I walked outta that house?" Might as well expose all his dirty laundry to the club. She was doing such a bang-up job of it on her own, Retro might as well jump in the ring, too. "That don't sound like reconciliation actions to me. Kids are good, though. I talked 'em through it, made them understand that with me out of that house, it was up to you to behave the way you felt was necessary. Told them that their momma wasn't a whore, and mind you—that was their word, not mine." She flinched at that and he nodded. "Yeah, sucks that I gotta defend you to my kids."

"*Our* kids."

"Are they? Are they our kids? Where are they? Do you even know? I do. I can tell you." He lifted a finger and pointed upstairs. "They're in my suite upstairs, playing video games and eatin' pizza. Called me mid-morning fuckin' *days* ago, told me they don't want to live with you after all. So now I got shit to deal with and it's your business, but you showing here and not even knowing they aren't at home? That don't look good for you, hon. Now—" He took a deliberate breath as he leaned forwards and put his fists firmly on each hip. "—get the *fuck* outta my house, because make no mistake, this clubhouse is mine. The club is mine. And those kids? They're mine, too."

With jerky movements, she slid the vest off her shoulders, folding it over one arm as she smoothed the leather with the palm of a hand. He thought for a moment that she might defy him and try to take it with her, but finally, she rested it gently on the bar top. Wordlessly, she stepped towards where he stood, and he shook his head vehemently, hair flying around his face, stinging his cheeks. She looked like she'd been slapped, cheeks pale and shining with the wet that kept flowing from her eyes. Then slowly, she turned and walked through the body-lined aisle that appeared before her towards the door, head down, shoulders slumped. Defeated. He knew it was a ruse, though, and waited, certain it wasn't done with yet.

Sure enough, just before she opened the door, she paused.

"Here we go," he muttered on a sigh, waiting. Twisted made a muffled sound next to him, but Retro kept his attention on the woman he hoped would be walking out of his life sooner rather than later. *She's gonna try one last thing.*

She didn't disappoint. "I love you, Jerry Rogers."

"Woman, you told me that you weren't happy in our 'loveless marriage' so do not think to pull that bullshit just because you have an audience." He straightened his neck, chin lifting high as he looked around the room, seeing nothing but support on every face, even from the ole ladies she'd ruled for so long. "Go home, Wanda. Go home and please, for the love of God, please try to sort out what you really want from your life."

It wasn't lost on him that he'd shared very nearly the same message with his sister not an hour earlier. Retro stared at the closed door for a solid minute, sounds in the room slowly recovering from the unwanted drama.

"Mudd," he called out and his VP yelled back a simple, "Yo?" Retro tipped his head toward the vest Wanda had left behind. "Secure that, wouldja? Lock that motherfucker up tight, as I do not see it being put to use at any time in the foreseeable future." He scanned the room, catching head tips and chin lifts from every man, and mouthed "I'm sorrys" from the women. Swallowing painfully, he nodded, flipped his hair back over his shoulder and held out his arms to either side. "Welcome to my life, brothers and sisters. Shit gets deep, then we pull ourselves out and clean it off. That's where I am right now, and it pleases me to see your support. Love alla y'all. Me and my kids gonna need that going forwards." He looked around the room again, meeting each set of eyes with a direct gaze. "Thank you."

The air filled with "no worries" and "you got it, brother" and "club, man, it's what we do" and each supportive utterance gave him a greater satisfaction and pleasure.

"You good, brother?" Twisted asked the question and Retro turned to him.

"Fuckin' serene, man. I'm good." He nodded. "Oh, yeah. I'm good."

"Beer?" Mudd held out a bottle and Retro accepted it. "She came in the back door while you were upstairs. I didn't see her until she was already parked at the bar, brother. Or I'd've dealt with her and told you later." He tipped his head side to side. "Maybe it's best this way. Public statement sets all the wagging tongues to rest, and now every member knows to turn her away if she dares show her face here again. That was a definite put-down, and you made it clear this is final. Shouldn't be any issues or questions in the future."

"Oh, yeah. I put a pin in it, for sure." Retro laughed humorlessly, the sound falling flat. "She cannot mistake me after that little encounter."

"You knew she stepped out on you?" Twisted's question seemed to slip out and he shook his head. "Sorry, man. Not my place to question you on shit like that."

"No, it's okay. We're all friends here." Retro grimaced. "Yeah, I knew. Kinda, at least. I'd heard rumors for a while, and then when I told her I was done, she confirmed it for me. Seemed to want to draw her own line in the sand, and I thought that was good, that it meant she was as done with this farce as I have been."

"You think your kids know?" Twisted shook his head. "You know all about my raisin', and everything that came from that shitshow. It's not a bad thing for kids to learn their parents are fallible, perfection is a hard model to follow, you know? How you handle this will give them more guidance on how life works than anything else possibly could. You can't turn away from those hard conversations, though."

"Anything about me say that I turn away from anything just because it's hard?" Retro gave him a half smile, seeing the glint of amusement in Mudd's eyes.

"Prez here ain't shy about any fuckin' thing, brother." Twisted laughed when Mudd put in his two-cents worth. "Learned that a long fuckin' time ago."

"True words," Twisted allowed. Then his gaze shifted to the stairs and sharpened, and Retro turned to see Nelda standing there. "Your girl's lookin' for ya."

"I see that," he said, already walking towards the stairs she was now descending. "What's up, baby girl?"

Nelda was fifteen, his oldest, and smarter than any child had a right to be. She was also entirely enamored with a man currently on the tail-end of his prospect period. Knowing she was his president's daughter and her tender age, Buzzkill hadn't behaved with anything other than strict appropriateness, but even before the current mess with Wanda, Retro had decided to get Nelda out of town for a while.

Twisted and Penny had offered to foster her for the summer, and plans were to haul her and her bags down to Twisted's house next weekend. She was excited about the chance to get closer to Penny, someone she'd heard stories about for a long time. Retro was expecting her to want to stay in Birmingham now that he'd split from her mother, figuring she'd try to care for her younger brothers, but they needed to learn how to cope with the change, just like she did.

"Daddy." She stopped there, brow furrowed with an expression of unease. "I heard Aunt Bekka talking."

Fuck. Serious shitshow tonight. "Yeah? She's upstairs right now. Penny and Twisted came to town, and Penny's with her."

He waited, but she held her silence close, lips trembling as she tried to bring her emotions under control. This was about more than whatever she'd heard Bekka say. Something told him she'd been present for the showdown with her mother, and her next words proved that true.

"Is Mom okay?" Blinking fast, she was fighting true tears of pain, unlike Wanda's parody earlier.

"She will be." He held there, giving her space to ask whatever else was troubling her.

"Who's Clara?"

He hadn't expected that punch to the gut, and the love of his life's name on his daughter's lips wasn't something he could ever have prepared for. Chin to his shoulder, he turned away and roughly cleared his suddenly clogged throat. "I—I…" He couldn't go on, couldn't put words to anything that was in his head right then, and in his heart, he cursed Wanda for making him appear so weak in front of his girl.

"Oh, Daddy." Then Nelda's arms were around his waist, her face buried in his chest as she sobbed. "Why would Mom try to hurt you with something that matters so much?"

Wrapping her up tightly, he held her close, rocking them slowly side to side. After a few moments, he struggled to clear his throat again, finally croaking out a broken, "I don't know, baby girl. Maybe because I hurt your mom? I didn't mean to. I never meant to. I just cain't…like I told you kids, I just cain't anymore. I've give all I can. Give until I'm empty for her. I'm sorry."

"What are you sorry for, Daddy?" Nelda pushed back and glared up at him, reddened eyes ringed with clumped and wet lashes, but her gaze flashed with anger. "You didn't do anything. Anything. If what I heard was true, then she went into the arrangement with you with her eyes wide open. She's the one who wasn't satisfied, and she's the one who's cast shame on herself. Not you. Never you. You don't have anything to be sorry for. Me and the boys, we'll be okay. Because we got you, and you'll break yourself into pieces to make sure that's the way it goes." She paused and her arms tightened while he stared down at her, astonished at the words flowing from his little girl's heart. "Well, won't you?" He nodded, and she gave him a shake, rattling her own bones in the process. "Then it'll be okay. Sure, it's not right now, but it will be. But her doing that to you?" Nelda's head flew back and forth, hair just like his, a cloud around her face, his eyes in her face angry as they stared up at him. "That's not okay and won't ever be okay. She's wrong, Daddy, and that's not me sayin' that because you're my favorite." She rolled her eyes slightly and sniffed as she choked on a tiny laugh. "Which you totally are. But that's not the point."

"What is the point, baby girl?" His voice was rough, raw, but filled with strength and pride, because this girl in front of him was his. *I made this*, he thought with awe. "Because sure as shit, you got one. I know you do."

"The point is…" She tossed her head again, taking a step backwards, her arms falling away finally, "You're awesome, and right now, she's not acting like a grown person should. That's on her, not you, so don't you say you're sorry for something that doesn't sit on your doorstep. That's not you, that's her. Me and the boys? We know it." She gestured towards the room behind them, an open space surrounding this encounter as a polite buffer he knew didn't really provide any privacy. It didn't matter that his men heard his girl talking, because her words were true, and it was good for them, and him, to hear it and know he had their support.

"Our real family is here, Daddy. They know it too. We all love you. Do you hear me? We all love you."

"I hear you, Nelda girl. I caught your meanin' loud and clear." He smiled at her and reached to dust the remaining wet from her face with the pad of his thumb. "Now, tell me what you overheard your Aunt Bekka say."

"She said a man hurt her." Nelda's back stiffened and her chin came up, and in that moment, Retro truly recognized himself in her for perhaps the first time. Really saw his influence and another wave of pride swept through him. "I don't care who he is, or what she thinks he is to her, you need to find him and fix his attitude, Daddy."

Oh, yeah. She's my girl.

***

Trina

Katrina Fainburg shifted the strap of her bag from her shoulder as she climbed into her car. Fingers crossed as she turned the key, she breathed a tiny sigh when the engine started up without issue. Sitting behind the wheel, she buckled in as she looked across the parking lot, watching tall, beautiful women strut their way to vehicles already idling, shadowed profiles behind the wheels thrown into sharp relief as the interior lights flashed on, then off.

Waitressing at The Promised Land wasn't the worst job she'd ever had, and the tips were good most nights. Tonight she'd worked a private party, and had seen even more bills than normal in her envelope at the end of the night. Probably a quiet way to ensure she didn't talk about what she'd seen, because actual contact wasn't supposed to happen, even in the private rooms. The groom-to-be had been embarrassed by his behavior and had assured her more than once he hadn't come there for that.

Still, it had been interesting to watch for the few minutes, the dancer not upset by her presence at all, even as...occupied as she'd been.

A horn shrieked from beside her and Trina jumped, whirling to look out the passenger window. One of the bouncers sat in his car, looking irritated at something. He was staring straight at her. She glanced around and saw the rest of the lot had cleared while she was lost in thought. With a tiny wave, she put her car into gear and pulled into the scant traffic that was Birmingham at 4:00 a.m.

It was about a fifteen-minute trip to her apartment, and she weighed the time against how many days it had been since she'd talked to her mother. Mind made up, she swung into a laundromat on the next block and locked the car behind her as she got out. This place had the only pay phone she'd found, and she hoped it was still in working order. After hearing the recording when she picked up the receiver, she got a few dollars in quarters and settled onto the folding table under the phone. Money slotted in, she dialed the number from memory.

Two rings later and a man's hello filled her ear, making her smile broadly. "Dolph, what are you doing there? It's good to hear your voice." Dolph Chulpayev had always been a welcome and stable influence in her life, one of her mother's closest friends and almost like family. "I've missed you."

"And I you, sweetkins." He called her by the nickname he'd used since she could remember, and Trina grinned as she imagined the dimples in his cheeks when he said it. "It is late, are you well?"

"Yeah, just got off work. Thought I'd take a chance Mom would be up." She made a face, frowning at her reflection in the window. "Is she sleeping?"

"She is. Should I wake her?"

"You're brave to offer." They both laughed, her mother's early morning grumpiness was legend. "But I'll pass. If she'd still been up, that would have been one thing." A few years ago, her mother started suffering from insomnia, something Trina shared, as did Dolph. "Tell me all the things, mister. We're well beyond the normal chatting window, so you better fess up on all the pretty women you've been wooing."

He laughed, deep and rolling, and so filled with pleasure at her teasing, Trina vowed to call him more often. Every important milestone she could remember had images of Dolph associated with it, and he deserved better.

"Oh, Katrina, there are no women in my life other than you and your mother. Don't you know you're my world?"

She laughed quietly and leaned her head against the wall, staring up at the ceiling as she folded her legs on the table, getting comfortable. "How's work?" She sighed, not because she missed home, but because starting over in a town where she didn't know anyone was hard. Harder than she'd expected. "How's Atlanta?"

"Atlanta is as it ever is, and work is work. I'd much rather hear about your life, sweetkins." His voice softened, turned cajoling. "Is the apartment sufficient? Do you need money? How is the diner?"

She winced, because she *had* worked at a diner, but that was two jobs ago. The economy was tanking, according to all the financial analysts, and she could see proof in the way work was. Or wasn't. Less money for consumers meant less eating out, which meant fewer waitresses needed. She hadn't shared that change with her mother, because she knew if she confessed working at a strip club it would have earned her a scolding and offers to "just come home," which she couldn't do...wouldn't, because this was something she'd longed for. Freedom from the expectations of everyone back home. Not family, because it had always been just her and her mother. But between Dolph and his cousins, Trina hadn't been able to go anywhere without someone there, taking care of her, even if it was unwarranted and unwanted.

"I made great tips tonight. Let Mom know I'll be sending some cash home." That was what she did. Everything extra went to make her mother's life just a little easier. The government's disability check didn't cover essentials, much less splurge items like a new couch. Something she knew was needed, because the last time she was home and slept on it, a spring had played punch-the-kidney against her back all night.

"I'll tell her. Is all truly well, Trina? You sound...sad."

Oh, crap. If he thought she was sad, Dolph would be here tomorrow to try to fix whatever it was. She faked a yawn, following it by a forced sigh. "No, no. Just tired. I'm gonna head home and get some sleep." She smiled at his grumbled response, words lost in the static of the line as the recording told her to deposit more coins. "The phone's about to cut off, but I'm glad I got to talk to you, Dolph. Love you."

"Love you, t—"

She cradled the handset for a moment, then settled it into place and unfolded from the table. A vehicle with dark-tinted windows slowed as it cruised past just as she was settling into the car and she used her mirrors to track as it drove away, noting when it turned at the next corner.

Home and bed awaited, but she still had the few blocks to drive to the lot where she parked, then the long walk to the apartment building. She yawned, this time for real, and pulled out onto the now-deserted street.

***

Retro

"Well, that was quite the ending to the evening." Penny's words came from beside him and Retro glanced over to see the tiny redhead standing near his elbow.

"All that shit happened near five hours ago, woman. Seems maybe the evening is longer than my troubles can reach. Gimme a break." He shook his head and leaned over to grab a bottle of water from a cooler. He twisted the lid to crack the seal, retightened it, and handed it to her. "Thanks be to God. What did you find out from Bekka?"

"Nelda's something, isn't she?" Penny shook her head slowly as she opened the water and took a long drink. "Girl was mad as a wet hen on your behalf. Good to see. She's got a steady footing under her, and that's due to your influence, Retro. Good job, daddy man."

"Yeah, my girl is the tits. I'm proud as fuck of her. Real proud of her and my boys. Now." He turned to face Penny head on. "What did Bekka share?"

"Bekka's a facile liar." Snorting a laugh, she took another drink of water before she slowly recapped the bottle. "Once she got herself under control, she tried to lay a glib line of shit on me. Did not fly, I tell you what. That's one brand of bullshit I ain't ever gonna buy. I let her go on and on, spinning herself tighter and tighter in her own web. Then I let loose on her. We had us a come-to-Jesus moment, and I hope she doesn't soon forget it."

He shrugged and shook his head. "Won't take. We've done this dance with her before. You might think it's stickin' for a time, but she's slick as a greased hog, and it will not stick." He eyed the ceiling near the stairs, towards where the room Bekka had camped out in. Hosting not only the IMC group, but his kids and his sister had put more than prospects out of their beds, and he had some members to thank tomorrow. The ones who'd needed it were offered a free cab back to their house on his dime, and all had done it with good grace, knowing the only reason they'd intended to stay at the clubhouse and away from home was to avoid drinking and driving. "Y'all get settled into a room?" He looked to see Twisted still talking to his men, the IMC members clustered at their president's back. "You get tired, you go on up, doll. You're safe here, and you know that."

"I do know that. Now I wanna know why you think she's too stubborn to learn?"

"I don't know, maybe because I've known the woman her whole life? She's always been like this, you know? She's not an addict, but she is hooked on the mental high she gets from the pain. Been self-harming since she was little, and we didn't see it. Now she looks for pain." He shrugged. "I've accepted it, thought I'd found her a solution in that club she goes to. Laid down the laws, and they assured me it would be followed. Simple stuff, but figured if there's no breakin' the skin, then there's no chance of infection settin' in. I'd learned from her past mistakes, so at least one of us can be taught. Man didn't respect her limits and tore into her. She didn't come clean and got sepsis. We nearly lost her from that, and I thought she was afraid for maybe the first time in her life. Nearly died, but still it didn't take." He traced along the edges of his teeth with his tongue, considering his words. "Parents age, you know, and their style changes with time. When Bekka came along, they were tired, I think. So they put up with her bullshit, as you called it. For her, this is just the normal situation. She fucks up and gets in trouble, she runs to one of us and we clean it up for her. Rinse and repeat. Even if there's years between the troubles, they still circle back around." He yawned widely, not bothering to hide his weariness. "I got enough of my own troubles, in case you missed that shit goin' down."

"Mmm." She hummed and leaned close, pressing her cheek to his shoulder. "Nelda passed along that tidbit of knowledge. You shoulda taken the bitch's rags when you walked out."

"Ain't tellin' me nothing I don't already know." He shook his head. "Seriously, I'd like to understand what drove her here tonight. Bekka I get, because this? This shit is her standard operating procedure. Wanda? I got no fuckin' clue. Nelda tell you she had her boy toy over? Had a party?" Penny nodded and he grimaced. "She share anything else? All I know is what the boys said. Nelda won't speak about it since I picked them up."

"Not much that flatters her momma." Penny stared up at him steadily. "Now, back to Bekka."

"Jesus, you're like a goddamned dog with a bone."

"Uh-huh. Might as well give in, brother," Twisted said from Retro's other side.

He turned his glare that direction. "Y'all gangin' up on me now?"

Twisted smiled. "No, brother. But lemme tell you what I see. Can you stay your tongue for thirty seconds and lemme run things down for you?"

Retro held his gaze, irritation bouncing around inside him. This was his friend, one of his best, a man he'd ridden to war for, and someone he trusted beyond measure. *I can take this from him.* He nodded.

"Okay, so here's what I saw. You treated your woman nicer than most men in here would have, if theirs'd've pulled that same shit. You showed care with how you spoke, until she pushed, and at that point, she'd more than bought whatever came her way.

"Your sister, you did the same, and when you realized she was hurtin', you moved what you needed to in order to get her safe and cared for. You comforted your girl when she heard ugly words, and when you found out she'd dealt with more ugliness in her momma's house, you held it together in a way that told her you believed in her. That she was strong enough to bolster you, and brother, that's a level of givin' I hope to have for my own kids one day.

"Being the big man don't always mean being the meanest in the room, sometimes it's about bending and showing others that you won't break, and give them hope they won't, either.

"My woman, the one sitting right here? Hell, you've cared for her a dozen times since we rolled up uninvited. Moving us to comfortable seating when I know you'd far rather range along the edges of the crowd. Had her served, more than once, and that's a show of respect I very much appreciate, I'll tell you that now. Thank you. Even just now you saved her fingers from the bottle top, something she can handle no problem, but you paved the way.

"That's just the man you are, and that's the kind of kids you're raising, and I know you didn't just find that strength holed up inside yourself one day. I've met your brother, and he's the same. A good man, through and through. You were both raised like that, and it shows." Twisted paused and took a breath, and Retro braced.

"That's the kind of raisin' your sister had, too, whether you saw it or not. You're older enough I bet you were out of the house by the time she was into trouble the first time. Am I right?" Retro nodded, keeping his mouth shut. So far Twisted had hit everything just right, and it pained him to see things laid out like this. He could deal with someone telling him his faults, but praising him? That came hard. "Your sister's in the shit, and there ain't no bout adoubt it, as Po'Boy would say. I think she needs a change of scenery. Me and Penny—" He stepped around Retro to sling his arm over Penny's shoulders. "—been talkin' and we think we'll keep both of 'em for a bit."

"Both?"

"Yeah, you were loanin' us Nelda already. We got ample room for Bekka, no problem. I'm here for you, brother." Twisted held out his hand and Retro gripped it, holding on. "I'm here, and I'm gonna be here. You need me, you got me. Don't matter the what or why."

"You're a good man, Twisted." Now Retro was the one blinking fast, forcing back the wet in his eyes. "I'm proud to call you friend, and brother."

"Backatcha, man. Backatcha." Twisted released and stepped behind Penny, pulling her back against his chest. "Me and my ole lady are hittin' the hay. You good, brother?"

"I'm good." He reassured them both, smiling as they turned to walk up the stairs in lockstep, exactly how they'd been since they'd met not even two years ago. *Not as good as you are*. He looked around. The clubhouse main room had quietened, a few brothers clustered near a pool table, Dancer now on station behind the bar. *But I'll get there*. He flicked a finger at the man, smiling when the prospect came in his direction. "Relieved, brother. Go do your thang."

"Thanks, man." Dancer tapped his shoulder gently. "Later."

***

An uneven pounding on his bedroom door woke Retro the next morning. He rolled up on one hip, elbow to the mattress as he reached out to grab his phone. "Fuck," he muttered as he looked at the time, which was way too early for as late as he'd made it to bed. He stretched, coughing and clearing his throat.

"What?"

His shout at the door was answered by the doorknob turning, and Nelda's voice asking, "You decent, Daddy?"

"Gimme a minute." Bare legs slung over the edge of the bed, he wiggled his toes for a moment before he bent to grab the jeans discarded in a pile nearby. Eyes closed, he wedged his feet into the legs and stood, yanking them to his hips before he zipped up, button still undone. "Good."

Eyes still closed, he wasn't ready for Nelda's sneak attack from the side, and they both nearly toppled to the floor. He reached out with a hand to the wall, the other around her shoulders. "Jesus, baby girl. What the hell?"

"Sorry. Sorry. I'm just excited."

"I got that. What makes this level of excitement acceptable at eight in the goddamned morning? Girl, I didn't hit the pillows until nearly five, and that little bit of sleep makes your old man a tired and grumpy bear."

He pretended to growl. "More grump than you're ready for, I promise you."

"Untruth, Daddy mine." She gave him a squeeze and then flung herself away, the compression of the mattress springs testimony to where she'd landed. "Untruth. You're never too grumpy." He turned and looked at the door to see his two boys hovering there, Isaiah and Jeremiah Jr.

"Come on in, Saya. Jimmy, you too. You boys might as well join in whatever fun is it your sister's cookin' up this morning." He screwed his face up into a ferociously comical scowl. "You put her up to this?"

"No, sir," came from Jimmy, both boys crossing quickly to him for a hug before they joined their sister on the mattress.

"Lies and prevarications." He shook his head. "You both got that face. Stop makin' that face. Just ask whatever it is you want to ask." He yawned and rested a hip against the dresser. "God." He rubbed his face. "Y'all are terrible slaves. One of y'all shoulda brought your old man a coffee, at least." Saya made as if to get off the bed and Retro grinned at him. "That's my favorite boy, right there. You'd run all the way downstairs to get me a coffee, wouldn't ya?"

As Saya nodded, Nelda pushed up on her elbows and glared at Retro, eyebrows drawn down over her eyes. "Daddy, this is important."

"So is coffee, and that is a full truth you will understand much later in your sweet life." He shook his head at Saya, giving the boy a grin. "It's all good, Saya. Sit your ass back down." Louder, in a firm voice, he demanded, "Now ask already before I expire of curiosity. Y'all know how much your daddy needs to know all the things. Tell me all the things."

"Saya and I want to go to Louisiana, too." Jimmy stared up at him expectantly.

"You ask Twisted?" Retro hoped not, because that would make it easier to tell the boys no. Wanda might have a deserved shit fit if he shipped all three of his kids out of town for a couple of weeks. "What about Mom?"

"I called her. Mom said if you okayed it, she didn't care." Nelda's words were thrown out there like a challenge and he angled his glance at her, lifting one brow in caution. "She did, Daddy. Her words, not mine. You always say context matters. Well, there's no mistaking her context, seeing as she already had someone else at the house." Saya made a distressed sound and Retro lifted both brows, more displeased with Wanda than his daughter, but she needed to mind her words to keep from hurting her brothers unnecessarily. *I'll chat her up later.* "Sorry, Saya," Nelda mumbled and sat up fully, reaching out to wrap her arm around her youngest brother. "I didn't think."

"Not cool. Saya shouldn't have to hear that from you." Retro picked the boy up, letting his son wrap both arms around his neck. "Gimme a big hug, boy." Thin arms squeezed. "You want to go visit Twisted and Penny for a couple of weeks?" Saya's head moved up and down, face still buried in Retro's neck. "Aunt Bekka will be there, too." Saya reared back in his arms, eyes wide in pleased surprise. He cupped Retro's jaw in both hands, cradling his father's face as he aligned their foreheads and pressed forwards. Retro stared into the eyes of his youngest child, the sensitive one of the bunch, the boy who wore his heart on his sleeve and would do anything at all for the people he loved. He wished, as he'd wished every day for so many long years, that Saya would speak, would say anything, wished with his whole heart to hear his son's voice lifted in more than laughter. "You want that, boy?" Saya's eyes brightened, the corners crinkling as he nodded slightly, careful not to lose connection with his father. "You ask Twisted?" Saya nodded again and leaned back, turning to point towards Jimmy on the bed. "Jimmy asked? What'd Twisted say? You sure he wants the three of y'all all at once?" Saya nodded and flipped his hand towards Jimmy who nodded, too.

"Yeah, he was makin' coffee this mornin' and I asked him. I didn't wake him up, Daddy, I promise."

"What'd he say, exactly?" Retro gave Saya another squeeze, feeling his heart fill even more with love when his boy collapsed on his chest, trusting his father to hold him safe. Retro dipped his chin and pressed a kiss to the crown of Saya's head. "Exactly, mind."

"He said," Jimmy's voice dropped an awkward octave, imitating Twisted even to the cadence of his speech, a trick his boy had learned early on and one that never failed to make Retro grin. Each of his kids had a talent, and he'd done the best he could to encourage each of them. Nelda's was her quick mind and ability to observe and notice details. Jimmy's was mimicry, but he also had a nearly flawless memory for spoken conversations, something that had annoyed Wanda to no end. Saya's was his empathy, the facile reflection of someone's emotions, but in a way that took them to a better place. Like he had his father just a moment ago, by giving Retro a quiet interlude where he was his boy's sole focus. "I'd've asked yer daddy myself had I but tho't on it. Hell, yeah, boy, you and your brother are welcome at my house. We got room, and I got time. Clear it with your daddy, and get ready. We roll out at nine." *Well, that explained the rush to wake me, at least.*

"Daddy says yes." Saya crowed with silent laughter at Retro's words, arching his back until he stared at the ceiling. Jimmy's response was more restrained, but no less joyful, and Retro shared a grin with his daughter. "You already packed?" She nodded. "Good. Now, let's head down so your old man can get some coffee in his system before he has to say goodbye to his kids. Bring your bags and helmets downstairs." He set Saya on the floor. "Make sure you got enough drawers, and take a suit for swimmin'."

"Already packed, Daddy. I helped the boys. They've got underpants aplenty." Nelda pushed off the mattress and came to him, curling into his side. "I love you."

"Love you, too." Jimmy gave him a sideways hug on his way to the door, Saya trailing after him. Nelda disengaged, and Retro reached out a hand, staying her a moment. "Mind your words about your mother. You can feel whatever you need to feel, and I'd never tell you otherwise. But you need to let your brothers have the same freedom. It's hard on everyone."

"Not her." Nelda stared up at him and he was struck by how much she'd grown over the last six months or so. A little taller, sure, but her face had matured and now he could truly see the beauty she would grow into. "She's acting out, Daddy, and it's unbecoming. I could see if she was just mad at you and was hurt, but she's behaving in a way that disrespects me and the boys, too. I'm fifteen, Daddy." He nodded when she paused. "Her boy wasn't even ten years older than me. It's like she feels you stole her youth away or something."

"Maybe I did." He shrugged. "There's more at play there than you know, and that's as it should be. I'm not always a nice person, and that is a hard thing for a man to admit to his kids. A man wants his kids to always look at him like he could move the world if needed. Daddy should be a superhero, and not just a man. I'm just a man, and your momma knows that better than anyone."

"If I have to make my mind up based on the evidence I have, then I'll do that. You're not doing this to hurt her, or us. You put off doing this to keep from hurting us. You are *not* the bad guy in this scenario." She shook her head, lips pressed tightly together. "I love her, but she's acting out."

"Was it your idea for the boys to go to Louisiana, too?"

She nodded. "It will give her space to do what she needs to do without the boys having to see." A shrug, something he could see masked her own pain. "This way I won't have to worry about them, either. Penny told me last night it would be okay, and Aunt Bekka was excited at the idea. This only leaves me worrying about you."

"Don't worry your pretty little head about me, baby girl. Daddy's fine. Maybe for the first time in a long time, your daddy's doin' a little bit of okay." He pushed off the dresser and reached out, smoothing her hair back as he bent to press his lips to her forehead, holding the caress for several moments. When he pulled back, he said, "And you're the best big

47

sister there ever could be. I hope you know how proud it makes me the way you take care of your brothers. Proud and happy that you're mine. I look at you every day and wonder to myself where the magic came from that let me make you. I'm so lucky, Nelda." Retro cleared his throat. "Now, come on. Let's go. At this point? I really need that coffee."

Nelda's laughter trailed behind as she ran out of his room and Retro stood there a moment staring at the door.

"I've got the best goddamned kids in the whole world."

Chapter Two

Retro stood in the parking lot long after the group of bikes had ridden out of sight. It had taken more than a single hour to finally get them on the road, but the laughter that had rolled through the clubhouse was good to hear. It seemed his breakup with Wanda had put more of a damper on the place than he'd thought. Or maybe his pairing with her had done that. *Either way, I'm done with that shit.*

When they finally pulled off the lot, Nelda was astride behind Penny, Saya behind Twisted, Jimmy rode with Wildman, and Retro had found himself inordinately pleased to see Bekka relegated to riding behind the newest member IMC had with them on the run. Privately, Twisted had told him the man wasn't new to the life, that he was a patchover from a support club, but Retro knew Bekka had clocked the tIny slight. *Good for her to get a set-down from someone not me.*

"What now, boss?" Mudd was standing beside him, shoulder to shoulder, and Retro glanced over at him for a moment, trying to read his mood. "What's on your agenda for tonight?"

"You got something in mind?" He turned and Mudd moved with him as they walked back to the clubhouse. "Other than sittin' around here and drinkin' beer? Which I would not be opposed to, just so it's known."

"Noted, brother," Mudd said on a laugh. "Naw, I thought we could go out and shake the dust off. Do you good to see and be seen, and for everyone to have a little blowout."

"Where exactly do you propose we do this blowout?" Retro stomped his feet, clearing dirt off his heels before he walked into the clubhouse proper. The double tap of Mudd's boots echoed behind him, a courtesy to the clubhouse whores who cleaned the place as needed. Of course, like a lot of clubs, their prospects would be assigned the duty before and after any party, giving them a chance to serve in a different way. Preparing the face of the club for visitors, and dealing with the detritus of whatever had happened during the evening, gave them a fresh understanding of what it took to keep the joint property running like it should, and Retro had found it made for more compassionate members in the long run. "Where'd you wanna go?"

"Out. Definitely out somewhere. Somewhere else, as in not here." Mudd shook his finger at Retro, making him laugh. "And you don't get to bail early and come back to crash. You're in this with us tonight, Prez."

Ten hours later Retro sat beside a wide, low stage with a good portion of his club, watching half a dozen women shake their asses and tits. His choice had been to go to a friendly bar and shoot some pool, play darts, drink a little, let the boys flirt a bit with whatever tail was present, and then go back to the clubhouse to end their night.

His choice had been vetoed. Soundly defeated in a one to twenty-two lopsided fight.

The grin on his face felt foreign, the relaxed state of his shoulders unfamiliar, and he realized Mudd had been right. He'd needed a night with the boys, just him and the trusted brothers who wore his patch. This would set his world right again. The good day had started with the early morning chat from his kids, and while it killed him to know how much they'd seen, he suspected it was better for them to have it out in the open, too. *Fuckin' Wanda.* Noise from his side alerted him and the woman's hand on his shoulder didn't startle him too badly. *Thank God, woulda sucked to punch a stripper for offering a lap dance.*

"Next guy, honey. I like to watch, sure as shit, but I'm not gonna be your best customer for a dance." Her lips pursed in a pretty pout and he stared at them for a moment, trying to visualize how they'd look wrapped around his dick. Glossy and shiny from her lipstick, he imagined seeing the color on his shaft, a high-water mark that would let him reach for the back of her throat. *Nothing.* Shaking his head, he pointed to the member seated to his right. "Next guy."

Maybe I'm fuckin' broke inside. He hadn't found Wanda attractive for a while now, which meant he hadn't been laid in months. And now, when a beautiful painted lady offered a ready-made fantasy, he not only turned her down, but found it wasn't a hard decision at all. She didn't do a thing for him. Retro looked around the rest of the club, gaze flicking from woman to woman. *Nope. Nope. Nope.* There'd been a waitress across the room earlier he'd found interesting, but she'd handled customers on her side, and then disappeared a short time ago, probably shift change and gone for the night. He sighed.

Leaning forwards, he laid a hand on Mudd's shoulder to gain his attention, pulling his gaze from the whirling tassels in front of him. Eyebrow cocked in a "what the fuck" look, an irritated-looking Mudd thumbed at the woman who'd already moved on to the next man seated along the edge of the stage.

Retro grinned and said loudly, "Takin' a walk outside. Need to get some air."

Before he could stop him, Mudd reached out and poked a member and a prospect, then pointed a finger at Retro. He saw Mudd's mouth move, but couldn't hear him over the noise from the music and club patrons, but knew what he was doing as soon as the two men stood. Retro patted the air with his hands and the two looked from him to Mudd and back again. He patted the air again, pointed at the back door and held up one hand, showing them all his digits. "Five minutes," Marlin mouthed to him, and Retro nodded.

In the hallway along the backside of the building, Retro caught a noise at the edge of his hearing, sharp and short, it was a retort that didn't echo, the brief concussion absorbed by the padded walls. He slowed and listened intently, waiting. It came again and then was followed by a woman's trembling voice counting out, "Five." Retro rolled his eyes, realizing he'd stumbled on some backroom antics the woman was probably being well compensated for.

A moment later the doorway opposite where he stood opened and a figure stumbled out, pulling the door closed behind them. Not a dancer, this was a waitress, set apart by the different outfits they wore. She stood for a moment, then gave a shaky sigh and let loose the tiniest sob. She seemed not to see him as she pulled in a deep breath, then another, and he watched as her shoulders lifted, squaring as she worked to pull herself back together.

It was the waitress he'd been missing, and he felt a tiny lurch in his belly at the rough trade she seemed to like. *Not that I'd be opposed normally.* Right now, it just felt dangerously close to what his little sister needed.

"You okay?" He couldn't have derailed the question if he'd wanted to, and then he was looking into the deepest blue eyes he'd ever seen. Indigo near the center, they lightened to a brighter color around the outside edges and were set off by dark brows that matched her raven hair. His cock gave a twitch when he looked at her lips, red and puffy, and if her teeth worrying at her bottom lip was any indication, they'd been bitten that way. No gloss, no shine, nothing like the dancer from before, but Retro found he wanted to kiss her in that moment. Wanted to take, and taste, and see what she would give him back.

She stared at him a moment. Then her gaze flicked to the floor and stayed there as she nodded.

"You sure?" He wanted to earn another look from her, wanted to see those eyes again, wanted to see if he could interest her in anything more than a quick glance. Before she could answer, the door at her back opened and a man stood there, still threading a belt through the loops of his pants. She didn't move, didn't jump at the sudden nearness of the man, and Retro got the vibe that this had happened before.

"Back to work, Trina." Arrogant tones threaded through the man's few words. His stare hadn't left Retro's face, and with the same arrogance, asked, "Can I help you?"

"Naw, man. Just having a chat with this pretty girl here. She was helping me find the bathrooms." He dipped his chin to look into her face. "Point the way again, please?" Her shaking hand lifted and she indicated a nearby door, clearly marked with a cock and balls sign. "Thanks so much." Retro paused, then decided he wanted to at least hold her name in his mouth, finishing with, "Miss Trina," giving her greater respect than the asshole behind her had.

Said asshole spoke again, his voice now dripping with anger, painting red stripes across Retro's vision with every word. "Trina, you want another five? Go sell booze. That's what I pay you for. Not playing peeping Tom, and not a tour director." Then he set in motion the actions of the next fifteen minutes, causing Retro to react as he'd never done before. Not since Clara. The man put his hand on her shoulder and gripped roughly, making her cry out as he yanked her back against him, hips thrusting against her ass. "Unless you want a private party with the boss. Go sell booze." Then he shoved her hard. A hand in the middle of her back made her arms pinwheel as she stumbled and fell to her knees with a tiny cry. Smaller than the sob had been, still Retro heard it, attuned to her as he was.

Fist met face, and it was on, the cowardly manager not offering much in the way of a challenge. The bouncers were a different beast, and Retro found himself strung between two of them with a third in front and he ducked and dodged, striking out as he could with fists and feet until his men heard the commotion.

Ten minutes later, they were standing near their bikes on the lot, laughter and stories circulating freely amidst his men, his brothers, the ones he could trust to always have his back. The bouncers were positioned just outside the door, iced towels held to eyes and lips, watching them, phones in hand a promise of police if Retro and his boys didn't clear quickly.

Retro scanned the lot one final time as he sat astride his bike. Movement in the alleyway behind the strip club caught at his attention and he saw Trina jog out into the light, shoulders shaking, hand covering the bottom of her face as she fled to a small car. She got inside and drove off the lot in such a hurry her lights didn't come on until half a block down the road. *Fuck*.

Leaning close, he told Mudd, "I want you to find out everything you can about a waitress named Trina from here. I suspect she just got canned."

"This was over a woman?" Mudd reared back, chin up in surprise. Retro nodded. Mudd grinned, the expression spreading across his features slowly. "Fuck yeah, I'll find out anything I can."

***

Trina

Curled on her bed, toes scrunched into the blanket she was underneath, Trina squeezed her eyes closed so tightly she saw sparking arcs behind her lids.

Tonight had been the absolute worst. First, her section of the club had been nearly empty, most of the men settling nearer the stage. She knew she'd been taken off that section because she wouldn't play Andy's games, and as the manager of the club, he had the ability to override the floor shift leader when it came to where waitresses were assigned.

Then when he'd caught her watching another private party show through a crack in the door, he'd ordered her into his office for a talk. *Some talk*. Her bottom still stung from his belt, but that wasn't anything to the sting of her embarrassment at what the man in the hallway had witnessed.

She'd suspected he'd heard it all when she escaped out of Andy's office, finally. His warm brown eyes had stared at her with compassion, and she'd been mortified when he'd spoken to her, making it clear her humiliation had a witness. Then Andy had come out, made a spectacle about what he'd been doing, and acted his normal brand of asshole to her. She'd watched, fascinated as a change came over the man standing in the hall.

He'd uncoiled in a flash and hadn't given any warning before he was on Andy, Trina still crouched on her knees behind them. Fist around Andy's throat, he'd struck him again and again before the bouncers heard the commotion and came to see. Then it had been three against one, and he'd still held his own. Silent, mouth drawn sideways into a contorted grimace, he'd battled them, pushing the fight away from where she was frozen. His hair swung wildly as he ducked and wove, his fists hitting their targets again and again, only glancing blows from his opponents landing on his torso.

He'd been magnificent, until the moment Andy had kicked at her, yelling something she hadn't heard over the fight. The man had whirled, distracted, that had been all the bouncers needed to swarm and take him down. It had been only moments later when he'd whistled, the piercing sound echoing up the hallway. Men approached at a run and Trina had shrunk back, plastering herself to the wall, unable to look away as he'd risen from the bodies and men, standing still amidst chaos to sweep the hallway with his gaze, stopping when it landed on her. His lips had tipped up on one corner, an impossible grin crossing his features as his eyes tracked down and then back up to stop again on her face.

Andy had shoved her again and Trina lost the man's gaze, shrinking against the wall as the shouted words finally made sense.

Fired.

She'd forced herself to stop by the diner on her way home, finding to her surprise that there was an opening not yet advertised, and they'd rehired her on the spot. Her first shift was tomorrow evening. Which was good, because there'd been no tips from tonight, no cash to tide her over until her tiny check arrived.

Now, safe and hiding in her bed, covered to the bottoms of her ears, she let her mind wander back over those moments. His few words to her had been sweet and kind, his attempt to get her out of trouble with Andy ill-advised, but so caring she could create whole scenarios where he was the hero rescuing her from this life. "Miss Trina," she whispered, and smiled, even as she snuggled into her pillow.

That night her dreams were filled with brown eyes, sweet smiles, and hair that created a curtain around her, keeping her safe and happy.

***

Retro

Third night in a row he'd parked his ass on a stool at the bar of the strip club, watching. He'd left his minders at a table near the stage, knowing the titty show was the reason Marlin and Crazy Mike didn't mind this assignment. And as much as he didn't like taking them away from something more productive, he understood Mudd's position. *"Damn, Retro, you got in a fuckin' bar fight in that place when I let you out of my sight for five minutes. I ain't down for letting you run around by yourself like that. Suck it up and let the boys do their jobs."*

So he had, and tonight he might have hit pay dirt. The bartender on previous nights wouldn't cough up anything on Trina, if that was even her real name. Mudd hadn't been able to turn up anything on her, but Retro wasn't letting himself give up hope. *Yet.* His reaction to her had been troubling, and something he wanted to keep as much on the down low as he could. At least until he could understand more about her. *Where's she from? What's a woman like her doing working in a dive like this?*

The blonde behind the bar headed his way again and he smiled at her. Flicking a finger at his glass, he said, "I'll do one more, pretty thing." She nodded and ducked her head, hiding the smile that floated across her features. "Hey," he used a surprised inflection, as if he'd just remembered something important. "I met a girl in here not long ago. She was a waitress. You look like you've a head for faces and names. Am I right?" She studied him as she dropped a couple of cubes of ice in and then tilted the whisky bottle over his glass. He counted to five before she ended her pour and there was barely enough room in the glass for her to give it a shot of soda. Generous to a fault, and that was something he could use to his benefit. "She had some trouble with a customer." Lies, but if he said she had a problem with the man who Retro was making sure would soon be the ex-manager of the place, this source would clam up tight. "It was a mess. She was cryin' when she left." He accepted the glass when she slid it his direction, lifting it to his mouth for a shallow sip, hiding his wince at the bite of the liquor. "Nice girl. You know if she's okay?"

"What was her name? I haven't worked here long. I don't know all the girls." A man down the bar called for a beer and she lifted a finger to let him know she'd heard him. "A waitress, right? Not the talent?"

"Yeah, yeah. Waitress. Little thing. What was her name…" He pretended to think hard, then snapped his fingers and said, "Tessa? No, that's not it. Tisha?" He shook his head. "I don't got no head for names. Not like you. It started with a T though. I remember that much."

"Trina," she supplied with a nod. "Sweet girl. It's too bad what happened. She was good with customers."

Retro's belly set up a slow roll, because the grief in her voice was real and that combined with her use of past tense had him on edge. "Trina, yeah. That's right. What happened to her?"

"Some customer acted an ass." He suppressed a grin, because she was talking about him and didn't know it. "She encouraged it, I guess. Andy, the manager, said he gave her a week off without pay. But a man came in the next day and told him she wouldn't be back. Told him to lose her number."

"That happen often? Someone dictating the business side of things? Was it family or something? Learned she worked in a joint, and didn't like it?" He could see that, and it would be his reaction if he ever learned Bekka, or God forbid, Nelda worked in a club like this. *Protect the ones we love*. He nodded.

"I don't know." She again lifted a finger to the insistent beer-lover down the bar. "But Andy was told to mail her last check, she wouldn't be back. It's too bad, like I said. She was good to work with. Honest and sweet, and that's not a combination we get here too often."

"Yeah." He nodded and watched her walk away. He leaned over the bar and dumped about half his drink into the sink before grabbing the soda nozzle and filling it with pop. Softly, eyes on the dancers working the crowd, skin and smiles aimed at any man with money in his hand. "That's a good combination, but not one I'd expect to find here."

***

"Uh-huh. Yeah, got it." Mudd pushed back from the bar, shoulder hunched up, phone still pinned to the side of his head as he waved Retro over. "Yeah, got it, brother. Much obliged."

"What's up?" Retro rocked his head side to side, neck creaking with the movement. It was already days later and he was still stiff from the bar fight. *Gettin' old*, he reminded himself, and grinned wryly.

"Found her. Katrina Fainburg, from over in Atlanta. Former waitress at the strip club, emphasis on the former, because you were right about her gettin' canned. She's now the proud owner of a waitress apron from a local breakfast and dinner place. No family in the area that we can find, which is interesting given what you learned from the chick behind the bar there about someone carin' for her. But based on her name, there's a chance that family tree might just stretch to the Georgia on the other side of the world." Mudd laid out everything in clear, concise language, as he and Retro had taught all their men.

"Russian mafia in her blood?" That struck too close to home, and memories of Clara's body wavered in the edges of his vision. "You fuckin' serious? No way would the bratva allow one of their own to be treated like she was. No." He shook his head and scoffed far back in his throat. "Not buyin' it."

"I only know what I'm told, boss." Mudd stared at him. "You want the address and her schedule or not?"

"What the fuck do you think?" Retro held out his hand in a mute demand.

Fifteen minutes later, Retro rolled off the clubhouse lot at the head of a two-bike escort, something he felt was far too showy for a Friday evening. At the diner, he waved the men in when they would have stayed outside, laughing at the insinuation that he might need some alone time. "Boss," Dancer said with a grin, "you bled for her. Least she can do is blow you."

"Jesus, you're a raunchy crew." He shook his head. "Come on in. I'll buy dinner. You motherfuckers need a goddamned life."

"Nope, we all got good lives." Dancer laughed. "It's our job tonight to make sure our prez gets himself a good life, too." That drew Retro up, his steps slowing. Dancer's eyes narrowed and he turned to face Retro fully. "Boss, I've been a prospect for eleven and a half months, and in all that time, you have only once had a night when you didn't deal with club business. I've been half convinced the sayin' all work and no play didn't apply to you, not when you went day-in and day-out without blowing off steam. I get it, brother." Retro liked hearing the man own that word, and liked how Dancer felt comfortable enough to lay the truth out there for someone he cared about, ignoring the difference in their standing within the club. It told him that Dancer was locked in even better than he and Mudd could have hoped. "You been makin' choices for your kids, and living to do for them. You know my story, and I'm a hundred percent certain you'd back any brother's play if they had the same situation. But a few nights ago, I got to see a different man, the president and leader the boys all talk about peeked out and I'm more impressed than I was before. I like being part of this club, because what we do matters. And you proved that again at that damned strip club." He shrugged and stepped back, swinging a hand out towards the diner. "Now, let's go see if there are any spoils of war we can collect for you, brother." Dancer grinned. "She's a pretty piece, right enough. Even if you aren't ready to be searchin' for a new ole lady, it doesn't hurt to catch yourself a sweet distraction."

"You're smart," Retro said mildly, shaking his head. "A regular fuckin' Einstein." His eyes landed on the bare leather over the man's chest where his nameplate would go, once he had one. "I like you, Dancer." He pulled out his phone and tapped out a message to Mudd, getting a Y in response. "We're doin' church Sunday, be sure you're there in plenty of time to clean up after whatever kinda trouble raises its head from tomorrow night. Service to the club, brother. Now," he stepped around Dancer, already calling him Einstein in his head, "let's see what kind of trouble I can rustle up tonight."

Installed at a corner booth, Retro stretched his legs out under the table, and hooked his elbows over the back of the bench seat. He'd taken the wall side of their round table, letting the other men sort out who slid to the inside and he took this minute to study the patrons. It wasn't late yet, so the rowdy drunks weren't out in force, but he noted a table two spots away that held four men. They'd been quiet when Retro and his boys had walked in, but now the volume level was beginning to climb, and the slurred words and loud laughter highlighted their boozy attitudes. *Something to watch.*

He'd picked this booth because the waitress in view as they approached the diner was flitting from table to table on the other end of the building, which meant it was likely Trina would be assigned this swath of tables. He hoped. *Fuck Mudd if he sent me on a wild goose chase.* That thought fled his mind when the kitchen's swinging door opened and a woman carefully backed through, a tray full of plates held with both arms.

Legs climbing from her sensible shoes up under the swishing fabric of her skirt, and her waist tucked in just right showing her hips weren't as lean as he'd thought. She had a sweet, round ass under the fall of red, the signature color for the servers at this diner chain, and something that looked good on her with all her dark hair. She turned, intently focused on the tray that looked too heavy by far for her to hold for long. The door swung open behind her and a man stepped up close, reaching over her shoulder to plop another full plate on top of the already teetering pile.

Retro did not miss how the asshole let his crotch brush her ass, also marking Trina's practiced twist of avoidance. *Fucker.* She got shit on no matter where she went. *Wouldn't be like that with me.* He shook his head, dismissing the wild idea. He wasn't in the market for anything. This was just him satisfying his curiosity about the woman he'd failed to protect the other night. His chin tipped up as he considered his thoughts. *Why would I think I failed? She ain't mine to protect.* "Not yet," he murmured, pulling Dancer's attention.

"What, boss?"

"Nothing."

Digging his heels against the sticky linoleum flooring, he settled himself in to watch. Sure enough, the mountain of food was for the table of drunks, and the closer she got to that quartet of testosterone, the more he had a bad feeling. She slipped in close and said something to one of the booth's occupants as she balanced the tray on her shoulder.

Two of the men sat back, considerately making room for the plates she started placing in front of them. *There's always one, sometimes a duo.* He noted how two of the men were dipwads and stayed angled over the table, elbows firmly set in place. In the outside seats, they were on opposite sides of the surface, and their postures were antagonistic enough Retro noted it. These were either good friends in the midst of a disagreement, or they weren't friends at all.

Plates deployed as best she could around their standoff, Trina tucked the empty tray under one arm with a smile and he overheard her ask them, "Will there be anything else, gentlemen?" Sweet and professional, nothing out of the ordinary in that exchange.

Then one of the dipwads made a mistake by reaching out to wrap his meaty hand around the top of her thigh, thumb buried between her legs. Trina screeched and tried to jerk backwards, but he had the fabric of her skirt in his fist, and she couldn't go far without being willing to leave it behind. On his feet in an instant, Retro loomed over Trina from behind, chest against her back and hands on her shoulders to steady her as he glared at the dead man.

He knew Dancer and Crazy Mike had climbed to their feet from the noise behind him as well as the wide-eyed look on three of the men's faces. Dipwad hadn't released Trina yet, so Retro didn't pay the rest of the men any mind, just reached down and laid claim to the man's wrist, grinding down on the fine, fragile bones until he heard and felt a satisfying crunch that made the asshole let go. Retro carefully put Trina behind him, the sensation of her fingers winding through his belt loops satisfying in a way he didn't have time to focus on yet. The man had grunted and yelled, face going ashen as he tried to get away from Retro's grip.

Dipwad was not successful.

Tightening his hold, Retro twisted until he felt a tendon stretch and pop under his hand. Then with the benefit of the crippling pain he knew the asshole was experiencing, Retro jerked the man out of the booth and into the aisle between tables, laying him out on the floor. He ignored the table that was now in an uproar, three men shouting at him to stop. From the corner of his eye, he saw the kitchen door swing wide, the asshole cook standing there with his fucking idiot mouth hanging wide open.

A man at the other end of the diner had his phone out, either live streaming or recording. *Out-fucking-standing.*

Retro was astonished at how fast things had escalated, and knew it was time for damage control. *Mudd's gonna rip me a new one, if I don't.*

"You think you're gonna grab any other random woman by the crotch, douchenozzle? That shit don't fly, motherfucker, and you're goddamned lucky I've left your fucking tainted arm attached. You don't touch a woman without her permission, ever. She gives you that permission, you hold that carefully, like it's a goddamned precious thing, because it's hers to grant. What you don't do"—he flung the man's hand away from him with force, gratified by the shout of pain the movement elicited—"is touch a woman that's not yours in any shape or form. She yours? This woman behind me? This waitress just tryin' to make a goddamned living serving food to ungrateful limp dicks like you? She yours? Don't answer, because I know she ain't. Know why?" He pulled himself up, chest puffed out and elbows akimbo, fists slamming against each hip. He wanted to intimidate, wanted to scare this crew senseless, because as long as they felt they held a right to behave that way, his Nelda wouldn't be safe. His Bekka wouldn't be safe. And his Trina wasn't safe. *And that shit don't fly.* "Because she's mine."

63

With the camera pointed at him, Retro couldn't turn and give it his back, not without repercussions because of his patch, but he wouldn't put Trina closer to the fuckers still gawping at him from their position over asshole laid out on the floor. More damage control, something Mudd was better at than him, but Retro knew he could do a fair job when put to the test. Conciliatory was the way to go, with whatever live audience the fucker with the phone had going on. *Sure, now I'm a fuckin' peacemaker.* Teeth gritted tight, because every word went against what he wanted to do, Retro asked, "You gonna eat or go? Gonna eat and put this shit aside, then it's all good and you've learned a lesson. You gonna go, then..." He paused, thinking, then twisted to look over his shoulder until he caught sight of her pale face and asked Trina, "What's the cook's name?"

"Umm...Gary. His name's Gary." Her voice trembled on the verge of tears and Retro reached back to pull one hand free of his belt loops, clasping it gently in his fingers. Hers were chilled, cold to the touch, and he knew it was the adrenaline dump from everything happening so fast, the uninvited hand on her body, followed by violence right in front of her. *Part of it's my fault.* He wanted to make it better, somehow, so placed her palm on his side, using touch to flatten it against his shirt, holding it in place.

"You wanna leave, Gary there will get you some containers. You'll pay for your goddamned food, motherfuckers, and tip my girl. Now—" He leaned slightly forwards, pulling Trina with him, belly warming when she rested her other hand on his back. She didn't know what the gesture meant. He did, knew to his bones her unconscious movement meant she had his back, but the mere fact she wasn't running away screaming told him she had at least a grip on what he was trying to do for her. "Get off the floor and apologize."

"You broke my fuckin' arm." The man probably meant it to sound threatening, but it came out more a puling whine and Dancer snorted behind him. "Why'd you do that?"

"One, I didn't break it. If I'd broken it, you'd know it. I put you on your ass and in your place because you touched what wasn't yours." Retro shook his head. "Two, because you deserved it." He looked at the table and the man who'd been posturing angrily earlier had slid back in his seat, seeming to take in the confrontation with pleasure. "You." The man pointed to his chest and Retro tipped his chin up in acknowledgment. "You know his momma?" The man's face lit up as he instinctively understood the plan, and he nodded. "Call her." Trina's hand flexed under his and Retro threaded his fingers through hers, clasping tight until she settled.

"What? No. I'm a grown man, I don't need nobody calling my mom on me."

"You weren't acting like a grown man." That bit of insight came from the video specialist on the other end of the diner. He'd ventured closer by twenty feet, the camera now angled towards the man pushing to his feet. "You were acting like a dick."

"Mrs. Thompson? Hi, this is Troy. Yes, ma'am, it's been too long." Retro listened to the man going through the polite motions with the mother of this asshole and grinned. They were clearly southern boys, had probably grown up together, and if this woman was anything like Retro's own mother, then dipwad here was in for a tongue lashing, and not the fun kind. *This is gonna be good.* "Paul got into a fight. No, ma'am, he's okay. But the man who handled him wanted you to know what he was doing." He paused, then said, "Let me put you on speaker." Fingers tapping on the screen, he laid his phone down and said, "Mrs. Thompson? Can you hear us?"

"I can. What's that boy done now?" Oh, yeah. She already sounded pissed.

"Ma'am," Retro said, rocking back on his heels a bit as he took control of the call with a smirk. "I had to put your son in his place because he grabbed a woman where no man should. She's a waitress, trying to serve the food he ordered, and he just grabbed her out of nowhere. So, I took it on myself to teach him a lesson."

Silence from the phone, then a wavering, "Paul? My Paul?"

"Mom." Paul tried to talk, but that's when the shouting started as Mrs. Thompson laid into him. Retro grinned at a few of her more inventive non-cursing curses, as she educated her Paul what he'd done to her by his actions tonight.

Retro gestured towards the camera guy, who'd wandered another few feet forwards. "You gettin' this, man?" He nodded and Retro grinned. "I'd be obliged if you'd end it before the cops get here."

"No one's called the cops," Gary the cook said with a sideways smile, tentative as if unsure he had a voice here. *You should worry, buddy.* "I've got a scanner back here and haven't heard anything."

Wonders never cease. Retro nodded at the welcome news, tuning back into Mrs. Thompson's tirade. Time to bring this to an end. "Ma'am?" She paused, and he continued. "Do you think Paul's teachable? You think he learned from this?"

"I hope so, son." Oh, yeah, she was a true southern woman, wanting to mother the good boys.

"Then my work here is done. Troy, thanks for helpin' out with this. Paul, eat, don't eat. It don't matter to me, but if I see you again and you're acting like a fuckwad, we'll have a different ending to the encounter." He leaned closer and Paul reared back, hand still gripping his swelling wrist across his chest. "You understand what I'm sayin'?"

"I understand."

Retro nodded then turned to the video guy. "I think we're all done." The phone stayed steady on Retro for a moment then the man smiled, backed away, and turned the phone on himself to do some kind of signoff to his viewers. *Live stream then.* Retro glanced over his shoulder at Crazy

Mike who was already on his phone. He'd be connecting with a friend they had in another club, getting him to track the recording down and wipe it if possible.

Video guy went back to his table, the other waitress picked up the coffee carafe she'd placed on the countertop and stepped over to top off a customer's mug. Gary went back into the kitchen and came out a minute later with a check and a pile of to-go boxes, picking up the tray Trina had dropped on his way. Back to normal, back to work, back to boring—which was safe and very welcome after that tense handful of minutes.

Retro stood through it all, Trina's palm flat on his back, fingers of her other hand wrapped trustingly around his. Seeing the table of four decided to pay and leave, after they'd had gathered up their food and vacated, he looked at Gary, projecting as much menace as he could summon, which Retro knew was considerable. "Same treatment comes to men who rub up on someone uninvited." Gary blanched and nodded, gaze darting to the floor as he retreated to the kitchen once more.

Retro swept the diner with his gaze a final time and then pulled Trina around in front of him. He took a big step backwards, trusting his brothers to wing out, and move back in, giving him a moment of relative privacy with the woman. She stared up at him with wide blue eyes, mouth pressed into a thin line that told him the chill and trembling in her fingers was due at least In part to fear. *Fuck. That's on me.*

"You okay?" Her head moved side to side, and then she closed her eyes, swallowing so hard he watched the muscles of her cheeks move with it. She nodded slowly, top of her head nearly touching his chest with each movement. Her hair fell on either side of her face, thick tendrils escaping the messy bun pinned on top of her head to hang in curly waves, and he stilled his hand from reaching to touch, to caress. *Not mine to take. Not yet.* "Trina, are you okay, honey?"

"Thank you." She sniffed and laughed softly, swiping her nose with the side of one wrist. He realized he still held her other hand captive, and gave it a squeeze that brought her eyes back to his. "Sorry. It's just been a rough few days. Yeah, I'm okay. Thanks." She huffed out a quick breath. "Thank you."

He gave that practiced flip of his head, settling his hair behind one shoulder as he looked down at her. This woman was about as far from okay as she could be, if what she was fighting to hide was real. "You ain't okay." He shook his head, shushing her when she would have spoken. "Shhhh. Were you working two jobs before, or is this one new?"

She blinked and lifted her chin, clearly expecting censure. "Depends. Money's money, and I have some hours to fill now." Trina rolled her eyes slightly, mouth pulling to one side. He liked that she was quickly regaining her sass. "So, if you happen to know of anyone hiring, I'm available."

"What do you do other than waitress?" He settled his ass against the lip of the plate glass window, noting how Dancer had turned and was watching his vulnerable back. *Good man.* Crazy Mike was placing an order with the other waitress, up near the counter, keeping everyone in the diner at bay. *God, I got good men.* "Any other skillsets I can tout?"

"I push a mean broom." She tried to smile, losing the battle somewhere in the middle. "Menial work, mostly. I learn fast, can follow instructions, and I'm dependable." The hope in her expression slayed him, and he was suddenly in a hurry to leave. Not to get away from her and whatever this instant attraction was between them, but to dig into her past and learn more about her. The sum total of his knowledge about Trina would fit on the head of a pin right now, and he wanted to find out everything that made her tick.

"How can I contact you when I find something?" He wrestled against smiling when her lips mouthed the words "when not if" and he nodded, because he'd meant what he said. "When," he confirmed, and she clamped her mouth closed, lips rolling between her teeth. "You got a phone?" Retro frowned when she shook her head. "What do you mean?"

"I don't have a cell." She shrugged. "There's always something more important to spend the money on."

Chin up, he looked over at Dancer who had overheard and was already moving away with a nod, headed for the door. Retro carried fresh burners with him everywhere, stocking them was part and parcel of the information business. Being able to make and take calls without being tracked could be critical to the continued usefulness of any given source. "Yeah, life can be a rat race." Not having a phone meant she was at risk, because if something happened to her wreck of a car—and he noted right then that she needed a better ride—then she'd be at the mercy of whoever happened by. Knowing she didn't have a phone meant he wouldn't sleep at night, wondering about her. His boys had phones, even Saya. His was a special kind with unique controls to allow him to text easily, since he couldn't use the voice features. But a cell phone was a safety net in this world. For Trina to not have one? *Not acceptable.* "But you gotta be safe, yeah?" She tipped her head to the side and studied him a moment. "Trina, you gotta be safe." A moment later and Dancer was back inside, fitting the battery into the back of a new phone and sliding the flat case into place. He powered it up and tapped around on the screen until Retro's pocket vibrated and he nodded.

"Why are you being so nice to me?" She retreated a step and he missed the heat from her touch. Their clasped hands stretched between them, a fragile bond he wanted to keep.

He pushed his bottom lip up in a slow smirk designed to distract and sighed as she shook her head. "I gotta have a reason?" Retro offered her a crooked grin; he hadn't been surprised when she didn't fall for the ploy.

"Everyone has an agenda." Her fingers twisted and she tried to release his grip from her hand. "What's yours?"

Fingers tightening down on her for a moment, he held on to give her a squeeze and then released, letting her retreat again. "No agenda. I found I have a profound interest, and I won't try to hide that. But no agenda." He gestured behind her and she looked to see Dancer holding out the device in a silent demand. She took it automatically, then stared at the phone in confusion. "Keep it on you. I'll call when I find a job for your consideration." Crazy Mike gathered up the bags of food containers and stood next to the door. "We'll take our leave now. I done took up too much of your time here at work." They were the only ones on this end of the building now, the other patrons having moved or left. *Fuck.* His little drama would mean fewer tips for her, and she'd just admitted to being tight enough on money that one job wasn't enough. He reached for his wallet, flipping the chain out of the way with a movement as practiced as the one he normally performed with his hair. Five bills landed on the table. "Tip for your trouble."

"Uh." She sounded so lost he turned back to look at her. Gaze fixed on the money on the table, her lip trembled. *Goddamn it to hell.* "I don't know what to say?" Her questioning tone was cute, but her expression of pain and confusion wasn't. He didn't want to look too deeply at why he felt compelled to set her world right again, he just did, and accepted that as part of whatever this was.

"Say you'll pick up when I call." He shrugged, and she looked at him, tiny line centered between her brows.

"How will I know it's you?"

Retro grinned and dug out his phone, lifting his chin towards the one in her hand. He navigated to the missed calls list, pushed a button and hers rang. She looked down at it and her eyes went round. Then, mouth open, she lifted it so he could see the screen. It said "Retro Calling ..." and the image showing was an intimate vignette of the two of them not five minutes ago, her palm on his chest while he stared down at her with a look of pride and adoration. He ended the call and grinned at her. "Now you'll know."

***

"Mister Secretary, is there any past business to take care of tonight?"

Mudd's voice was filled with boredom, because this was the part of church they just wanted to get through. Past business generally was about tidying up the timeline of decisions, or about finding a resolution for something they hadn't been able to handle the last meeting. Protocol demanded they run through the routine, and Retro found it soothing. A simplicity and cadence that was predictable, because in an ever-changing world, the parliamentary procedure remained the same year after year.

Paper shuffled and Marlin called out, "No old business."

Mudd looked at Retro and patted the pocket on the front of his vest. "Mister Secretary, is there new business on the docket?"

"There is, Veep. We have a prospect who has completed all requirements as laid out in our by-laws and is ready to come to the floor to have his fate decided. To continue, we need to conduct a full vote with all active members present and in good standing. At this time, do we want to open the door and the floor?" That was aimed at Retro, but he held his tongue, giving Mudd a chance to respond.

"We do. Make it so."

The doors opened, folding back against the wall until there was an archway of about twenty feet that looked out into the main room of the clubhouse. They were in the outer office, one generally understood to be less secure and not soundproof, but it gave a good view of the rest of the clubhouse once the barriers were stowed away.

"Bastards," Mudd stood and waved his arms, hands curling in a "come here" gesture every man understood. "Members in good standing only. Dues owed and prospects other than Dancer need to head to the lot." There was a shuffling of footsteps while the only other prospect they had patched stood and looked at Mudd, apparently shocked he was being excluded.

That Buzzkill might be a questionable patch. Retro shook his head. "Fuck you waitin' on, boy?" He rested his hands on top of the gavel, fingers folded around the handle. "Are you a goddamned member? No. Then get your ass to the lot and stand there until someone comes to get you." Moving faster than Retro expected, the man turned and trotted towards the door. He muttered, "Fuck. At least he moves quick when he's kicked hard enough." Louder, he called out, "Dancer, need you to come up here."

As Dancer made his way through the crowd, careful not to jostle the members who held glasses, bottles, or cans, Retro started the recitation of the man's accomplishments. "While he was a hangaround for two months, Dancer made himself useful by working on more than one member's bike. We voted him to scrub status, and gave him a set of blacks with a support patch. Took him to a party out of town, and he conducted himself with grace. Made him a prospect then and there. That's been nigh-on a year." Retro pointed towards a circle painted on the floor near the wall. "Get in the round, prospect."

The circle they called a "round tuit" was most often used for punishment, putting a prospect on display who didn't move fast enough to do the bidding of a full patch member. Three incidents in the round within a month meant a man would be busted back to whatever status he'd had previously, either scrub or hangaround.

"Not that you need the reminder to get your ass in gear, because you don't put off even the hardest of tasks. Man scrubbed the thrones in the clubhouse this morning before I was even out of bed, and that's the kind of service we like to see. He gets right on it, not around to it whenever it pleases him. He's in this because the club matters, not because he matters to the club. Even though he does. That's just not his way, is it? No, he's a dude who puts a hustle on it, ain't afraid to lay things out for his brothers when needed, a solid keeper of secrets, and born again as our patchover."

Murmuring came from all around the room and Retro met the eye of every man. He checked again to see Dancer was already in the circle, face aimed at the wall.

"Simple silent vote. Give me an emperor's up or down, life or death. In or out."

Retro held out his hand, made a deliberate fist and held it for a beat, waiting until every man mirrored the gesture. Then he tipped his thumb out sideways, even to the floor, holding that another moment until there was a sea of fists and thumbs in front of him. Without warning, he tipped his upwards, showing his vote with his actions, no words needed. If there were a total of three downward votes, it was a passing vote and the prospect was given another thirty days to earn his place, no questions asked and no exceptions. More than three noes and they'd be stripped of their vest and back to hangaround status, if they could stomach the demotion. Bama Bastards didn't patch lightly, or easily, and all votes were honest and binding.

He studied the upwards pointing thumbs, not finding a single one turned down. Needing verification, he asked, "Mudd, you seein' this shit?" He heard an inward suck of air from Dancer who was still blind to the proceedings, probably because those five words could mean either of two things, and it made Retro grin a little to leave him suspended in limbo for a minute. Mudd nodded and lifted his fist a little higher, the movement matched by every man with a vote to keep Dancer. "Okay." Retro dropped his fist and asked, "You get what I needed?" Mudd reached into his pocket with two fingers, pulling out a scrap of fabric. "Mister Secretary, do you have the rest of it?" Retro held out his hand and accepted the new vest with the full set of patches from Marlin. "Okay."

He turned and watched Dancer for a moment, seeing the man's ramrod straight posture, shoulders back, and chin up. No matter what the answer had been, he would have accepted it. *He's a good man.* "Einstein." Retro grinned, because of course there wasn't a response. *Not yet.* "Hey, Einstein, turn around." That got Dancer's attention and he twitched, then stilled. "Yeah, I'm talkin' to you, Einstein. Get a round tuit." Dancer's head jerked to the side and he guardedly eyed Retro over his shoulder. "Yeah, you. Turn around, Einstein."

"Drop your vest." Mudd's shout was echoed by a dozen other men, and it made Retro swell with pride to know Einstein was so well regarded. "Drop it, brother."

With a broad grin finally bursting forth on his face, Einstein shrugged out of the ill-fitting prospect vest, but he didn't just hand it off and grab for his colors. He did something that made Retro nod as he heard approving murmurs swell around the room. Reverently the man folded the vest, folded it and tucked in the edges so the prospect patch was completely protected by the worn leather of the garment.

"Respect, man. I love seein' that." He reached out and took the folded leather, passing the man a vest so new it squeaked as Einstein pulled it into place. He rolled his shoulders a couple of times, settling it over his skin and bones, and Retro could see in that moment that this man would someday be important for the club. "Welcome, brother." He pressed the nameplate into Einstein's hand. "Figured you'd want to sew this on yourself." Eyes closed, Einstein nodded, and Retro reached out to pull him into a one-armed clinch. "Welcome, brother."

He passed him off to Mudd, who pounded his back before passing him off to the next man, and the next, and Retro basked in hearing the same murmured greeting repeated again and again, solidifying the reason he'd built the club from the ground up.

Brotherhood, belonging, trust, and honor. It meant everything to men like them, and Retro soaked it up for a moment, watching the bonds being built all around him.

Brotherhood.

Chapter Three
Retro

He sat sideways on a loveseat near the back door, socked foot propped on a cushion, other foot flat on the floor. His phone was balanced on top of his jeans-clad thigh and he twisted it like a whirligig, around and around. It had been more than a full day and the woman hadn't called. He was still sourcing her a job that he could stomach, Mudd having a good old time reminding him how his brother went through the same thing with his woman, his angst about her working around men the topic of many a humorous story shared between the clubs.

It ain't that. He sighed. It was, but he wasn't going to admit his own feelings of jealousy.

He and Mudd had paid a final visit to the strip club owner today, leaving there with a good assurance that Andy would be terminated with prejudice, meaning he wouldn't be able to circle back for a job in a few months. Retro flexed his fist, bruised knuckles aching with a good reminder of resolution to another of Trina's problems. The asshole cook had assured them he'd learned his lesson, spitting his promises through a mouthful of blood to gain mercy.

"Call her."

Retro picked his head off the back of the couch and twisted to look up at Mudd. "Not that simple, brother."

"It is that simple." Mudd shrugged. "What's holdin' you back, man? You want her, you go get her. That's what you do. It ain't like you to sit around and look constipated because you're not working whatever angle's up in your head."

"I don't look like that." He snorted. "I'm just tryin' to decide what job to offer her."

"So you *were* thinking about her." Mudd threw himself into an overstuffed chair nearby, toeing his boots off before he turned to settle his feet on the end cushion of the couch. "I knew it."

"You think you're so smart." He chuckled. "What am I thinking now?"

"You're deciding between the dry cleaners and the mechanic shop, and you'll land on the mechanic shop because there's more opportunity for her there. And it fits better with her exhibited skillset, because getting mustard stains out of someone's sportscoat wouldn't be very satisfying. Managing three mechanic bays and ordering for the shop would keep her just busy enough to leave every day feeling like she made a difference, without being overwhelming." Mudd shrugged. "I'm callin' it now. Shop."

"That's where I was leaning," Retro admitted as he looked down at the phone, setting it spinning on his thigh again. "We got a shift with only ugly fuckers on it? Because I'll move them all to days, and that'll be where I drop her for sure."

He didn't have to look up to know Mudd was laughing, the sound advertised his amusement. Retro didn't look up to see when it trailed off and stopped, either. He kept his gaze on the phone, willing it to ring. Mudd was silent for long minutes, and Retro listened to the familiar sound of men coming and going from the kitchen area and out front, then back inside. And the phone still didn't ring.

"What's goin' on in your head, brother?" Even more familiar than the noises around them was Mudd's quiet voice, and the trust built over decades of friendship finally pulled Retro's attention away from the phone. His patch brother was studying him, head cocked to one side, a puzzled expression on his face. "Talk to me, Jerry."

"I've seen the woman a grand total of two times. Spoken to her twice. There's no earthly reason she should be under my skin like this. Me sittin' here, free from Wanda finally, livin' my life in the midst of a day I've been dreaming about for years, and I'm sittin' here waitin' on the phone to ring. Trying to decide if it's too needy to text her first, and then wishin' I'd already given in and done it. What the fuck is wrong with me, man?" He huffed out an irritated laugh. "That's what's in my head, got me tied up in knots over here. I don't even know the woman, but I want her here, under my arm, in my bed. Want her to meet my brothers, my kids. My *kids*, Rodney. The fact I even got that in my head is shocking and scary as fuck, but I can't get past it. I *want*. So much. So *fuckin'* much. Maybe more than I've ever wanted anything in my life."

"What do you see happening with her? Is this a rebound thing? Drop Wanda, find someone who needs rescuing and latch onto her?" Retro was shaking his head before Mudd finished speaking, holding his peace when his friend lifted a palm. "No, brother, listen a minute," Mudd urged him. "Think it through. Don't answer based on your gut, as good an indicator as that anatomy usually is. You've been in the middle of some shit over the past months, and maybe this woman, this Trina is a way to anchor yourself. If that's so, then great. She seems like good people, and you could do worse."

"I did do worse." Retro didn't shy away from calling a spade a spade, even in his own life. "Made my own life hell because I wasn't enough something for my woman. Cuckolded, shamed, the only thing I have to show for those years are my kids, and thank God they look like me, or I don't know what I'd do. So yeah, I did do worse, brother."

"Be that as it may, Wanda can't set the bar for what you bring into your life now. What is it about this woman that has you spinnin' in circles?" Mudd sighed. "She's pretty. Boys say she's sweet. She stirred something inside you, that's for sure. But why her?"

"Pretty doesn't touch her. Pretty isn't in the same room with her. She's a class above. Gorgeous and shy, genuine and sweet. She brings out the protective side of me, makes me want to smooth the way for her. Brings out the possessive side, because I'm not kiddin' about shifting mechanics around if they do one damn thing out of line. That man grabbed her, brother." He shook his head again. "Only took me half a heartbeat before I reached for Betty. I tell you what." Dirty Betty was his private name for his Glock, the weapon that was so much a part of him he felt naked without it at his back. Jaw tight, he fought the remembered anger swelling inside him. "That little boy doesn't know how close he came to takin' a dirt nap. If we'd been in a less public place, I can't say it wouldn't have gone down differently."

"Whoa." Mudd's mouth made an *O* of shock. Then he laughed low, bleeding off the sudden tension between the two of them. "You aren't kiddin', are you?" Retro shook his head back and forth slowly, gaze locked on Mudd's. "Fuck, man. That's…"

"Fast. I know." The phone buzzed under his hand and he nearly dropped it in his haste to grab the device. Disappointment swept over him as he recognized the number as a local political source, and he looked up at Mudd to see a dark frown on his face. "Not her." With a tap of his thumb, he sent the call to voice mail. "I won't rest until I talk to her again."

"Then make the call, Jerry. Make the call and get things rolling between you, because the way you are now, you'll eat yourself from the inside out before you settle." Mudd sat upright and reached out for his boots, stomping his feet back into them. "Make the call, and then come see me over there." He pointed over his shoulder at the pool table. "I'll whip your ass, get you drunk, and send you to bed."

"Sounds like a deal."

***

Trina

"No, Mama, this kind of thing doesn't happen to me." Trina fingered the money on her nightstand. Nearly four hundred dollars in various currency, mostly twenties, lay there, still stacked in a tidy pile, edges all lined up evenly. "He was unlike anything I've ever encountered."

"Trina, honey doll, maybe he's the one." The hissed eagerness in her mom's voice when she said "the one" made Trina grin. She still found it cute when her mom would get wound up in her dizzying excitement over something simple.

"You and I both know that's not how life works, Mama." Trina yawned and leaned back on a locked elbow. "He's super nice, true, but he's just a guy like any other. Now, I'm bushed from working, and I have the breakfast shift at the diner tomorrow, so I should get to bed."

"No rest for the weary," her mother agreed, and Trina blew a soft kiss into the phone as her mom did the same. No goodbyes, this was their traditional ending to any phone conversation, a superstition her mother had followed all Trina's life.

Toes scrunching, she let one shoe drop to the floor, followed quickly by a thud from the other. Knees to chest, she curled in the middle of the bed, staring blindly ahead. Still holding the phone, she tucked her hands under her pillow, fingers wrapped around the thing she wouldn't admit to herself felt like a lifeline.

Retro. His nickname fit him perfectly. Such a mix of gentleman and warrior, she hadn't been able to properly breathe around him. First when he'd rescued her at the club the first night, and at that rude memory, she felt the smallest twinge of pain in her bottom. The discipline wasn't something she'd agreed to, but when offered the choice to take it or walk out, it hadn't required much thought to bend at the waist and take it. Rent had been due, and as jobs go, it hadn't been the worst. Most of the customers weren't too handsy, and even if most of the dancers held themselves aloof, it wasn't like she had started working there to make friends. Some of them were nice, to her at least.

Still, Retro hadn't hesitated to leap into action either time, and that confidence in his own ability should be frightening. It meant he fought a lot. Trina stretched out a hand and fumbled with the twisty switch on her lamp, finally plunging the room into darkness. A tiny glow crept around the edges of her pillow, and she pulled the phone out and looked at it.

There was only one number saved, and she already knew it was listed as Retro, a name that matched the piece of sewn cloth on his vest. She wasn't an idiot; she knew what he was. A biker, probably a criminal, and someone who would be dangerous to know. But he had been her personal savior too.

"Like four times," she whispered, ticking her fingers up as she listed. "Arrogant Andy," that was the night shift manager at the strip club. "Paul the prick." The man who'd grabbed her at the diner, the pain from his grip excruciating, hurting and burning until she couldn't have gotten away without help. "Lunatic landlord." The money on her table would ensure at least another month's rent on her tiny one-room efficiency. More than covering rent, just the money he'd given or gotten for her would be food, and maybe a brake job on her aged car. "Phenomenal phone."

She fumbled the phone and it dropped, screen down on the thin blanket. Trina shut her eyes and snuggled into the pillow, relaxing her body muscle by muscle.

"Hello?" Even muffled, the masculine voice was unmistakable.

"Oh my God," she breathed, staring at the phone.

"Trina?" His tone sharpened, and she could imagine the look on his face from before, when he was cutting that rude customer down to size.

"Trina?" There was a mumbled conversation. Then she heard him, voice so crisp he didn't need to raise it to get respect, just being who he was garnered him attention enough. His bearing said this was a man who needed to be attended to with full focus. He said, "Trace it, Mudd. Fuckin' trace it. She dialed me, but she ain't talkin'. I bet that damned asshole from the strip joint knows where she lives, and God knows who else. Could be nothin', I know. But, it could be anything."

Trina suddenly realized she was the one causing him distress and that made her throat tight, bitter salt burning the back of her nose. "Retro?" She tipped the phone upright and slipped it under her head, nestling her ear on the speaker. "Hi."

"Oh, thank fuck." He sounded genuinely upset, but not angry, more as if he were fearful. "Naw, it's good, Mudd. Thanks, brother, I got her finally. False alarm." The background sound changed and a moment later he asked her softly, "I'm real pleased to hear from you. You doin' okay?"

"Yes." *I could listen to him talk all night.* "I'm okay. Are you?"

He huffed out a tiny laugh, sounding surprised. "Huh. Yeah, I'm good." He fell silent and she lay there, waiting, realizing a few seconds later she was listening to him breathe. "What are you up to, Trina?"

"About to go to sleep." She curled up a little tighter, knees to chest. She flexed and pointed her toes, feet still aching. "I didn't mean to bother you."

"Honey, hearing from you is the far end on the scale from things that bother me. I'm glad you called. I don't have any news on a job yet, but I've got some irons in the fire already. Might have something for you to consider within a couple of days." He breathed, and she got lost in the regular beauty of just that soothing sound, heavy and deep, steady. *Dependable.* "What kind of a place you got? Tell me where you lay your head." These were a kind of get-to-know-you questions, and that soothed her nerves, because if he wanted to know her, there might be something here like she'd been imagining.

Instead of answering him, she asked a question of her own. "Where are you at now?" She squeezed her eyes tight, blocking out the tiny room where she lay on a single bed that took up more than half the space in the room. She knew it by heart anyway. Tiny sink scarcely large enough to wash both hands in at once, and the smallest crockpot ever made sitting on the narrow counter beside. From the ceiling over the foot of the bed hung a set of cheap fabric shelves she'd found at the local resell store, her non-uniform clothing stacked in two of the openings. Uniforms on hangers dangled from a loop of rope pulled through the crack of the bathroom door. "I bet it's nice."

"This you tellin' me you aren't somewhere nice?" Retro's voice softened, trying to coax words from her and she squeezed her eyes tighter. "Trina, are you safe? It matters a lot to me that you're safe."

"I'm safe," she lied. The wood framing the door was soft and old, and all it would take was a hard shoulder to the jam and the surface mounted deadbolt would pop loose. *Again.* "It's just nothing fancy. I bet you're in a much more interesting place."

"Okay." He dropped the line of questioning and something told her his acquiescence was a deliberate ploy and they'd be returning to the topic before long. "Okay. Well, I'm standin' on a back porch of sorts." She heard boots on wood, another steady sound, pacing along with a determined stride. "Headed up the stairs now, because it's two levels. The top one adjoins my bedroom here."

"Where's here?" She swallowed. "Not that you have to tell me anything. I know what you are." *Oh, Lord.* She'd just blurted those words out there and didn't mean to say anything close to that. But it had felt like she'd been so demanding and she just wanted him to not hate her for being such a noisy goose.

"And what am I, Trina?" His tone was carefully modulated, steady in a very different way, rigid with steel and potential anger. "What do you know me to be?"

"A good man." Trina forced truth into her voice as much as she could, because she believed down to the soles of her feet that he *was* good. He'd proved that twice over just in how he handled people who weren't good. "I know you're good because of how your friends treat you. They wouldn't stick by you when fists were flying if you weren't. If they didn't trust you."

"That's not what you meant, honey." She heard him breathe out, not a sigh exactly, but close. "Always say what you mean to me."

"You're a biker." Her mouth flooded with bitter spit and she swallowed the burn down, hoping she hadn't messed up so much he'd hang up. Just listening to him breathe made her feel safer than she had in a thousand days. "So, of course, you don't have to tell me where you are. That's all I meant. I don't want to be the reason for anything bad to happen."

"Why would something bad happen if I told you where I am?" He sounded genuinely curious and she rolled her eyes, still closed tightly.

"Because we're on the phone." She almost added a "duh" but controlled herself at the last second. "And people listen on phone conversations all the time."

"So you're tryin' to protect me?" The lilt in his voice made her think he was smiling, because he seemed the kind of man who'd echo his smiles in his words.

"Well, yeah. You're a good guy, and this is your phone, and I don't want to be the reason anything bad happens to you." She paused, then gave voice to the final reassurance she had inside her. "Ever."

"Got it. You're a protective little thing. I like that a lot." Rolling smoothly as velvety chocolate, his voice wrapped around her and Trina relaxed into the pillow, imagining he still held her hand. "Where I am, because the phone I gave you is safe, super safe as long as you don't let anyone do anything to it—so keep it close, yeah?" Trina's throat made a strangled sound and he laughed. "Keep it close, and it's all good. Where I am is where I'm living right now, in the house the club keeps for itself. I have a bedroom suite here, and right now, I'm standin' on the balcony off that suite, staring up at the stars and wondering where you are. Can you see the stars from where you are, Trina?"

"I can imagine them." There were no windows opening out from her room, so the only stars she saw were on her hurried walk home from the free city parking eight blocks away. "Do you want me to imagine them?"

"Yeah, honey." The endearment slipped along her skin, warming her from the inside out. He seemed to hold those things close, and she thought it was more important than anything how he'd slipped up and given her one just now. "Imagine the stars blinking overhead while you stand next to me here. My arm across your shoulders, holdin' you close. You can lose yourself in the sight, because I'll keep you safe. You feel that, don't you. That's why you're so protective back to me."

"Yeah." He'd nailed it in one try, putting words to this tiny seed of something that he'd planted inside her. "That sounds nice. Safe."

"How's your knee?" His question was as soft as the other words, but it seemed to come out of the blue.

Trina reached down and ran her fingers over the broad bandage she'd taped to her skin. "It's okay. Healing. How did you know I'd hurt it?"

"You fell on the carpet at that club, got a rugburn, right?"

"Uh, yeah. Sort of? Your powers of observation are uncanny." She choked a hysterical giggle off before it escaped. *Imagine what it would be like to have them turned on me in a different setting.* She had an idea that Retro wouldn't allow any falsehoods in a relationship, probably especially in an intimate situation. *No fakin' it with him.* "What do you do for a living?"

"Did you do more to it than the fall I saw?" His voice had regained that careful tone, and she paid close attention to his words. "Was it something that happened in that office? I heard him belting you, Trina. Was there more that happened in there?"

"I fell, that's all." She decided to share a tiny bit more. "Arrogant Andy, that's what I call him in my head, I don't know what his problem was with me, but he got it in his mind that it was okay to do that. That thing. You heard." She squinched up her face until lights flashed behind her eyelids. "I tripped over my own feet and fell in the office, and then tripped in the hallway. It's no big thing." She paused, then tried out his name, wanting to see how it fit inside her mouth. "Retro."

"Mmmm. Say that again for me?" He could have been wedged in behind her with the heat his soft request brought to her. It rolled through her, settling low in her belly, tendrils licking between her legs that made her back arch and toes curl.

"I bet he's a furnace in bed." She shivered.

"What?" He sounded confused and her eyes popped open, blackness receding because of the line of light under the door.

"Oh, God. I said that out loud." She yanked the phone out from under her head and stared at it in dismay.

"Trina?" From this far away, his voice sounded tinny, and she wanted what she'd had before, so she flipped sides and put her back towards the door, phone back to her ear. "What'd you say?"

"I said it's no big thing." She tried to backtrack, stymied when he laughed low and sexy, which brought her mind right back to the "furnace in bed" thought, and followed it up with a "beast in bed" which made her imagine other things in rapid succession.

"Trina, you okay? You're breathin' funny, honey."

"So this house you're at, it belongs to the club? Do you like being part of a club like that? Doesn't it keep you from doing normal things?" *Oh, way to go*. She'd just insulted him after imagining him naked and doing glorious things to her body. Things she'd read about in books, but never expected to have a chance to practice, because her experiences had shown her that reality was far and away different from fictionalized romance. "Not that I'm judging."

"I wanna go back to where you were thinkin' about what I'm like in bed." And that right there proved he had better than average hearing, because he'd caught what she'd said, just been shocked she'd mentally put him in her bed like that.

"I'm sorry I said that. I didn't mean to make you uncomfortable."

"Oh, Trina. The only thing uncomfortable about this conversation is the distance between us while we're havin' it. I'm enjoying every moment here with you. I just wish you were actually here, with me. Now, say my name again, like you did a minute ago, like it matters to you who I am and that I like you. Say my name, honey."

"Retro."

"Mmhmm. That's the tone I wanted. So Arrogant Andy, and I gotta say, that is a choice moniker you picked for him, what he did wasn't anything you wanted?"

"What? No. No." She shook her head. "You have a way of surprising me with questions, so you get the honest answer. No, I didn't, but it was my job or *that*. And I needed to work. Need."

"You like waitressin'? Enjoy workin' in the service industry? No shame in that game, because it makes the world go 'round and gives a body plenty of people time if that's what a body wants. So is that a good job for you?"

She rolled to her back, elbow in the air to hold the phone close. "Not really. The people are the hardest part, you know? I'm not really a people person. But it's easy to find a job like that, and they're at least steady hours with a regular cash option if you're good."

"You're good," he muttered, and she preened. "I watched you at the diner before that guy fucked things up for me, and you were easy with everything going on. I bet you do okay on tips."

"That was an especially good day for tips. Thank you." She paused, then pushed ahead. "What do you mean he messed things up for you?"

"Oh, darlin'." Her breath caught in her throat because that was new, and unique enough it made her fingers tremble with the beauty of his voice saying things like that to her. "I had plans of talking to you and gettin' to know you. And I am, so that's all good, but it certainly did derail the timeline I had in mind."

"So you came there to—what? Talk to me? Was it because of what happened at that other club? Because you need to know that's not what...I'm not like Andy might have suggested." Eyes squeezed tight, Trina lifted her top lip in anger because Andy had messed everything up all the way down the road. "So if that's what you're after. If that's why you were asking...if what he did was what I wanted, then you should probably take back this phone and we'll call it a day. I can mail it to you, if you want. Just text me an address or something." By the time she finished, Trina was back on her side, knees curled to her chest. With her free hand wrapped around her legs, she held herself together with effort. "I can return the money, too."

"What's your address?" She froze at the edge of anger in his voice. "Gimme a goddamn street or apartment building or something, because as nice as it is to have you in my ear like this, I'm feelin' like there's way too much room between us for this discussion. You're rewriting things in your head, Trina, and dammit, you've had a shit few days and I don't want to fuck up and make things worse." She didn't respond, watching the light under the door. It wavered as if she were underwater and she realized her eyes were wet, tears flowing down her cheeks. "What's your goddamned address, Trina?"

"I'm sorry." Her voice choked off, and she tried clearing her throat, not finding much success in relieving the tightness there. "I'll find a way to get you the phone and everything. It was nice to talk to you."

"Trina, if you hang up, I swear to fucking God—"

"Bye, Retro." She pulled the phone away from her ear.

"Trina, dammit." Tinny and small, his angry words came from the speaker. "Goddammit to fucking he—"

She disconnected the call.

***

Retro

Tongue tucked firmly into one cheek, Retro slowly lowered the phone from his ear, fingers straining as they clamped around the device. He tipped his chin up and stared at the cold stars blinking overhead. He knew if he stood here long enough, he'd get to watch them wheel and turn, aligning and realigning as they moved through the heavens. Dead, cold celestial bodies, light shining through space for eons after their time had passed.

With careful control, he took a breath and held it for a three-count, then let it out slowly, pushing it out from between his tightly pursed lips. Shoving the useless phone into his pocket, because he knew sure as anything that if he tried to call Trina right now, she'd have already turned off the device he'd given her, he propped his forearms on the railing, eyes still on the night sky.

I pecked around the edges of too many things.

Unblinking, he watched the lights of a jetliner traverse the expanse of the sky.

I dug deep too fast, tried to figure her out too soon.

Noise swelled and waned from the clubhouse underneath his feet, the door downstairs opening and closing a dozen times as his men came out to do whatever it was they needed to do.

I shoulda taken more care.

"Boss?" Mudd called up from the base of the stairs. "You need anything?"

Chin still lifted, he nodded. "Yeah." Somewhere in those stars, there was light that hadn't yet reached earth. Hadn't been seen by any man, alive or dead. Hadn't begun its first oscillating wave across the universe. Somewhere in that mass of blinking lights was a new star, not caring about whatever fates had decreed would be its final outcome. *Death is inevitable. But, life?* "I need a goddamned address." *That's for the living.*

Chapter Four

Retro

Idling up the street, he reflected for the hundredth time what a mistake it had been to say a goddamned word to Mudd. He could have gotten the address himself for a fraction of the grief the man had laid on him.

A quick glance in his mirrors showed he was at the head of a column of eight bikes, each ridden by one of his men. And not a single one of them was there at his request.

Fuckin' Mudd.

A week since he'd spoken to Trina, which was seven days too long in his books. But, it had taken time to find out everything he'd wanted to know. Time to deal with the things he wanted to settle before he saw her again. And if he were honest, he had needed time to sort out his own head.

Trina had pulled at him like a siren and in the moment, he'd reacted far outside of expectations. He'd responded to her physically, emotionally, and any other "ly" word he could dream up. At the diner, he'd proudly claimed her in public, in ways that couldn't be mistaken. Risked jail, or worse, and jeopardized his brothers and men doing the same as they defended him. Mudd had observed him with little sideways glances for two days, and Retro couldn't say he blamed him one bit, because he hadn't recognized his own actions, so far from the measured pace he normally set as he guided his club down the road.

Something about Trina made him reckless, willing to take a leap of faith about a woman he didn't know at all.

So Retro processed things in the way that felt right. He researched.

Address, work history, credit history, family history—hell, he knew how often she got the oil changed on that piece-of-shit car she had bought for hundreds more than it was worth because she didn't have anyone to haggle on her behalf. Mudd had worked alongside him for hours and hours, leaving to catch a nap at home so he could see his kids, then back to the clubhouse to tweak the web of information Retro had pieced together.

They tackled it as if she were an enemy they needed to take down, or a potential ally who required vetting before the first sit-down happened. He'd amassed a ton of info, and all of it pointed to him being a hundred percent right about one thing: Katrina Fainburg was a good woman.

She normally worked at least two jobs but could barely pay her bills, because she sent most of her money home to her mother, like clockwork every month. She would be the first coworker to chip in when someone needed help, and the last one to ask for assistance on her own behalf. She'd been known to offer someone the shirt off her back, a gesture done without any thought for her own comfort or safety.

She was quiet, kept to herself, was registered to vote, and donated money to a local animal charity. About the only flaw he could find was her car was still plated in Georgia, which was where her mother was from. No father in the picture at all, her birth certificate listed the shut door of "unknown" on that line. Cautious conversations with her mother's neighbors gave them a picture of a simple woman who'd raised her daughter until her daughter could raise herself. Deloris Fainburg had been on disability for years, and going back to when Trina was about twelve, the handwriting on checks to pay bills had changed from her mother's shaky loops to the daughter's tidy script.

Now he was ready to attack the problem head-on.

Because over the course of investigating her, his fascination hadn't eased off, hadn't slackened at all. If anything, it had grown more intense. He was done with that, tired already of eking out tidbits and snippets of her life. He needed to see her, to talk to her, and wasn't going to wait another day to make it happen.

She'd gotten off work about two hours ago and should be home right now.

I'll make her talk to me. He glanced at the lights in his mirrors again, pleased with the tight ranks on the column behind him. *Maybe I can break free that way.*

He needed to not have his head muddled by a woman, because there were things active in the region that his men should be acting on. In a way, this was his last-ditch effort to break the hold she had on him. *Do I want to break it?*

In his whole life, Retro had loved one woman. He'd been faithful to two, keeping Wanda a priority while they'd been together. *What the fuck do I need?*

Another block slid past under his wheels while his brain worked overtime, second-guessing everything.

I've never acted like this. Never felt the need to jump the creek the minute I see something I want. Some kind of instant love hadn't ever been in the cards for him, not since Clara. *Not in my stars.* He glanced up at the few shining beacons visible amidst the streetlights and buildings. The connection to Trina had been immediate and strong, overriding his basic survival instincts. Even in the days since, while forcing himself to stay away from her as he looked into who she was, he'd found himself obsessively wondering if she were safe, warm, tired, hungry, sleepy, or— *please God*—lonely.

I'll see what happens when we're face-to-face again. He would keep his hands to himself and just talk. He settled his shoulders, gripping the handlebars tightly before relaxing his hold. "We'll see."

He noted the dense clusters of observers every half a block or so, groupings of men who eyed the column as they rode past, heads on a swivel to track progress, and every one of his own men reciprocated. This was not a good part of town in anyone's way of reckoning. *Maybe Mudd wasn't such an idiot, after all.* He marked more than one set of hands that fell to a ready stance. If taken as gospel, that move telegraphed how they'd have weapons at the ready, and he not only worshipped at that church, Retro was well able to preach a message if needed, and took the opportunity to settle his own protection, not giving a shit which eyes caught the movement. Black Betty rode easy on his six, holster fitting to his body like a glove.

Only another two blocks and the column of bikes would be at the building he and Mudd had tracked her to, the address indicated in her employment records from the strip club. Half the places along the streets looked abandoned, and the other half probably should be. Retro was tense, not nervous for himself or his men, but at the thought how every day Trina braved these streets to get herself a little bit of money that scarcely saw her through.

Fist raised, he pulled the column to a smooth halt. There was no parking anywhere close, but he didn't need it. Not for this. He killed the bike's engine and stood up, feet firmly on the pavement on either side of the machine as he looked around. Deliberately catching and holding the gaze of anyone still on the street for a long moment, he swept the area. Most of the people had disappeared inside, fading away like late morning tendrils of fog, the ones who remained marked by more than himself.

Finally, he saw what he wanted and locked gazes with a man he knew well.

Mudd's position was behind him and to the right, and he heard a whisper, "Come on, fuckers. Come on. Bring it."

Head shaking back and forth, Retro patted the air, using a "simmer down" motion every one of his men would understand. Heel to the kickstand, he leaned his bike over as he sat on the saddle, untying the bandana that had been in place across the bottom half of his face.

"Fuck, boss." That from Einstein, no dirt on his patches yet, but Retro was already accustomed to the name in his head.

"Show them shiny faces, boys." This was a deliberate act on his part, because by uncovering their features, he told the men staring from the corner that he didn't mind being identified for whatever was going down. It had the desired result as three men broke from the group and walked towards where he sat.

"Greg," he called out, lifting his chin at the man in the lead. "How's it shakin'?"

Gregory Popova, affectionately known as Pooka to his grandmother, had been an organized crime staple in Birmingham for as long as Retro had been around. The man smirked and angled his head in a brief nod. "It shakes. You're—" He looked around the neighborhood as if surprised by where he found himself. "—not normally one to slum it with us riff-raff." A broad smile split his face and he reached out a hand. "Well met, Retro."

Holding up a single finger, Retro made a production out of removing his fingerless glove, knowing Greg would understand the respect inherent in the gesture. Finally stretching out his bare palm, he firmly returned the offered shake. "Good to see you. I wasn't sure who owned this part of town anymore." Which was his out for not having called first, and gave Greg a deferential nod at how well he'd kept his organization's infiltration under wraps, because if Retro didn't know he'd moved in, then it was likely no one did.

"That is good news." Another smirk and Retro laughed at the pleased expression. "So what brings you to my neck of the woods?"

"I needa see someone who lives here." He thumbed over his shoulder to the address Mudd had surfaced. "Just...comin' to pay a visit. I was planning on relocating them, but if you're here, then things are less dire than I expected." He lifted a shoulder in a lazy shrug as he scratched at one cheek, every movement intentional and a silent aspect of the ongoing conversation. *See me? See my hand? See how comfortable I am? See how I'm not reaching for my piece?* "Might still relocate. Hard to tell yet."

"My building, yes." Greg looked at him with interest. "Mostly populated by streetwalkers and their handlers. That doesn't seem your..." The man's mouth pulled to the side in a moue of distaste. "Speed."

A cold ball of rage burned in his belly as Retro listened to the man describe the residents of that building. "I know you aren't sayin' my friend's a whore." He said the words evenly, calmly, but noted the instant Greg's shoulders went back, the verbal challenge acknowledged and accepted.

Shaking his head, Greg said, "I just call it how I see it, just sayin'."

"Hey, Mudd." Retro waited a beat, knowing Mudd would have given an unseen chin lift in response. "What's it mean when someone finishes a sentence with 'just sayin'?"

"Really means 'you dumbass.' Or so I've heard."

Greg's eyes widened and Retro stared at him. "So back to my point, I know you aren't sayin' my friend's a whore, you dumbass." He let his mouth twist into a snarl. Straightening his posture, he leaned forwards, teeth grinding hard before he spit out, "Well, lookie there. I fucked it up and said what I really meant. Guess I'm not real great at subtleties."

"Fuck, man. Fuck." Greg held out his hands in a warding off gesture. "No offense meant, Retro." It was always gratifying when someone backpedaled like this. "I mean, sure. Yeah. I've got some tenants who are normal citizens, hard workers, always try to pay their rent on time. I bet your friend falls into that category. No offense."

Straightening his legs, Retro pushed up and off the bike, standing inches taller than Greg. From that position, he saw the group at the corner begin to move, heard the men at his back shift, jackets and vests rustling, sliding as weapons were loosened. With a fist raised, he stilled his men, not surprised when Greg did the same.

"None taken." Retro gave an inch with that rigidly-spoken lie, because he was pissed as hell. "But now I'm sure you won't be upset if I move her." He crooked a finger over his shoulder. "Mudd, dispatch two for me." Mudd called out two names and Retro heard boot leather hit the street as his men closed in on his back. "Good to see you, Pooka." Using the man's childhood nickname underscored to everyone how long Retro had known him, and reminded Greg that Retro knew his family. Well. The good part? That might have been a second lie, but it rolled off his tongue easily in the moment.

"Let me know if you need assistance with this, my friend." Friends were good as family to this man, and him naming Retro as such meant the same to his crew as if Retro had called him brother. Dipping his chin, Retro acknowledged the word for what it was—an olive branch for the man's unknowing misstep.

"Should be good to go, but will do." He gave the man his back, trusting his men to protect him if needed, and arrowed straight towards the door in the center of the two-story brick building. Built in the 1960s, the structure was showing its age with crumbling mortar and cracked wooden window frames. He knew the insides had probably been chopped up again and again to turn a six-family structure into something that could house about fifty instead.

Pausing at the door, he turned back on a whim and asked, "You happen to know which unit Trina Fainburg is in?" Greg's response was so surprising, it took Retro a moment to take it in. His face went slack and paled, then turned red and his fingers balled into fists held rigid at his sides. Retro already knew the info, but asking was one more way to wedge information out of Greg, and Retro saw Mudd mark the recoil, too, knowing it for as big a tell as it felt. She was somehow important to this man, but Retro had found nothing in her history that would have advertised it. "I can knock on all the doors, man. No worries."

"Are you sure you got that right? Your business is with Katrina? What'd you mean?"

Retro moved away from the building by a handful of steps, studying Greg closely. "Yes, she is my business." His statement declared ownership without laying it out more, and Greg rocked backwards with the words. Every reaction layered on another surprise, and Retro found himself trying to play catchup in all kinds of ways. "Why do you want to know?"

"She's a…" Greg paused and seemed to be searching for words, something Retro wasn't used to from him. "Friend of the family."

Fuck. Maybe Mudd had the right of it after all with his theories of the Georgias.

"Good." He decided to take it at face value, where he could acknowledge the security that association offered her. "Then you'll be happy to know I'm taking care of any of her problems. In fact, all her problems are now mine." That would open the door to see how much Greg actually knew about this friend of the family he was so quick to claim. "And I've found her alternative employment." He hadn't, but at this point, if she'd be willing to move into the clubhouse, he'd pay her to stay there.

It hit him again how fast this was moving. How quickly he'd fallen under the spell of a tiny woman who had no expectations of him, and who might not find his offers attractive. *Don't fuckin' care.* Something about her settled him in a way he needed. With the first glimpse of her face, Wanda's had been wiped from his mind. With the initial slide of Trina's hand in his, his heart felt like Clara had been laid to rest, finally. It didn't matter he hadn't known Trina but a handful of hours in total; she'd owned him from the first smile. Didn't matter all he'd done was innocently touch her in full view of a dozen people in a diner. *I'm in this.*

Retro finished speaking to Greg, giving him the benefit of this sudden knowledge. "She's mine."

"Was unaware she had problems." Chin lifted, Greg studied him a moment, then with a nod, said, "Top floor, back right. She's in 2B4."

"Much obliged." Retro turned to stalk inside.

***

Trina

The building breathed around her, sounds of comings and goings constant as they always were this time of night. She held no illusions as to her neighbors, and wasn't put off by the careers represented within the walls. Few of them followed the trade by choice, and even if it had been their favored option initially, who was she to judge someone for taking what they wanted?

Her tears had ceased, finally, scratchy streaks of salt drying on her skin. As she'd done every night, Trina had tried to analyze every word spoken by Retro, trying to bolster her belief she'd done the right thing. Hanging up on his call had seemed correct at the time, but now she could scarcely remember the reasons.

I don't even know him. She forced her eyes closed, burrowing a little deeper into the pillow. *It's not like he's my boyfriend or anything.*

The raw anger reverberating through his voice had her trembling by the time she'd finally tapped the button to end the call. It had set something loose, swirling inside her to stir fear and anxiety. Not a memory, as such, because her mom had never been one to raise her voice. But something along the edges of her mind, stories about a story, maybe? *Who knows?*

The overlapping sound of hurried footsteps in the hallway made her open her eyes, studying the strip of brightness from underneath the door. A shadow appeared, blacking out a growing portion of the light as the footsteps slowed becoming a measured pace, and stopped. Trina's breath stuck in her throat because in this moment, everything seemed to hang in the balance. There was no good or bad, just the potential for so much. With her pulse pounding in her ears, she clutched at the blanket with suddenly nerveless fingers.

This is when everything changes.

No knock, nothing so abrupt as a thudding fist against her door, just a graceful resumption of a conversation she just been wishing had never been terminated.

"Trina, honey, from where I was standin', I could see a million stars. The sky was covered, edge-to-edge, and it was so beautiful. So fuckin' beautiful, it took my breath." He paused, and she licked her lips, waiting. "Then I remembered your eyes, dark blue like the nighttime sky, and I'm no poet, but for you I'd like to try. See if I can figure out how to tell you what you feel like to me. There's been a hole in my soul for a long time. Someday, I'd like to tell you about it. If you decide you wanna hear. But the point is, meeting you has filled in that hole."

"You don't really even know me," she called out, then bit her lips to keep them closed.

The wood of her door groaned as if he'd had to lean against it, weakened in some way by her acknowledgment of his presence. *That's me reading way too much into something I can't even see.*

"I know you're a good person. I know how inside you feel like you don't deserve much, but you're wrong. I know you work hard. I know you see the best in people. I know you smell like some mix of wild berries and vanilla, and that's my new favorite scent in the whole fuckin' world. I know I wanna learn all the rest of you. All the things I *can* figure out about you, I wanna. I know you make my heart race. Make my brain work overtime trying to come up with ways to make your life easier." She heard him pull in a deep, slow breath, and she matched it, muscles relaxing. "I know you, Trina. I do. Now open the door, baby."

She rolled up to sit on the edge of the mattress, flicking on the light beside the bed. Staring at the door, with some trepidation she stood, reached out, and turned the locks, disengaging the chain as she asked, "What do you want from me?"

The knob twisted under her fingers and she yanked her hand back, gasping as the door opened. Retro stood there, illuminated from behind with a slight glow, and from the front by her weak light. Hair down around his shoulders, he tipped his head to one side and she watched a smile spread across his face, the beauty of it making her knees weak. Then he blew her mind with his response, giving her a glimpse of so much she hadn't believed possible. "Everything."

She stumbled back a step and settled on the bed, staring up at him. "I don't understand. What are you...how did you find me?"

His expression softened, lines in his face easing as he stared at her, gaze roving her face as if it had been far longer than a few days since he'd last seen her.

She reached up, self-consciously smoothing her hair away from her face. She'd been plodding back and forth to work, holding her head up because that's what she always did. Her shift at the diner had been long and exhausting, and Trina hadn't bothered with her hair after discarding a favorite slouch hat she'd worn on the walk home. "Hi."

"Hi, Trina." He released a slow breath, and she was reminded of those moments of being on the phone with him, listening to him breathe, and feeling safer than she ever had before. No matter he'd been miles away and she'd been in this room where hearing gunfire was an every night occurrence. She'd felt safe.

"I...uh..." Before her bravery could leave her standing flatfooted with nothing to say, she blurted out what she'd wanted to say to him two seconds after she'd turned off that darn phone. "I like how I feel around you. Like you'd take care of me. I'm sorry I hung up on you. I was enjoying our conversation." She paused, felt the weight of his gaze on her, then finished with the understatement of the year. "A lot."

"I enjoyed our conversations, too. I like talking to you. You cut right through the bullshit and lay it on the line, and that's rare." A grin creased his cheek and she warmed from the inside out, because she'd made him smile. "Rare, special, and something I like a fuck of a lot about you. Won't lie, I was pissed as hell you hung up on me, but most of that was hurt feelings, because if you could sever the connection like that, then maybe you weren't in the same place I was." He paused a moment, then shook his head ruefully, as if he were arguing with himself. "Same place I am."

"And where..." There was noise from outside the building and she looked towards the street, as if she could see through the walls and doors between there and here. It stopped, and she glanced back up at him, finding him scanning her room with an analyzing look. "Where are you, exactly? I think that'd help me understand why a man like you would be standing here. Now. Because in my world, this doesn't compute."

"I want you to be with me." His gaze locked on her face and Trina's cheeks burned under his focused attention. "Yeah, that's where I am. Smackdab in the middle of missing a woman I've never really gotten a chance to be with. Which leads me to wonder if she'll let me get to know her. The secret her that she keeps inside, not all the pieces I can find out from everyone else. The person she wants to be." He shrugged, the movement slow and elegant, the leather of his vest swinging freely around his hips and she saw something underneath his shirt shift with the motion. "But I can't do that if I gotta traverse across the city to see her. So then I was wondering if she'd let me keep her for a few days. Asked myself if she'd give me a couple of days at least. I know there's work, and you can't miss, because that's the kind of person you are. But I wanna keep you for a couple of days anyhow. Can you do that for me?"

She'd do nearly anything for him; he just didn't know it yet. She didn't understand her own feelings, but she'd accepted them over the past few days where her mind kept returning to thoughts of him again and again.

His head slowly tilted to one side, gaze still fixed on her. "You're open to it." He nodded sharply as if he'd just needed to say it aloud to believe. "What do you need to bring with you right now? Got a purse or a bag?" He smiled again, that slow spread of pleasure across his face that curved his cheeks and crinkled the corners of his eyes—and made her heart pound. "'Cuz if you're down for it, I wanna take you on a ride. Wanna ride with me?"

The phone was packaged in a box along with the cash, because she hadn't been able to force herself to spend it. In her mind, it was Retro's money, earmarked to go back to him without fail, because she'd feared he had invested in a false image of who she was. But by his appearance here tonight, and the things he'd said, she wondered if maybe he did know her.

"When you say 'be with me,' what do you mean? For a ride?" What he'd asked felt weightier, more important than a tiny moment out of his life and Trina needed—*needed*—to understand the intent behind the question.

Palms propped on the doorframe to either side of him, Retro filled the opening, broad shoulders taking up the space with a caged power she could feel radiating off him. He leaned forwards, towards her, then back. She found herself inclining, body arcing in a mute desire to intersect with his, something she'd never ask for nor expect. On the next mutual sway, he muttered, "Fuck it," and released his death grip, stepped into her room and kicked the door closed behind him. She stared up at him as he seemed to suck all the oxygen out of the space, leaving her gasping in tiny sips of air, gaze angled far up where she saw his eyes seem to catch fire, pupils dilating as his lids lowered over his warm gaze.

With a hand to either side of her waist, he effortlessly picked her up and deposited her in the middle of the small mattress. Then he was on the bed and braced himself over the top of her, hips aligned as if by magic while her legs fell apart and he nestled between her thighs as if he'd always been there.

"Oh." She couldn't have stopped the bow of her back if she'd tried, couldn't have gotten in the way of the avalanche of feelings that had her hips rising against him, meeting his hard thrust and holding tight against the grinding pressure of his weight against her. "*Oh.*"

He fell to an elbow, chest pressed tight to her breasts and his free hand cupped her jaw, thumb stroking across her lips in a prelude she couldn't wait to have conclude, as long as it did with his mouth on hers.

Then he kissed her. As Trina's eyes closed so she could lose herself in this once-in-a-lifetime moment, she saw the soft confusion in his gaze and sighed in sad understanding, because why would a man like this settle for someone like her? His mouth moved, lips plucking at hers, teeth raking gently at the edge of her mouth and then along her jaw, sucking kisses falling on her neck as she arched under him again, hips rising in a swell of primal demand.

Every touch branded itself on her heart, as did the echoing sighs from him as his hips rolled and dipped, rigid cock precisely where it needed to be to get her off with all her clothes on. "Fuck, baby." His mutter was liquid and quivering, leashed emotion evident in every shaky sound. She turned her head and found his mouth as he worked along her collarbone, drawing him to her with a tiny lap of her tongue against his closed lips.

An instant later, she opened to a more demanding kiss, lips parting as he speared inside. The taste of him was everything, sweet and spicy, tinged with the faintest trace of yeast from whatever beer he'd had earlier in the evening. She wanted more, slipping her tongue alongside his in a bold move that earned a groan from deep in his belly, the sound rattling through his chest and into her mouth where she swallowed it down, keeping it as evidence she wasn't the only one so affected.

Retro arched up and shifted to the side, creating unwelcome space between them she'd mourn later. Right now, she was still caught in the moment, taking everything he was willing to gift her with. His fingers were busy at her waist an instant later, tugging and loosening and then he flattened his palm on her belly, sliding down and into her panties as he kissed her hard, pulling back to lay a line of kisses along her jaw, mouth to her ear to grit out something that was as much a demand as a request, but she believed in her soul was her decision. Voice hoarse, he told her, "Wanna touch you," and goose bumps danced across her skin as she nodded, giving in immediately, not that she'd ever had any intention of denying something she needed. *Needed*, or she would go up in flames right here in this bed with him, his hard body pressed all along hers.

Head angled, he took from her mouth again, tongue gliding and lapping slowly as his fingers parted her, the slippery touch of his rough fingertips a contrast that tweaked every nerve in her clit into standing at attention, waiting for the barest brush of his skin against hers. He teased her, slipping alongside, then diving to her entrance where he circled, and circled, seeming to wait for some signal. Trina lifted her hips, chasing his touch with an undulation that pulled every muscle taut in anticipation.

No more hesitation, he plunged inside, deep and curving, thumb finding and pressing against her hooded clit, every connection between her legs tied back to her heart and lungs, the ability to breathe suspended even while her heart beat out a rapid tattoo. In and out, and in again, his hand forced her legs wider, broad palm owning the space between her thighs. Then in again, fuller, more of him inside her and she opened her mouth to cry out. Retro's lips trapped her shout, mouths slanting together, keeping this between the two of them, no need for her neighbors to know this kind of ecstasy lived so close, no need for her to slink in a walk of shame later, because he'd protect her. He would. *He will.* Fast and steady, he thrust into her, the wet sounds of this coming together muffled by the fabric of her clothing. Her skin buzzed, licks of lightning racing along her tensed muscles, burning her up from inside. She could smell her own arousal on the air, musty and rich, drawn to the surface by his skillful fingers, by his desire to make her feel good, and she breathed it in, letting the knowledge that he wanted this carry her higher and higher.

"Come for me, baby," he urged, biting at her lips hard enough to sting. "Come all over my hand." More pressure, deep inside as he thrust hard and held, fingers finding and exploiting something that she'd never felt, a burning excitement that built inferno-fast, flashing over before it exploded through her. Chin lifted, she clamped her teeth together, head thrust back into the pillow as her body went rigid, his fingers inside her feeling impossibly huge, an intrusion she'd longed for without knowing, needed without words to put to it, and she wondered if this was why her emotions and body had reacted to him so strongly, if his ability to play her like a violin was tied up in her soul recognizing him.

"Yeah, that's it," he whispered roughly against her ear. "Fuck yeah, baby." Weight on her legs anchored her in the moment; he'd thrown a leg across her, grinding against her hip and groaning deep in his throat. Mouth to her neck, he bit and kissed, teeth latching onto the curve of her shoulder as he buried his fingers a final time, palm pressing tight to her clit. "Mmmm. Ah, God." His breathing was fast and heavy, and she found the echo of her pounding heart in his beating so rapidly against the inside of his chest.

His touches changed to lazy, endless caresses, lips moving across the skin of her shoulder and throat, up to her jaw, lips finally settling in place against hers. Breathing settling slowly, he sighed heavily, sounding pleased and contented and happy all rolled into one, and she pulled back to blink at him. Head up on a hand, he was propped over her on an elbow, a satisfied smile in place on his face. Fingers slipping from inside her, he stayed there, hand covering her sex in a move that could only be called possessive. "I want you with me."

She blinked, trying to track back to whatever conversation had sparked this interlude, finally finding the thread in her memory. "*Oh.*"

"And by with me, I mean with me all the time. Life's too short to give up a moment with you." A shadow darted across his face, grief followed by a sad resolve. "I know it too well. So, I want to pick up and go from here. This moment with you is exactly what I've wanted. I wanna make you feel good, keep makin' you feel safe. I wanna give you all the things that you need. I wanna become the man you deserve, wanna do so much with you."

"What..." She took a breath that caught in the middle when he stroked her softly, fingers slipping and sliding. "What does it mean to you? What you're asking? What would I be?"

"Mine. It means you'd be mine. Means I get a chance of a lifetime right here, you in my arms." He brushed his lips across hers, side to side, nibbling along the way. "You'd be mine."

"I'm crazy to consider this. It doesn't make sense, Retro." She shook her head and tried to shift away from him, but he kissed her again, tongue dancing against hers in a way that was distracting. His hand had moved to her hip and he tugged her tightly to him again. "You're crazy to offer something like this. You don't know me." Trina tried to resurrect her earlier argument, with about as much success.

"Fuck that noise. I *do* know you. I'm going into this with my eyes wide open." He scoffed and then grinned down at her. "You're cute when you frown like that." Trina tried to smooth out her brow, giving up the effort when he laughed aloud, the sound bouncing around the room in a way that made it seem larger than it was, as if he had the ability to bend matter with his mind, granting her a bigger living space through will alone. "No, Trina. I'm serious. I didn't come to you a week ago because I wanted to take some time and sort out my head. I'm a cautious type normally, and you were making me cast that to the winds. I wanted to understand everything I could about you. So, I looked into who you are."

She tensed, because that sounded invasive, and not in a good way. "You what?"

"I got a guy can help you do the same with me, if you want. But I'm happy to lay anything out there you ask about. I got history and I got a family, and I got wants and needs. You and me, we're a lot alike in some ways—"

"And entirely different in others," she interrupted with a mutter, and he laughed again, burying his face against her neck. His hair tickled her nose and she huffed it out of her face, drawing another low laugh from him.

"Yup. We are. And that's okay. There's something between us that don't care about same or different. You feel it as well as I do. So if you want to check me out, I'm an open book on most things for you." He shrugged, the mattress moving, shifting beneath them like sinking sands underfoot. "Not where the club's concerned, because that impacts more than me. But for things personal to me, then yeah. Ask away."

He rolled over the top of her, pausing mid-motion to kiss her deeply, devouring the tiny noises she let escape at how good it felt to have his mouth on her. "But right now, we need to get goin'. Come on, beautiful. Grab your bag or whatever."

He moved to the sink and washed his hands, then unfastened his belt and pants and yanked a handful of paper towels off the roll, swabbing at the inside of his jeans. He ducked his head into the bathroom and tossed the trash, then turned back to her. She saw the root of his penis as he tucked himself away and she blinked. Still half hard, he looked huge, and she experienced a distinct tingling vibration between her legs. Trina pushed to her feet and turned her back to him as she refastened her pants, head ducked, trying to ignore her body's reaction to him.

"What's this?" He was beside the table, head angled down towards the package she'd addressed to him. Not like he could have missed it, and it wasn't as if she'd had enough warning to hide it. With economical movements, he ripped it open. He stared into the ruined box and papers, then reached down to retrieve the phone, putting the battery back into place and booting it up without a word. Then, moving slower, face blank of any emotion, he dug the money out and stared at it for a long moment, thumb sliding the bills back and forth in his grip as if he were counting the cash. "That fuckin' hurts."

"What?" She was startled, because that wasn't the reaction she would have predicted. Anger, sure. Disappointment, maybe...but never in a million years would she have expected pain.

"The phone I get. I can understand you wanting to cut off that line of connection. I pushed you harder than I should have, and you shut me down. But I've spent the past week consoling myself that at least I made part of your life easier." His gaze lifted from the bills to her face and he studied her for a moment. "But I didn't, because you didn't trust me. You didn't know me, and I shoulda seen how that would go down." Reaching out, he gripped her hand and folded her fingers around the money. "Please, Trina. Please." He used the grip on her hand to pull her towards him and she went willingly. An arm banded around her shoulders and held her tightly while fingers to her chin lifted until she was staring up into his face.

They stood like that for a long moment, gazes locked while he searched for something in her eyes. "I'm sorry." She didn't say what for, hoping he'd understand.

Retro proved himself again in that moment because he smiled, the curl of his lips so soft and secret and something she hoped was just for her. Then he dipped his head, mouth on hers for a kiss that matched his smile, sweet and tender, and every gentle caress she'd ever wanted.

"Forgiven," he told her, lips moving against hers with the single word, and she wanted to remember how this felt, wanted to keep the dark taste of him in her mouth forever. "Now..." His arm gave her a squeeze, palm of his other hand just above her ass, pulling her hips close against his. "Much as I wanna do the horizontal Mambo with you." She gasped when he thrust forwards, each delicious inch of his front pressed against her as he swayed them to silent music. "I wanna do it somewhere I don't have to leave two of my men in the hallway for your safety. So come with me, Trina. Say you trust me enough to get to know me, and come with me. Ride my bike with me, and if you don't understand what that means, let me know so I can educate you, because it'll be a big deal to my men to see me put you on the back of my bike. They'll be expecting it, seein' as I changed out seats to have a place for your ass, and strapped a second helmet on. I want you to understand you're gonna be the topic of some attention, and not a bit of it will be bad. I fuckin' promise you I'll have the head of anyone who makes you feel uncomfortable. Come with me." He kissed her again. "Come with me." A hip thrust followed by a tug on the back of her knee, drawing her leg up as he opened her to him again. "Come with me." A kiss combined with the stroke of his renewed erection against her heating core. "Come, please."

"Okay, okay. You're a gifted negotiator." Trina laughed softly when he tried to pull away to look down at her only to find her fingers were wound in the fabric of his shirt, holding him as firmly as he'd been holding her. "Okay. Show me your world."

"You got it," he whispered, eyes shining.

***

Retro

"Favorite food?" Chin tilted towards the ceiling, Retro smiled at her latest question. Trina had taken him at his word, plying him with inquiry after inquiry, mostly the "get to know you" things she'd initially assured him were on all the dating websites. Hearing that, he'd pestered her to use his computer to log into whatever accounts she had set up to change her status, only to find she'd been bluffing and didn't have any.

"Meat." He waited a beat, listening for it, and smiled again at her lilting laughter. "You didn't expect me to say something froufrou, did you?" Her head in his lap shifted back and forth, pitching innocently against his rock-hard dick. She likely didn't realize what proximity to her did to him, not yet. *She will.* For tonight though, they were in the room he'd promised she could stay in at the clubhouse tonight. An anonymous space, not his bedroom, and he was determined to keep their interactions as innocent as he could manage, locking down his desires and keeping a tight rein on the touches he allowed himself. He'd pushed Trina hard enough already with throwing caution to the wind in his desire to kiss and touch her. *Course, in return I got to see what she looks like when she comes.* He liked the contented feel in his chest at the thought.

This was the room Nelda used when she stayed over, and Trina might have looked sideways at the juvenile decorations, but she hadn't come out and asked. He wanted her to ask. Wanted her to have as deep a burning desire to know him as the one he held in his gut for her.

"No, not froufrou. But meat is so predictably male. All meat? Like, anything would do? Roast versus steak versus barbecue doesn't factor?" She moved again, and he knew she was looking up at him so he broadened his smile. "What's funny?"

"Meat for any meal, and you're right, there are different demands for different situations. Generally speakin', I like a good steak. Keep it rare for me, just introduce the cow to the fire. Show it to her from a distance. Hell, you don't even gotta walk her past it."

"Bloody and raw." She made a disquieted sound in her throat. "I'm a well-done gal."

From his position lounging sideways on the bed, Retro reached out and laid his palm on her belly, feeling her muscles jump and jerk underneath his touch. Fingers drawing a slow circle against the silken material of her shirt, he allowed himself a minute to caress her like that. "You are done well, darlin'. That's for sure. The man upstairs outdid himself with you." She shifted, and the fabric slipped out from underneath his fingertips, leaving him to encounter a broad expanse of soft, warm, sleek skin. "Mmm. You like this?" He took advantage of her offering and resumed drawing circles, finding and evading her bellybutton, giving himself permission to dare a skate to the side to trace along the curve of her hipbone.

"Yeah." Her response was soft and breathy, and he lifted his head because he needed to watch. If she was aiming to have his fingers inside her again tonight, he would give up his chivalrous ideas and oblige.

Gladly.

Eyes closed, lips parted just enough he could see the pink of her tongue as it slipped along the inside of her bottom lip, she was gorgeous and needy. So fucking needy, and he hadn't felt like this in so long, wanting to give her everything, but that wasn't the whole of it. It wasn't only that she wanted his touch, but that he couldn't deny himself the same, not when she was so close, under his hand, right here and ready. *Slow*, he reminded himself.

"I like it, too." Wider spirals across her skin, chasing the retreating fabric up her ribcage until his fingertips found the edge of her bra, trailing side to side, marking that barrier as if it were the outer edge of a cage he was bound within. Down, down, down until he dipped underneath the waistband of the soft pants she'd changed into after their ride. They clung to her like a second skin and he'd been envious of them. In the darkness underneath was warm skin, soft and smooth, and she fit his hold like she'd been made to be handled by him. "Like it a lot, Trina."

"Why are you being so nice to me?"

There it was, the question he'd been hoping she'd ask again. The one she had to be sure enough of the answer before she'd brave the query, and the hours of back and forth were worth everything if it'd brought them to this so soon. The ride, her leaning against him, trusting him with her body, and now, trusting him with her emotions. Her heart.

"I need to answer that question with one of my own. You game to answer?" Her eyes opened and unerringly found his, her expression open and guileless as she nodded. He suppressed a groan, because every movement rubbed up against his dick, which was very glad at the attention, but not something he wanted her to notice right now. She might get the wrong idea, and he didn't want that, didn't want to risk losing the ground he'd gained over the past hours.

Glancing at the windows, he saw the first faint oranges of sunrise tinting the horizon. When they'd settled on the bed, he'd drawn the drapes to the sides so they could watch the stars, and now it gave him a measure of the time they'd spent here, learning the other in tiny bites, questions and answers that had given him great satisfaction.

"Okay, then. You been in a serious relationship before?" *Before me*, he meant, and from how her eyes widened, he knew she marked his meaning. She shook her head. "No?" Another headshake, this one slower, eyes dipping to the side as a memory crept up on her. "You sure, honey?"

"I was sixteen. He was thirty." Trina cleared her throat. "My mom's friend didn't like him, and I've always trusted Dolph." She shrugged. "It wasn't a relationship so much as the possibility of one, so I don't count it really. But I think it could have been. I was in love with the idea of being in love, and I would have made it fit what I needed."

Dolph. He noted the name, so he could feed it to Mudd since it wasn't one that had come up in their inquiries.

"So the answer is no, yeah?" She nodded and he smiled, flattening his palm on her belly, chasing away the goose bumps with his touch. "The first woman I loved, I met when she was sixteen and I was eighteen, and her daddy thought it was too big an age gap. I can't imagine what he would have done if I'd been nearly twice her age. What'd your daddy think?" Not a test, but it was a questioning salvo to see how well he and Mudd had done their homework.

"I don't know my father." She changed the language and he noted that, wondering why. "My mom is complicated, and it's not a comfortable subject." She'd tensed under his hand and he soothed her muscles with soft strokes, thumb brushing along the underside of her breasts. "So you've loved more than one woman?"

Truth, or sidestep? He studied her face, found himself unhappy her expression had grown distant, closed, so he decided to give her the truth. "Yes. Two. One was that girl I mentioned. Later on, I got married, but not to her, and my wife wasn't one of my loves."

She twisted around so she could look up at him directly. "You were married?"

More truth? She might run, but he'd already told her he didn't love Wanda, so maybe she'd stick until he could unveil everything. "Am. Physically separated for a few weeks now." She'd gone still under his touch, and he could see her heartbeat speed up, her rucked-up shirt vibrating over her heart. Retro's hand slipped underneath to rest between her breasts, palm covering her sternum. "It wasn't a marriage I chose." Faster and faster, her pulse pounded. "Wasn't a woman I loved. I finally had enough of her playing around and moved out, but we weren't ever together out of love, not on either side." He shook his head, pinning her with his gaze. "We've got kids, and I love 'em. More than I can say. Worth it all, just to get my kids out of the deal." The skin around her eyes softened and he liked that she gave him that, showing him it mattered to her that he valued his kids. No surprise if talking about her lack of a father was still painful. "But I never loved her."

Trina's mouth opened and closed. Then she swallowed hard and forged forwards, and he braced because whatever she was asking was important. "She was unfaithful?"

"She was." He tried not to scowl at having to expose his humiliation, then gave her a knowing smirk, suddenly understanding the unasked part of her question. "I wasn't." Trina blinked up at him, and he laughed hard enough to jostle her head on his lap. "Surprised you with that, didn't I?"

"No." She huffed out a breath and he laughed again.

"Fuck that noise. I shocked you." She started to shake her head and he stopped her with a touch on her cheek. "I'm not a womanizer. Me telling you that my boys would be alert to the message of me putting you on my bike? That's part of it. But Wanda—" That tiny line appeared between her brows and he smiled, smoothing it away with the pad of his thumb. "My gonna-be-ex's name is Wanda. What was your thirty-year-old love's name?"

"Daniel." She nuzzled against his palm. "Wanda sounds like a bee, and not a good one. Pardon my French."

"Yeah, she's a bitch for sure." He smirked at her. "'Pardon my French.' You're fuckin' cute." He laughed at her pursed-lip moue. "Oh, yeah, way too fuckin' cute. So the bike. In the seventeen years we've been married, I've spent sixteen of them riding alone. She got pregnant with Nelda, my oldest and only girl, and she refused to get back on my bike again. So me letting you cuddle up behind me was a bigger statement than you probably realized." He smiled down at her look of shock. "Yeah, I know. Did you like that ride we had?" They'd spent an hour roaming the darkened countryside around Birmingham before he'd turned the column back towards the clubhouse, and when he'd parked at the front door, Trina's face had been shining with excitement.

"Yes. Oh, yes. I loved it." Over the past few exchanges, she'd relaxed again, head propped on his thigh so she could look into his face. The honesty of her expression floored him, and he hoped he'd never see anything other than this kind of raw emotion from her.

"God, I love that about you. You're not fake. You feel it, you show it. Simple as that. You liked the ride, and so you can't imagine anyone ever not wanting to do that, and you give me that kinda goodness without shying away." He stroked her hair away from her face, hoping he showed her half as much as she was giving him. "Wanda wanted different from the life I gave her. She was raised in a big house, people all around telling her how pretty she was. Nothing I could offer would ever be half what she wanted."

"Why did she marry you then? If you didn't love her, why did you marry her?" There was wet in Trina's eyes and he could only wonder at the source, but she'd asked good questions, and he owed her real and honest answers.

"I had something her daddy wanted, and he could give me something I needed in return." He shrugged. "It was business, and I thought it'd be enough. Thought all I needed to do was work at it and I could make it good for her and me." He glanced at the window to see deeper reds now stitched in layers along the horizon. The sun would be peeking over that edge before long. *Time to finish this while we still have shadow courage.* "I was wrong. It took me a while to accept that. Probably five years ago, when my youngest was toddling around, I realized she wouldn't ever be what I needed. And I couldn't be her ideal, either. I stuck with her until I couldn't anymore. Something happened recently that reminded me there are better things in store for us all."

"What happened?"

He sighed at her question and shook his head. "That's a story for another night. It's late, and we've talked through a lot. You tired, Trina? Wanna nap, or you want me to cook you breakfast?"

"Would you let me get away with that? Avoiding a question just because it touches on difficult things? Don't be fake, Retro." He stared at her for a moment. "Well?" She shoved her elbows into the mattress, wedging up and off his legs, the beginning phases of a glare on her face. "Would you let me get away with it?"

Shaking his head back and forth, he smiled slowly. "Nope."

"Don't treat me like a fool." From the set of her jaw, he knew she wasn't joking. "You said you looked into me, my background, my family. You know about my mom?" He nodded, not saying anything because what person wanted to be told exactly how much a body knew about them. "I like you, Retro. I want to get to know you better." He glanced at the sunrise still changing colors outside, the stripes of color beginning to muddle together on the edges. "But, if I ask, and you don't answer, then I'll know you either don't trust me or I've ceased mattering."

"Hey, that's not fair. I haven't pushed you on anything you didn't want to talk about."

"Because you didn't have to. You already know it all." She shrugged and wiggled towards the edge of the bed. "I haven't got any secrets."

"You got secrets a plenty, Trina. I don't know shit about anything that matters, baby. What do you have that you feel it taints you in a way you gotta pay it back again and again? I know a little about your mother, just from people who know her, that's all I did there because I wanted it from your lips, not from a stranger on a phone." She'd halted, legs dangling off the edge of the bed, chin tucked over her shoulder so she could stare at him in surprise. "And there I go, shocking you again because you thought I'd just taken all that. I didn't. I only learned enough to know I wanted more, and more, and then decided to get it from you, just like I figured you'd want. What secrets do you wanna share? Tell me."

"My mom's not smart." Wet hit her eyes and she blinked furiously to clear them. "All my life, I knew she wasn't right. But at one time, she was. You talk to people who knew her in high school, they'll all talk about how smart she was. Nearly valedictorian of her graduating class. Missed it by a half a point. Then, about the time I was born, something happened to her. It's not genetic, because I've had tests run to check for all the usual things. She thought it was fun, me coaxing her mouth open so I could swab her cheeks." He reached for her and Trina shook her head, dark hair swinging around her shoulders. "It feels weird, talking about this. I'm trusting you, Retro, trusting you and I don't even know your real name.

How messed up is that? I don't know your name and yet I trust you more than I do all the people I grew up with."

"Jeremiah Rogers. Family calls me Jerry. I got three siblings, a brother Isaiah who's in an MC, too. A sister Miriam who lives a boring-ass life back where we grew up. She's president of the parent-teacher committee, if you can believe that, and she and our mom pack care boxes for the town every Christmas. Our youngest sister, Rebekka, is trouble with a capital T, and right now I've got her parked in Louisiana at the home of a friend in yet another club. Bekka's a mess, but I'm hoping I can help her sort her shit out. My kids are great, I love 'em more than life itself. I'd do anything for them." He nodded firmly, letting her see the honesty of the words. "Anything. Nelda is fifteen and she's way older than she should be thanks to the shit her mother has pulled over the past few years. My boys are good, sweet kids. Jeremiah Junior, Jimmy, he's twelve and the negotiator. Got me wrapped around his fist." He held out a clenched hand with a grin, turning it back and forth to demonstrate how malleable he was for his boy. "Little man can twist me this way or that to get what his brother or sister needs. He's the kind of kid who won't ask for himself, so when he asks for others, it's harder to say no, and they all know it.

"Saya, my little boy, he's my heart. He's named after my brother, Isaiah. He's eight and doesn't speak. Smart as a whip, that boy can work math problems around me and turn me dizzy with how smart he is. But he don't speak. I'd give the world to hear his voice say my name. Call me daddy. Love him anyway." He smiled at Trina, loving her stunned expression again. He liked surprising her, turning her ideas about him on their heads and pulling her in deeper with him. *Want her deep as I already am.* "Love him because of it. Still, Jerry. That's my government name. I like hearin' Retro from your lips, though. But, woman, if you call me anything, I can guarantee I'll come runnin'. Promise." He nodded at her and reached out a hand, letting her see the depth of his pleasure when she took it, fingers pressing into place between his, fitting perfectly.

"Something happened to my mother. Something bad." Her whispered admission felt like a bomb in his gut because it didn't make any sense.

"She wasn't always that way, but there's no accident I can point to. I've always been afraid that something…someone happened to her. But I never had the courage to take it any farther."

"You know who might know?" He tugged hard, pulling her across the covers and back towards where he lay, reaching for her when she was close enough, bringing her up to sit on his lap, shoulder tucked against his chest. He turned her to face the window and laid his cheek on top of her head. "You got any idea what was goin' on?"

"No." She shook her head, emotions thick in her voice. "No clue."

"Want one? This right here? These kinds of questions are what I'm good at, what I do best. You wanna know and the info is available by hook or by crook, I can get it for you. Want to know who your dad is? I can try for that, too." He breathed deeply, pulling the scent of her into his lungs. "Berries and vanilla," he whispered. "Check out that sunrise, baby. Ain't that something?"

"It's beautiful." She used the same soft tone of voice to respond. He reached out to the light on the table next to the bed, tugging at the chain pull to turn it off. With a loud click, the room was plunged into darkness, making the varied hues outside seem even more brilliant. They sat and watched the sky lighten and change colors, the gold of the sun finally peeking into the room. "Yeah," she told him finally on a long, outrush of breath. "I want to know."

"You got it."

Chapter Five
Retro

"There ain't no expiration on this request, man. You hear anything at all, you give my number a call." Retro leaned back, heels of his boots propped on the edge of the table to hold himself in place, balanced up on two chair legs. "Let me know what it's worth to you. This is personal, not club." There was silence on the other end of the call and he rolled his eyes. "You think I don't know what you're doin', Sparks? Fuck you. I got more sources than you, and I'll pull them in before I let you silence me into a bad deal."

Laughter echoed up the line and he grinned at the sound. Sparks was the president of a Florida club where their main claim to fame was an *in* with a federal agent. The man was well aware that Retro had more, better connections in that same building, so his ploy had been doomed from the beginning.

"I should know betta than tryin' to hustle a hustler." Sparks made a noncommittal noise. "I'll see what I can find out, brother. We'll sort it out, yeah?"

"Mmhmm. Like I said, obliged." Retro disconnected and tossed his phone to the surface of the table, the rattle loud in the silent room. It was the middle of the afternoon and so far the prospects were the only ones stirring, other than himself. Trina was still sleeping, and hadn't that been a hard feat, peeling himself away from her. Before finally dozing off, she'd mentioned working this evening, which meant he'd need to either take her, or run her back to her car. From her description, the lot she used was close enough to her apartment so he could use the trip to make a case for packing more things into the tiny bag she'd used last night.

He tipped his head back and stared up at the ceiling. Drowsing next to her had been more refreshing than the last handful of full-night sleeps he'd had by himself. She'd snuggled her ass back against him, cheek on his folded arm underneath her head, and he'd been in awe that he was the one holding her. *So fuckin' fast.* Not too fast, though. He'd already questioned himself enough, losing days with her in the meantime. If she was down for it, he planned to keep going, full-bore ahead.

What she'd shown him was enough to earn his loyalty for life. Good and true, sweet and kind, she was exactly what he wanted. Throw in smart and cute, and he was wrapped up in her in a way he hadn't been since Clara. *And I wasn't but a kid then*. Age didn't matter, though, because he'd been infatuated by Clara from the moment he'd first seen her at a party. Pursued her relentlessly, against both their families' wishes, convinced her to take a chance on him, and then she'd been the one chasing him. *Not that I ran far*. Retro smiled sadly. *Her old man just fucked everything up.*

Trina's family situation was interesting in an odd way. He'd found that she was a hundred percent correct with everything so far. Her mother had been pregnant and carried her, delivering her in the old downtown hospital. All the records had been moved to the county courthouse, but he had a resource already digging through the dusty boxes there. Not that he expected to find more on physical records than he had the electronic. He'd gotten access to her doctor's records about the pregnancy. Every step along the way was normal, matching what he remembered about going to the visits with Wanda.

Except the beginning.

Trina's mother had been nearly six months pregnant when she first went to the doctor. Still, he had a memory of at least one other pregnancy that had started like that, and Isaiah's wife's pregnancy had been normal. Her delivery, not so much. He had a poignant memory of his brother's face at the funeral, one arm cradling his tiny baby girl, and one holding the hand of his little boy. Sammy was nearly fourteen now, Faynez six, and Isaiah, also known as Hoss, was rocking the single parent life. "Boy's a fuckin' spider monkey," he murmured, mind rolling back farther to the moment he'd fallen in love with his nephew. *Sammy's a good boy.*

So Trina's mother not having prenatal until more than halfway through the pregnancy wasn't unheard of, just uncommon.

He reached out for his phone, glancing at the screen and marking the time as he dragged the device back towards him. One tap on his speed dial and he was listening to the short double-ring that told him his daughter was already on her phone. Ending the attempt, he texted her to call him in five minutes, getting a **Yus da** back.

Jimmy picked up on the second ring. "Hi, Dad."

"Hey, son, how's it going?" Wind noise in the background told him his boy was outside somewhere and he smiled. Jimmy would rather be in nature than inside, and he probably had Saya right there with him. "You havin' a good time at Uncle Twisted's place?"

"Yes, sir. We're goin' fishin' again today. Penny—" Retro made a quietly scolding noise and Jimmy changed his phrasing, "Aunt Penny said me and Saya aren't allowed to come back inside unless we dunk Uncle T at least once. He said we could not and just say we did, but Saya won't lie, so I guess Uncle T's gonna take a swim." His boy laughed, the sound so light and easy that something inside Retro's chest loosened, a tension easing because if his son could be happy like this, then that meant Wanda hadn't fucked everything up for all of them. "He's not best pleased by the idea."

"Oh, I just bet he's not." Retro let the sound of his smile echo through his voice. "Sounds like you're still having a good time. I was gonna come get you Wednesday, you ready to come home?"

"Awwww." Retro didn't let the disappointment hurt his feelings, remembering well how it was when he was a kid, farmed out to relatives who had places nearly exactly like his family's farm, but to a kid, the strange spaces were filled with far greater wonders than could ever be discovered at home. "Do we hafta?"

"You wantin' to stay on a bit? I can talk to Uncle Twisted and Aunt Penny and see what they say." He offered the hope, but tempered it with reality. "Gonna have to come home sooner or later though, so don't set your hat on stayin' there indefinitely."

"I won't. I've been helping Aunt Penny with Missy. Aunt Bekka's helping, too. It's been a lot of fun. Saya says hi, Daddy." Retro grinned. "He says he'd like to stay extra, too." A pause and he filled in the blanks for himself, chuckling when Jimmy proved him right by saying, "He likes Uncle T."

"Most folks do." If they didn't have a beef with his club, that was. Twisted was known throughout the region as a hardnosed bastard, but Retro had faith the kids would never see that side of him. "Who's Missy?"

"Uncle Po'Boy's girlfriend's sister's little girl." Retro tried to draw connections from that convoluted sentence.

"Uncle Po'Boy's niece is down from Minnesota visiting?" Far easier way to identify the child than the connect-the-dot version Jimmy had offered. "That's good. I know his Crissy has been missin' that little girl a lot."

"You know Miss Crissy?" Before Retro could respond, Jimmy scoffed, sounding so like Twisted Retro wanted to roar with laughter. "Saya says of course you know Miss Crissy. You know everyone."

"That I do, son. That I do. Saya's right there with you?" Retro waited for an affirmative sound. "Tell that boy his daddy loves him."

"Daddy loves you, Saya." Retro smiled at the care his Jimmy had with Saya, and he mourned the time surely coming when Jimmy would be too cool for his little brother. *Hope that never happens.* "He loves you, too, Dad."

"Your sister around? I tried to call her, but she was on the phone."

Jimmy blew a brief raspberry. "She's been talkin' to some guy she met on that game she plays." Retro narrowed his eyes when he heard Nelda's aggrieved squeal in the background, knowing that meant Jimmy was telling tales she didn't want carried to her father's ears. *Oh, ho. I've got the scent now, girl.* "Uncle T threatened to take her phone away, and Aunt Bekka told Nell if he didn't, she would."

"Did she now?" He settled the legs of his chair to the floor, feet dropping with a thud. "That's something." For Bekka to give a shit was new, and for her to do anything other than fly the "you're stifling your girl's free spirit" was unlike her, too. "Tell Nelda to call me. I wanna hear all about her new beau."

"Nelda," Jimmy shouted too close to the phone and Retro squeezed his eyes closed for a moment to keep from laughing. "Dad wants you to call him. In a minute. Not now. I'm on the phone with him now. No, he doesn't want to talk to you right this second. Nell, stop it. Nelda—"

"Daddy, it's nothing. I'm smarter than that." Retro smothered another laugh when his girl took control of Jimmy's phone. "You know I'm not stupid."

"Well, hello to you too, sweetheart. And how's your stay at Uncle Twisted's going?" From the sounds of things, he was missing quite the show and he imagined her head back, staring at the sky like she often did. *My girl, through and through.* "You goin' fishin' with the boys, too?"

"Daddy, it's this guy who knows a girl whose mom is one of the judges for the squad." Retro tipped his head sideways, smiling. "I'm just trying to scope out the competition."

"Now that, I believe." *My girl.* "You get what you need?"

"Not yet, I had to talk about that dumb game for too long. I'll call him tomorrow about something and see if I can find out when the secret practices are happening, because we all know they're having them. Stella"—that was one of her best friends from school—"said she saw the cheer coach's bus parked at the church. I bet it's happening there."

"You let me know if you need me to lean on someone for ya." He knew he didn't hide his laughter well enough when she scolded him lightly.

"Daddy. I can handle this on my own. I'm pretty close to getting everything he knows."

"I know you can, baby girl. But the question to ask yourself is, do you have to? Or can you get someone else to work the angle for you. You think on that and let me know. But meanwhile, go fishing. Have fun. School will start before you know it, so take some summertime for yourself." He paused and sighed. "While I have you on the phone, I got something to tell you. Pass it along to your brothers, if you think it's right." She was quiet and he gave her a moment, then said, "I met someone. You'll hear about it, I'm sure, because I put her on my bike."

"Daddy?" Soft and questioning, she put a lot of emotion into that single word.

"Yeap, I know. That's how it is. I didn't want you to hear it from anyone else." He tucked his chin, studying the battered surface of the table. "You'll meet her when you come home."

"To the clubhouse?" Oh, yeah, his girl was already tired of the little-to-no privacy at the house, just as his members would have been chafing against the need to stay PG-13 in their displays, Mudd and Rhonda being one of the biggest fans of an adult-only zone.

"Nah, I'll have us a house by then, too. No more stayin' at the clubhouse."

"Mom know yet?"

He chuffed a laugh. "No fuckin' idea, baby doll. No idea, and less concern."

"What's her name?"

"Trina. Short for Katrina. You'll like her, I think." Movement at the doorway had him glancing that direction and he saw Mudd standing just outside the door, his attention on the second-floor landing. "So you go fishin', you do your network trawling, and you be good for Twisted and Penny." He paused a beat. "How's Aunt Bekka doin'?"

"Twisted's threatened to beat her butt about a dozen times. I think she's afraid of him."

"Fuckin' finally, someone she's afeared of." He laughed. "What's he gettin' riled up about?"

"She's taken to hiding when there are guests. He wants her out where he can see her, his words." Nelda didn't back away from the previous topic, carrying on as if they hadn't stopped. "You like this Trina a lot, Daddy? Enough to introduce her to the boys?"

"Yeap. And that should tell you everything you needa know. So what guests is Bekka hiding from?" Tit for tat, he'd trade Nelda all day long if it meant his girl would be okay with his woman.

"Crissy's brother-in-law. She likes the little girl, Missy, but she keeps ducking Bob. He's a nice guy." She made a tisk sound. "Little bit too nice if you ask me. Talks funny." Nelda laughed and he heard Jimmy in the background. "Just a minute, Jimmy, and I'll ask him."

"I bet he thinks we talk funny, too. He's from Minnesota, so everything down this way's gonna be different for him. He stayin' in town long?"

"This week for sure. After that, I don't know. Hey, Daddy, Jimmy wants to know if you'll take them fishing when we come home." Away from the phone, Nelda said, "There, I asked him."

"Tell the boys we'll all go campin'. You too, don't think I didn't notice how you said 'them' instead of us. So yeah, we'll get some fishin' and hikin' in this summer." He took a breath. "Nelda?"

"Yes, Daddy?"

"I love you, girl. You'll like her, I promise. I wouldn't pick someone that would have the potential of hurting you or my boys. You want me to, I'll see if I can swing it to bring her with when I pick you guys up. Think on it, okay?"

"Yes, Daddy. We love you, too."

He disconnected and then dialed another number immediately. Two rings and a man picked up. "Cheerleadin' tryouts here for Birmingham Central, who's the best coach? Which one will impress judges just with their name?" The man grunted and Retro laughed. "Yeah, I know. Not my usual ask, but my little girl's got her sights set on something."

"She cheer?" The man coughed, a rattling sound far down in his chest.

"Naw, she's workin' some info for something. If I know her, there'll be a payoff though. So it's worth my time to see if I can prime the pump." Retro laughed. "She's her old man's girl, that's for sure."

"I'll let you know."

He disconnected again, then pulled up a contact and tapped a button. The video connection stalled. Then he heard a buzzing that indicated the other end was being alerted to a call request via the private application they used. A moment later, a man's face filled the screen and Retro lifted his chin. "Tell me what my sister's doin' duckin' a chance to strut in front of someone."

Twisted shook his head, hair tamed in a braid. "No fuckin' idea, but she's pissin' me off, man. I do not like rude, and her ditchin' supper and shit is rude to Penny."

"You need me to pick her up?" Retro studied Twisted's face, noting the smudged half circles under his eyes. "Penny's okay, right? The kids behavin'?"

"Yeah, everything here is right as rain." Twisted sighed. His voice dipped an octave, exposing his pain when he said, "Po'Boy's gonna patch out."

"You knew it was comin'." Retro shook his head. "Fuck, man, we had this conversation scarcely a week ago. I told you then and you said you already knew."

"Knowing and hearin' it from his lips are different things. Same coin, different currency. He's pushin' Wildman." Retro nodded, because that made sense and lined up with what he already knew. "I'm in favor."

"What's the problem then?"

"Wildman's got no old lady. What happens if I promote him and he's dandy, and then he finds himself a piece that don't want nothing to do with the life?" Twisted shook his head. "I don't need to have a bunch of back-and-forth crap in my officer ranks. That's bullshit and exhausting, and I don't have fuckin' time for such."

"Borrowin' trouble that ain't even in the wind yet." Retro flicked his fingers at the camera. "Not like you. You sure Penny's okay?"

"Yeah, she's good, brother. She's enjoyin' havin' a full house, and keepin' busy is good for her. Her momma's wantin' to come visit soon."

"Ohh. You met her fam yet? I don't think much about them, because her uncle *was* the club, you know? But his sister is her momma." Retro considered before adding anything, then pushed forwards. "Her fam didn't want the life for her."

"Oh, yeah. I fuckin' know. Wrench isn't shy about sharin' that shit. Mother*fucker*." Twisted pulled in a breath. "I can stare down a gun from three feet away without breakin' a sweat, but the idea of meeting my mother-in-law is fuckin' terrifying. How the hell does that even compute?"

"One is the life, and one is love. Penny matters, so of course you're gonna be careful with her. You'll be fine."

"Fuck you. I do not need you tellin' me I'm gonna be fine. Why don't you tell me about that little Russian girl you got holed up in your clubhouse instead?" Twisted snorted laughter at whatever he saw on Retro's face, but he'd been stunned, no doubt. "You think you're the only one with their finger on the pulse of the Gulf Coast?"

"She ain't Russian. And she's not holed up, dammit. She's here with me. And Twisted—" He eased a little closer to the phone, staring fixedly into the camera. "You gonna need to mind your tone when you speak about her."

"Fuck." Twisted shook his head. "Brother, I was just there and saw you dealin' with an unforgivin' piece of ass that I wouldn't wanna touch with another man's dick. You don't have the best track record here. You sure about that statement? She's with you?"

He nodded. "She's mine."

There was a brief and weighty pause, then Twisted hummed softly. "Well, alrighty then." Twisted glanced to the side, then back to the camera. "You tell your kids?"

"Told Nelda. She'll pass it on to the boys if she feels it's good to do so." He knew what Twisted was really asking. "You're good to tell Penny, if you feel so inclined."

"Oh, I'm inclined." He chuckled darkly. "I'm very inclined, because this is the best news she'll have heard in a while. Get me some lucky shine bringin' this to my Penny." Retro laughed at Twisted's impertinent grin. "I'm headed out, brother. I'll keep your kids safe. And I'll do my best to knock some sense into your fuckin' sister. Penny likes her. I'm not sure why." Twisted paused, then shook his head, mouth pulled to one side as if he'd tasted something foul. "Get me info on Wildman, wouldja? I need peace."

"Sounds good. I'll do what I can to bring you that peace, brother." He paused and flicked two fingers at the camera again. "See you when I see you."

"Ayeap."

The screen went black and he sat back, blowing out a long, slow breath. Raising his voice, he called, "Mudd?"

"Ya, boss?" His second in the club, and first in friends stepped into the office. "Got a need?"

"We know who marked my sister up?" Mudd nodded. "Close the door. Tell me."

***

Trina

"Baby."

Retro was about to kiss her again, his fingers softly stroking along her cheek made it impossible to open her eyes, but she could feel him getting closer and closer. She wanted him on her, in her, and she rocked her hips to no avail. Oh, please.

"So fuckin' cute."

She lifted her chin, waiting. Kiss me, Retro.

"Hate to do this, because you're sleepin' so well, but you gotta get up, Trina baby. If I know anything about you already, it's that you stick to your obligations. Sweetheart, wake up."

He finally brushed his lips across hers and she couldn't help but moan softly at how sweet he was. How kind and gentle and gorgeous, and he'd come to see her. He'd come to her, out of all the women in the world, he'd come to her. He'd touched her, and the look in his eyes told her how much he loved her.

I love him, too.

"Trina, wake up."

She blinked, surprised to see Retro's face hovering close. He was seated on the edge of the bed and leaned across her, arm locked to prop him up. His hand cupped her jaw, pad of his thumb tracing along the swell of her bottom lip. "What?"

"You told me not to let you oversleep." Heat from his body next to hers radiated all along her side. "If you're still plannin' on working at the diner tonight, it's time to get up." Still lost in the dream, she pressed her lips against his thumb. "Fuckin' cute. Too cute for your own good. We gotta pick up your ride and then you gotta get to work."

"Mmm. Okay." She twisted in the bed, looking around for a clock and coming up blank. She blinked several times and finally shook her head, giving in and asking, "'S time's it?"

"Four. You said you had to be there by six, so this gives you a chance to shower. You want some coffee?" She nodded and he smiled. "Milk and sugar?" Nose scrunched she shook her head. "Just black?"

"Like God intended." He grinned broadly at that and she felt a sense of achievement at his expression. "There's a shower?" He tipped his head towards a door she hadn't paid much attention to last night. She studied it for a moment and looked back up at him. "Mmmkay."

"You sleep good?" His thumb was tracing along the edge of her bottom lip again and she dipped her tongue out, lapping at it until he offered it with one brow lifted high. Trina rolled it in her mouth, teeth nipping along the side. "Damn, Trina. You wake up sweet."

She gave it a suck then smiled at him around his thumb. He retrieved it, brushing a soft caress along the seam of her lips. "I slept very well," she whispered against the touch. The last thing she remembered was lying beside him talking the merits of space travel, with Retro advocating for learning more about the earth they lived on before they spent all that time and money to explore nearby planets. He'd been playing with her hair, and that soothing touch along with the steady beat of his heart under her head had conspired to put her right to sleep. "Did you? I kinda fell asleep on you."

He bent close and brushed the tip of his nose against hers, eyes holding her gaze the whole time. "I slept amazing." His lips touched hers in another soft caress. "You can snooze on me anytime you want."

She stretched, arching her neck, smiling when he chased her mouth for another kiss. "I should get up."

"You stretch up against me like that again and I'll be the one up."

She smiled at his grumbling, then looked around. As she woke up more, the *where* of where they were fell back onto her like a load of bricks. "This is your biker place." She closed her eyes, thinking, finally coming up with the word she wanted. "Your clubhouse." *This whole thing is just a little weird.* "Do you live here?"

He studied her for a second and the intensity of his expression made her feel like live wires were routing electricity just underneath her skin.

He sighed and gripped her waist, lifting and sitting her up next to the headboard. He shifted to his knees, climbing onto the bed so he straddled her shins. She bent her knees, tucking them close to her chest, not sure what was happening but it seemed big and part of her wanted to feel as protected as possible. Retro scooted even closer and covered her hands with his. She shivered to feel how strong and hard his hands were. Heat flared where he touched her, and the grip was solid, ungiving, effortlessly managing to keep her where he'd placed her.

"No, I don't live here. Not normally." He began talking without preamble, jumping to the core of her unassuming question. "I've had a bedroom suite here since the club started." He pointed to the wall at her back. "It's up the hallway. This is one of the rooms I keep for guests. My daughter stayed in here most recently. I've been parked here at the clubhouse since I split with Wanda, and it's past time for me to get my thumb out of it and latch onto a house. I need to do that for my kids, if nothing else. They won't give a shit as long as it's got internet and their dad, and I can make sure I tick those boxes on the list. I can't have them staying here full-time, and they've told me they're done with livin' at their mom's place. I looked at a couple of houses online earlier, did a virtual tour of one, and I've got the paperwork coming tomorrow so I can sign for it."

"A rental?" She shook her head. "Sorry, it's not my business. It just seems like that's fast."

"It *is* your business. Did you not hear me ask you to be with me yesterday? That's here, or wherever we wind up. You don't have to go back to that apartment except to collect your things. And yeah..." He shrugged as she stared at him, struck speechless by what he'd just revealed. "It's fast, but if you throw enough cash at the seller, they're motivated to make haste with the transaction."

He wants me to what? She ignored that piece of information and focused on the rest of the topic. "You're buying a place? Without seeing it?"

His lips curved slightly as he nodded. "You wanna see it?" He paused a moment to consider something, then smiled more broadly. "Sure thing. We'll go look at it, first thing in the morning. I wanted to see it, but I didn't want to leave you here. You wouldn't have been alone, because I got a couple of brothers hanging out on the main floor, but I didn't want you to wake up in some strange place without me, without knowing anyone, and get scared. So I sorted out something that let me do both things." His fingers tightened around hers. "I'll take you to work tonight, bring you back here, and we'll wait to pick up your car tomorrow until after we look at the house."

"That's a lot of money." Relentlessly, she kept her mind from wandering down the path of thought about why he wanted her approval on a house he was getting for his kids. He was right, it was too fast, and she didn't know what to do about that. So she disregarded it as best she could.

He laughed. "I didn't tell you where it is. Could be in the worst neighborhood, one where they practically pay a buyer to go through the deal. Jumpin' to conclusions there, and I see your head working overtime."

"But...when did you start looking?" He wasn't wrong about her leaping to conclusions, but he was the one pushing her to consider things she didn't understand. She'd liked his wake-up call, a lot, and it wasn't a far leap to imagine getting the same or better every day. *I don't even know him.* She winced at her internal lie. She knew a lot about him after last night. As promised, he'd been an open book for any question. They'd talked about subjects as diverse as music tastes and political leanings, two areas where they weren't a match. At all. But when it came to family and friends, loyalty and devotion, their morals and tenets of faith were side by side. He'd been clear about what he'd wanted from her, too, and after their superhot session earlier in the evening, she'd been shocked when he hadn't asked for more. Hadn't pushed her at all. Then—as if he'd read her mind—he'd told her that he didn't want her to think that was all he was after, and the expression on his face had taken her breath away.

Everything. She remembered what he'd said when he came through her door. *He wasn't kidding.*

"Today. I called my kids and told 'em about you. Nelda made me realize I would have three kids and my woman on my hands in a few days, and I needed to sort my shit, so I called a friend of a friend. I knew he had a place up for sale, and if we like it, it'll work out for both him and me. The place can even come furnished, if we want. Which is good, because I don't want a damn thing out of that house I shared with my ex. But we can decide shit like that when we look at it." He smirked as he looked at her. "You're takin' this well."

"You're buying a house." He nodded, that smirk still firmly in place on his face. She needed to know for sure, because if she took him at face value and then found out she was wrong, it would destroy her. *He's already become so important to me.* "So your kids can live with you."

"And you." His thumbs stroked across the backs of her hands, trailing a soft touch across the bumps of her knuckles. Back and forth, mesmerizing her. "You're an important part of this puzzle, Trina." The echo of her thoughts made her shiver and he chafed at the skin of her arms with his palms, chasing away the goose bumps along with some of her fear.

"And so I can live with you." He shook his head and her stomach dropped. *So much for hoping I was right.* She decided to seek clarity, because his refusal was confusing, he'd been running hot, hot, hot, and now he'd switched to cold? *That doesn't make sense.* "What? That's what you just said."

"It'll be your place, too. You won't be living with me, we'll be living together. Might seem a small distinction, but it's important. Important to me, and I wanna make sure you and me are on the same page, darlin'." She blinked at him, the difference not lost on her. Living together meant she'd be invested in more than just the relationship he wanted. She needed to let herself believe, because—*I want it too.* Living together meant a sharing of everything, starting with the decision on the house itself. "I don't expect any issues with my kids, but we'll work through whatever happens. You're part of this now."

"It's so fast. You. Me. This." She pulled a hand away from his grip to gesture around the room, only lasting a moment before he recaptured it. "A house with kids?"

"Yeah. Gotta get them settled before school starts, so it's got to be fast." He smiled at her. "You and me, it feels right, and don't try to tell me you got it any different in your head. So, yeah, it might be fast, but you're locked in for me. I can no more imagine walking away from you than I can consider not bein' part of my kids' lives." Her heart beat faster at the idea, pounding with a rush of terror and when his gaze dipped to her throat, he nodded. "Yeah, I don't like even thinking anything like that. Anything where I'm not a part of something with you. And I see you're the same. It's fast but it's right, and I ain't goin' anywhere. You aren't either, and I know that down to my toes, because I see it in your eyes. I feel it in your touch, the way you give to me when I'd bet the farm you never gave to someone like that before."

She felt her cheeks heat and knew they were flooded with red.

"Baby, you threw an arm over me last night and held tight, grumbling if I moved around. Even in your sleep you wanted to be close. I nearly picked you up and toted you to my bed, but I didn't want to scare you or wake you, and a single night in here with you was worth everything. I slept good, you slept good, you woke up cute as shit, and woman—if you're gonna be sweet like that when you roll outta bed, I need to develop some kind of immunity to it. You could ask me for anything and I wouldn't be able to tell you no to save my life. So fuckin' cute, and I want that every day. Give it to me, yeah? Trina...it's fast, but right. Tell me you know that."

She stared at him, her belly rolling nervously, but for all the right reasons. She couldn't find an ounce of fear inside her about this, about him keeping her and her keeping him, just excitement and a deep affection that surprised her. There was only one answer that felt right, and she gave it freely, leaning forwards to press her forehead against her knees, covering her face as she said, "Yeah, I know it is."

"Don't hide from me." He gripped her chin and lifted, bringing her gaze back to meet his. "Don't ever hide from me. It don't matter what you got to say, you give me your face when you say it." His thumb traced that well-worn path across her lips and she dared to press a kiss to the tip, which made his lips quirk up to the side, the half-smile falling away when he shook his head. "But, darlin', especially don't hide if you're giving me everything I wanted."

"Everything?"

This time he gave her a full smile, the effect making her stomach roll and dip in the best of ways when he repeated the word that seemed to sum up whatever this was they were building.

"Everything."

***

It felt like the longest shift she'd ever worked at the diner.

Starting from the time Retro dropped her off in front of the doors—and never mind she was supposed to go in the back—when he kissed her until her knees were weak. Tongue sliding into her mouth in that way she'd already come to expect, lapping at her lips as if he couldn't get enough of the taste of her, and she felt the same, because he was addicting. This man who'd blown in like a Gulf storm and taken over her life.

He'd set her upright, holding her shoulders while she swayed towards him, soft laughter through his smile at how addled she was just from a kiss. "Bodes well for me, when I finally get you into my bed." That had been his whisper into her ear before he'd leaned back and turned her with a businesslike, "You're gonna be late clockin' in." Then he'd swatted her butt, just hard enough to sting a little, before he'd climbed back on his bike.

She'd been left standing on the tiny cement landing in front of the doors, watching him ride away, bracketed on either side with men she'd seen at the clubhouse, but hadn't met. *Not yet*, she'd thought, internalizing her belief in what she'd told him. This, her and Retro, Jerry to his family, wasn't too fast, or too unlikely, or too anything except right. *And there can't ever be enough right in this world.*

Pete had stared at her when she walked in, his head going back and forth like a metronome as he looked between her and the place the bikes had disappeared, then back to her. He'd only asked her one question that wasn't to do with an order, and she'd noticed how he'd kept his distance from her physically, where before he would have been all up in her space. "So, you and the biker, huh?"

Trina had lifted her chin at that, waiting for whatever putdown he'd thought up. She'd been surprised when he'd nodded and just said, "He's a cool dude. Good for you."

Then had come the hours of customers. Solo diners, businessmen doing the right thing by filling their bellies with a pre-drinking meal. Families where the parents looked exhausted, the kids were hellions, and in the end, there were cracker crumbs everywhere to be swept and wiped, clearing the space for the next round of patrons.

Retro has kids. Her head circled back to that with every family she waited on. Nelda, the oldest, followed by Jimmy and Saya. And ex-wife that was a "pain in everyone's ass" as he'd put it. Family in the small town he'd grown up in, friends all over the country, and already some of the names were becoming familiar. Twisted and Penny, hosting his children for a couple of weeks in the summertime. Wrench, a man Retro felt he'd had a hand in shaping, and was proud of as if he was a son.

She was in the kitchen stacking clean plates out of the dishwasher when she heard the sound. Trina lifted her head, excited gaze meeting Pete's panicked one, and she smiled broadly.

The echoing rattle of motorcycle exhaust died away outside. Rushing to the swinging door, she lifted on her toes to peek through the window just in time to see Retro stand up off his bike, hand lifted to tug away the bandana tied around the bottom of his face. He was smiling wide, laughing at something one of his men had said. Helmet and bandana removed, his hands worked at the back of his head and then he shook his head, hair falling around his shoulders. With his strong jaw, straight nose, and striking hair—Retro was a sight to see. *He's gorgeous.* She smiled, feeling that good quiver in her belly again. *He's mine.*

He scanned the interior of the diner as he came through the front door. Then his eyes landed on the window and she knew when he'd seen her. The smile on his face changed, softening, and he wrinkled his nose as he tipped his head towards the same corner booth he'd occupied the first night he'd come into the diner. *He's mine.*

She was still standing there on her tiptoes when Carolynn walked past, the other waitress on shift heading towards the booth on Trina's end of the diner. The woman was the worst about trying to lay claim to a big table, sometimes only bringing water and place settings but demanding half the tip. Carolynn sashayed up to the table and Trina got to watch as the men's faces all closed down, going from relaxed and smiling to stoic in a breath. Retro shook his head once and said something too low for Trina to hear. Carolynn persisted, swaying her hips as she shifted her weight side to side in a move designed to bring the men's attention to her boobs and hips. Retro shifted in the seat, turning away from her and the man next to him spoke up, louder, less careful of the waitress' feelings. "The fuck you still doin' here, honey? Man said he ain't interested and asked you politely to move along."

Carolynn responded, her ass twitching to the other side in her skirt and Mudd, Trina thought that was his name, laughed, the sound ugly and mean. "Bitch, you could offer to suck his cock right here and he'd still turn you down. His woman's workin', and you ain't her, so mosey yourself back to where folks need you." He pointed down the diner with two fingers, flicking his pointer finger down at the last minute so it looked like he was flipping Carolynn off. "Shoo. Get on. Don't embarrass yourself."

Trina stepped away from the door, ducking down so Carolynn wouldn't know she'd been witness to the humiliation. With a deep inhale, she stiff-armed the door, checked on her other tables first, then hustled to where Retro sat. "Hi." He looked up and the moment his eyes found her, he smiled, that soft, sweet expression he seemed to only have for her. "Are you guys eating or just want coffee? I don't get off for another hour. I didn't expect you this early." She clamped her lips closed, rolling her eyes at herself. "Hi."

He reached out and drifted a soft touch down her arm to her hand, fingers wrapping around and holding on for a quick squeeze. "I'll eat supper with you later, but these boys need menus. Coffee for all of us, though. You have a good day, baby?" She nodded, digging in a pocket for her pad and pen. "I missed you." He plucked at the hem of her skirt, fingertips brushing the skin of her leg in a there-and-gone flare of heat. "I like you in a skirt." She'd ridden on the back of his bike to work in pants, changing in the bathroom after he'd left. "But, you ain't sittin' my bike like that tonight. It's too exposed."

"I can put my jeans back on." She ducked her head. "After work, I mean. I'll be right back with the coffee." She started walking away and then stopped, turning back to face him. "I did. Have a good day, I mean. And—" She took in a steadying breath. "I missed you, too. And I liked that you didn't want Carolynn to wait on you, that you told her I'd take care of you. I will." She nodded. "I'll take care of you." Through it all, he stared at her, a crooked grin lifting one side of his mouth. "So, I'll go, but I'll come back." She took a step backwards and flicked her thumb towards the counter where the coffee machine was. "This is me, going." Retro's grin spread to a smile that made her belly dip and buzz in that good way again. "Because if I don't go, I can't come back." She stopped and closed her eyes, dropping her chin to her chest. "God. I'm so—"

"Smart?" Retro's voice came from right in front of her. "Beautiful?" She opened her eyes to see he'd made the short trip to where she stood. "Funny as fuck?" He crowded her, getting so close she had to look up to hold his gaze. "Sweet? Because if you were going to say any of those things, I'd agree with you." His face dipped closer and she got to see his dancing, laughing eyes up close. "Mine?" He unknowingly echoed her thoughts from earlier and she held her breath. "Because that'd be true, too." He kissed her quickly, a firm press of his mouth against hers, followed by a glide of his lips towards her ear. "You don't have to be anything other than yourself with me, Trina. Because what I want? You already got it goin' on. You're real, and that's everything to me. So you go on and do your thing. We're not in a hurry here. You go and do, but you got it right. You'll come back to me. You'll come back, and I'll be here. Always."

"Damn." Drawled by one of the men at the table behind Retro, that single word held every emotion she was feeling right now.

***

Retro

He studied the numbers painted on the curb, lifting his hand off the throttle to pull the column to a halt. There was a car parked in the driveway up near the house, and he could see a business placard on the door. It was too far away to read the name, but the outline matched the realtor's sign in the yard.

Big, the white two-story house sat well away from the street at the top of a slight rise. He looked at the surrounding homes and liked what he saw. With well-kept yards, these were lived-in homes, not rentals, a house halfway down the block even had a pile of bicycles on the front yard which meant kids.

He heeled the kickstand down and ran a hand along Trina's lower leg, wrapping his fingers around her calf to give her a squeeze. It was something he'd found himself doing yesterday, too, at every chance along the way. Just a touch, a caress, a way to connect with her that wasn't her holding tightly to his belt loops.

The engines of the bikes died, and he listened to the men behind him sorting out their strategy. They'd leave Einstein to stay with the machines, just in case. He turned and gave a chin lift to Crazy Mike. "Hey."

"Yeah, boss?" The quick response made him grin. The men knew that this was important to him. Knew that whatever house he chose would be with more than his kids and woman in mind. The club would be part of the equation, always, as it should be for a man who lived and breathed for his colors and patch, for the men who followed him without question, for the men who battled for a right to have a place in the rank and file, who held their heads high with pride because they were a Bama Bastard, and that was how it should be, too.

"Garage is around back, should be a four-bay, which will give us plenty of space for personal repairs." The club owned mechanic shops, but those were busy with citizen jobs all the time, and they'd managed a makeshift shop at the clubhouse by moving in a big storage building, which worked fine for quick jobs. For something where a member was rebuilding a bike, or doing a custom build, the garage here might offer a better solution. "Pool and pool house are back there too, so check those out while you're lookin' around." Trina's muscles flexed under his hand and he smoothed a touch up and down, holding her ankle loosely. "You and Marlin go see what you think. Me and my woman gonna take the inside tour, we'll meet you out back, yeah?"

"You got it." Crazy Mike lifted a crisp two-finger salute to his brow, then led the men across the lawn towards the driveway and around the house.

"I like the look of it from here." He tipped his head back slightly, making it clear he was talking to Trina and not Einstein. "Hop off, honey, and we'll go give it a look-see." He held a hand up and waited, smiling when she placed her hand trustingly in his. She was steady on her feet, and he frowned down at the multihued canvas sneakers on her feet. "Need to get you some boots, baby." He heeled the bike over and stood up, stretching his back with one eye on Trina, smiling with satisfaction when her expression made it clear she appreciated all of him. *Tonight*, he promised himself, and grabbed her hand. "Come on."

Downstairs matched his virtual tour, so he let the realtor do her spiel while he focused on things that were new to him. Then it was time to change floors, and this was more new, because the online video hadn't featured much. There were five bedrooms, all upstairs, three with a private bathroom, something he knew Nelda would appreciate. Two were connected by a Jack and Jill bath, and he made a mental note to put his boys into those rooms, because Jimmy and Saya were joined at the hip most of the time anyway.

Trina kept hanging back when he was looking at most of the rooms, seeming shy as the realtor spouted off the features built into the home. "Can you give us a minute?" The woman nodded, already headed back towards the stairs, her heels clacking annoyingly as she rattled her bones down the steps. "Jesus, baby, you wear shoes like that?" He pointed towards the empty stairs, catching Trina's hand with his other one to pull her towards the master bedroom, the one he wanted to explore without an audience.

"Do you like her shoes?" The hurt in Trina's voice pulled him up short and he swung around to stare at her. He shook his head. "Because I don't normally. They aren't practical for what I need or do—" She paused a long minute, then finished softly, "—or like. So no, I don't own shoes like hers. But if you liked something like that—"

He cut her off before she could say something that would piss him off, because if she insinuated he liked the realtor, he would definitely have been pissed off. "Fuck, no. I don't like those shoes. They don't do it for me. I like simple, easy, and comfortable, and those weren't any of that. I like you, like your style, which is kinda like mine. I wear what I wear because I like it, or it can take a long day of riding and come out of the dryer without embarrassing my woman when I'm with her. Plus, her shoes were noisy as fuck, and that'd be annoying fast. That's the kind of shoe—" He cut himself off, shaking his head, staring at Trina whose features had softened into a smile he liked, something that told him she liked what he'd said and he'd given her what she needed, and that pleased him.

"That's the kind of shoe your ex would like, is that what you were going to say?" He nodded. "So you don't hate my shoes?" She held one leg out and he glanced down at the colorful canvas that covered her foot, shaking his head again. "You said you wanted me in boots, and I think that'd be cool, but then you asked about those sky-high heels with all those straps, and I wasn't sure for a minute what you wanted from me."

"Boots will keep you safe on the bike. Road hazards, stones, all kind of shit flies up off the road at us, and boots keep your feet from getting bruised up or worse. That's all I meant, baby. And you should ask sooner if anything I say makes you feel anything other than cherished."

"Your tone about her shoes confused me." She rolled her eyes with a tiny smile. "Awed and terrified all at once."

"Jesus, did you see them? If you wore shit like that, you'd be taller than me." Trina laughed aloud at that blatant lie and he smiled with pleasure at pulling that sound from her. "Scary as fuck. No, I don't like 'em. Do me a favor and never develop a fetish for that kind of footwear. And if I do anything that makes you wonder or question what I'm thinkin' or feelin', then spit it out, okay? Better out than in, and that's a saying for more than the fart jokes my boys make." He smiled but let it fade as he kept the layer of serious in his voice that he hoped would tell her he meant everything he said. "If you get concerned about what I mean, ask me and I'll tell you. I'm an open book where you're concerned, Trina. I want you to ask. I want what I say to matter, and for you to *want* to clarify so we're on the same page. I want it so fuckin' bad, I cain't even tell you. I want to matter to you, and I—fuck, I just want to matter to you." He shook his head. "That's all."

"You do." She stepped closer and placed her palm on his chest, between his pecs, right over his heart, as he'd done to her, and he liked what it said that she used the same gesture to calm him. "You matter more than you know."

"I wanna know." He reached up and covered her hand with his. "I haven't had that in a long, fuckin' time, baby. I wanna know, because that makes me less afraid I'm the only one in this. I haven't had someone give a shit about me like this, and I'm scared as fuck I'm gettin' it wrong. So you asking me shit, that doesn't annoy. In fact, it tells me you're in this with me, and we're finding out each other as we go. Fast and right doesn't substitute for understanding and comfort. It's real, but fuck, it won't be easy. We're sidestepping a big chunk of the 'get to know you' shit, your rounds of twenty-questions aside. So you think it, you ask, and I'll do the same. That's what was behind my question about her shoes. I wanna know you."

"Same." She smiled and her fingers flexed, spreading, and he threaded his between, wrapped his hand around hers with a squeeze. "Same."

"Soooo." He drawled the word out long enough to make her grin up at him. "Let's go see our bedroom, yeah?" The light in her eyes brightened and he laughed, staring down at her smiling face. "Where all the magic'll happen, right?"

Her gaze dipped, then lifted to meet his again, and he saw her steel herself to be brave, smiling wide when she asked, "We don't have to wait to move in to make magic, do we?"

"Jesus, my woman's horny. We better get this tour over with, so I can take her back to my room and have my way with her. Come on, quick like. Double-time." He tugged her hand, pulling her along the hallway at a trot, shaking his head when she laughed softly. "Let's see what our future love shack looks like."

In the bedroom doorway, she stopped and he paused, giving her a minute to take it in. Furnished and decorated, he thought it looked more like a hotel than a private residence. There was a built-in dresser along one wall underneath a wide-screen TV and low lighting from recessed sconces in the ceiling to highlight the centerpiece of the room, an enormous bed with a poufy comforter, probably a hundred pillows that served no purpose he knew of, and a padded headboard that gave him a thousand ideas of things to do to Trina's body. *Mmmm.* Time to clue her in, just in case she'd missed the first memos he'd given her.

"I could wake up next to you every morning in that bed and never get tired of it." Her fingers tightened in his, but he kept his gaze off her, letting her look her fill if she wanted. "High bed like that? Bend you over the foot and take you from behind, make it easy for both of us to crawl up and collapse when we're done. I ain't young anymore, but you make me want everything. All the lovin' from you. Lean back against that headboard, let you ride me, slow as you like, givin' me a show and I'd fuckin' love that, baby. I'll treat you like an empress, Trina, you let me. I wanna feel you all over my body, wanna taste you a dozen times a day, you let me. This is as real as it gets. You want me, you got me, and I'm all in. Let this be the start of it all." He turned and faced her, linked hands stretched between them. She had shining tracks down her cheeks and he forced himself to stand still while her chin trembled, her lips quivered, and she wept openly with the sweetest look of devotion on her face. "You want me?" She nodded immediately, quickly, ends of her hair flipping through the air. He smiled and took a deep, steadying breath because finally, fucking finally, he believed. "You got me."

He backed towards the bed, drawing her along with him as he propped his ass on the edge and spread his thighs wide. She stepped between his legs like she'd always belonged to him and knew what he wanted, and he smiled up at her, the position giving her an inch or so advantage. "Retro," she breathed, her eyes darting back and forth as she scanned his face. "It's a big house."

"I got a big family. Got a woman whose mother will wanna visit, got a brother with two heathens of his own he'll bring down for holidays, and my kids have friends. This house is in the same school district they've always attended, so that's a huge plus in my book. Gotta take care of my kids." He smiled when her expression softened. "You like that my kids matter to me." It wasn't a question, but she nodded anyway. "In my head there's no other way to be. It's what my parents taught me, and I learned well. Any kids we have together would get the same from me." He knew he was jumping the gun with that statement, but he wanted to ride the rush of this first wave of discovery. Her eyes got wide and he grinned. "Make of that what you will. There ain't no 'my kids come first' or 'my woman comes first' or 'club first' because in my head, it's all important. It all holds places of criticality that I cain't...won't change. It's all important to me, because all of it matters. My brothers under the patch, the men who ride with and behind me, who depend on me to keep them and their family safe, my kids and family who depend on me to keep them fed, sheltered, and safe, my woman who'll depend on me for anything she needs—it's all important to me." He shrugged. "So yeah, it's a big house, but it'll be what we make it, which is a home."

He settled a hand on either hip, tugging her close enough he could rest his chin between her breasts, staring up into her face. Her fingers threaded through his hair and he closed his eyes, letting her see how much he liked it when she touched him. Her heart beat fast, thudding against her ribcage from the inside, and he wondered if he'd gone too fast, too far, dropped too much on her shoulders with what he'd said. Then Trina blew him away, because she used her grip on his hair to turn his head, nestling his cheek where his chin had been and kissed the top of his head.

Then she spoke, and he listened with every fiber of his being.

"I always wanted a big family, and you come with one ready-made. Three kids, which is a lot, but I've missed out on parts of their lives that I didn't know I'd want. Let me meet them, make them love me—" He made a sound in his throat and she shushed him absently. "Shhh. I'll make them love me, meet your men, because I know like four names so far, figure out how to get to work from way out here—" He started to interrupt again to tell her about the job and she kissed the top of his head again, quietening him with another soft, "Shhh." Her heartbeat slowed and she took in a deep breath. "My mom would love this place. Meeting the rest of your family sounds terrifying, but I'll have your kids on my side by then, I just know it. I'm good with kids. And I want one. One that would be ours, because...well, just because. If you give me you—" Her voice lowered, shaking as her heartbeat sped back up and he listened to the silences between the words that were filled with so much information. "Then you can't leave. If we're in this together, like it feels, then it's..." She took a beat, and finally whispered, "...forever." Another deep breath and her fingers resumed movement, running through his hair, caressing the back of his head, tips tracing the curve of one ear. "I'm not anything special, Retro. What you're saying is I'd be special to you. I've...like you said, we're a lot alike. I've never had that, and I'm going to mess up."

He jumped into the gap then, ignoring her attempts to shush him. "I'm not going to give up on this, Trina. We'll argue, and get sideways, and then we'll figure it out, like we need to. We'll figure it out, and I'm not going to run. I'm not a man who gives up just because something's harder than I expected. I won't run." He repeated his words, each laced with emphasis, hoping to convince her that he wasn't whoever had fathered her. He wasn't someone who would make her raise a child on her own, wouldn't do that to her. "I won't run." Pulling against her grip, he lifted his face to her and reached up, locking his fingers behind her neck to bring her down. "You're special to me."

Their lips met, and it was like an inferno that had been banked back for days, finally given enough oxygen to roar to life again, consuming him. Pulling her into his lap, he twisted and lay her on the bed, coming down over her, keeping the connection between them hot. He took her mouth again and again, head slanting to find a different angle, tongue slipping between her lips with a firm thrust that she met with her own. It was powerful and so arousing he found himself panting into her mouth. He drank from her over and over, repeating each movement that made her gasp, his hand on her breast, tweaking the nipple through her clothes until she arched up against him, and he knew he could have her here and now, forget the realtor waiting downstairs and the men wandering the grounds. She was gone and he could do what he wanted, if he didn't care about what she felt like after. But he did, and he knew she'd be mortified if they made love now.

Slowly, deliberately, he eased back the intensity, ignoring the needy noises she made in her throat, steeling himself against her hands on his back, his ass, at his waist to pull him closer. He gave her his weight, anchoring them against the arching roll of her hips, until he was the one shushing her frustrated cries, their roles reversing as most good relationships did. He pulled back until his forehead touched hers, noses brushing softly with each breath, her eyes opened and were so dark, so filled with want and need he nearly gave in. "Soon," he promised and tried not to smile at her groan. "Soon, baby."

He kissed her again, soft and slow, palm gliding down her side until he gripped her ass. One leg between her thighs, he pulled her up and ground on her for a moment, the pressure a bracing agony. "So fuckin' hard to wait." Her knee lifted and hooked over his hip and now he was the one groaning in frustration. Hand curving around her ass, he found her core and pressed the seam of her jeans against her, a scraping caress from his nail dragging along the fabric threads making her gasp. "Got me hard as a rock, and ready to go, but we need to wait."

"Why? Retro." Her rising cry told of her frustration matching his and he wondered again at his reasoning to wait. Then one of his men laughed loudly outside, the realtor's voice carrying through the windows as she joined in. "Oh, no," Trina whispered, grinding against his leg a final time before she fell back onto the mattress, panting as her muscles relaxed.

"Yeah, all that." He dipped his head and trailed kisses along her throat, spending more than a few moments thinking about marking her now, so his men wouldn't wonder what was between them, but he shook his head. "So, the house. I'm a fan. You like it?"

"I've seen the bedroom." She laughed. "I like it."

"Bullshit, you were right beside me when we walked through." He gave a bounce on the bed, grinning when she giggled at being jostled around. "Good mattress. Plenty of spring under your ass."

"I wasn't really paying attention downstairs." Her chin tipped to her neck and he lost her eyes as she angled her gaze to the base of his throat. "Sorry."

"No sorries, doll. What had you distracted? Living room, a big-ass family room, nice-sized kitchen that opens out onto the backyard patio. Decent dining room and the table they have in there will seat more than a dozen with all the leaves put in. Bunch of built-in shit in the laundry and mudroom." He shrugged. "I like the open layout. It'll let me keep tabs on my boys." He settled his weight on the bed next to her, lowering himself so his head was even with hers. "Now, tell me what had you distracted."

"How much is this place? I don't have any money saved, not really. I can't help out with buying it. Not at all." The line was back between her brows and he reached up to smooth it out with his fingertip, cradling her jaw to bring her gaze to his face.

"I found you a job. It pays good, a competitive rate, and I think you'll enjoy it. No requirements for knowledge going in, which means it's entry level, but there's plenty of room to grow. Regular hours, too, which means you'd have nights free for me." He smiled at her, liking how her gaze went to his mouth and lingered there, telling him without words how much she'd liked their kisses, enjoyed what he did with his mouth, and was probably wondering what else he'd be willing to do. *Everything you want, baby*, he teased in his mind. But this was a serious moment, so he kept those thoughts to himself. "It's a club business, but this ain't a 'gimme' job, because we've been advertising for someone for weeks now. It's hard to find people we can trust, so we've been limpin' along. You'll be helping us out, really. And that's no lie."

"What is it? Are you sure I'll be okay at it?" The tentative note in her question drilled between his ears and he fought against grinding his teeth. People like that club manager had stripped down her confidence, making her feel less than so often it was ingrained in her. *She'll fix that.* He knew he didn't have to fix it for her; she'd do it once she wasn't surrounded by idiots and assholes.

"Yeap. Full confidence in you. One of our car and bike repair shops needs someone to organize shit. I saw your place, saw how you straightened things in the diner. It's probably perfect for you. Repair jobs are broken down into different categories, each category has a predefined time slot it needs. The job's lining up the need with availability on a calendar. Then the mechanics note what's needed for the repair, and you order the shit so it's ready when the gig is scheduled. Organizing shit." He shrugged. "Full confidence."

"I can do that." Her breathy whisper and shining eyes told him how excited she was, and he angled forwards to catch all that in a kiss, her soft sigh when he pulled back payment for everything.

If she only knew how she owns me.

"We should head back downstairs and I'll give you the nickel tour. Then we can look out back, see about the yard and pool and shit." She blinked. "There's a pool in the backyard. Did you miss that?" She nodded, eyes wide, and he laughed. "Come on, then."

Surprised when she moved towards him, he held his place and accepted the kiss she pressed to his mouth, letting her lead when she slipped her tongue between his lips, dipping inside for a taste. "Thank you." Breathed against him, her words were confusing, and she must have seen it on his face, because she smiled. "For not giving up on me."

He wrapped her up in his arms and rolled to his back, pulling her onto his chest. Fingers in her hair, he brought her head down and gave her a promise before he kissed her silent and boneless against him. "I'll never, not ever give up on us, baby. Us. You and me, we're in this together. We're a team. The Retro and Trina team."

When he finished kissing her, she relaxed so her head rested on his chest and he cradled her against him for a moment, shouting with laughter when she heard her say softly, her words nearly too quiet to hear, "Go team."

Chapter Six

Retro

"Anyone surprised?" Mudd's question made Retro snort, because the man did like to ask questions he already knew the answer to. "Not me, but anyone else?"

"No," Marlin answered with a laugh. "Think we all knew this was coming. It didn't make any sense to have a division in the clubs like they've been laboring under for the past months."

Standing in the doorway, Retro glanced back at the TV and studied the message cast up there for everyone to see. With a sigh, he read it aloud for the benefit of the members still out in the main room. "Caddo Hobos have a new president. Ace cut his own officer patch and handed it over during open church tonight following the officers' vote. Wrench is leading the CoBos as of today." He glanced around, seeing pondering looks but no surprise, which was good. For a club that traded in information and knowledge like the Bastards did, it wouldn't be a good sign if any member had missed signs pointing to this change in leadership. "Means a lot of our network will need tweaking, make sure they're up on the new knowledge. This puts us in the know in our region, because CoBos will hold it close until after Incoherent is informed." He made a show of looking at his wrist, pretending to consult an invisible watch face there.

"Which will happen in three—" He bopped his head to an unheard beat. "—two—" Another beat, more elaborately carried out. "—one." As if on cue, his phone buzzed in his pocket and the men around him laughed aloud. He grinned at them, dug it out and answered with a confident, "Good news, brother."

"Fuck you." Twisted sounded annoyed and Retro understood. Replacing anyone in a club was hard, no matter the reason for the leaving. He'd had to fill in a hole a while ago when a member had been killed at a rally in Florida. The man had ridden down with unpatched friends for a weekend of fun, and over an imagined insult of spilled beer, had been targeted, stalked, and taken out. Killed in a way that had given Retro nightmares for weeks, stories about the cops finding individual teeth in bloody piles along the roadway enough to curdle any man's stomach. He shook his head, stuffing down the pain associated with those memories, focusing instead on the here and now.

Twisted would be looking ahead to when Po'Boy dropped his patches, and that should be what Retro touched on tonight.

"You asked me for some info, and I found it." He had talked to Twisted a dozen times over the past weeks; his kids staying on in Louisiana a great cover for all the things Twisted needed from him in an unofficial official capacity. "Gimme a second while I get private." He motioned to Mudd and stepped around two members in deep conversation, one pointing animatedly towards the TV.

Walking quickly, Retro made his way across the main room, down a short hall, and into the smaller office used for these purposes. Soundproof, bugproof, isolated on a separate network, electrical system, and using a different HVAC unit than the rest of the clubhouse, few people not full patch members knew about this room. "Give me another moment, brother. I'm bringing Mudd in." That was how they worked, because it didn't swing things in their favor to only have one member in the know on something sensitive. He, Mudd, Crazy Mike, and any of his other officers would always call in another to witness. Mudd already knew what he was about to disclose, but using the system would give Twisted the illusion that the information was so critical Retro had held it close until it was time to deliver. Exclusivity cost, even for friends.

Most of what Retro traded in were markers, future favors to be called into play at his discretion. Knowledge leveraged against knowledge for the club's benefit. Twisted wanted to know about the member considered for officer position, but without the man knowing they'd checked up on him. Standard request, but it would still cost Twisted, no matter they were friends.

The door opened and closed, Mudd stepping inside as he locked it behind him. "Here," he said, loud enough for Twisted to hear, another intentional tactic they used to make the person on the phone feel they could depend on their own hearing. In reality there were two built-in touch-screen surfaces in the walls where Mudd could display or write messages without the person on the phone knowing anything. They never did video from inside here, keeping all their secrets close to the vest.

"Here's what I know. Wildman is a patchover from a club over in Baton Rouge, you pulled him and a half dozen others, eating away at the foundation of that club until it imploded, at which time you scooped up the rest that were worth anything. He's a good man. You learned that from the boys in Baton Rouge. But he's not without a past. His brother was an officer in a club down in the Keys." This was the new info for Twisted, and Retro didn't expect it to be welcome. "Wildman was in line for an officer position there until a passing swipe from a hurricane took out about half their clubhouse. He took it upon himself to organize a crew to first repair all member houses, and then the clubhouse. Earned the loyalty of a bunch of men, and their ole ladies, and we know that carries its own kind of weight. His brother felt he was too much competition and called in a paper on him."

"You're fucking with me?" Twisted's voice was hoarse with shock and Retro understood. Finding out that a man, someone who's been a trusted brother and patch, had an assassination attempt on them would be hard to swallow. That it had been by blood also in the life, made it more so.

"Nope, this is truth that I know." That was his bond, that he stood behind his words, that the person who'd bought and paid for them could take each uttered statement to the bank. "Wildman got word about what was going down, and he confronted his brother in the clubhouse. Assassin got to his home and took care of the rest of the paper, waiting on him to come home. Killed his pregnant wife in their bed, and then hunkered down in the kitchen. Meanwhile, back at the clubhouse, the brother demanded a beatout for Wildman, then known as Ogre for all the wrong reasons. Note that Wildman didn't know what'd happened to his old lady at this point."

"Hold on, man. You're tellin' me his brother, his fuckin' *blood* brother had Wildman's wife killed? Family? And her carryin'? Are you shitting me?" Anger rode the edge of Twisted's voice and Retro nodded, taking in his outrage and holding it close, because in there echoed the good in this man. Twisted might be ruthless and brutal when the situation called for it, but blameless family was sacrosanct, and all the clubs in their regions knew it.

"Yeah. So the brother, the veep for this piece-of-shit club, wants a beatout but can't get anyone to pony up the muscle, so he winds up fighting his brother solo."

"I cannot imagine Wildman was down for that." Twisted made a disgusted sound. "That's fucked up, Retro."

"Indeed. Kicker is that veep, his brother, got his feet tangled under him at some point. Way I heard it and from the vids I saw, Wildman wasn't anywhere close to the man when he went down. Fell hard, awkward, side of his head hit the corner of a cabinet. Died two days later." He paused for a breath and looked at Mudd who nodded, confirming Retro hadn't forgotten anything important. "Man called a bus for his brother, followed it to the hospital, dealt with the cops there because both the brothers were fucked up from the fight. For all Wildman didn't want to rumble with him, he'd known if his brother was willing to pay for paper, he had to be in it for real. So there were a hundred cops asking a hundred questions each. Some of the video I saw surfaced then and helped clear him. Then he went home to see why his wife wasn't answering the phone, the paid killer was still there waiting. Wildman dealt with him in a final way, and then tried to call the club to come help clean up. But they weren't picking up for him anymore. Not after the fucked-up shit that had gone down. The expectation was he wouldn't want anything to do with them, and can you blame him if it were true? They'd known it was bullshit and still stood by when everything went down."

"Jesus, it's like everything lined up against him." Twisted whistled low, soft and rattling in a cadence that almost was familiar. "I can empathize. Who'd he get to help clean shit at his house?"

Retro glanced back at Mudd with one eyebrow lifted. They hadn't talked this through, so he wasn't sure if he'd have Mudd's support on what he was about to do. He lifted a hand and pointed a finger at himself, not surprised when Mudd's head dropped back and he puffed out air towards the ceiling. With a grin, Retro answered Twisted's question, aware too many seconds had ticked past for this not to be telegraphed as critical information. "Bastards assisted him."

"What the fuck? He met you after I patched him, and swore he didn't know you. The man could not have lied to my face like that." Twisted's anger edged into his voice, rattling around like a growl deep in his chest. "He told me flat out he'd never met you. Never laid eyes on you, except at a distance when he was my prospect. How the hell did you do that?"

"He didn't know it was me, and I didn't know it was him. I'd had some trouble in Florida, not as bad as it got, but bad enough. My network was fucked up, people moving in and out following storms and fires, and I had a friend of a friend call in a marker he held." Retro shrugged and then laughed soundlessly at Mudd's antics, finger repeatedly dragging from side to side across his neck in a clear request to kill the conversation now. "They were short on manpower, so I supplied what was needed, but you know me." Twisted made a sound Retro took to be agreement. "Yeap, so I took it on, but there was a lot in it for me and mine. All kinds of information to be had about the dominant in the area, how they dealt with support clubs, how they dealt with pop-ups, which was lethally, and that in fact was where the killer had come from to begin with. Imagine this if you will—" He waved one palm through the air theatrically, knowing he was performing only for Mudd, and not caring. "Support club veep is a douche but he pays his dues to the dom. Might be off the backs of his own members, but he pays his dues, so he calls for an eradication, doesn't give details too deep, just enough surface to make it plausible. He's got the money for the paper, so the dom MC spins it up and assigns it. Then they find out *all* the background. So *then* they're hiring someone to help come in and deal with everything. That someone is me. I get all the lowdown on the down low and make a pile of money to boot. And now, I got your marker, because I gave you everything you asked for. The man's loyal, good to the bone, knows his way around shit situations and isn't afraid to stick his neck out to do the right thing. You could do worse than promoting him, brother. And if you don't want him..." He left that last sentence to trail off, waiting for the sound that would tell him story time was over.

Twisted laughed, a guttural sound that came from deep in his belly, and Retro smiled, cocking a finger and pointing it at Mudd. "Worth everything to learn that, brother. If you find out more..." It was Twisted's turn to trail off and Retro grinned at the manipulative bastard as he pulled an imaginary trigger.

"You'll owe me another marker if I find out more. Anything else is outside the scope of the original request, and you know it." He pulled a chair out from under the table, leaning back with eyes closed. "He's a good one, brother. You already knew it."

"Aye, I did. I just wanted confirmation."

"And now you got it." Retro waggled his fingers at Mudd who took the hint, leaving the room and closing the door gently, cutting off the sound of the men in the other room. "Po'Boy give you a timeframe yet?"

"Nope. Just soon. Asshole." There was a fondness in Twisted's tone that belied the name calling. "Kids are about ready to come home, I think. Your sister, though, she's turned into a real help with Penny. You cool if she decides to stay here a while?"

"Yeah. Keeps her out of trouble. As long as she's useful, then that's good." He studied the screen, flicking icons on the computer connected to this private network. A calendar flashed up on the wall and he looked at the dates and events noted. "I'm closing on a place in two days." It would probably take that long to move money around his various accounts so he could pay cash for the house. "What if I come to get the kids on Thursday?"

"Stay until Saturday, we'll make a party of it?" Twisted's voice dropped. "Penny wants to meet your woman. You're bringing her, right?"

"Wouldn't think of doing anything else." He smiled. "She'll love the ride, long as she can hide behind me if the bugs are out."

***

Trina

Retro and three of his men walked into the diner about an hour and a half before her shift was up. This was the third night in a row, and she smiled at him as she headed towards the corner booth she was quickly beginning to think of as his.

"Hey, baby," he called as she got close, reaching up to slip his fingers around her wrist, then down to clasp around her hand. She didn't resist as he pulled her to stand between his knees. "How's your day been?"

She tried to keep her cool, but his touch ignited a heat and need between her legs. It didn't make any sense, because before him, she'd been celibate for a long time...years, any attraction to a man vague and casual in an "oh, he's hot" kind of way. She and Retro hadn't had sex— she couldn't say hadn't slept together, because that had happened several nights in a row now—but when she was around him, it was all she could think about. She'd been so tired after they saw the house, then went back to her apartment, and then her car, by the time they'd eaten supper last night, she'd been ready to collapse, and he'd known somehow. Lying next to her, he'd played with her hair until she'd fallen asleep, staying that way until he woke her to get ready for work. *No nookie for me.*

All day she'd caught herself fantasizing about his hands of all things, visually measuring the width of his fingers and remembering how they'd felt inside her the one time he'd touched her like that. *I'm just frustrated.* She shoved those ideas out of her head and greeted him, aware from the way his grin had spread that she'd been slow...again. Because once she got around him, her head filled up with him, and she lost track of everything else going on. *This can't be normal.*

"Good. Not too busy, but busy enough." She shrugged. "Menus and coffee?" She nodded at the three men, not recognizing them.

"Yeah, that'd be good. Trina, these are folks from out of town. Mason..." The man on the outside of the opposite side lifted a finger and she noted the phoenix tattoo on his arm, striking and bold colors making a statement of some kind. "Fury." Positioned on the inside of Mason, the redhead gave her a smile and tip of his head. "And this old troublemaker here—" Retro flung his arm around the shoulders of the man next to him. "—is Hoss. My brother." She froze in place, that name familiar enough to make her search back through her memories to try and find it. "Isaiah Rogers."

"Oh, Lord. You're his brother." She looked down to where the spaghetti stain from a food-throwing three-year-old decorated her uniform shirt, and a coffee stain was splashed across the skirt. "Hi." She glanced up to see the handsome man next to Retro smiling at her, his face soft. "Hi," she tried again, hoping her voice was stronger, "I'm Trina. Katrina Fainburg."

"Hi, Trina." Hoss disentangled himself from Retro's rough embrace and held out his hand. "It's really good to meet you." His fingers wrapped around her hand and they had barely started the downslide of the handshake when Retro reached out and separated them, flinging Hoss' hand away while keeping control of hers.

"Mine, asshole." The other men in the booth laughed, and Trina stared at Retro, mouth open. "Baby?" She swallowed and blinked. "Gimme a kiss." More laughter, and Trina scarcely had a chance to react before his hand was at the back of her neck and she was drawn down until his lips hit hers in a soft, sweet caress. "Better," he murmured against her mouth, renewing the kiss for a moment, then releasing.

"Oh, I'm lovin' this." The man introduced as Mason was smiling broadly when she glanced at him, giving a fist pound to the man next to him. "Never thought I'd see the day when Retro got tangled up in a woman."

She frowned at that, because if these were close friends, they knew he had been married—was still married, for that matter. Her confusion must have been apparent, because Mason leaned close, palm flat on the table in a gesture that looked ritualistic. "Oh, yeah. I met Wanda. Didn't like her for this man right here. She wasn't ever the right fit, and anyone with eyes could see how things were with them. Found out a while ago the deal your man had to make,"—her belly warmed at how he just called Retro hers as if it wasn't a question, but something he knew as truth—"and I understand, because we all do what we have to when put up against decisions like that." She marked his words, deciding to wait to ask Retro what had pulled him and Wanda together. He'd told her it was something her father had that he'd needed, but he hadn't gone beyond those words. Mason's little speech made her wonder. "But just because a body's content with their choices doesn't mean they're the right ones in the end. I like you for him, and that's truth spoken. Met you. Like you.

The way he's holdin' on to you means he's all in on this. The fact he's introducing you to me and mine, that's big too, sweetheart." She smiled at that and realized Retro's arm was around her hips, and he'd pulled her close, his head resting against her side. "Introducing you to his family without warning? That's just him being a thoughtless asshole, and you'll have to overlook that."

"She'll have to overlook his shit all the time." Hoss threw in his two-cents' worth and it made her smile, because he swayed in the seat, bumping Retro's shoulder, which in turn bumped her.

"That also is truth spoken." Mason's smile was relaxed and real, and she saw from the lines on his face this wasn't something he had all the time, and wondered at the man's life. "So well met, Trina Fainburg. I like you for him, and expect to see you around."

"Thank you." She dropped her hand to Retro's shoulder and gave him a squeeze, looking down to find him staring up at her. "I'll get that coffee. Be right back."

When she returned with the mugs, two to a hand, hot ceramic burning the backs of her fingers where she held the handles, the men were in an intense discussion, cut off suddenly as she approached. They sat back, and she realized how far over the table they'd all been leaning, talking. Menus retrieved and handed out, an unspoken question when she offered one to Retro and he took it.

"I'll feed you later, when we get home, but I'm hungry now." He smiled. "I closed on the house early. Everything worked out and the timing fit my day." Shifting around in the booth, he dropped the menu to the table so he could dig out a wad of keys, each labeled with a paper tag. Selecting two, he removed them from the main ring, adding them to a smaller ring in his hand. "Front door, back door. The tag on one has the code for the garage. Boys'll get remotes keyed tomorrow for your car and my truck." He smiled up at her as he pressed the keys into her palm. His voice was soft when he told her, "We got a house, momma."

She clutched them to her chest, trying hard not to squeal loudly, but knew he saw the pleasure on her face when he laughed, gripping her waist to bring her into his lap, turning sideways on the seat so he could wrap his arms around her. Face buried in his neck, she clutched at his shoulders with her hands, holding tightly. Part of her had expected something to happen: the deal to fall through; the seller to back out; the HOA to bar the sell. Something. He'd explained the financing to her that first night, walking through his plans so they could be her plans, too. She'd asked about the money, because according to state law, half of it should be Wanda's, and he'd talked about the prenup her father had insisted on and the language there that protected both of them. So, his money was his, and hers was hers, and they'd never had a joint account in the whole time they'd been together.

Somehow that had been the most telling thing he'd said about what their relationship had been like. To have been together for that long and not have anything that tied you other than marriage and birth certificates. She'd thought it sounded miserable, and when the tears appeared in her eyes, he'd known, somehow. *"Don't cry for me, baby. I made my bed."* A statement she'd never understood before, but which now seemed incredibly sad. She'd offered to sign whatever he needed, right then and there, and he'd laughed hard at her, falling to his back in the bed as she'd rolled up on an elbow, palm flattened to his chest, his heart thumping slow and steady inside him.

"I would. I will." It was a promise, and she needed Retro to know she meant every word. "I don't want your money. It should be in trust for your kids anyway."

"I know you would, sweetheart. But I don't want that with you." His hand at the back of her neck pulled her down to his shoulder, arm going around her to hold her close. "I want everything with you." Pressure on top of her head turned into a soft smack, a sweet gesture of affection that said so much more than words ever could. "And when I put a ring on that finger, you're gonna know I'm all in."

She froze because that was new territory for them. They'd talked about a lot of things, family and friends, property and holdings, but it had been a clinical conversation, the family part sounding far in the future. Babies and growing old together seeming too much for the now of what they were building. A wedding? Not even on her horizon right now.

"Don't you go quiet on me now, Trina. You're feelin' something, you give it to me. We talked about that, didn't we?" She nodded, the fabric of his tee slipping under her cheek, the heat from his body baking through, something she could depend on, his strength feeding her strength in this. "You feel it, you wonder what I mean, you think I'm a crazy loon, you say it straight out."

"You want to get married? You're not even divorced yet." She hadn't meant to say that last part, but it was on the air between them and she knew she'd exposed too much when he went still underneath her. "I mean…it's not something I'd thought about."

"I had a feelin' it bugged you. I just had a feelin'." His muttered words sounded angry, even as his strong arm tightened around her, contracting to give her a squeeze. "I talked to someone the day after I met you. The state drags their feet on things, but I'll have it sooner than you think, Trina. I'll be shut of her for good, outside of the fact she's half the parenting for my kids. What'll make it better for you? In my head I'm already done with her, so she don't factor in any decisions I'm workin' on right now. She sure don't factor in anything with you and me, but you sayin' what you said tells me it bugs you more than I knew. You wanna wait on anything more between us until I got that paper, I'll do it. It'll kill me, most likely." Another squeeze to let her know he was kidding. "But I'm content with what I have from you right now, and I don't expect that'll change. Do I wanna love on you? Oh, fuck yeah. And I will, because you and me, we're separate from her shit. But with you, now I'm the one wondering, because if you wanted to hold off, wanted to wait, wanted to close one relationship before we open another one, I'm down for that. Do anything for you, baby. Anything."

Another squeeze and she slipped her arm over his stomach to hug him in response. "Everything." She smiled when she spoke, because he'd know. Of course he would; he was the one who'd opened her door with that word on his lips. "Everything, Retro. That's all I want."

"Only everything." He pretended to grumble, not pulling it off because of the laughter rumbling in his chest and she smiled to hear it. "My woman's needy and wanton, and she wants everything." Another soft, sweet kiss to the crown of her head, and he whispered a promise, "She gets what she wants. That's my guarantee to you, baby. You want it, you got it. Only everything."

She whispered it to him now, lips against his skin, eyes closed as she sat on his lap in public, not caring who saw. "Only everything." He made a sound and she smiled, because she'd surprised him somehow and that was rare. "That's what you give me, every day. Only everything."

"Woman," he growled, and she grinned at his mock annoyance. "You're killin' me here." His voice wasn't quiet, wasn't private, and she knew he did that on purpose, to bring his friends into their moment in some way, because these men at the table mattered to him, and she loved he'd made sure she got to meet them. "Now I wanna fuck you, and you're at work, and I ain't doin' you against a bathroom wall." He gave her a final squeeze, shifting so she sat up facing him, her eyes locked on his smiling face. "This time." Her cheeks heated and she knew he liked the fact she blushed so easily, so she wasn't surprised when he chuckled, the sound dark and promising, like so much about him. Retro might be a rough and tumble guy, might be a man's man in every way, and the caveman inside him might like showing her off and having people notice what was his, but he was also sweet and kind, and careful of her feelings in a way she'd never had in her life. Not once. "You good, baby?"

"I'm good." She was, too.

"Well, I'm not," Hoss said, his grumbling not at all pretend. "I'm starving here. What do you guys serve that's good?"

Trina stretched up to touch her mouth to Retro's, smiling at the satisfaction in his expression when she did so. "Specials are meatloaf, which I'd pass on if I were you, and a tenderloin sandwich, which is really delicious. We do serve breakfast all day, so if you're in the mood for that..." She stood and turned to face the table, trying to not react when Retro's hand dipped lower, curling around her leg before he slid it up and up, under her skirt. *Oh, Lord.* "Then it's a safe choice. Oh!" She jumped when he pinched her lightly, tightening her thighs together to try and keep his hand at a safe distance from her privates. "Uh. The Manhattan is really good, one of my favorites." His fingers trailed heated circles on her skin as he retreated slowly, each touch ratcheting up the desire that had been simmering in her middle. "Retro,"—she decided to attack this head-on, since he didn't seem self-conscious or fazed about discussing private time in front of his friends—"if you don't want to make good on that bathroom wall promise today, then you need to stop it now."

She learned a moment later that was the right approach when he tipped his head back and laughed, loud and long, the sound coming from his gut as the muscles in his neck worked in a gorgeous way she could watch all day long. Mason, Fury, and Hoss laughed too, but their eyes were on Retro, like hers, taking in the sight of her man—*my man*—responding freely to her teasing. *Worth any embarrassment to see that.*

Two hours later she was coming out of the women's room, zipping her bag closed over her folded uniform, new biker boots from Retro on her feet, when she saw Hoss waiting at the end of the hall. After an initial brief pause, she resumed walking towards him. "Hi," she said unnecessarily, because she'd seen him not five minutes ago when she told Retro she would be ready as soon as she changed.

"Thank you." Said without preamble, his words surprised her and she shook her head, confused. "My brother's been going through the motions for a while now, and I didn't even realize how bad it had gotten. Shit happens gradually, and you get used to it, and it worsens, and you get used to that, too. Bad coated on top of bad until that's all a body knows. That's where he's been for years, when the only light I'd see on his face had to do with his kids, but I didn't realize how much he'd closed down. I don't know the last time I saw him like this. So..." He shook his head. "Full of life." He shrugged and grinned, that expression making him look even more like his brother. "I like the look on him. And I've got you to thank for all of this. So, thank you."

"It's not one-sided." She hesitated to show how broken she'd felt before Retro barreled into her life, but decided Hoss might already know. *They're brothers, after all.* "He's opened doors to a world I didn't know existed. Just by being himself, he's already made my life richer than I deserve. I'm more than half in love with your brother, Isaiah. We know it's fast. We've talked about that until the sun came up more than once, but just because it's fast doesn't mean it's not real. I believe him, and I believe in us. The 'us we're building,' that's what he keeps saying, and it's true. Every conversation, every time we're together, it layers on another bit of foundation for what's between us." She shifted, hitching her bag a little higher on her shoulder. "You're welcome, I guess, because I didn't know him before, so I don't see what you do. But I know"—she touched her breastbone, a steady pressure to center herself—"in here, I know what he means to me, and what I want for him." She decided to give Hoss a little more, hoping he'd understand. "He promised me everything, and what he doesn't realize is he's already given it to me. Just by being with me, and being who he is, he's everything I need."

"And that right there? That's why he's got that look on his face when he sees you. Because whatever he's giving you, you're giving it right back." Hoss sighed and pushed open the door into the diner. She saw Retro through the windows, standing next to his bike and staring inside where they stood, head cocked to one side as he tried to decide what was going on here in the bathroom hallway. "I like you for him, and from what you've said just now, I like him for you, too."

He held the doors for her and Trina thanked him softly, the pain in his eyes as he'd said the last words heavy on her mind.

Retro had shared about his family, explaining about his sisters in detail, drawing Miriam's life for her in broad strokes of words that told of a steady and safe existence, one where she was happy and fulfilled and he saw it, even if it wasn't what he needed.

Bekka had taken longer, because her world had somehow twisted through and into his in ways he wasn't entirely comfortable with. But she got it, why the youngest would rebel against the successes of the older siblings. Not something she'd experienced, but it made sense, how being held up against someone else's life could make you want to do something—anything other than what had been covered before.

Isaiah's story had been told slowly, with long pauses between, as if it pained Retro too much to disclose all at once. Two brothers following similar paths, finding relief and comfort in their clubs when their personal life went to the crapper. She thought Retro might even feel guilt over being married unhappily, when he knew Hoss would give anything to have his woman back breathing air. "Not to be," Retro had whispered into her ear. "And it kills, babe. It fuckin' kills."

"You good, baby?" That was his question as she approached his bike, hand out for her bag. She ignored that and stepped close, lifting her chin in a move she knew he wouldn't ignore, and he didn't, bringing his mouth to hers in a kiss so sweet it made her eyes watery, and—like he saw everything—he saw and recognized it for what it was. Grief for his brother, and love for him. "You're good," he answered his own question, hand in her hair tipping her head back further, giving him a chance to ravish her neck, hitting all the sensitive spots he'd learned. "So fuckin' good."

A moment later, her bag was strapped to the rack he'd installed on his bike for that purpose and he'd lifted her to the seat, letting her settle on the leaning bike as he secured her helmet. He turned back to the other men, already astraddle their own rides. "My house, not the clubhouse." That was evidently enough of an instruction to the men because with simultaneous nods, they started their bikes. He settled in front of her and waited a moment for her to grip his waist. The rumble of the bike no longer startled her, and she leaned forwards to rest against his back, ready to ride.

It took thirty minutes to get to the house they'd toured only a couple of days ago, and as she had every time she was on the bike with him, she enjoyed the ride. Retro kept touching her, draping his arm over her knee and leg. The possession in each caress made her smile. She reciprocated, having already learned he liked when she did, fingers smoothing his shirt across his belly, curling high under his arm so her hand could touch his throat in a glide. He initiated a new touch tonight, his hand capturing hers and bringing it high on his thigh in an echo of his hold on her leg earlier. She laughed aloud when she heard his groan as her fingers danced up and up, grazing across his prominent erection.

The next red light gave him a chance to lean back and turn his head, helmets clacking together as he told her in a voice rough with desire, "Fuckin' hell, woman. Killin' me slowly. I fuckin' like your hands on me." The light flashed green and they were off again, her fingers daring a firm stroke up the shaft outlined in his jeans. He'd captured her hand again then, bringing it down his thigh in a clear de-escalation of her fun.

Then the house appeared, lit up from within, windows on each floor shining in a welcome she hadn't expected. There were bikes parked in the street and along the edges of the driveway, and Retro carefully threaded between them, his brother and friends following behind him in single file.

Faces she knew appeared from the shadows around the pool, the rippling water seeming to glow with the lights built into the sides. Mudd waved from the patio and she lifted a hand in response as Retro made a circle in the drive, backing towards the garage. Kids shouted and played as they swam, and someone had set-up a bouncy house in the yard, the sound of the blower keeping it inflated loud when the bikes shut off.

"It's a party," she marveled as Retro's fingers worked under her chin in their post-ride ritual. He liked taking care of her, and this was one of the things he always did. He'd told her it settled his mind to know he helped keep her safe by putting on and taking off the helmet, and she didn't mind, and had told him so.

Bandana still in place across the bottom of his face, he told her, "Whole club's excited about this move. Draws a line under the differences between before, and now." He reached behind him and hung their helmets on the handlebars without turning around, his motions so practiced and smooth she knew he'd done it a million times in his life. "Between unhappy me, and me happy." His words reminded her of what Hoss had said and she glanced over to see him staring at them with a smile on his face. No sadness there, just pure pleasure for his brother, and she loved knowing Retro had that from him. "Between me without you, and me with you." Retro cupped her jaw, thumb brushing back and forth underneath her eye, softly caressing the apple of her cheek. "My empress. You good with this, baby?" She smiled, and he dipped his head, resting his forehead against hers. "You're good," he assured himself, and she nodded, careful not to break contact.

"I'm so good." The corners of his eyes crinkled and she knew he was smiling. Trina reached up and found the tie that held his hair back, easing the ponytail free so his locks hung around their faces. Then she tugged the bandana down, uncovering his smile. "You're good, too."

Eyes closing briefly, he told her, "I'm so fuckin' good, I can't explain. Deep and wide, that's what I'm feelin' for you. Ain't none of this for show, baby. It's just me." His eyes opened and stared at her, pupils dilating wide. "You ready?" She nodded again, never losing the touch of his skin against hers. "Here we go."

He stood upright and picked her up, swinging her around a moment before he settled her on her feet, body sliding down the front of his until she was on the ground. "All the women are inside, probably. I asked Mudd's woman to get the kitchen and shit stocked, threw some money at her and got out of the way, because that woman can fuckin' shop like nobody's business. She's gonna have waited on putting away some things, if I know her. Rhonda will wanna know what you want. So be prepared to take your place in this, baby. You're my empress, their queen, and the beehive needs to know you're the one to follow. They'll take their cues from her, and she's club to the core. I trust her as much as I do Mudd, and that's sayin' something."

He set his hands on her shoulders and bent down, bringing his face level with hers. "That's your place, baby. You're their queen to my king. President's ole lady has a part, and Rhonda can help you figure things out." She'd known the hierarchy within the club was role-based, so this wasn't a surprise, but the fact that any part of it would fall to her was. At the involuntary shake of her head, he made a dismissive noise in his throat. "Yeah, it is. I see you winding up to set it aside, but I don't want you to do that. Try it on, Trina. You don't like it after a good test run, we'll talk. But you try it on and see. I think you'll do well. I was born for this, and the mantle fits me like a glove. Knowing what I know now about what keeps a club healthy, wealthy, and wise, I believe that I've chosen well. My gut tells me you're gonna be what those women in there need. Wanda—" She must have let something slip through at that name, because his expression softened even as he bulled through. "—she wasn't cut out for it. She saw it as her due, not a privilege. And that right there should tell you what they've put up with from my ex. Wasn't ever an honor, not with her. You, my sweet, my baby, my love, you're day to her night, and I've never been prouder to say I'm someone's ole man than I am to tell it to my friends. And my family, and I'm not forgettin' I saw Hoss jawin' at you. You can bet we'll talk on that later, but he wouldn't have taken the chance it'd piss me off if he hadn't felt deep about whatever it was he said. Now, you go in there and you own it, because this is our house, and you and me, we're gonna be the king and queen this club deserves." He kissed her, the movement of his lips on hers fierce, demanding, and the look on his face when he pulled back, proud. "I fuckin' love you."

Chin high, she swallowed hard and nodded then turned to face the house. His swat on her ass scarcely registered as she walked away, stunned into silence by his declaration, voice pitched to carry and the way the men moved out of her way, she knew it had, and they'd heard. *He loves me.*

***

Retro

"Smooth," Hoss said from beside him and Retro reached out to smack his chest without turning from watching his woman walk away, ass swaying in that mesmerizing way she didn't even know she did. "She's something else. Where did you find her, Jerry?"

Retro smiled, only turning from his study of her when the door cut off his line of vision. "She's made for me, ain't she?" He pulled in a deep breath. "Luckiest man in the world." He looked around the backyard, grinning widely when he saw kids racing between the bouncy house and pool. "What do you think of the place?"

"Fuckin' big, but I get it. I started something with my house a bunch of years ago, and now a half a dozen Rebels have big compounds. Facilitates communing with our brothers, for sure." Hoss tipped his head towards the garage. "That's a nice touch. What are you planning on doing with all the space?"

"Nelda will be driving in a year, but that'll still leave me a bay for bikes. Talked to Mudd, we're going to spring the cash for tools and a lift, make it a place where men can bring their bikes and family, work together on a project bike, or sort out an issue before a ride." He heard a commotion in the pool and turned to see two men with women on their shoulders, having a chicken fight, the women shrieking with laughter. "Yeah, this was a good buy."

"Where are Nelda and the boys? I expected to see them here." Hoss made a face, mouth twisting to the side. "Heard through the grapevine Wanda's got a live-in at her apartment already. You okay, brother?"

"I do not give a fuck about her." He wove threads of steel into his words, hoping Hoss would read the silent request to leave her out of anything they had here today. "Or what she does, outside the places where it touches on my kids. She's out of my life, and if you saw that woman walking away from me just now, you'll know I'm the richer for it."

"Yeah." A fond smile curled Hoss' lips. "Envious, man. Glad as fuck you got that for yourself, though. The kids, you didn't ever answer me, but I'm guessin' from your response that where they aren't is with the witch."

"Hell, no. They've already picked where they're gonna live, and we got paperwork making its way through the courts now. Way Wanda's actin' she might as well sign 'em, because she ain't gonna sue for shit and win. Kids are in Louisiana, hanging out on the bayou with Twisted, Penny, and their crew." He paused, then sighed, hating the next topic with a passion, but it had to be said. "Not sure you heard the shit Bekka got herself into. Did Miriam talk to you yet?" He'd filled in their sister the last time she'd called, and as she often did, Miriam had declared herself, "Washing my hands of her for once and all." He didn't know if that included banning mention of their little sister in her presence this time, or not.

Hoss tipped his head back and gave the same heavy sigh Retro had used. "Fuck no. What now?" He thrust his hands through his hair impatiently. "What the fuck did she get into now?"

"I had her hooked up with a local S&M scene, but she took the show elsewhere, and then showed up at my goddamned clubhouse in front of guests all marked up. Penny, Twisted's old lady, got involved, and Bekka boo-hooed her way into an invite to their place. I tell you what, every time I talk to Twisted, it sounds like she's on his last nerve, and when I talk to Nelda, I get the same feeling, but then Penny's all chill and shit, and recently I find Bekka's talked her way into another week beyond what the kids are staying. She's babysitting or something. One of Twisted's men has family in from out of town, and I guess she's helping to keep their little girl occupied. Brother, I do not know what to do with her. We're going to have to come to an agreement at some point to let her twist in the wind of her own decisions, and Bekka's gonna have to grow up and be an adult."

"Yeah, let me know when that happens. I keep thinkin' she'll wise up and figure shit out. Hell, the way things stand now, my Sammy is more mature than she is. He's growin' up to be a special kid." Hoss reached out and rapped his knuckles against the wall. "Knock on wood he stays that way."

"With you as his daddy, it's a no-brainer. Spider Monkey still playin' that hockey?" Hoss grinned when Retro used his favorite nickname for his nephew. "You got good kids, brother. Real good. How's that little Faynez?"

"Too cute for her own wellbeing, and I'm gonna have to steel my heart against it. I've seen what your kids do to you, twisting you this way and that, and if I don't get in front of it somehow, she'll do the same with me." Hoss' hands moved in unconscious patterns and Retro smiled.

"You working again? Painting those mini-me's you got runnin' around the house?" As Isaiah Rogers, Hoss was a well-known artist, and the movements he was doing now mimicked actions needed to get paint on canvas, something Retro had watched him often do back in the day. He'd stand in awe at the ease with which his brother translated something mundane he'd seen into art that would take your breath away. "You are, I'm gonna want some of that beauty for my home, brother. Tell me you're working again."

The smile on Hoss' face faltered and Retro knew the word that caused it. "Again" underscored the fact there'd been a before, and now his brother was stuck here, in the after. *Nothing can change the past.* He reached out, gripping Hoss' shoulder tightly, pulling him close for a moment. Wordlessly, the two brothers mourned the losses of the one, and unspoken promises of support and love were transmitted through that embrace.

Finally, eventually, Hoss pulled away and cleared his throat. "I love ya, Jerry. You come up and visit and bring your family. I like what you're building, and I want Sammy and Faynez to see love like that woman has for you. She say it yet?"

He shook his head. "Not in so many words, but I see it every day in all the things she does." Chin to his throat, he said, "I don't mind waitin' to hear it. Those words were currency in Wanda's book, and she spent it as if she printed it. Throwaway, nothing I had to work for. Trina?" He lifted his head, staring towards the house, trying to catch a glimpse of her through the windows. "Ain't nothin' throwaway about anything she does."

"She's gonna be good for you." Hoss waved across the pool where Mason and Fury had found a circle of acquaintances. "I should go do the good officer thing and introduce the new international president around." He cut his eyes towards Retro, who stood there, stock still. "I'm sure the past-president knows everyone, but still."

"Are you fuckin' kidding me?" Without looking away from Hoss' face, Retro broke through his shock of the info Hoss had just dropped to whistle high-low, repeating the sound once. "We hung out at the clubhouse, we sat a meal, I introduced you to my woman, and you've been sitting on this fucking news for all that time? It's like you aren't even my brother, man. I'm disappointed." Footsteps grit against the cement behind him and he asked, "Mudd, you hear anything about a change in leadership in the RWMC?"

"No, boss. I haven't heard anything to indicate a passing of the mantle was imminent. We got faulty info on your own brother's club?" Retro nodded. "Well, that just sucks balls, man. You should work your sources harder, Prez. You been slackin' on the job, man."

"Apparently." Retro tried to hold back the laugh, and failed, glad when he heard Mudd's chuckle. "So, here's what you're going to do, oh brother of mine." Hoss tipped his head to the side, smirking at the men. "You're going to bring Mudd right up to speed with everything, while I go offer my congratulations to the new international president of a North American prominent dominant. A man I've known forever, and count as a friend, and who bought my dinner tonight." He sighed. "Fuck, you're an asshole."

"Love you, too, Jerry."

* * *

Trina

Walking into the kitchen had been like stepping into chaos owned by strange women, but not the bad kind. It wasn't the catty behind-closed-doors snippiness the dancers exhibited against each other in the dressing room, and wasn't even the petty jealousy she'd dealt with in breakrooms from other waitresses when she was having a good shift with decent tips. This was the chaos of family, and friends, and working together towards a single goal.

Now, late into the evening, food served, consumed, and clean-up all done, she was seated on the floor between Retro's feet, head leaned back, enjoying him idly playing with her hair. He'd picked an overstuffed chair off to the side, and with her back and feet aching from a long workday followed by hours of unexpected entertaining, she'd opted not to slouch on his lap. Her position still gave her access to him, his heat and touch, and Trina wouldn't have wished to be anywhere else if she'd had a genie's bottle to rub. Across the room, Rhonda caught her gaze with an exaggerated eye roll at something Mudd was saying and Trina giggled, lifting her water bottle to her mouth to stifle the sound.

A tug on her ponytail told her she hadn't succeeded, and she tipped her head back to look up at an upside-down Retro. He was smiling, eyes soft as they often were when he looked at her, and she loved that expression on his face. His declaration earlier had taken her off-guard, and she still hadn't fully processed the words. Sure, she knew he had feelings for her from everything he did, the care he took with her, the way he coddled her—but love? Part of her argued that was a whole different level. Most of her was of the opinion she'd already known it, and reciprocated, and that he knew it. It had felt good to hear it said straight out, no hesitation and filled with a confidence only Retro seemed to muster.

"What's so funny?" He bent over and kissed her upside down, heat from his mouth making her sigh. "Hmmm?"

"Rhonda's nice. I like her." He'd pulled back so she could see his face, and Trina liked the satisfaction in his expression as he smiled down at her. "I didn't know what you meant, earlier, but I think I see it now. You made it sound like...I don't know, but whatever I expected, it wasn't anything like that. It was just people. People who were already inclined to like me, because of things you'd told them about me. You make everything easier, Retro. You are too sweet to me."

"Just sweet enough," he argued with a tip of his head. "Life shouldn't be hard. It's work, sure, otherwise we wouldn't appreciate it in the end, but working doesn't mean hard, it just means effort. That's not to say there's never any politics involved, because there are. You'll meet women from other clubs and be expected to be our queen and above anything they might try to start. That's them being insecure, and you holding your ground. Not a bad thing, just a thing, you know?" She nodded, because it made sense. "And it wasn't me talking to the women you met tonight. What Rhonda learned of you, she picked up from her ole man, not me. Same for the other women. I told you my men would mark who you were to me the moment we walked out of that apartment building. I claimed you, right there, whether you knew it or not. You've been mine since. Hell—" He smirked at her, the expression so filled with sweet teasing she wanted to kiss it off his face. "You've been claimed since I bled for you in the hallway of that strip club. That was me making a physical statement of interest in you, and every man with me knew it as such. I know, because they've made no bones about telling me so."

"I don't understand. If you didn't tell them about me, how did the other women know so much?" She shook her head. "I only know the names of a handful of the guys." She lifted her head and turned sideways to face him, chin resting lightly on his knee. "I've been..." She trailed off, and then took a breath and finished, setting aside her fears for a moment in favor of honesty, knowing how much he valued it. "I've been so wrapped up in you when we're together, I don't pay attention to who's around, really." She rushed on, shaking her head slightly. "I'm going to be terrible at this."

"You're already a champ. You just don't realize it yet." His roughened fingertips stroked down her face, traced a zigzag line to her lips where he brushed a soft caress. "How you are with me, that's what's earning my men's loyalty to you. I hand-picked every one of them for my club. And they kinda like me." His lips quirked sideways. "There's gotta be a smidgen of mutual trust and faith for them to follow me like they do. That means they like you for me, because of how you are. Pillow talk gives their women access into the club a lot of people don't think about. So they're tellin' their ole ladies about how you are, and because it makes their men happy, those women are happy. They're gonna wanna keep you around. I told you they suffered under Wanda's reign, and tonight you showed them how different you are. Pitchin' in and helpin' like you did? That's earning your place. I'm proud of you, Trina. I've thrown a fuck of a lot at you, and you just keep on truckin' like it's no big deal. I know it is, though. I moved you, changed your life, barged into your work, told you you're gonna be a stepmom to three kids, promised you more if we get lucky that way, and still haven't fucked you." His eyes heated and she smiled. After what felt like a long pause, he bent close and, voice low and vibrating with intent, told her, "That changes tonight."

He lifted his head and whistled, two low and one high. Conversation around the room ceased and the men's heads all turned to look at him. Enunciating clearly, he said two words: "Good night." Smiles and chuckles all around as the men and women climbed to their feet. Murmurs of goodbyes between them, and Trina started to push up, but was held in place by Retro's heavy hand on her shoulder. She settled back into her position between his feet.

Then his men and their women paid tribute to their king. She watched in awe as the first man approached. It was Hoss, and his brother gripped Retro's offered hand and pulled him upright. Retro held up one finger and Hoss grinned, then Retro bent to her and, hand on either side of her waist, wordlessly picked her up and placed her beside him. Then he and Hoss embraced, deep voices reverberating as they muttered in each other's ear. Hoss stepped to her next and she was surprised when his arms went around her, holding tight. "You'll do," he said in a rough whisper. "See you again soon."

The process of first acknowledging Retro, then her, was repeated a dozen times as every person there said goodnight. As the sounds of motorcycle exhaust faded, and silence fell in the house, Retro pulled her in front of him, her back to his chest, and burrowed his face against her throat. Trina shivered and arched her neck for him, enjoying the way his mouth moved against her skin.

"You been upstairs yet, baby?" One of his hands had moved to a breast and he was caressing her gently. His other arm banded her belly, hand gripping her hip to pull her back against him, hips thrusting gently, a rhythmic promise of more.

"No, not yet. There was so much to do down here." Her whisper hitched in the middle when he ground hard against her ass.

"Let's go to bed." Teeth to her shoulder, he tightened his grip on her breast until she arched into his hold with a soft cry. "Fuck, yeah," he muttered and grasped her hands, lifting her arms up as he twisted them both around in something close to a graceful pirouette, ending with her breasts against his back. He crouched in front of her with a brusque, "Climb on."

Using his hands for leverage, she gave a little hop to land on his back and wrapped her legs around his hips, his hands bracing her securely. Up the stairs, two steps at a time, he turned towards the master suite they'd toured just a few days ago. "What about locking up?"

"Boys took care of that on their way out." This was said with confidence, but she hadn't heard any exchange that indicated it had been a request of his.

"When did you tell them to do that?" He shook his head and she released her grip on one of his shoulders to gather his hair into a hank, draping it over his shoulder so she could kiss along the side of his neck.

"Mmmm. Like that, Trina. That'll earn you anything you want, you take initiative like that." He ducked through the door and shifted under her, kicking it closed. "Don't have to tell them shit like that. It's just something I know they did. We're club," he said simply. "And always got each other's backs." He stopped at the foot of the bed and patted her ass. "Slide down, baby." She did, unwrapping her legs from his waist, finding the floor with her bare toes as he turned to face her. "Been torture of the best kind, waiting for this,"—he bent her backwards over his arm, holding her hips tight to his—"and now, I'm gonna have my fill. It's just you and me, Trina. You and me and all night, because we've both been so patient, holding off until it was right. This, right here, this is right. You've had a chance to get to know me, and I've done the same." He kissed her between each softly spoken phrase, lips plucking at hers in tiny caresses she wanted more of. "We put in the time, because this isn't for the now, it's for the ever, you know what I mean?" She nodded, trying to steady her breathing. "What we're building here, ain't gonna break. And now, gonna make love together, and that'll tie the knot on it all. You wanna be mine?"

"Yes," she whispered, staring into his eyes, returning the earnest intensity. "Please, yes."

Her plea earned her a crooked smile and he kissed her hard. Tongue sweeping in to slide against hers, he possessed her mouth, hard hands holding her tight to him. "Gonna try to go slow, baby. Try being the operative word here. You make me crazy." He kissed her again, deep and wet, until she was moaning deep in her throat, the vibrations rattling up into her mouth and he made a needy noise in response. "On the bed, sweetheart. Get on the bed and let me unwrap my present."

He made sure she was steady on her feet, hands on her shoulders anchoring her until the room stopped swaying around her. Turning to face the bed, she put a knee on the mattress, intending to crawl to the center, but froze when his hand gripped the inside of her thigh, fingers and thumb moving against her in knowing ways. Angling her head to look over her shoulder at him, she took in the look on his face as his gaze traveled from where he touched her up to her face. Smile gone, he looked so serious she wasn't sure what he was thinking for a moment, then he told her, giving her everything, like he had since they'd met.

"Gorgeous and giving, this body, that mind, that mouth is mine. It's mine, and you better not ever think of leaving me, baby, because I'll scour the earth to find you. You're mine, and I keep what's mine." Her heart leapt to her throat, beating as fast as a bird's wings. These words, this sentiment, echoed hers so closely it was startling. "I'll treat you like my empress, that I promise you. I'll make you happy, Katrina. Live to make you happy, but you're mine from here forwards. Tied to me tighter than a ring and vows could ever do." She quivered as he took a breath, blowing it out slowly, his fingers moving higher, pressing the seam of her jeans against her core. "I ain't perfect, not in any way, shape, or form, but I promise you this. Right here and now, I promise you. You'll want for nothing. You'll have everything you desire, somehow. I'll make you happy. I'll satisfy you in bed and out, and you'll fuckin' own me. You own me, and I'm yours just as much as you're mine. Now." She lost the heat from his hand. Then her ass cheek stung as a loud slap racketed through the room. "Get up there and lie back, baby. Let me love you."

She stared at him for a moment, trying to memorize the expression on his face, filled with such beauty, honesty, and depth of emotion. Eyes intense on her, he lifted his chin, simple hope bare on his face. That speech was Retro doing what he did best, making sure she knew he wouldn't let her fall, that he would catch her, always. This was the man she hoped would always be hers, laying claim in a way that couldn't be mistaken.

"You make me crazy, too." She shifted a hand, then a knee, gaze locked on his face as she moved up the mattress. "I'm yours." More shuffling of knees and hands gained another foot of distance between them. "And you're mine." She turned and rose on her knees, facing him. Hem of her shirt between her fingers, she lifted and watched the look on his face change from hope and love, to dark desire and hunger. "Mine."

Chapter Seven

Retro

He watched Trina scramble up the mattress, flipping to her back and pushing up on her elbows so she could look at him.

He'd never forget the look on her face when he spoke his vows to her. As he'd stated, this would lock her to him, and everything he'd said had weight and power in his mind. If she wanted it, he would move heaven and earth to make it happen. The trust and belief in her expression had nearly taken him to his knees, would have, if it hadn't been for his hold on her, the heat from her pussy baking through her jeans, a promise of its own.

Moving swiftly, he shrugged out of his vest, folded it and placed it on the dresser. Respect to the patches was respect to the club, and his vest never hit the floor, never hung from his apehangers, never draped over the back of a seat. Something their prospects were taught from day one, because cuts left unattended were fair game for other clubs, and the last thing a member wanted to do was have to admit they'd lost their colors because of stupidity. Losing them by force wasn't shameful and would bring the club's wrath to bear on their behalf. But losing them out of inattention only to be mocked and humiliated by another club? A beatout would be the least of that member's worries. So even in the privacy of his own home, Retro followed protocol and treated the fabric extension of the club with respect. He made a note to have a chat with Trina about his vest, because for a woman new to the life, it might be tempting to try it on for size, something he couldn't allow. Women weren't club; they were the surrounding strength that allowed the men to do what they needed to do, but patches were reserved for members. Retro made another mental note to get her a support shirt, and to petition for a Property Of vest. No way would he stomach seeing Wanda's damned First Lady vest on her, because she'd made such a mockery of the title. He'd burn that shit first, not wanting any hint of taint to transfer. No, Trina would get her own set, and he'd sort out what that meant later.

Club handled, it was just them in the room now, and he lifted the hem of his shirt up and over his head, gathering his hair out of the fabric with an economy of movement that would have told any observer how long he'd worn his hair so. When he'd moved off the family farm, he'd grown it out, first in a silent rebellion that seemed so juvenile in review, then kept it long because he liked it. Liked how he looked, how it felt, and how it set him apart from most of the population, a physical barrier of difference. Just as being in a club did, but in a more idealistic form, the standard one-percent designation making sense when he tore things down to their core.

Movement against his chest caught at his attention and he stared down, abruptly fixated on the ring dangling from the still-swinging chain. He'd worn it for decades, always keeping it close, thinking about Clara every time he looked at the metal. For an instant he was back in that hospital, leaving her room for the final time, the words of her father ringing in his ears.

Trina made a noise and he looked up at her, seeing her gaze locked on the ring. Kept close to his heart, the only thing it could be was a memento, and he knew she saw it as such by the pain on her face. *Fuck.* The last thing he wanted to do was bring Clara into their bed the first time they were together, but he'd never taken it off, always worn it. Staring at Trina, he reached down and gripped it in his hand, so tight the metal bit into his flesh. He was readying himself to bring it over his head, breath coming faster, gut rolling as in anticipation when she moved across the mattress. On her knees in front of him, she leaned close and covered his hand with hers, face lifting for a kiss.

"Don't," she whispered, and he shook his head. "No, don't. It matters to you, and I'm not unaware that you had a life before me. You are married, still. Have kids, and told me you loved one other woman. That ring—" Her fingers tightened around his. "—this ring matters, and I'm okay with that. You're a passionate man, and I've seen that over and over while I've been with you. You love deep, and your trust and loyalty are unshakable. This is for that woman you loved, isn't it?" He nodded, swallowing hard. "Then leave it on. Give me a fraction of that kind of love, and you won't have to wonder if it's worth it. I'll prove myself to you."

"It's not that. You never have to prove a goddamned thing to me, Trina. You're everything for me, all I need or want." He shook his head. "I hadn't thought about it until now. I wear this all the time, but maybe here…maybe I don't want to."

"You do, or you wouldn't have hesitated." She kissed him again. "Do what makes you feel right, Retro, but know that I'm okay either way. To me, it's a symbol of the kind of love you're capable of, and that's a treasure to be cherished." She shifted backwards, opening space between them and he swayed towards her, halving it again. "Your experiences have made you the man who stands in front of me right now, and that's the man I want." She touched his face, trailing paths of heat and electricity. "The man I want to love." She blinked slowly, then smiled. "The man I love."

Eyes closed, he reached for her, wrapping his arms around and pulling tightly as he lowered his mouth to hers, kissing her until he'd branded the feel of her into his brain, until he knew he'd feel her lips under his every time he thought of her. "You're mine, Trina." She gasped, and he took impatient advantage, thrusting inside, roughly fucking her mouth. "All of you, mine."

Fingers to his belt, he loosened it and his pants, then stepped on the hems, pulling them down before toeing off his boots. Socks and jeans abandoned in a pile, he wrapped an arm around her again and leaned her back, looming over her as he maneuvered her into the position he wanted: center of the bed, head on a pillow, waiting for him.

The next hour was spent discovering her, article after article of clothing discarded to the floor, bared skin covered in kisses and bites, marks left in his wake. Retro was hard only moments into it, his cock rewarded with occasional grazes of her skin, or her fluttering fingers until he grumbled softly and swatted her hand away, not wanting to blow too early.

He found the spot on her side where a firm touch made her gasp, and a graze earned a giggle. He marked her there with a fierce bite that had her groaning his name. Her breasts were an erogenous zone of their own, and each caress of his fingers made her arch against him. He fed her into his mouth, pulling her tit deep with a hard suckle while he flicked the tip of her nipple with his tongue. Legs falling wide, she dug her heels into the mattress, making wanton pleas mixed with his name on a hiss as he nipped and bit, plumping with his hands, bringing her titties together so he could go from one to the other, giving each sloppy, loud kisses.

He straddled her waist and used the slippery fluid from his dick to slick her tits and then fucked them slowly, bringing her hands up to hold herself for his pleasure. The look on her face was awed as she watched the crown of his cock slip in and out of view and he thrust farther, closer to her mouth, doing it again and again until she gave into temptation and darted her tongue out, lapping at him. "Fuck yes, baby." Her gaze lifted to meet his and on the next thrust, she opened her mouth and he slid between her lips into the hot cavern of her mouth where she sucked hard, making him shout out, the sounds an unintelligible mix of her name, guttural groans, and the word "Fuck," over and over.

He abandoned her tits then, leaning over and reaching to position her head, fucking down and into her mouth until the muscles of his back and ass shook with the strain of holding back. Not once did she try to pull away, the trust in her motions making it better for him as she let him set the pace, pulling back to give her a chance to suck air around the knob of his cock, spittle slicking her lips and chin, fingers stroking the shaft she couldn't take, other hand between his legs, rolling his balls and tugging on his sac. He was close, nearly lost to the electric jolts flooding up his muscles when he pulled away. Her disappointed keen was music to his ears because it meant she'd been as into it as he was, not something she'd been suffering through for his pleasure.

Stretching out over her, he held her thighs together with his legs, cock sliding between into the tight embrace of skin and muscle. Then he took her mouth a different way, her puffy, swollen lips hot against his mouth. Her avid suck of his tongue made his dick jerk and twitch because she was so goddamned perfect, and he told her so, the litany of praise never faltering, telling her about how he saw her. "So fuckin' beautiful, Trina. You're everything I could want. My empress. There'll never be another for me. You're it, and you're perfect, and I want to be inside you so goddamned bad. Want to fuck you, oh hell yeah, I do. But this is what I needed, time to play, time to learn you, my queen. I needed to see your face like this, flushed and sweaty and so goddamned gorgeous because you love me. You know me, inside and out, and you aren't afraid of a bit of it, aren't afraid of me or what I am, and that's so big, so fuckin' big. My lover."

He kissed her again, hard and deep, working for every sound she gave him, eating her moans down, enjoying her writhing body underneath him, heat from her pussy scorching his cock as he fucked her thighs. He put his mouth to her ear and whispered a question he should have already asked, but hadn't, and being the man he was, Retro couldn't do what he wanted without her express consent. "Baby, gloved or ungloved?" She shook her head, hips rolling up against his next thrust and he was the one groaning now. "Lover, you gotta tell me. This isn't my decision, never just me, because you're too precious to me to risk. I need your words. How do you want me inside you? Gloved, or ungloved?"

"I want you," she whispered, turning to face him. "I want everything we've talked about, and nothing is too soon. I want you, Retro. Don't stop, don't wait. Come inside. Please, come inside."

That was all the permission he could ever ask for, and he vowed right then to always ask, to never take her for granted, because complacency would kill a relationship, and he never wanted to give up one iota of the excitement of bedding her, loving her, being with her in the small hours of the morning.

He changed position and with a swivel of his hips, fell between her legs, Trina lifting them high to wrap her heels around his ass, opening fully to him. Propped up on one arm, he reached down to find her hand making the same trip. Twining his fingers through hers, he guided her hand to his cock, letting her wrap them around his shaft. "Put me in you, baby. Bring me home."

Heat engulfed the head of his dick, an inferno that promised even more once he was inside. She stroked him. Then her fingers fell away. He could feel the press and wriggle of her hand between them and he reared up on both arms to look down, seeing her work her clit side to side, unable to wait for him to start. "I got you, baby," he promised and bent his neck, lips to a nipple with a hard suck as he thrust inside on a slow, deliberate glide, pacing himself as he pushed into her tight heat, breath caught in his chest until he was seated deep. Ripples of sensation worked up and down his shaft, muscles of her pussy walls clenching and releasing around him as she adjusted to his girth.

"God, Retro," she cried, her hand on his neck, fingers of her other tangled in his hair as she cradled his head to her chest. Her hand moved and he switched sides, focusing on the other titty as she offered it up to his mouth, letting him feast his fill of her. Then he shifted again and angled his knees wider, preparing before he started to move in long, deep strokes, punching hard into her the last couple of inches on every thrust. He was captivated watching her breasts lift and sway with every movement. She moaned his name again, her mouth opened and closed, and her pupils dilated wide, darkness taking over her eyes as she eagerly participated in everything he was giving her. "That's so..." Her voice trailed off and he pounded harder for a few strokes, fucking so deep and fast she slid on the sheets and he had to scramble after her. "So good."

Without prompting, she put her hands over her head, palms flat on the headboard and he watched the muscles in her arms bunch and strain with the effort it took to stay in place. "Gonna give it to you hard, baby. Wanna watch you take me like that." She nodded, strands of hair draped over her sweat-sheened face. "Love this look on you. Wild. Untamed. This is a side of my Trina I haven't gotten to see before." He dipped down for a kiss, biting her bottom lip until she whimpered in his mouth. "I fuckin' like it, baby. Fuckin' like it a lot. Love it, so much."

He placed a palm beside hers on the headboard, holding himself up as he wrapped his other hand around her waist, rocking back on his knees to change the angle so he could pull her back onto him. Flesh slapping together, the lights in the room seemed to dim, illumination focused on her face, cheeks flushed red, mouth open as she whispered his name repeatedly, over and over, "Retro, Retro, please. Love you, Retro. Please."

"Gonna feel me tomorrow, baby." He changed the angle again, slipping his hand around her hip until he mashed his thumb against the root of her clit, staying away from the unhooded bundle of nerves to stroke and play with the rigid part up over her pubis. He knew when he hit the spot just right, because she clenched up all over, tightening inside until she gripped him hard, pulling him deep while he stroked in and out. The next adjustment had him hitting a spot inside that drove her crazy, nails on her hands digging deep into the padded headboard while her hips lifted like pistons, pounding up and against him as she came hard, thrashing and undulating on the mattress, a sudden flood of wet making it a sloppy fuck and he loved that, the moment she fell apart gifting him with an image of her he didn't want to lose, ever.

Overtaken with pleasure, her face twisted, tendons standing out in her neck as she called out a babble of words too fast to pick apart. The sight of her like that broke something in him and he crashed down on her, hips hammering at hers as he fucked her hard, chasing his orgasm like it was a living thing, hunted and captured, and then he was rising high, his soul soaring, balls drawn tight to his body as he came, shooting deep inside her, painting her inner walls with his pleasure.

"Fuck, Trina. So goddamned good. So good." Her legs around his hips tightened while her hand in his hair flexed, bringing his face to her neck and he latched on, sucking hard, knowing he was marking her and loving how she encouraged it, tiny mewls of desire falling from her lips. "My Trina. My baby. Mine. Fuck, you're perfect for me, baby. Mine."

***

Trina

Retro stayed buried deep, hips moving lazily, tiny thrusts in then out that sparked nerves inside her with pleasure. He was the right kind of heavy, the right kind of hot and sweaty, and his ejaculate running down her ass held the right kind of promise. The fact he'd paused nearly in mid-act to gain her approval for what he wanted to do had sealed the deal for her, because it reinforced what she already felt deeply in so many ways. He wasn't going to pressure her into anything, wouldn't push, would wait until she was ready to give, and she'd never dared to dream of finding someone like him. The skin of her neck tingled and pulsed and from the way his gaze kept dropping to that spot, she knew he'd left a love bite in plain view. Glancing down, she saw more dotting her breasts, and Trina smiled.

"What's that grin for?" One corner of his mouth lifted and he dipped his head to brush his lips across hers. "How you feelin', baby?"

"Good," she promised him, losing herself in his kiss for another moment. "So good."

"You're fuckin' stupendous in bed." He nipped at her bottom lip, the sting making her gasp. "Stunning." Another kiss, another bite. "Perfect."

"You're sweet." She wanted to dodge this topic if she could, because talking about sex so openly felt weird and from the heat in her cheeks, she knew she was already blushing. "We...uh...were loud. I'm glad we're alone."

He lifted from her and she felt exposed, naked under his gaze that raked her from where they were joined up to her face. Retro's expression went carefully blank, and that was as telling as a frown on any other man's face. "Nothing we did was wrong or bad, baby. I'm gonna wanna fuck you a lot, and we won't always be the only ones in the house." He stared down at her and she struggled to hold his gaze. "Outside of closing the door, I'm not going to worry about who knows we're havin' a good time in here. Kids, friends, family—when we wanna play around, I'm gonna play around. If you're not down for that, let's get that into the open now, so I don't fuck up until we figure out what's comfortable for you."

"I wouldn't say it'd be messing up, exactly." She shrugged and wrinkled her nose. "It would just be weird if your kids knew we were having sex." She chewed on her lip a moment, then amended her statement, "Or your men."

"You think they got any other message when I kicked them out of the house tonight?" She winced and slowly shook her head, because the expressions on every face had been knowing. "Then does it matter if they're here or not? I'm not sayin' I'll bend you over a table at the clubhouse and we'll fuck in front of them..." He trailed off and now he was wearing a frown. She stifled herself, biting back the image that had flashed through her head because the idea of having sex where someone could see them was more than intriguing, which was weirdly at odds with her reticence at having someone able to hear them behind closed doors. "Trina." His voice was soft and careful, speaking her name just as his cock flexed, reminding her they were still connected intimately, and she squeezed down around him. "Rhonda likes to give a little show once in a while, so you may occasionally be treated to the sight of her going down on her ole man in the clubhouse." She tensed, trying to keep her breathing steady, because the idea of that was interesting, too. "One of the reasons I couldn't have my kids living there. We have party-dolls who come on weekends, and not everything happens in private. Most ole ladies don't come on those nights, but Rhonda does. Says it's fun to watch. She's a bit of an exhibitionist." Trina blinked up at him, the idea of being so open about something like that shocked her to her core. He ground against her and she realized his cock was growing hard again, swelling inside her, filling her. She tightened around him, bearing down until he hissed. "You worked in a strip club, what did you think about the women there?" Blinking at his subject change, she opened and closed her mouth, trying to find the right words. "Don't think about it, just spit it out, Trina."

"They were beautiful. Proud of their bodies. I liked watching the men watch them, the way they'd get so engrossed they didn't notice anything else. A bomb could have gone off and they'd have never known, because they were caught up in watching." She raked her bottom lip between her teeth. "I didn't mind working there. They weren't the nicest people back in the dressing room, but it was a competition for them. Work the dance, work the pole, work the crowd. Get the biggest tips and draw, and they'd get a better timeslot to dance." She paused, wondering if she should share what she'd just remembered.

"Spit it out, baby. Don't think." He was demanding, and he underscored the challenge by thrusting against her, sliding deep until the wiry hair around his member was grinding against her clit.

She gasped and said, "I saw them sometimes giving private dances. The door of one room didn't close right and would open a crack if you weren't paying attention when you shut it. One girl—" She trembled at the memory. "She was on her knees and he was doing to her what you did earlier, with her mouth and his...you know."

"He fucked her face." She nodded, blinking as she glanced to the side. "Eyes on me, Trina. I'm intrigued by this story. Tell me more."

She looked up at him. "She made these noises, and he called her a 'good girl,' told her how good her mouth was, praised her, and she stared up at him." She smiled and decided to tell him the rest, the part that had been her secret for so long. "It was hot."

"You saw other private dances, too? Tell me about one of those." He shifted, gliding out and back in, working his cock into her slowly. "Tell me while I fuck you, baby. Tell me what you saw, what turned you on. Because you *were* turned on, what you saw made you horny. I see it, I see you. Did you want that, want a moment where someone saw, where someone watched you getting off? Do you want that, baby?"

"Maybe?" She shrugged one shoulder, lifting her leg when he tugged at the back of her knee while she focused on how good he felt inside her, over her, his hands on her, eyes staring at her with reverence and interest, and heat. What she was telling him wasn't an idle curiosity; it had stirred something deep-seated, and she wanted to give that to him, tell him everything. In a rush, she said, "I saw another girl bent over, hands on the bottom of a chair. The man's back was to me, and I couldn't see much, but his pants were down. She was the one talking, and the sound of them making love was loud."

"You saw his ass? Muscles moving and clenching?" He drove deep, pulsing in shallow thrusts so he only withdrew by a fraction of his length before plunging back inside. "Heard how wet she was, sloppy for the takin', and them fucking like that I don't doubt it was probably loud. You liked watching, baby? Did it make you wet? Get you primed? Did you touch yourself? Play with that pretty, pretty pussy until you came like a faucet? Tell me you did, because the idea of that is enough to break me right now. Fuck, Trina, that's so goddamned hot."

"I did," she whispered, closing her eyes to blank him out, not wanting to see his face at her confession. "I went to the break room right after."

"Fuuuucck." He groaned the word out slowly while he sped up, his balls slapping against her ass. "Eyes on me. Fucking hot, baby. So hot. You went to a place where you could be caught playin' with yourself. Did that make it better? Make you come harder?" He grunted and his knees spread her legs wider, hips twisting and rolling, his shaft filling her just right. "Fuck, baby, fuck. Fuck me back, Trina. Fuck me back."

Her hips rose in response to his plea and she gasped at the changed angle, finding and matching his fast rhythm, holding nothing back. Gasping at what he was doing to her body, what they were doing together, she was honest. "Yeah, just knowing someone might come in. I don't know why that made it better, but it did. It did." She shook her head and lifted her chin, breathing hard, fingers of one hand threaded through his hair to pull him close. "Please, Retro, please."

He dropped down and pressed his mouth to hers, tongue spearing inside in a cadence that matched his thrusts, matched the pace of their bodies meeting, her rising as he fell, catching him in the cradle of her legs every time. She was panting when he broke free, lips to her ear. "Gonna get you an audience, baby. Just talkin' about havin' someone watch makes you hotter than a fuckin' furnace, and I wanna see how you get off on the real thing. Way you're revved up right now, you'll be more than I can handle. I just know it. You got any other fantasies? Because if they get you goin', I'll do my best to make 'em happen. Tell me, baby, tell me."

"Uh..." She stumbled over her words, focusing on the powerful feeling of him pushing deep, then the loss of withdrawal. This was different from before, more frantic, but still a discovery because he was definitely into the idea of her wanting to be watched. Something she'd only admitted to herself, not expecting it to become reality, but found a deep well of excitement with the tease of possibility. "What if they didn't just watch?" Soft and slow, she tripped and paused between every word, and the groan he gave her at the end of her question was answer enough.

"No one fucks you but me," he told her immediately. "This pussy is mine. But you want someone to play, someone to eat you out while you suck on me?" She pulled in a breath because she hadn't imagined that, but now that he'd said it, she could see it clearly. "We can add someone to this in a limited fashion, but you're mine, make no fuckin' mistake." He thrust deep on the word "mine" and stayed planted, his cock jerking inside her as he groaned through his climax.

"Yours," she assured him, smoothing her palms up his arms to cup his shoulders. "Yours, only yours."

"Fuck, baby. Made me crazy with all that sexy talk." He shook his head, sweat-dampened hair hanging around his face. "I'm beat now, though. So goddamned good." He smiled as he swooped down for a kiss. "But I'll take care of you before I crash." She tipped her head to the side, staring at him, not sure what he meant. "I'm not afraid of my own spunk, Trina. Gonna eat you now."

She groaned when he slipped out of her, then gasped as he made good on his statement, mouth latching onto her with a loud smacking kiss. He paired his two middle fingers together and thrust inside, crooking and curving them in a way that set her belly buzzing. Then he locked his lips around her clit and sucked, finger-fucking her slow and deep. Her toes curled and she gasped, hips rising and falling to meet the movement of his hand. His other slipped under her ass and lifted so she arched her back, bringing her sex to his mouth in a way that let him crowd his tongue inside along with his fingers. "Retro, I'm gonna…"

"Mmmm." He hummed against her, the vibration starting the rumble and tumble of her fall down the slope. She turned her head to the side and found the mirror over the dresser was angled just right to see them in the bed. His muscular back shifted and moved between her legs, his arm pistoning back and forth as his head bobbed slightly. She cupped her breasts, remembering how he'd framed his cock with them earlier, wishing she'd found the mirror then so she'd have that memory, too. Then she imagined watching someone else like this, falling apart under their man. Rhonda's face imposed over hers in the mirror and that was it, all the impetus she needed to soar, Retro's name on her lips. "God, Retro. Please."

He rode her hard during the peak, thumb pressing and flicking her clit, fingers diving deep in a scissoring movement she felt all along her sensitive insides. Finally slowing, he gave her clit a soft kiss then lifted up on his knees, sitting back on his heels as he used a corner of the sheet to wipe his face. "Fuckin' love you, Trina." His voice was gruff with emotion and she held out her arms, gladly taking his weight and returning his sweet kiss.

"I'm yours," she reminded him, and he laid his mouth on her neck over the mark he'd made earlier. "Only yours."

"Mine," he agreed, and shifted so he lay beside her.

"I'm gonna get cleaned up." He nodded, fingers drifting down her back as she sat up on the side of the bed. "You need anything while I'm up?"

"I'd take a washrag." She looked over her shoulder at him, meeting his gaze. "I'm serious, Trina. You want that, I'll get it for you in a way that's safe and makes you feel good. You want it?"

She nodded slowly, not missing how the corner of his mouth turned up. "Yeah," she told him. "I want it."

"You got it."

Chapter Eight

Retro

"Shit you not, man. My ole lady's gonna kill me one of these days." Mudd's preen was over the top, as he no doubt intended, telling about his and Rhonda's latest escapades at the local swingers club they frequented. "She's fuckin' glorious when she's into a scene."

Retro considered the opening, glancing around at the crowd and decided now would be a good time to broach the subject. They'd be off to Louisiana tomorrow morning, and then would spend a couple of nights with Twisted and Penny, close quarters all the way. Twisted had offered the IMC clubhouse to put up his men, and he'd accepted gladly. It was past time to bring his kids home, his most recent conversation with Nelda filled with snippets of talk about an IMC prospect, which meant she was attaching to someone. *At least it's not one of my boys anymore.* He grinned.

"Trina's got a li'l kink in her." He kept his voice quiet, knowing Mudd would note the delivery and respond with the same. "We had an interesting conversation last night."

"Oh, really? Do tell." Mudd tapped the table and twisted to catch the eye of Buzzkill, assigned to the bar tonight. They were in that middle period of the early evening where a few men were starting to drink seriously, a few men had stopped in after work to talk to their brothers, and a few were gearing up to go out. All the traffic in and out had kept the prospect hopping and Retro was glad to see the man had adopted the pace Einstein always maintained, a quick trot instead of a saunter. Mudd lifted two fingers and Buzzkill nodded, reaching down into the cooler to collect two bottles to bring to their table. After he'd retreated to the bar, Mudd turned back to Retro and picked up the conversation. "What'd y'all talk about that's got you grinnin' like a fool?"

Mudd knew Retro liked to watch, and also knew that all attempts to convince Wanda to participate had fallen flat. Retro had stayed faithful to Wanda through it all, but that didn't mean he hadn't looked his fill when he had the opportunity. "She got to see some live show action at the strip club, liked what she saw. It's got her wondering what it might be like to be the center of attention." Mudd's forehead wrinkled, eyebrows lifted to his hairline and Retro chuckled and nodded. "Fuck yeah, it's like my perfect woman just got a little more perfect for me. She was downright interested. Revved her right up."

"And you'd be okay with that?" Mudd stared at him with a piercing gaze. "Someone watching you fuck your ole lady? I mean, it turns me on to know someone's there, looking on, seeing how jazzed she gets ridin' my cock, but it's not for everyone, brother."

"The idea is not a turnoff, but would have to complete a proofing run to know for sure." He lifted his beer and pulled hard, revisiting the feeling he'd had during the discussion. "Definitely not a turnoff, but I'd want to control the scene."

"Wouldn't expect any different, comin' from you." Mudd laughed softly. "Stiffy city here, just from the thought." He adjusted his cock behind the fabric of his jeans. "She lookin' to jump in the deep end right away, or gonna just dip her toes in?"

"I'll figure out a way to start her slow and safe, make sure it's a desire not just a fantasy." He shrugged. "Either way, hot as she was? I'm a winner."

"Skirts," Mudd stated firmly, nodding with certainty. "Easiest way to mask public sex and give a woman a sense of privacy. Mid-length. Unless you wanna be sure to show off the goods. You say the word, man, and me and Rhonda will be a willing audience, no matter the setting. You wanna start off private with just us? My ole lady won't say shit that would embarrass your woman. She mentors folks at the club. Has just the right touch for newbies."

"Might need Trina to watch, first." Retro grinned as Mudd quirked his eyebrows in a blatant leer. "And I know you'd be down for that, too."

"Oh, yeah. My woman does love to put on a show." Mudd took a drink and smacked his lips. "Skirts." He repeated himself with a grin. "God's gift to exhibitionists."

Retro had enough inspiration and the start of an idea for tonight. There would be the normal crowd here, and all he had to do was swing by the house before picking Trina up to set the stage. If she felt too nervous, they could retreat to his suite here, or go home. Either way, he'd make certain she wasn't overwhelmed by anything. *Fuck.* If he didn't stop thinking about it, he'd be popping wood like Mudd had. "Okay. Back to business. I heard through the grapevine"—their phrase for any well-sourced gossip or intel—"that Po'Boy's gonna drop his patches while we're over visiting."

"Why would he do that with us there? That doesn't make any sense, boss." Mudd frowned, but accepted the change of topic without question.

"Who better to chronicle an exchange of power in the main dominant club in our region? Twisted knows if we see it, we say it, and we don't fuck with the story. It actually makes a lot of sense." He shrugged and drained the beer, setting the empty to the side. "We were the ones who refused to circulate that damn picture from the sham cutting last year, so if people hear it from us and see it's amicable, then that'll cement it in everyone's mind."

"Fuck, man. I'd forgotten about that."

Last year Po'Boy had his colors stripped from him in an effort to trap an enemy into exposing themselves. It hadn't worked the way it was planned, mostly because business from his pre-club life had come home to roost before Twisted and Po'Boy could put things fully into play. If Twisted had asked Retro, he would have told him it was a fucked-up, rushed plan that was doomed to failure. *Nobody asked my opinion.* He smirked. *Maybe this is him showing me he can be taught.*

"Yeah. I can't help but think that plays into things. I get why Po'Boy's patching over, but still, it's something else to see, you know?" Retro shook his head. "End of an era."

"Changing of the guard, for sure." Mudd glanced around the room. "You tagged ten plus us to go, right?" Retro nodded. "Einstein in that group?" Retro nodded again. "Good, I like him. I think it'll be good for him to see us out of our territory again, goin' a different direction and yet still well respected. He's solid, brother. Rock solid."

"Yeah. Did you hear the shit that happened with his old club?" Mudd shook his head. "Lemme get him over here, tell you himself. It's fucked up." He whistled softly, a cadence all their prospects learned, and as expected, Einstein was so fresh off his probie period he looked up same as Buzzkill. Retro called him over with a tip of his head.

"Yeah, boss?" He might not have come at a trot, but he hadn't wasted any time making his way across the room, and Retro appreciated it. *Another sign of respect.*

"Cop a squat. You need to spin a tale for Mudd, here. The note you got from your old friends." Einstein had come to Retro right away, because while it was old club business, he knew the fact he no longer wore their colors made it new club business, too, given who'd reached out.

"Eh, fuck." Instead of seating himself in a nearby chair, Einstein hunkered down, knee to the floor and looked up at Mudd. "President of the Monster Devils sent me a message." Monster Devils was his old club, an old-school organization that had changed leadership so often in recent years they'd lost all history and stopped adhering to protocol. Part of that was why Einstein had moved away from them, coming to Alabama to bring his woman back to her family, and to gain a position in a good, solid club like the Bama Bastards. "Said the business that had me itchin' to leave had gotten worse. No more selective shot calling, just out and out war. 'Shoot on sight' was the phrase he used." He shook his head. "That's fucked up, man. Officers, leaders, they expect to be put on notice if someone's gunnin' for them. Foot soldiers know their role, and in a battle they might catch one. But to be walkin' down the street and get popped? That was my worst nightmare, and it's like I knew it was comin'. They're bleeding members, and I think part of the man's ask was to see if there'd be a place for him here."

"The fuck you say?" Mudd barked a laugh. "Yeah, prolly not happenin'."

"As I expected, but it's not my place to tell him such. I'm nothin' but a soldier here, and I know my role." He shrugged and his gaze came to Retro. "That's why I informed my president of the communication right away. Your call, your convo, and I'm outies. I like my place here, brothers. I find myself unwilling to risk it for a man in a club that had no loyalty to their members, and you know all about it because you heard it from my lips. This would be a hundred percent our call."

"Still, I'd like to know. Your recommendation would be...?" Mudd left it hanging and Retro studied Einstein's face, seeing a flash of anger there followed by resignation. Whatever he was about to say wasn't what he wanted, but because he was loyal to the Bastards, he'd voice it anyway.

"Hear him out. The why of the war might sway you, because it's something he's been forced into. He can be a dick, but isn't too bad a guy if you know what I mean, mostly badly influenced." Einstein shifted, changing position as he sat back on his heel, physically divorcing himself from that statement. *Interesting.* "His ole lady's a piece of work, and thinks she has a bigger voice than she should have. Problem is, he doesn't nay-say her much." His mouth twisted, a fleeting expression of disgust there and gone in an instant. *But it was there.* "She's a fuckin' piece of work. Slid into her position on her back, with no respect to anyone in her way."

"Well, that's a recipe for a mess." Mudd's voice was quiet and Retro glanced at him to see he was glaring across the room towards Buzzkill, who was chatting up a party-doll. "Women do change the fabric of a club, for better or worse." Retro frowned. Her back was to him, but she looked oddly familiar. "Boss man, you stay right here. Lemme deal with this shit."

Einstein spun to look and stood, his body blocking Retro's view as Mudd took to his feet, walking quickly away. "What the fuck is going on?" Retro asked even as he kept his seat, because Mudd was his trusted second, his best friend, and when he said to let him handle something, Retro tended to do just that.

"I don't know." Einstein shifted and Retro caught a glimpse of Mudd, hand on the arm of the woman, swiftly escorting her towards the door. "It's no one I recognize."

Retro stood and looked over his shoulder. "Fucking hell." The woman was Wanda's sister. *What the fuck is she doing here?* Tipping his chin up, he stared at the ceiling for a minute. There were few reasons for her to be in the clubhouse, and none of them were good. If she was here, it would be at her father's request. Retro hadn't spoken to the man for nearly a decade, and wasn't about to break that streak, which was probably why the man had sent his youngest into the fray instead of reaching out himself. He looked back just in time to see Mudd reenter the room, studying something in his hand. Probably a note from the woman, or maybe even from the old man himself.

Closer, Mudd's gaze lifted and locked with Retro's. He tipped his head towards the main office and without asking anything, Retro preceded him, reaching back to slide the door after Mudd stepped through. Hand out, he accepted the paper, not looking down. "What's he want?"

In the dark days after Clara, Retro had been freefalling, the club a group of five men, four of whom shared interests and were building loyalty between them. They'd needed something to believe in, needed something to set them apart from any dozen riding clubs in the territory. One of their members got sideways with a Florida dominant club, and Retro had stood at the front of their little cluster facing down the barrel of a gun one night, threats and accusations thrown around like candy at a parade. He'd stood his ground, talked down the dom's shooter, and then proceeded to cull his own group by one.

Cops got word of what had gone down somehow. Retro had always suspected one of the rival clubs had dropped that dime, and his man's bloody cut surfaced in the hands of a widow no one had known existed. It hadn't looked good for him, and Retro, still Jerry at the time, had stood on the steps of the county courthouse with an overpriced lawyer, listening to realistic prospects for the outcome of his case, which didn't have any echo of "dismissed" in them. He'd been looking at a solid nickel, just on circumstantial, the local DA having every expectation of a conviction even without a body to show off to jurors.

Wanda's father had chosen that moment to approach, dismissed the legal eagle with a wave of his hand, and introduced himself, making his affiliations clear. Then he'd laid out his proposition, and Jerry had known instantly he wasn't in any place to turn it down. Marry the man's daughter, keep the club out of east Birmingham, and feed him information about any dealers or distributors who came into a broadly defined swath of territory. Even then, small as they were, the Bama Bastards had been known for the quality of their intel, and the old man had banked on those skills only becoming more valuable. Wanda had been nothing but trouble for the man, and after he'd caught her in bed with his lieutenant, he'd carved her fate in stone.

One handshake later, the charges were dropped, every file closed and permanently redacted. Wanda had wanted a big wedding, but she'd gotten a quick civic ceremony instead. Part of the deal was giving the old man grandchildren, so Retro had set out to do that straight away. Wanda hadn't disliked him yet, and things were at least amiable.

Nelda and Jimmy made the old man malleable for Wanda, which meant she had a steady supply of what made her happiest: money. Retro didn't give a shit, because at least she wasn't spending his, and her old man had plenty, both from inheritance and his many, varied businesses.

Then Saya was born, and within a short time, it was clear he was different. He babbled a bit, but it got less and less, falling silent with no physical reason found. Retro didn't give a shit; he loved his youngest son just like he loved his other kids, without reservation.

He knew Wanda didn't feel the same, and other than how that might touch his boy, he didn't give a shit how she felt about his beautiful boy. But all it had taken was overhearing Wanda talking to her old man one time for Retro to ban the man from seeing any of his kids. Saya had been about three at the time, a cute, bright little boy, who simply didn't speak. To Retro it was more that his boy saw the world differently, but to his father-in-law, he'd been a flawed model needing a reset. What he'd suggested showed how ruthless he really was, and Retro didn't want to risk having any of his kids around the man. The fact Wanda hadn't argued with him was less about her being cowed, as she'd later claimed, and more about how she'd portrayed caring for Saya as a burden.

So Retro had bartered his future for a wife, gaining both the best things in his life, and the worst experiences he could imagine.

"What's he want?" Retro crumpled the paper and shoved it deep into his pocket. "She wasn't here on her own doing, am I right?"

"Yeah, the old man wants to talk to you. Seems Wanda's been crying in his ear, and he's tired of it already. Zofia said she's broke and angry." Mudd smirked. "And heard you bought a house and moved a newer version in already. That seemed to be the theme, the fact Trina's younger came up like three times in the short walk back to her cage. I suspect Wanda's playing the wounded woman card, and her daddy's buyin' it."

"*Outstanding.*" His tone meant it was anything but.

"Yeap. What will you do about this?" Mudd's stance was easy, relaxed, but conveyed a sense of being ready for anything.

Retro was silent for a moment as he studied the face of his best friend, knowing he'd do anything asked of him. He huffed a sigh and looked towards the window, seeing the kid's playground through the glass. He smiled as a thought hit him.

Mudd chuckled darkly, "Oh, hell. What's that look for, boss?"

He smirked. "Let's just say I have an idea of how to drive home to daddy that his little girl's not what she seems. We got a name for her boy toy? Nelda said he was only a few years older than her, so if she wants to wander into ageist territory, I can play that game, too."

"Yeah. Of course I do. Some shit touches you, I'm gonna do what I can to sort out info on it. I got a name and contact info. He's a play for pay boy on the side, too."

"Oh, ho. I did not know that." Retro laughed and shook his head. "Even better, because our money's greener than Wanda's IOUs right now. Her daddy will be having a late dinner tonight, like he does every Wednesday. His closest associates over to lick his boots." Walking to the desk, he pulled out a piece of paper. "Here's what we're gonna do. And I guarantee you it'll shut her up for good. Lawyer said he's got the paperwork ready to sign, so let's send it with the boy toy. Pay him to courier as well as fuck up her night."

"You got it, boss." Mudd's grin was evil and Retro returned it.

"Then, you get on the horn with Rhonda. I'd like to see what I can stir up with my baby, and your pretty woman's gonna play a part. You down for some public display tonight?" Mudd's grin ratcheted up a notch, turning sly and Retro laughed, pleased with the response. "Oh, yeah. It's goin' down."

***

Climbing from the bike in front of the clubhouse, he held her hand while Trina stepped off the pegs, and then he retrieved a small duffel from the sidebag. Inside, he led her to his normal seat near the wall and kissed her deeply before he pulled away and placed the bag in her hands. "There are two skirts in here. I'd like you to go up to my room and change out of your jeans. Pick one of these to wear. And, baby?"

He didn't have to wait long, her breathy whisper telling him she was already turned on by his demanding words. "Yes, Retro?"

"Forget the panties tonight. I want easy access." He'd cupped her throat with his hand, thumb on her pulse to feel it pounding faster and faster, and he knew the moment she swallowed hard in reaction to his words. "I put some sandals in there, too. Tried to think of everything. Now go." He swatted her ass softly, hearing a quick inrush of breath as she reacted. "And come back to me." Without waiting on her to move, he sat, which put his face level with her crotch. Smiling, he curled his tongue out, lapping at the air, then glanced up to see a stunned expression on her face. "Go," he said, winking at her, "come back, and we'll have some fun."

He and Mudd hadn't planned the next few moments, but he couldn't have orchestrated anything any better. As Trina turned, she stumbled and came to a halt, staring across the room to where Mudd had Rhonda backed against the wall. His hand was buried under Rhonda's skirt, and he'd pulled one of her tits out and framed it with her bra and shirt, mouth sucking hard while Rhonda leaned her head back, eyes closed, lost in the moment. Trina looked back at Retro and he smiled, giving her another wink. She might not have gone at prospect speed up the stairs, but she didn't dawdle, and that alone told him this was something she wanted.

Once she was out of view, he lifted a hand to Buzzkill. As the only prospect the Bastards currently had, he was permanently assigned the bar on party nights. Next week they'd planned an open-house evening where he knew there'd be a half a dozen hangarounds lining the walls, each of them hoping for a nod. He and Mudd had already talked through who'd they'd like to tap to make the next move, planning to onboard two prospects at the same time, because it wouldn't be long before Buzzkill's vote came due. Even though Retro had a few passing thoughts of concern, the man had done passable well enough Retro expected to put him in the Round a prospect and have him exit a member, and it would be easier to bring two probies on. *Competition is good for the soul, too. Maybe they'll try harder if pitted against the other from the get-go.*

"Yeah, boss?"

Retro didn't turn his head, addressing Buzzkill while keeping his eyes on the stairs. "You know what my woman likes to drink?" A humming response was a yes, and Retro grinned. "Bring one now, and then another in fifteen minutes. Get me and Mudd a couple fingers of the blue, if you would, and whatever Rhonda usually drinks, too." Retreating footsteps were his only response, and Retro let the smile drift off his face. She should be back any minute, and he wanted to be the first to see her. Neither of the skirts were short, but she'd probably be self-conscious about going commando, and he wanted to watch her wrestle her way down the open stairwell. Crazy Mike and Marlin were in on the plans, and were stationed to either side of the stairs, prepped to look up and see if they could catch a glimpse of her sweetness. Retro hoped to get an idea from her responses to how far he should push tonight.

Buzzkill loomed over his shoulder, four glasses tucked between his fingers. Two were bright red like a child's drink, and two were the warm amber of good scotch whisky. "Thanks, brother."

"No worries, Prez. I'll be back in fifteen with two more for y'all's ole ladies."

Movement in the upstairs hallway captured his attention and he watched as Trina floated into view. She'd picked the longer of the two skirts, one that had more flip and flare to the swing of fabric beside her knees, and he grinned. The other would have been more difficult for him to manage, so he was glad she'd selected as she had.

Eyes fixed on him, she skipped down the stairs, the hem of her skirt lifting and swirling around her legs. She had a hand on the banister, and not a care in the world about controlling her possible exposure, and he knew she'd flashed them when he heard Crazy Mike swear under his breath, "Oh dear sweet Lord, thank you."

Retro was ready for her by the time she got to him, arms up to catch her and draw her into his lap. "Hey, baby," he greeted her, then kissed her mouth softly on his way to her neck. The shirt she'd changed into left his mark there exposed, and he laved it with the flat of his tongue for a moment. "You look good enough to eat." Trina stilled in his lap and he laughed, chuckling deep in his chest when she shivered. "Not on the menu tonight, baby. I thought we'd start with something a little more tame."

"Tame? Like what?" Her breath stirred hair on top of his head and he knew she'd turned away from the open room.

"You saw Mudd and his old lady earlier?" He bit down on her neck just above his mark, clamping down with his teeth until he felt her move. Taking that for a nod, because he knew she'd witnessed their exchange, he released and kissed down to the notch of her collarbones. "He had quite the show goin' on. Told you Rhonda liked being watched. Nothing wrong about enjoying a woman's body, is there?"

"No," she breathed, already revved up, unsteady fingers threading through his hair. "Nothing wrong."

"Woman enjoyin' herself is beautiful to see. Don't you think so?" Retro lifted his head and stared into her eyes. Cheeks red, she angled her gaze down. "Baby, don't you think so?" She nodded and he ran his lips along her jaw, one hand slipping down the outside of her leg until he could trace bare skin with his fingers.

She gasped, then said, "No. I mean, yes. Rhonda was so beautiful. Is beautiful." Her words paused every few syllables, shaky breaths interrupting her speech.

He cut his eyes to the side to see Mudd seated in the chair opposite, back to the room, Rhonda perched on his lap with legs spread to either side of his thighs. Her skirt covered everything, but he could see the movement of Mudd's hand underneath, fabric draped around his wrist.

"Lookie here. What do we have to see?" Fingers to Trina's jaw, he turned her head and watched her face, seeing the instant she recognized what was happening. Breathing irregular, she blinked slowly and her tongue appeared, lapping at her top lip in an unconscious reaction. *Fuck yeah*. Retro leaned forwards and held Rhonda's drink out. She smiled her thanks as she took the glass from him and sipped from it before leaning back against Mudd's shoulder. Mudd gave them a grin so devilish Retro found himself smiling back. Retro gathered up Trina's drink and matched Mudd's pose, handing it to her as he turned her to face the other couple. She squirmed in his lap, glass held low over her lap as Retro kissed along the side of her throat.

Her legs were tucked inside his, but that was no barrier as he found the hem of her skirt again, fingers slipping to the inside of her leg, careless of how the fabric draped. Trina fixed it fussily, all while moving it out of his way and giving him a direct route to her pussy. *Fuck yeah*, he thought again, tracing along her pussy lips from front to back. Trina's awareness was divided between what the couple was doing and the movement of his hand, and hadn't paid attention yet to the fact what he was doing could be on display to the whole room.

Trina gasped and lifted her drink to her lips, sipping noisily. He delved deeper, humming when he found her slippery and wet. "Oh, honey. That's exactly what I hoped for." Mouth to her ear, he whispered. "Turned on and excited, and I am right there with you. So fuckin' sexy." He lifted his hips, pressing his rigid cock against her back. "So fuckin' good." He drew some of that slick up to her clit, circling slowly until she shifted impatiently. He looked at Rhonda who had her head back, eyes closed as her hips shifted, fucking herself on Mudd's hand. *Time to make it clear it's okay to watch.* "Rhonda, you feelin' good, honey?"

"Oh, yes. So good." She lifted her head and flashed a smile before draining her drink. "I love this."

"Give us a show?" He posed it as a question, giving Rhonda an out in case she wasn't feeling like being a demonstration, but as he'd expected, she happily sighed and inched her skirt up. Flashes of skin on her legs, the movement of Mudd's fingers, and then the fabric was out of the way and he had an unfettered view of Mudd penetrating her pussy, rosy lips closing over his fingers, effortlessly taking what he gave her.

Trina stiffened in his lap and he kissed up the side of her neck. "See how beautiful she is?" She nodded, her eyes never straying from the exhibitionism in front of them. "Imagine that's you." He flicked her clit, then pushed down and in with two fingers, picking up speed until he matched Mudd's pace. "Imagine my mouth on you, eating you out for anyone to watch, fingers inside, driving you crazy with my touch." The material of her skirt bunched up around his wrist, and he knew Trina wanted more touch of skin on skin when he felt her shifting it around, cool air drifting down to where his hand was between her legs.

Mudd called out, low and guttural, "Wanna see anything you wanna show me, Trina. I'd love to watch you."

The fabric moved again as one of her legs slipped sideways to dangle down the outside of his. "You want this, baby? My hand in you here, like this?" Retro thrust his fingers deep into her pussy again, holding there to curl and stroke while his thumb toyed with her clit. "Want them to see?"

Crazy Mike walked up behind Mudd's chair and bent over, murmuring something in Mudd's ear. He nodded and Rhonda smiled up at both men. Retro knew they'd all played together in the past, so he wasn't surprised when Crazy Mike pulled Rhonda's shirt down, bringing both titties out, tweaking her nipples while he stared down at Mudd's fingers moving in and out of her pussy.

"I do," Trina answer him finally and Retro had to think back to what he'd asked.

"Then show them." He kissed her throat and slipped a hand up inside her shirt to toy with her breast, fingers reaching under the fabric of her bra to cup and plump one. "Show them, pretty baby."

"Oh, gorgeous," Rhonda said, her voice high and wispy. He glanced up to see she was staring at Trina, and he looked down to see his own hand matching what Mudd was doing, flashes of Trina's pussy visible around him. Drawing his fingers higher on her sex, he spread her labia wide while he diddled her clit hard and fast, making her gasp and groan, her knees lifting involuntarily. Retro took advantage and slipped his whole hand down, circling her entrance with one wet fingertip before plunging inside using hard and fast movements.

"See how they look at you?" Trina lifted her head from his shoulder then, staring across at the faces turned her way. "You're beautiful takin' your pleasure like this." Crazy Mike had crouched beside Mudd, mouth on Rhonda's breast, hand on her thigh, thumb caressing her skin near where Mudd's hand still worked. Marlin was stroking his cock through his pants, eyes only for Trina. Mudd and Rhonda were also watching Trina, desire for her evident on both their expressions. "So fuckin' gorgeous, and you're mine." He pushed far inside her as he latched onto the side of her neck. "Mine. All mine." Her pussy clenched around his fingers, her grip on his arm tight, then tighter, and he knew she was coming without making a sound. "Come for me, oh yeah. Come for me. Mine." He reached up to bring her mouth to his, thrusting his tongue between her lips. She quivered and shook, the clenching easing by fractions until she was lax and loose in his lap. "Fuckin' mine," he murmured against her, withdrawing his fingers and flipping the skirt to cover her as he turned her in his lap. Cheek to his chest, she breathed heavily, fingers clutching his shirt. "Mine." He kissed the side of her face, then the top of her head.

Buzzkill set down two more glasses of whatever red concoction he'd made, and then retreated.

Eyes closed, he listened to Rhonda's noisy climax in Mudd's lap as she clearly enjoyed the attention the two men were lavishing on her. When he looked up again, Mudd had covered her, rearranging her clothing much as Retro had Trina's. Crazy Mike and Marlin had both retreated towards the pool tables, and were involved in a discussion with a party-doll sandwiched between them. He watched as Marlin unfastened his pants while Crazy Mike bent her over, positioning her face level with Marlin's crotch. A moment later, her short shorts were down around her knees and Mike was inside her from behind, pumping hard.

"Trina, check it out." He angled her head towards where they were and another inrush telltale of breath made him grin. "Yeah, she's into it. Watch how she yanks on Marlin, tryin' to get him down her throat. Crazy Mike's givin' her a poundin' she'll feel tomorrow, too. What she wanted, and they needed. You see that? She's beautiful, taking what she wants."

"They're just…right there." Trina's voice was soft and wavering. "She doesn't mind it being right there?"

"Not her. She gets off on it. If we'd have gone much longer, she'd have been over here begging to eat Rhonda's pussy." Trina went still, another tell of hers. *Fuck me, that's another turn-on for my woman.* "Oh, yeah, she enjoys that, too. She's sweet, always asks first, as if Rhonda's gonna turn down head. The gal likes that we don't judge her, take her as she is. She's just here for a good time, and then goes home. Boys use condoms, every time. Without fail, because that's what she's asked for." Trina moved restlessly and he soothed her with a palm up her thigh, fingers dipping to graze along her pussy lips, still wet from their play. "You want to try that out sometime, she'd be down for it, probably. Like I said, she's one to ask, so it'd be good to return that inquiry if you're into it."

"She'd...I couldn't. That's too...I don't know." Her breathing had sped up again, and Trina was panting as he started finger-fucking her slowly. "Oh, Retro. God."

"Wanna ride me, baby? Right here? Or wanna go upstairs?"

"Upstairs, please." Her immediate response settled him, because he'd expected this to be a lot for her, and her obvious excitement at watching the two men go at the one woman meant the reality more than matched her imagination. Still, that she wanted him now, with urgency, was gratifying, too.

"You got it." He stood with her in his arms, skirt draped around her knees and bunched under his arm, so she was covered. "Grab our drinks." He bent so she could reach, then stood straight. "I'll see you in the mornin', Mudd. Night, Rhonda. Thanks for the show."

"Get you some, boss man." Mudd's lazy smile said Rhonda's hidden hand was busy in a way he liked a lot. "We'll be headed up to our room very, very soon. Trina, sweetheart, thank you for your trust tonight. And thank you for not makin' my lady feel bad for what she likes. It takes a confident woman to make room for another like that, and I do appreciate you. Now—" He groaned and arched his neck, Rhonda's face buried in his chest. "You go and make my boy happy. You gave him something you don't even know, tonight. He's been tellin' me you're perfect for him, and I've begun to see it." He groaned again. "Fuck, woman, that's hot as fuck. Do it again, baby."

Retro took the stairs two at a time, catcalls following them down the hallway to their room. He planned to go slow once they got private, but Trina had different ideas, slipping from his arms and to her knees within seconds of the door closing. Her fingers tore at his belt and jeans, and she had him exposed and in her hands. Then her mouth was on him and all he could do was lean back against the door, fingers in her hair as she sucked him deep.

"Fuck, baby. Suck me off, yeah."

She went fast, not easing into anything, taking him to the back of her throat again and again, fingers wrapped around his shaft while she fluttered her tongue along the bottom of his cock. He looked down and smoothed her hair away from her face in time to see her eyes roll up to meet his. "So goddamned beautiful. You're mine, you hear me? You're mine." Lower, he saw her other hand disappear under her skirt. "Playin' with that pretty pussy, baby? You hot for this? You like suckin' me?" She made a garbled sound and closed her eyes as she forced her mouth farther onto his cock, nose tickling his pubes. "Jesus, baby. That pretty mouth is fuckin' hot as a goddamned furnace."

She gagged, forced herself past it, and swallowed around him with a squeal. Her arm was moving faster, hand on him following a ragged pace that had his balls drawing up.

"On your feet, baby," he ordered, and she opened her eyes with a shake of her head. "Yes, on your feet." He used his hand in her hair to pull her off him. "Wanna fuck you." Bending at the waist, he stared into her face. "Wanna fuck you hard. You gonna take it for me?" She nodded, fighting against his hold. "Up, and bend over. Just like the girl downstairs." The dark blue of her eyes was reduced to a thin ring, black pupil expanding in response to his words. "Gonna fuck you while you think about having a man's cock in your mouth like that. Like you were just giving to me." She nodded again and he released her, stepping to the side. "Hands on the wall." She spread her legs and angled towards the surface, palms even with her shoulders. "You wet enough, baby? You soaked?" Trina nodded, chin angled over her shoulder to look at him as he flipped her skirt up, exposing her ass and pussy to him. Rosy and blood gorged, her lips looked puffy and sensitive, and he could see the wetness glistening even in the low light. "Fuckin' gorgeous pussy."

He paused, hand on his cock, poised at her entrance as he asked the question he'd promised her. "Gloved or ungloved? I got a condom in my wallet, you want that." She shook her head and he made a tsk sound. "You know I want your words."

"Just you. Inside me. I want you to come in me."

"You got it," he told her, and pushed deep using a hard, fast stroke, not giving her time to adjust before he'd withdrawn and slammed back inside, repeating the motion, her pussy getting sloppy as she gave herself over to the act. He bent and spit, watching as his saliva slicked over her asshole before he twirled his fingertip around in the liquid, and traced her rim, pushing and massaging, testing her readiness there. "So fuckin' wet, already coatin' my balls and I love that. Love how wet you get for me. You like this, baby? Like me takin' what I want from you?"

"Yes, please," she told him, cheek resting on her arm, hair a wild mess around her head. "I want what you want. I want you. Want what you want, Retro. Please."

"Oh, be careful what you tell me." He grinned at her, not surprised when she tipped a little farther forwards, arching her ass up into the air. "This too, is mine," he said, and pressed his finger inside her hole. "You're mine." She tightened around him, pussy walls milking his cock with ripples as she came suddenly, her cries soft and hoarse. "I liked them watching, knowing I'm the only one who gets to tap this." His other hand went to her waist, yanking her back against him hard. "My pussy." She slid up the wall, shirt-covered tits pressed tight, and he bent his knees to power up into her, the pictures on the wall rattling with the force of him pounding her. "My ass." He twisted his finger around, going deeper inside, then shallow, then deeper yet. "My woman. All mine." Forehead to the middle of her back, he thrust hard, bottoming out and pulling another cry from her as her pussy convulsed around him. "Mine."

"Mine." She echoed his word and he groaned at the sound of ownership in her voice. "My lover." Teeth to her shoulder, he plunged deep and held there, cock shooting inside her, molten heat surrounding the head as he came again and again. "My Retro."

"Yours," he panted. "All yours. Every fuckin' inch of me, you own."

Knees weak, he breathed heavily as he rested against her for a moment before easing his finger from her ass.

"Wow." She sounded worn out, exhausted in all the best ways, and he smiled at the idea.

"Wow, indeed." She tightened around him and he tensed his abs, jerking his cock and making her gasp his name again. "Fuck, baby. You slayed me. Intense as fuck." He reached around and gathered her skirt up, finding and playing with her clit for a moment until she twisted to get away. "Love how you feel around me. Loved that, you takin' everything and giving it right back to me. You're fierce and hot, and everything—" He kissed the side of her head, nipping at her earlobe. "—everything I want in my woman. No gettin' rid of me now, I done told you. Stuck like glue."

"Not trying to get away." She shifted and he slipped from her body, her skirt falling between them as she turned in his arms. Head tilted back, she looked up at him. "Everything about you fits everything about me. Why would I try to escape?" She smiled and without looking away, gripped his softening cock, giving it a tug that sent zings of electricity down his legs. "Plus you're hot, good with this"—she gave him another gentle tug—"and sweet as candy to me. I say something last night that embarrassed me all to heck and back, and you went and turned it into reality in a way that got me what I wanted. A man who is good in bed, cooks,"—he'd made breakfast this morning, not something he considered real cooking, but she'd reminded him she'd been eating in restaurants for so long, anything cooked fresh and not from the diner was a novelty—"and turns the world upside down to make me happy? I'm not only not going to leave, but I'm going to think of another dozen ways to tie you to me." She smiled. "I kinda love you, Retro."

He kissed the tip of her nose, making her scrunch her face up with a giggle. "I kinda love you, too. Now, bed." She rolled up on her toes and pressed her mouth to his, then settled onto her heels, expression soft and sated. "You gonna clean up?" She nodded. "Meet you in bed?" She nodded again. "All right, baby. You do your thing."

***

Trina

She lay awake beside a sleeping Retro far into the night, rerunning scenes from the evening over and over in her head. Part of her wanted to be ashamed of what she'd done, what she'd allowed, but that was her past talking.

Dolph, her mother's best friend, only friend really, had hammered it into her head repeatedly what good girls did, and didn't do. He'd protected her against the boys of the neighborhood, standing on the stoop as she walked up the steps from their car, glaring over her head until their tires squealed as they pulled away.

Dolph had always been in her life. One of those puzzling things she tried not to think too much about. He hadn't gone to school with her mother, didn't exist in her yearbooks or family photos, but from the time Trina had been born, he'd been present. There was even a picture of him holding her on the steps of the hospital the day she'd come home.

That meant not feeling shame was a deliberate decision on her part, one bolstered by Retro's clear approval. He'd taken the time and effort to set it up, from the clothing selections, to the people he'd surrounded them with, to making sure she knew that every step along the way all decisions were hers. Even after she'd climaxed in his lap, he hadn't forced her to watch the two men with the woman, just drawn her attention to them, and then noted how she couldn't look away.

He'd learned a lot about her in a short time, and she loved how he held every nugget close, as if it were worth everything. *How'd I get so lucky?*

She'd still been tender from their lovemaking last night, and he'd used the right amount of force and pain to get her lost in her own head, something she hadn't any idea she would like, but he had. Somehow, he had, and he'd handed that knowledge to her.

In the shelter of the dark, his steady breaths at her back, she replayed the evening one final time through her head. The movie of Rhonda lost to what Mudd was doing to her, the knowing leer on the man's face as he drew Trina into their intimate moment, the way they'd watched her expose herself, Rhonda panting harder with every inch of flesh Trina showed, Marlin's eyes on her and only her, clearly ignoring what Rhonda and Mudd were doing—it all circled around, drifting back to a mix of Retro's reactions, and theirs, and hers, and his, always his.

Nostrils flaring as he'd thrust into her mouth, hair in disarray around his face, muscles taut with strain—he'd been magnificent rising above her like that. Praise flooding from his lips, painting her skin with glowing belief that she was right to own her sexuality. Him allowing her to hit her knees, not questioning if it was what she wanted, taking her at the word of her actions—that belief shored her up even more.

"You're mine, you hear me?" That question repeated in her head, every echo settling and relaxing her. The vibrato in his tone, the way it had rung throughout the room, how it had felt to be possessed in the moment, surrounded by him and his certainty that what they had was real and right—everything he did and was made her more confident. He was building her up without realizing it, every encounter or conversation easing her away from the woman who'd felt she had no right to be anything other than timid and retiring, taking what was given to her without question or complaint. If her father hadn't bothered to stick around, why would anyone else? Then Retro had come in and blown

those doubts away, showing her how he valued her, and giving her room to value herself.

Then his question, just as he'd promised to always do, giving her the option of him putting on a condom or not, even after he'd told her he wanted a child with her, had that image in his head already after only a few weeks. A man with children grown, wanting to start a family, to grow his family alongside her—wanting, not just willing—that was such a thrill. To be sought after, cherished, and desired, this was what she'd always needed in her life. No one had come close, and she knew now that's why they hadn't lasted. It had never been love before.

Not that Dolph knew she'd even had any relationships. She smiled. He would have had a fit if he'd known about the boys. She wrapped her fingers around Retro's wrist, holding tight. *He'd like this man*. Dolph was rough and tumble, and the men in his crew were much like Retro's brothers, in that they'd always had his back, would come at his call, and walked with one purpose. *He'd like my Retro*.

She snuggled into the pillows, finally closing her eyes, and—cradled in her man's arms—fell asleep.

***

Retro

He sat astride his bike and looked around the lot at the men readying themselves for the ride. Trina was already seated behind him, fingers hooked into his belt. She'd proven to be a natural rider, fearless, leaning into the curves and giving him room to maneuver the bike as he needed. This would be her first long ride, and he knew from the way she'd babbled over breakfast she was anxious. A thought struck him and he twisted his head to look at her.

"Hey, baby?" She stared at him through the clear goggles he'd made her put on. "You aren't worried about meetin' my kids, are you?" Color leached from her cheeks and he knew he'd hit on the reason for her nerves. "Nelda already loves you, just from hearin' me talk about you and what we got goin' on between us." Now her eyes were wide, and he grinned, because that was fear of a different kind. "Not that she knows everything we got goin' on, but the fact that you make her old man happy is gonna be enough for her and the boys. Promise you, they're gonna be huge fans in like five minutes. Max."

"You think so?" *Fuck, she's cute all tied up in knots like this.* "I really, really want to make a good impression."

"You already have," he assured her and touched his fingertips to his lips, then held them out to her mouth. The soft pursing of her lips against his fingers sealed the deal and he smiled at her. "You already have a fan in Penny, and Twisted said she's been talkin' you up to the kids. So you're well ahead of the game."

"She's Twisted's wife?" Something she knew but was asking for confirmation, so he nodded. "And she likes me because he likes me, even though he's never met me, because your men talked to his men, and shared that we were a thing."

"That's tangled as shit, but mostly right." He grinned at her, laughing aloud when she rolled her eyes. "My brothers told their friends that the witch was gone, and in her place I'd found a pretty, sweet thing that made me smile and laugh, and didn't get up in everyone's shit about nothing at all. And the part about me likin' you, and likin' how I am with you? Well, that'll be enough for them."

"So because I'm not your ex, I have their stamp of approval? That's all it took?" That tiny line appeared between her brows and he studied her for a moment.

Head shaking side to side, he started setting her straight, telling her what he knew as truth, something he realized she needed to hear from his lips right now, so by the time they got to Louisiana, maybe she'd even believe it. "You're thinkin' they're all comparing you to Wanda, and that's just not the case. Were they glad when I kicked her to the curb? Fuck, yeah. But that shit happened before I even met you. Timing is everything, yeah?" She nodded, but still looked dubious and hurt. "What they're comparing in their heads is me, to me. The me today who *isn't* a miserable asshole, who laughs and hangs out with them, the friend they'd been missing, up against that me from three months ago, a year ago, five years ago, who was pissed off almost all the time, unless I was with my kids. The me who never had time to do anything that wasn't full-on club business, because I was tryin' to hold things together for my kids. The me who felt like the weight of the world was sitting right on top of his shoulders, because I couldn't keep my wife from breakin' her vows every other weekend. The me who couldn't feel he was enough for anyone, because I stayed fucked up in the head. That's what they're looking at, baby. Me, not you, and the me with you is yards and miles better than the me without you. Trust me on that."

Now her eyes were brimming with tears, and he hated how that twisted something in his chest. "Retro?" He lifted his chin, unwilling to say anything else, feeling like he'd already said too much. Voice thick, she told him, "I like the me I am with you, too."

"Fuck, but I love you." With brusque movements, he ripped his helmet off and left it dangling from his fingertips as he leaned in to kiss her hard, relishing how she met him stroke for stroke, her lips sipping at his as he nipped hers. "Mine," he gave her their promise, and she smiled against his mouth.

"Mine," she agreed.

"Boss, we're ready to roll." He kissed her again, then a final soft peck at her lips before he turned to look at Mudd, settling his helmet back into place.

"Then let's roll." Fist in the air, he held it as, along with his, he heard motorcycles fire up all along the line. Engine rumbling under his ass, he leaned back so Trina put her head up alongside his. "Hold on." Her grip tightened in response and he grinned at the wild smile on her face. "Fuckin' born for this life."

He pulled out and onto the street, moderating his speed until the final bike joined the line, then he sped up as he angled towards the center line, making room beside him for Mudd. Crazy Mike was riding sweep on this run, to make sure they didn't lose anyone along the way. Just over five hours later they rolled off the interstate and onto surface roads in Mandeville, and he led the column to the Incoherent MC clubhouse.

Twisted and Po'Boy stood waiting on the lot, feet firmly planted, arms crossed over chests in matching poses, prepared to greet his group. Retro knew it was a point of honor that they didn't have a guard with them, and that they'd timed his arrival so well. He watched Po'Boy check his phone with a grin, and wondered if they'd had eyes on them part of the way. *Be an interesting bit of knowledge, now I just gotta figure out how to ask the question.*

The door behind the men burst open and Jimmy appeared, followed closely by Saya. Retro scarcely had time to get his kickstand down and climb off the bike before his boys were on him. Big as Jimmy thought he was, he still burrowed close for a tight hug before backing up a step.

"Daddy," he heard and looked up to see Nelda loping their direction, her long legs eating up the distance. "I'm so happy you're here."

"Jesus, girl, I think you grew a handspan while you've been visiting these folks. What have they been feedin' you?" He looped an arm around her neck and pulled her close, pressing a kiss to the top of her head. "Missed my kids somethin' fierce. I hope you had a good time, because this ain't never happenin' again."

Jimmy laughed, the sound so free and happy that his heart clenched in his chest. *How long has it been since he sounded like that?* He hated Wanda a little more, idly noting how he'd gone from tolerance to dislike, and now to actively hating the bitch. She'd done that, taken joy from his kids, pressing her agenda on them as she aimed to be hateful and mean, and they weren't like that, not deep inside. "Daddy, we had a good time. Uncle Twisted and I already done talked about next summer. We got ideas on what we wanna do."

"Well then, I guess Uncle Twisted and me better have a convo, but he's gonna be fieldin' his own rugrat by then, so we'll table the discussion for now. Maybe next year we make it a family vacation, and I come with?" He looked down where Saya was standing on his boot, fingers holding tight to his belt, cherub face upturned with an expression of such happiness, he had to swallow down a sudden lump, chest tight and eyes filling with tears. "Damn, boy, I love you." He hugged Nelda tighter and smiled when Jimmy rejoined them, his arms around his brother and sister, as was ever his wont, keeping them safe. "My kids are the best, and I love alla y'all. More than you know." He sniffed and bent his neck to drop a quick kiss against Jimmy's hair, snorting when it wasn't as far a stretch as it had been only weeks before. "Alla y'all grew a foot. Swear to God, my kids are giants now." He closed his eyes for a moment, listening to the giggles from his kids, Saya's head shaking back and forth in negation under his hand.

"I gotta say, they aren't this sappy when you aren't around." Twisted's wry voice came from nearby and Retro lifted his head to see his friend walking over, hand out. He unlooped his arm from Nelda's neck and gripped the man's hand, thumb to thumb as Twisted tugged him close for a back-pounding hug that took care not to dislodge his still-attached kids. "You got a good crew of spawnlings, brother. Be proud of them."

"I am, every single day. Blessed that these angels chose me for their daddy." He gave Po'Boy a nod, getting a grinning one in return. "I got someone for you all to meet. Trina, baby." He turned his head, finding her standing next to the bike, helmet off and fingers nervously smoothing her hair. "Come meet my kids."

She stepped around the front of the bike as he shuffled his trio of clingers in a half circle, facing her. "This is Nelda." He tipped his head to the side. "She's my princess, as you can see." Nelda untangled herself from him and gave an awkward wave that made him chuckle and shake his head. "Jimmy's my mini-me here, if you mentally add two foot in height, two foot in hair, and a few decades of attitude, you'll see what I mean." Jimmy turned in front of him and leaned back, shoulders against his father's belly in a protective stance that made Retro pause a moment. "And this tadpole here is my Saya. You met his namesake in my brother. This boy is my heart, and he knows it, don't you, boy?" Saya looked up and smiled, then looked at Trina. "Trina's the other part of my heart, and she means something special to me." At his words, Saya's face angled back up to him for a moment and then the boy unknotted his fingers from Retro's belt. He held his breath as his youngest made the first real overture, a shock because the boy didn't take to new people well, and seeing his arms thread around Trina's waist made Retro choke up again. She stared at him as she wrapped Saya in a loose hug, something he could break free from in an instant, and Retro loved how she was already taking care of his boy.

"Hi, Trina." That was Nelda, approaching from the side, hand held out like Twisted had done with him, but she kept her distance when they shook. "I've heard a lot of good things about you."

"Hi. I like your hair like that. It's cute." Retro studied Nelda for a moment, taking in the curls and tasteful makeup. She'd dressed up to meet Trina, and he loved that about his girl, how she'd marked this as a moment important enough to take care with. "I've heard so much about all of you, your dad loves you very much."

"I'm Jimmy." Still propped against Retro's abs, he waved. "Pleasedtameetcha."

"Hi, Jimmy." She released Nelda's hand and stroked the back of Saya's head, fingers threading through the strands in the way the boy'd always loved, and there was no way for her to know that would soothe him. *She's a fuckin' natural.* "This place is gorgeous. I've never been to Louisiana before. Did you have a good visit with your daddy's friends?"

Jimmy nodded. "The best. We went fishing and horseback riding, and fishing again. Dirtbikes and four-wheelers. There's a bayou about a quarter mile from Twisted and Penny's back porch. Just walk out with a line and a worm and you can catch a fish every time. It was great."

"That's awesome." She smiled broadly, then looked down. "Saya is it? I met your Uncle Isaiah. He's nice. Did you have a good time here too?" Saya tipped his head back and rested his chin on her ribs before nodding. "I'm glad. I'm also glad to meet you, officially. I'm Trina." He nodded again as her fingers slipped through his hair again. "Your daddy has all kinds of stories about all of you. I feel like I know you already."

"Trina, baby?" Retro called to her softly, loving this moment. "Come here." She disentangled herself from Saya with a final stroke of his hair, smiled at Nelda as she walked toward where he stood with Jimmy. "This is Twisted and Po'Boy, they're the national president and VP of the IMC. These boys are a big deal in their own mind." Both men laughed, as he'd intended, and he lifted an arm to her shoulders to pull her to his side. "They're close allies with the Bastards, and we're here as their guests." His gentle prompt that she needed to greet their hosts wasn't lost on her and she dipped her head in turn to the two men. "Trina's my ole lady."

As she'd been tutored by Rhonda, she held her tongue even when Twisted acknowledged her with a sideways grin, corners of his mouth lifting as he muttered her name, "Trina." Po'Boy followed with a blatant appraisal of her body, his gaze going down, then up, then down again before coming to Retro's face. "She'll do." He grinned and turned back to her. "Welcome, lady. We're honored to be the first to get a chance to know the Bastards' new queen."

Trina's murmured, "Thank you," was lost in the laughter as Retro's men left their bikes and approached, protocol having been observed.

The door of the clubhouse opened and Retro saw Penny peeking out, another woman's head positioned just over hers, eye to the crack. "Shiny Penny and Fearless Crissy, as I live and breathe." He moved away from

Jimmy and Trina to hold his arms out, catching the two women in a hug. "Good to see you two." Turning back to face Trina, he paused, because Jimmy had taken up the same position with Trina he had with Retro, back to her front. Saya stood beside her, hand latched onto the seam of her jeans and even Nelda stood near, some distance between them, but close enough to be obvious about her support. Just as he'd expected, his kids had already taken to her, and their approval of their father's choice was evident in how they wanted to make things smooth for her. "God, I love my kids."

"They're good kids," Penny told him. "I heard Wanda signed the papers." He stared at her as Penny's lips spread in a slow smile. "What, you didn't know?" Retro shook his head side to side once. "Well, well. This is something I'm gonna wanna remember. The day I knew something Retro didn't."

He barked out, "Don't fuck with me," and from the corner of his eye saw Twisted's head jerk up, staring at him because of the harsh tone of voice he'd used to speak to Penny. "Do not fuck with me about that shit."

Voice light and carefree, Penny called out, "Hey, Mudd, do me a favor and call Mister Willy? Ask him about the paperwork." Penny's gaze didn't leave his and he held the stare, waiting as he listened to Mudd muttering, then greeting someone on the phone. The one-sided conversation didn't give him any clues, but the person she'd told Mudd to call did, because William Genevie was the club's lawyer, and how Penny Dane Bell knew that, he could only wonder.

A minute later, Mudd was at his side, gaze cutting sideways to Penny, then over to their intent audience. Conversation had fallen away with the tension in the air, and Mudd's words were carefully modulated to keep them from reaching over to where the kids stood with Trina. "He said you're good, boss. Boy toy came through and earned his payday."

"And Daddy?" Penny inserted and when Retro glared at her, blinked innocently, the corners of her eyes crinkling as she clearly fought a smile.

Mudd studied her. "What do you know about that, gal?" She shrugged, and he turned back to Retro. "Daddy is not best pleased with daughter. She'll have to work to regain her place at his table."

Retro nodded, staring at Penny. "We'll have words later about how you learned this. Might be I'll have to put you on my payroll, if you can field that good of a network." She giggled like she was a teen and he laughed at the sound, surprised at how good he felt. "Now, come meet my woman."

The rest of the intros went well, Penny and Crissy disappearing inside with Trina and Nelda in tow, and it took a few minutes for Jimmy and Saya to wander off, but eventually it was just Retro, Mudd, Twisted, and Po'Boy walking around the outside of the clubhouse to the backlot, where the bonfire and grills were already set up for the night. He waited until they were in place, positioned near a back corner with a good view of the whole yard to ask, "How is Wrench doin' with the new mantle? I hear good things, but I figure you'll have fresher info." He smiled at Po'Boy. "That Crissy girl looks like she's happy as fuck, man. I'm glad for ya."

"I'm glad for me, too. She's the perfect fit between Wrench and me, I tell you what." Po'Boy shook his head with a sly grin. "Wrench is Wrench. He's good no matter what, but he was born to this role."

"What's been the fallout, if any?" Retro offered up a confession. "My Bastards haven't heard of anything except one member, and he wasn't no loss if you ask me. Be a wonder if he stays outta the pokey without the club to steady him." Alcatraz was the sole CoBos member who'd been noted as dropping their patch, and from what Retro had heard, it wasn't a surprise at all. "I know it's not IMC business, except as it impacts the territory, but I don't think this change is going to be anything except good."

"Yeah." Twisted nodded. "Peaceful passing of power is better than something that happens abruptly." He paused, then finished, his words laced with heavy meaning, "Like that little club down in Florida."

Retro carefully controlled his breathing, and from the corner of his eye, saw Mudd had done the same. There shouldn't be any way the Bama Bastards could be tracked back from the decimation of the leadership of that particular club, but those men had signed their own death warrants when they sheltered someone who'd killed one of Retro's own last year.

Working with resources across the United States, he'd pieced together information whisper by whisper, looking for the triggerman, coming up emptyhanded too many times. Then out of the blue, his friends in the Rebel Wayfarers MC had called to let him know the man, Tucker, a cut of theirs, had met his maker. Blood for blood, the way of the life.

With that information, he and Mudd had tracked back to where the man known by many names been given sanctuary, and laid plans that included using markers, some of them more than a decade old, going deep to exact vengeance.

"But you wouldn't know anything about that," Po'Boy said with a smirk, and Retro tipped his head to one side, face carefully blank. "Nope, didn't think you would. I gotta say, I'd like knowing my allies have balls and aren't afraid to deal with shit the way it needs to be handled. Was a new direction for that club who called the shots, and a good reminder to everyone of their bite."

"Dog that wags its tail yet still gots sharp fuckin' teeth." Twisted mused softly. "Not like some of those East Coast clubs, gummin' their way through shit. That's a mess out there, and we all know it. Makes a body wonder who's gonna spread their wings and push the shit off the plate." Now they'd moved from talking about Bastards business, to Einstein's old club, and the fact they knew where the man was from as well as Retro's distant connection through him, all told Retro that Po'Boy had been working his network hard.

"You gonna miss that when it's not at IMC's beck and call? The way Po'Boy sucks in rumors and inference, and spews out webs of scant truth and questionable conjecture?" Lines of tension around Twisted's eyes told him he was treading on uncertain ground, and he backed off slightly. Friends meant friends, but club was club, and they did not wear the same patch. *It's always good to remember that.* "He's a gem, ain't he? That Wildman, he was sure interesting to talk to when you brought him my way. Liked meeting that boy. He's a keeper."

"All my men are keepers." Twisted's diction was crisp and clean, not a bit of bayou mixed in. "And you are standing on Incoherent ground. Might be best if you remembered that."

"That, my friend, is something I never forget. Bastards stand with IMC, as always." He gave a little ground, expecting a return, and was not disappointed.

"IMC stands with Bastards," Twisted said clearly, then dropped back into the patois of the swamp, "Except when you piss me off. Po'Boy, you think we came at them a little hard?"

"Maybe a tetch." Po'Boy bared his teeth in a parody of a smile, and Retro was reminded again of who he was. *And why I love this game so much.* "But it's all between friends, am I right?"

"Oh, you're right," Mudd interjected. "You sure you don't wanna be a Bastard? Would be a right tight fit for a man like you."

"Man like me likes what he likes, and what I like is right here in Louisiana." Po'Boy's expression changed, becoming more grin than snarl. "Boys from Bama got them red necks. I like my boys to be bayou smooth."

Retro laughed. "What does that even mean?" Po'Boy opened his mouth and Retro cut him off. "No, don't tell me. I don't need to know that badly. My kids"—he turned to Twisted with a smile and a blatant subject change—"weren't too misbehaved, were they?"

Twisted beamed. "Not a lick of it. They're good kids. Helped out a fuckton with little Missy, and even Nelda got in a bit of fishin'. Penny liked having her here. They did all kinds of girly shit that I don't know what the hell they were doin' or talkin' about, but I was forced to ooh and aah over nail polish way too much to be healthy."

"Doubt your Penny had to do much forcin'." Retro breathed a little easier now that they were past the initial posturing and chest pounding. It was always the same, no matter where he went. When a body was known for something in particular, someone in the crowd would try to one-up until they got taken down a notch. He'd seen it happen repeatedly, and experienced much the same through past years. If a club gained a reputation for being badass and having a fighter, that meant they'd be challenged at every gathering by someone who felt their balls were a little bigger, their fists a little harder, and their bad attitudes a little more deserved. For the Bama Bastards, every rally, every meeting, hell just having a beer at a bar could turn into an intense "I know more than you know" session. He glanced at Mudd who grinned at him. And the Bastards learned from every single encounter. From this, Retro would be on the horn with his man in Florida to see who had been asking around, because knowing the source was as good as knowing the info. He was less worried about Philly since that club literally had nothing to do with his Bastards, but made a mental note to prep Einstein for whatever Q-and-A session might be in his near future. "I do appreciate you, brother."

Twisted nodded regally, and Retro stifled his grin, dipping his chin to his neck. "Our pleasure."

Music pounded out from the windows of the clubhouse, loud volume quickly moderated to something that would be edging just above a background level, an eavesdropping countermeasure he appreciated.

"What can my boys do to help prep?" He'd expected the head shake, but it didn't hurt to offer. "They can tote shit and take orders, if I tell them to." Not to say that any IMC patch could order his boys around, but if he asked it of them, his men would be happy to help. Balancing the tightrope of two clubs coming together like this was always a performance of push and pull, and something he and Twisted had perfected through the years. "Well then, can a body get a beer?"

Po'Boy lifted his chin and shouted, "Probie, unass now." As if waiting for the order, two men left the shadow of the clubhouse wall and walked within five feet, pausing as if there were a barrier surrounding the group. Retro nodded because it was a nice touch, as theatrical in its own way as his silent summoning and ordering. "Need some beer for our friends, go on and drag that barrel over here." Retro turned to see a half-keg sitting on top of a barrel in a tub of ice. "Get me some cups."

He stayed silent and unmoving, letting the IMC men arrange things to their liking. Retro expected to be handed a beer by one of the prospects, shocked to his core when Twisted did the honors. He flipped the spigot and filled one cup, then another, handing them by turn to Retro then Po'Boy, then a third for Mudd, and finally one for himself. The order wasn't lost on Retro and he nodded at Twisted, who simply grinned in response.

"CoBos makin' an appearance tonight?" He sipped the cold beer, appreciating it in the sweltering heat of the waning Louisiana evening. "And you sure you got room for my boys here? I'm happy to rent out some hotel rooms in town if you'd rather."

"Naw, we got plenty of room. Got some entertainment too, for after the ole ladies head home. It's not an imposition in any form. Probies will have the place cleaned up by the morning and we'll come back for breakfast, so we can get our feed on before rolling out and doin' our thang." He lifted a hand and brushed the foam from his mustache with a grin. "Coupla days, when it's time for you to head home, I thought we'll slide up the road with you a bit, make sure your spawn has a good send off."

Booze and women, two surefire ways to get the info tap flowing, and Retro knew Mudd had the same thought when he pulled out his phone and sent a quick message. Retro's phone vibrated silently in his pocket and he left it there for now. No need to telegraph it had been a warning sent to everyone on the run. That might leave a bad taste in Twisted's mouth. Instead, what he said was truth in its own way. "That sounds good, man. Was a nice ride, just long enough to feel it, but not so much even Trina was tired. She will be after we eat, no doubt, and we'll be ready for shuteye before it's too late."

"Trina. That short for something?" Po'Boy's question seemed idle, but Retro knew better than that with this duo. "Where's she from? I gotta say, I was one glad puppy to hear you were donesies with that Wanda shit. Shoulda kicked her long ago. I mean, I get why you couldn't, kids and all, but fuck, man, you lived eating from her table of bullshit for a long time. Where'd you meet this Trina?"

"Appreciate it, brother. Sucks to know that something you thought you were doing for the right reasons turns out to have been hurting the ones you love the most. I thought my kids would be better for havin' their parents stay together, but talking to them since just shows how wrong I was." He shook his head. "I suspect you already know everything you asked about, but I'll humor you."

"Oh yeah, humor me, because I can't ever be wrong." Po'Boy blew a short raspberry. "Fuck that, brother. I like you and I want to know that you've got a good one this time. Tell me, don't tell me, it don't matter nothin' to me."

"Katrina, and she's from Atlanta. That's where her family is still. She's a waitress by trade, but we're changin' that so she can work at one of our shops. She's a worker, and ten'll get you twenty she's in there standin' alongside whatever the other women are doin', elbows-deep in preparing supper. I like that. I like how she ain't afraid of me." He gestured around the lot at the clusters of black leather and denim-vested men. "Afraid of my life. It's nothing she's ever known, but fuck, man, she's made for it."

"Truth," Mudd put in. "Never seen a woman come in and win over so many of the boys. Not just our members, either. She charmed the Rebel Wayfarers who came to visit a couple of days ago, and we all know what kind of cynicism those boys carry. My ole lady's a big fan, and Rhonda's particular about who she lets in. I like her."

"That's a rousing recommendation." Twisted whistled soft and low and Retro noted when two of his own men nearby alerted, and grinned at the miscommunication. "I trust Rhonda's instincts, because the woman's never been wrong, long as I've known her. Atlanta's not too far for you. You been to meet the parents yet?"

Retro flicked his hair out of his face with a toss of his head. "Not yet. It's just her momma there, and Trina's been in Birmingham for a while so it's not like she's a chick just leavin' the nest."

"Speakin' of a chickie leavin' the nest." Po'Boy chuckled. "That Bekka's something else. I was expecting a troublemaker of the first order, but she's meek as a lamb, man. You sure she's the little sister I've been hearin' you complain about for years?"

Twisted made a rude noise far back in his throat and Mudd chuckled. Retro didn't try to keep the scowl from his face as he said, "Yeah, pretty sure she's the same pain in my ass as the woman I sent to stay out of trouble here."

"Well, there must be somethin' in the water here, because she's been sweet as pie. Those girly things my boy Twisted was talkin' about? She's all up in the middle of those, Nelda shootin' daggers at her or not. I think Bob's sweet on her, too, which tells me she's not a bad seed like you been makin' her out to be."

"Bob's the brother-in-law?" Po'Boy nodded. "And he's midwestern? A good old boy from up north?" Another nod. "And what in the fuck makes you think he's got anything to hold her up against? She's trouble with a capital T, dipped in the dye of the worst Birmingham has to offer, and then seasoned by bad decisions from the time she turned a teen. She'll be the death of our parents, I just know it, and forgive me if I doubt the intuition of a man I've never met."

There was a sound beside him and he turned to see a man about his age, lines of experience and what looked like grief weathering his face. Retro stared at him a minute then turned to Po'Boy who had an "oh shit" smirk on his face. "Let me guess. This is Bob?" A nod. Retro tipped his head back, staring up at the stars just beginning to make an appearance along the edges of the night sky. "Spectacular."

"So, yeah. Maybe this is bad timing and all that, but I wanted to come over and meet you." Bob's accent was drawling in odd ways, accents placed on different syllables, but Retro could make out the tone of hot anger that wove under and through the words. "Seeing as your sister speaks so highly of you, and so did Lewis and Bell here. But now—" He scanned down to Retro's boots, then back up to his face, gaze taking in the long, tousled hair that was his trademark. "I'm thinking better of that decision. I don't like a man who easily talks badly about family, because in this life, family is sometimes all we have. I happen to like Rebekka, and I put a lot of weight on what she says. Maybe in this case she's mistaken." He offered a respectful nod to Po'Boy and was already turning away, giving Retro his back. *Fuck.*

"Bob, wait." He didn't reach out, didn't touch him, but the words alone were enough to make the man turn back and wait. Anger was still evident in his expression, mouth turned down in a bulldog frown. "You got sisters, man?" He got a head shake in response. "Crissy's your sister-in-law, right?" No response and he ran through his memories to find the folder where this man's information existed. His wife had died, Crissy staying with them through the ordeal, and then afterwards, to help care for his little girl. "Did your wife think the sun rose and set on her, no matter what?" Bob made to nod and then paused, a tiny curl changing the set of his face as he shook his head once. "Siblings have a unique relationship on this earth. We love and loathe in the same breath, because we can and that's who we are as humans. I love my sister, Bekka. Love her more than she'll ever know, and want better for her. But she's gotta want that, and I've been frustrated because I couldn't make her see what I saw. Crissy came back here, came home, because her sister set something up for her, right?" Another nod, this one slower like Bob was thinking hard. "Because if she'd been left on her own Crissy wouldn't have made the same choice, am I right?"

"Yeah, my Rhoda said her little sister was the worst for making her own life better. Spent the last weeks of her life making certain Crissy would have what she needed to move on." Pain and love battled for space in his voice, and Retro ached for that evidence of the man's losses.

"Well there you go. You understand more than you know. My little sister needs something to change, or she's not long for this world. She's not an addict or anything like that, but her demons can be just as deadly. I don't want that for her. I want her to have what she needs." Retro held out his hand and waited, because the next move had to be Bob's. A firm grip met his, and their clasped hands shook up and down. "If that's you, and you're up for the challenge, and Crissy vouches for you—" He paused for the laugh he knew was coming, grinning when he heard it from more than one throat. "Then that's good enough for me."

"She loves you." Bob wore an earnest expression as he absently accepted a cup of beer from Twisted. "She's told me a lot of what's been going on, and it doesn't faze me."

"How long are you here for?" Retro wanted a chance to see Bekka with Bob so he could study the dynamics, because he wondered if Bekka had really told the man anything at all. She was into pain and that was a craving which didn't just up and go away. If she didn't have the outlet she got from scenes, then she'd go back to cutting, and that was a steady spiral down for her.

"Was only going to be here a week, doncha know. But I've already been here for two, and now Crissy's talked me into taking more vacation. I've got plenty, and it's not like I'm going anywhere else anytime soon. Missy will be back in school in a few weeks, and she keeps me plenty busy."

"I hear you, that's the main reason for my trip now, to bring my rugrats home. You get a chance to meet my kiddos?" Test of truth, because if the man had a single bad word to say about Retro's kids, he'd cut him out of Bekka's life no matter what it took.

"Oh, yeah. That Nelda's something else. She's real sweet with my little girl. Your boys have been really good to her, too. Playing and what not." Bob smiled fondly, the expression going a long way to reassure Retro. "That Saya can talk Missy's ear off, and that's saying something."

Retro locked into place, certain he'd misheard Bob. "Excuse me?"

"Oh, I don't mean it in a bad way. He's never bossy or anything. Real sweet with her." Another smile. "Nothing like getting to watch kids as they make friends."

Mudd asked, his voice as careful as Retro had ever heard, "When you say talk her ear off, what does that mean, exactly?"

"Well, just that he's not shy with her. Not like with everyone else. My Missy's a talker, and Saya surely keeps right up with her." Bob was looking back and forth between Retro and Mudd now, confusion writ large on his face. "What's up with you two? What's with the questions?"

"Saya doesn't talk." Retro said this slowly, because he wanted it to be a false statement so badly, he could almost taste the hope in his mouth. "He doesn't speak. Not to anyone."

"Well now, ain't that something? He doesn't talk, you sure about that?" Bob cocked his head to the side. "Because he's inside right now, playing dolls with Missy, and talking up a storm. I just came from there."

Retro bolted for the clubhouse, uncaring of how he looked, tossing the still-full cup aside, liquid and foam erupting in a wave that splashed against a wall. He pushed through the door and into the main section of the clubhouse, staring around the room. Nelda was nearby and took a step towards him, fear twisting her features. "Daddy?"

"Where's Saya?" He hadn't meant to bark the question like that, but he needed to know, needed to go, needed to hear this miracle if such existed. "Where are he and Missy at?" Nelda pointed to the stairs and he ran up them, trying to be quiet while still making his way at speed towards his boy. There was only one room with the door open, and he slid to a stop just out of sight of the occupants of the room and tried to listen over the pounding of his heart.

A little girl laughed. She shout-whispered something he didn't quite catch; it must have been a question because her voice rose at the end like Bob's had.

"No, my daddy's a hero." Soft, a choir boy's tenor, the voice was unwavering, strong and sure of the truth of what it was saying. "He's the best." Retro's throat closed tightly, hand shaking as he covered his mouth.

"My daddy's the best, too." Little girl sweet, all sugar and spice and everything nice, lilting and musical.

"We're the luckiest then, because we have good daddies." Rough around the edges, the promise of crackling teens far in the future, the boy's voice was unfamiliar and yet known, because it was everything he'd always imagined Saya's voice would be. "I love my daddy more than anything. Do you want more tea? Are your dollies thirsty today?"

He crept forwards then, needing to see to believe. Leaning against the wall of the hallway, he eased to where he could look inside the room. There his Saya was on the floor, a little girl in a pair of bib overalls lay crossways on a bed, head and arms dangling off by where Saya sat. Ponytail hanging over her shoulder, she looked up at Retro and smiled, the type of expression that only ever exists on a child's face, full of trust and honesty, and faith in humankind. "Is that your daddy?"

Saya turned around and beamed a smile at Retro as he nodded. Heart-stopping in that moment, because what if that nod meant he didn't get to hear his boy's voice again? What if Saya would only speak to Missy, like an invisible friend who came to visit when no one else was present?

Then Saya broke him into a thousand million pieces, putting him back together with every word, every breath. "That's my daddy. Hi, Daddy." A wave, and another smile, and that voice, that precious, precious voice, filling the air with love and magic and everything Retro didn't think he'd ever have. "Daddy wanna come play?"

"Yeah, yes. Yes, I'd love to play. What are we playing today?" Retro pushed himself off the wall, unsure at first if his legs would carry him the five strides to where Saya sat waiting. "I'd love to play."

***

Booted feet planted firmly on Twisted's back porch, Retro stared out at the silhouette of the trees against the sky. The moon was in the final stages of setting, so the definition wasn't as clear as an hour ago, but he didn't mind watching it fade. That just meant it was still traveling around the earth ball, and showed everyone with a mind to watch just how time marched on. *Saya talking.* "Jesus." He shook his head. *Miracles do happen.*

Isaiah had gone from being a normal little baby, full of cooing smiles to a sweet toddler who pointed and pulled faces to get what he'd wanted. Pediatricians couldn't decide on a reason, the audiologist said his hearing wasn't the problem, and the speech therapist proved his boy was smart, sweet as the day was long, willing to do whatever was asked—except speak.

And yet, tonight, here in Mandeville, Louisiana, he'd been treated to the sound of his boy's voice and laughter, and still couldn't wrap his head around what had happened.

Soft footsteps behind him told of someone approaching, probably female from the shorter strides, and when arms wrapped around his waist, he knew without a doubt who it was. "Bekka." He patted her hands and held onto one as she pulled away, keeping that connection. "Did you know he was talking to Missy?"

"No, Jerry. I would have called if I'd known." She leaned her head against his arm. "I'd have called straight away. That's amazing, isn't it?"

"Yeah." He breathed out, then in, reminding himself that time marched on. "It is amazing." He'd spent hours with the kids, sprawled on the floor of a bedroom with a rotating door of friends who'd come up to see for themselves, to hear with their own ears. Slowly Saya's words had come less often, his smile dimmed, and when he yawned wide enough to crack his jaw Retro had declared it time to head to Twisted's house. Just like he would have if Saya were still silent, because being a daddy didn't change. "It's like the moment I decided to change the course of my life, things started falling into place for me, you know?"

She hummed softly.

"Dealt with Wanda and only weeks later, I stumble on the woman who's holding my heart. Talk her into throwing her lot in with me, and you know that was some talkin' I had to do." He shook his head as Bekka laughed softly. "Moved out of the clubhouse into a home. A real, honest-to-God home like I've always wanted for my kids. A place where they can bring their friends and hang out, make a mess without someone climbing up their ass about dust or crumbs. Ride over here to pick my kids up, and get to watch them fall in love with my woman. Privileged to see her return that straight back to 'em. And then—" Voice rough, he broke off and swallowed, then cleared his throat. "And then tonight my baby boy called me daddy, and I got to hear him say how much he loved me. That's a fuckin' miracle right there, and if this ain't a good, fuckin' life, I don't know what is."

"Nelda okay?" Bekka's voice still held a note of wonder and he understood it completely. As a family, the Rogers had stood behind Retro as he fought against Wanda's wishes in order to get Saya evaluated, her stance that he was just a lazy boy who should have it beaten out of him not going far with any of his kin. Bekka had ridden with him to more than one doctor's visit, listening to the explanations, and then mothering on Saya afterwards, giving him more love than his mother ever had. *No wonder she's good with Missy*, he thought. *She's had plenty of practice with mine and Miriam's kids.*

"Yeah, she cried herself out and crashed a while ago." Nelda hadn't known, hadn't believed when Mudd first found and told her, and she'd stood in the hallway for a long time, hand covering her mouth to keep her sobs of relief and love inside, not wanting to scare Saya. Jimmy had been more stoic about the whole thing, taking it in stride in a way that made Retro wonder if he'd had an inkling all along. Not that it mattered a whit, because Saya was perfect any way he wanted to be. "She's a good girl."

"She really is," Bekka agreed, and he heard the love in her voice. "She's more than a little boy crazy, but she'll settle down. I have faith."

"How are you doin', Bekka? Really. No bullshit." He squeezed her fingers, folding her hand around his arm.

"I'm...good." Her tentative words were far from reassuring. "I needed this."

"What's this? What this are you talkin' about?" He wanted to nail it down so he could give it to her again, and again if it meant his little sister was getting her head on straight. "What did you need, baby girl?"

"You're going to take it the wrong way."

He shook his head. "Nope. I'll take it how you give it to me."

"I...ugh. It's hard to put into words."

"I got nowhere to be, little sister. You get it out however you can, and I'll be here, listening and tryin' to give you more of what you need."

"That's exactly what I don't need, don't you see?" She sounded frustrated. "If I always know I can fall back on you or Miriam or Isaiah, then I don't have to make any decisions. That safety net is what I count on."

"You're supposed to be able to count on family, baby girl." He shook his head again. "That's what we're for, because we're family and that's what we do."

"I don't mean it as a bad thing, Jerry. But here, Twisted's watching to see if I mess up, but not so he can clean up my mess. He's watching so he can kick my ass and make me deal with it. And Penny—" Her voice cracked and broke, and he could hear tears threatening in the thick sound of her throat. "She believes in me in ways I didn't know I needed. Not because she loves me, but because she likes me. Because she depended on me for a lot of stuff when we first got here. And I had to step up so I didn't disappoint her. But I didn't step up for her. I stepped up for me, just this once. I've never done that before."

He let that sink in, peeled away the resentment and let it resonate through him, finding echoes in all the emergency family meetings where they decided what to do with Bekka, what to do about Bekka, all without making sure what Bekka wanted or needed.

Even a couple weeks ago when she'd shown at his clubhouse, he'd already been aiming to check her into some kind of facility to try and help her sort herself out, but Penny had set her sights on bringing Bekka back here and nothing else would do.

She'd talked to Bekka.

He hadn't.

He'd just been ready to make a decision on her behalf, like he'd done a hundred times in the past. Since the first time she'd gotten drunk on muscadine wine in his parents' barn. Since the first time he'd seen the scars on her arms, on her legs, and thought she was on drugs, only to find out it was something else, something just as scary.

"She's an addict, but to pain," her doctor had once told the family while Bekka was tucked safely out of sight and hearing, speaking about her as if she wasn't capable of making her own decisions. And maybe at sixteen she hadn't been. But she was a woman grown now, and he'd been treating her the same all her life. No wonder she didn't grow up; she never was expected to. *Fuck*. He knew he wasn't the only one in the family that treated her like that.

"Say something," she begged, those tears no longer threatening, but flowing fast, his arm hot and slick with them from where her wet face pressed against him. "Please, Jerry. I'm sorry. Whatever I did, everything I did...I'm sorry."

"You stepped up, because she's your friend and she mattered to you." He couldn't keep the hurt from his voice, and knew she heard it when her body bucked hard, silent sobs wracking her frame.

"You matter too." Broken noises that slipped into sounds, and he waited patiently while it took her a full minute to get out those three simple words, giving her time.

"Oh, baby girl. I know I do. I'm your brother, I know. But you found something worth fighting for. Friendship, and that's beautiful to see. I'm glad you found that, more glad than you know. I didn't realize what we'd done, how we'd crippled you by wanting to help. Thought we were giving you the right mix of caring and tough love, but I think I understand what you mean. We helped but, on our terms, and that never let you learn what it was like to stand on your own." He took her hand in his, prying her fingers from his arm and wrapped it around her. "This is you finding your feet, and that's a beautiful thing. I'm proud of you, Bekka. More proud than you know."

"Really?" Still hiccupping with sobs, tension carried for years broke free from the anchors that held it in place and made her voice waver and shake with disbelief. "You're proud of me?"

"Oh, yeah. Proud, so proud." *Have I ever said that to her before?* He knew the answer was no. An owl hooted in the trees, the sound softly ferocious, because that was its nature. *Time for her to leave the nest long ago.* "This is you spreading your wings, and you're meant to soar, sweetie. So proud."

He stood there holding his baby sister, much as he'd held his daughter, staring out into the blackest night as she wept at his side, in his arms, and he'd never seen such bright hope in his life. Stars twinkled overhead, the flashing white and red of jets tracking through the sky, shine of eyes in the trees, cries of nighttime birds and croaking frogs. *Everything in life that's worth anything is right here around me.* He stood and breathed, and just existed in the moment in a way he never let himself do.

Voices called through the house, soft and respectful of the ones already abed, Trina laughing with Penny in the kitchen, Twisted tossing in an occasional observation that caused the women to laugh even harder. "I liked Bob." She stirred against him and the move meant she'd looked up at his words. "Seems like a nice guy."

"He's nice. He's not fake, and I like that a lot." She let him go and stood tall. When he glanced down, she was swiping at her face with both hands. "He's a good man, Jerry."

"You'll keep us updated on where this goes?" That was the first inkling he had of what he'd be doing tomorrow, which wasn't taking his sister home with his kids, or planning on how to come back in a week to retrieve her. *Might as well roll with it since this is clearly what she needs.* "Let us know if he's gonna move down, or if you're headed up to Yankee land?"

"I will." That told him she'd been thinking the same, and he wondered if she would have given it up if he'd told her no. *We'll never know, thank God.* "I love you, Jeremiah Rogers."

"I know you do, baby girl. And I love you right back." He shook his head as he fluffed her hair. "You're a mess. Good thing your man likes you as you are."

"Yeah." She breathed the word, no sound of tears now, just certainty that she was loved.

"I'm gonna go grab Trina and hit the bed. You met her, yeah?" She nodded. "Whatcha think?"

"Oh, you're askin' for my opinion now? This is a first. Someone call the paper." She laughed. "I like her a lot. She's good with the kids, so much better than the wicked witch was. And she's good with you. Handled you pretty deftly today when you were fallin' apart about Saya."

"I wasn't fallin' apart." He drew his brows down into a scowl. "I was just shocked as shit."

"Fallin' apart. Good thing your woman was there to handle you."

"Oh, fuck you." She smiled at his gentle teasing and he grinned, then gave her something he should have been saying all along. "I'm so proud of you."

Soft, low, and trembling, she whispered, "Means more than you know."

Oh, I think I've got an idea. He didn't say that, just shook his head as she turned to head into the house.

***

Trina

"It was an eventful day." His voice was gruff and low as Retro's arm tightened around her, pulling her back against him.

They were at Twisted and Penny's house in the guest bedroom that Nelda had been using, all three of the kids bunking together in a room down the hall. Nelda hadn't said a word as she cleaned out her things, giving her father an exhausted hug before she turned to Trina and wrapped her arms around her waist. Trina had carefully returned the embrace, not sure if it were a prelude to anything else, but Nelda hadn't said anything, just gotten her hug and then stumbled down the hall and out of sight.

Then Retro had disappeared, Penny pointing knowingly towards the back porch with a shake of her head. So Trina had given him the space he'd seemed to need, looking through baby registration sites with Penny until exhaustion made her head feel stuffed with wool. She'd made her excuses, retired to their room, and then stood at the foot of the bed for a long moment, not certain what Retro would expect. After a long tussle in her head over pajamas or not, panties or not, she'd thrown up her hands over her own indecisiveness and prepared for bed like she normally would, finally climbing between the sheets.

The windows were dark, and there were no lights in the room to tell her how late it was when he'd finally come to bed, folding himself in behind her as if they'd slept this way for years, not a double handful of days. He'd fit himself to her back, his hard knee hitched her leg higher, and had opened the door for conversation if she wanted.

"It was busy." She slipped her fingers around his wrist and gave him a squeeze. "You doing okay?"

"There's this charity thing Twisted wants me to go to tomorrow. I can take you into town to buy something to wear if you didn't bring something you think'll be presentable."

Okay, so they were clearly avoiding the fact something profound had happened with his youngest boy. And from the whispered exchange between Bekka and Penny, Trina assumed he'd had a troubling conversation with his sister, too. She set aside her worries and answered his question with one of her own. "What kind of event?" If he needed patience from her to give himself distance from whatever he was currently thinking about, Trina could do that for him. "Jeans and tops I've got covered, but if it needs a dress and heels, I'm out of luck."

"We can ask in the mornin', but I suspect your jeans will be fine." He tightened his arm. "Jeans and biker boots, which are hot as fuck on you, woman."

She smiled, burying her cheek against the pillow. "So you say."

"So I know." He hummed softly, mouth to the back of her neck as he shifted her hair to place his lips on her skin. Trina shivered with a sudden want that swept over her at the gentle touch. "I doubt I'll ever get my fill of lookin' at you, pretty momma." His hips pressed forwards and she pulled in a soft breath. He was hard, and she was certain he was also naked. "Wanna fuck?"

"We're guests here." She was rapidly losing her sanity, pushing back against him. She didn't know why that mattered, but it felt like something that should be said before her resolve melted in the feel of him here in bed with her.

"You think Penny and Twisted aren't fuckin' right now, you'd be wrong. I heard their bed squeaking to beat the band a minute ago. If you want, I'm down for it. If you don't—" He squeezed her again. "Then we'll talk until one of us falls asleep." She wiggled her bottom backwards and smiled at his dark chuckle. "That your way of tellin' me your preference, baby?"

"Maybe. If you don't think they'd be upset?" He chuckled again and she lost the arm around her waist. "What are you—" Fingers dipped under the gusset of her panties and touched her gently, briefly, slipping through her lips before they hooked the fabric and pulled it to the side.

Then his hard cock was there, blunt head nudging against her insistently. "Retro."

"Prop your leg over me," he ordered, voice gruff. "You're already fuckin' wet, and I love that. Now, you just gotta let me bring it home. You want me in you? In you like this? Bare and naked inside you? It's just you and me here, baby. You want me?"

Without giving another thought to who else was in the house, or to the fact his children slept down the hall, she opened for him, resting her calf on his hip as he found her entrance and eased inside.

Gravel rattled in his chest, and he muttered a drawn-out, "Fuck." His mouth grazed the back of her neck, teeth raking across her skin. "Not too sore?"

"No," she told him, breath catching between those two letters because he was inside her, hard, thick shaft spearing and stretching her until she couldn't have told him her name. There was just the rhythm he set, his body moving against hers, his fingers dipping and touching, playing with her as if they had all the time in the world. "So good."

"Oh, yeah. So good, baby. Love this." He shifted position slightly, but it translated into a huge change in sensation for her, and Trina bit her lip to quiet her rising cries. "Yeah, give all of that to me, baby. I want it all. You're with me, and we're here, and this, you and me, we're meant to be." Deep, fast, with long, steady strokes, he pushed in and withdrew, each movement equally devastating, her body's oxygen depleted because all she could do was pant out his name, fingers wound in the sheets. "Can't get enough of you. Never get enough of you. Meant to be, baby. You and me."

"You and me," she echoed him. "Retro, Retro. Please."

"Anything you need." Faster yet, the rattle and shake of the bed scarcely registering now. "You got it. You got everything."

He rocked against her, hard planes of his body fit to the curves of her back, hands roaming up and down, fingers touching her intimately. His mouth latched onto the side of her neck and she cried out again, the sound sharp and loud. "Retro."

"Yeah, baby. Come for me. You get yours, always. That's a promise, baby. Always. God, Trina. Gonna blow, gonna blow."

She wanted him to know it was good, so good and he was doing what she wanted, everything she needed. All the things she didn't know had been missing from her life, all these holes in her she hadn't realized until he'd come along and filled every one of them. Filled them up, made her whole, and all he had to be was himself. "You're mine, Retro." More a babble than a normal series of words, she kept going, hoping he'd make sense of what she wanted to say. "Mine, and in me, this is us, and what I want. Love you, so much. My heart and soul, you. Please."

Chapter Nine
Retro

Mudd backed in next to Retro, near where several others of their group had parked. Engine still running, he called out a question. "What's this thing for again?" Nelda was balanced on the seat behind him, and Trina rode with Retro. Jimmy and Saya were with some of the IMC wives and ole ladies at the clubhouse, playing with other club kids too young to attend an event that amounted to a long, drawn-out awards dinner.

Before Retro could respond, Nelda gave the answer. "It's an anti-bullying campaign. CoBos started getting involved last year when a boy got beaten up coming home from school." She accepted Mudd's steadying hand and stepped off the bike, her mouth never missing a beat. "On the bus, if you can believe that. The school knew who'd done it, but they didn't even suspend the other kids. Like the next day the boy's mom told someone what had happened and they posted it online and Ace saw it and realized the boy was the same age as his grandson. So then," her hands worked to removed her helmet while she kept talking, "he was going to head over to give the boy a fist bump or something, tell him it would get better, but then Wrench and a dozen others rode along and some neighbor took a picture of them talking to the boy and that got printed in the paper. So *then*," she handed the helmet to Mudd, who had a bemused smile on his face that Retro well understood, "there was a school board meeting and Ace decided to go and see what they were going to do about it, and they let him talk, and he promised to be there for that boy and any others who needed someone at their backs." She ruffled her hair around with both hands, settling it around her head with a final shake. "And then they gave the boy a ride to school on a bike, with like twenty bikers alongside. Three clubs, Daddy. That's good press, and Ace's no dummy, so he got the idea to make it more of an official thing." She stepped back and propped her hands on her hips. "So this is a fundraiser for the organization, to get it off the ground and running. Come on." Nelda flipped a hand towards the buildings behind her, on the other side of a huge parking lot awash with a sea of bikes. "We've got a table and everything."

"What do you mean we have a table?" Retro had leaned back against Trina, holding her in place while he watched his daughter. Trina's fingers were under his chin and he heard a click, then his helmet loosened. "And by 'we,' who are you talkin' about?"

"Daddy," Nelda said, taking a step back towards him. "It's probably the best press the Bastards could ever get, and you can't pass up good press." She grinned. "You can buy it, in this case, and that's what we've done. You just have to write a check."

He huffed out a sigh. "How much?"

"Grand. Cheap if you ask me. That's eight people and includes meals. Come *on*." Message delivered, she clearly had enough of his slowness because she turned to run through the parked bikes, stopping here and there to speak to someone she knew.

"Like father—" Mudd's laughter wasn't hidden, not even a bit, and Retro scowled at his best friend.

"Like daughter. I know, I know." He sat up and Trina removed the helmet, then the tie that held his hair back, fluffing it around his head much as Nelda had done her own. "And she ain't wrong. A thousand dollars is cheap to get in on a press release like this will have. We should look into what we can do back in Bama."

"Ayeap, already thought of that." Mudd gave a wave and walked away, headed towards a clot of bikers nearby.

"She's very smart." The bike shifted as Trina climbed off. "You should be proud that she thought about what it could mean to have the club's name on a table at this event."

"Oh, yeah. I'm not blind to my daughter's traits. She thinks around corners, too, not bound by any rigid box like other folks. I *am* proud of her." He smiled and held out his arms. "Proud of her very hereditary traits of intelligence and sweetness. That's what you'll have to look forward to in our kids, baby. Now come here and give me a kiss before we go in and you get all shy and shit."

Moving towards him, she said softly, voice lifting in a question at the end of the single word. "Kids?"

"Kid or kids, we'll take what we get, right?" He wrapped her up, arms banding across her back low and high, fingers tangled in her hair as he tipped her head back. "Meant to be."

"You are just…" She sighed and laughed quietly. "Something else, Retro. I kinda like you."

He kissed her hard and fast, stealing the laughter from her lips in the way that made her turn to jelly in his arms, knees weak and he held her up, would always be there to hold her up. His belly rolled and chest got tight as he thought, *Meant to be.* Lips working against her mouth, plucking, caressing, he took and took, and as she always did Trina gave to him, anything he wanted he could have, and he knew it. He eased back, slowed them both down, leaving her gasping his name along with air. Then he kissed her again, tongue sliding alongside hers in a hot glide because he loved that look on her. Dazed and more than a little drunk just from the taste of his mouth.

"I fuckin' love you." He paused a moment, then asked, "You want my name? Would you take it if I offered it to you?" Trina stared up, blinking through a sheen of wet. "You want that?" She nodded. "Wanda signed the papers day before yesterday. They were filed today. By Monday I'll be free to offer you that. If you want it."

She breathed in, then out slowly. Gaze fixed on his face, she looked between his eyes, back and forth as she gauged his seriousness. Then just as slowly, she told him, "I want it."

"Then we'll do it." He kissed her again, soft and slow, a confirmation rather than a conflagration. "We'll do it."

"How did we get here?" She leaned against him, cheek pressed tight to his chest.

"Well, we rode my bike—" He paused when she lightly smacked his side with the flat of her palm. "From the back hallway of a strip club, to today it's not been easy. But when a body recognizes the other half of their soul, they'll turn over every brick and open every door to get what they need. I needed you, baby. Needed you in a way you may not still understand. That's how we got here and the ride—" He lifted her, loving how she instinctively wrapped her legs around his waist, owning her place with him and giving him what he needed by her immediate acceptance of what he did, how he was. "—ain't over with." He rested his forehead against hers. "Keep ridin' with me, baby. Yeah? Keep ridin'."

"You want that?" He studied her for a moment, then realized she was going back to his words about a joining in the government's eyes, something her family could understand tying them together. "You want me to be yours?"

"Woman, you're already mine in all the ways that matter to me. But if you want my name, if you want to say words and exchange rings, then by God, I'll get you what you want. What you need." He gave her ass a squeeze with both hands, loving the grin on her face even as she squealed. "You're mine. That's what I need. You with my name? That's something I'd like. Mr. and Mrs. Rogers. Sounds like my old man and Ma, but I wouldn't mind it one bit. You're mine." He shook his head and kissed her gently, a press and slide and then he was staring into her eyes again, seeing more of that sweet wet there. "I'll tell the world."

Hand in hand, they strode towards the building, Trina following along as he paused amidst the various groups of men where he caught sight of a face he knew. They made their slow way inside, stopping at the door to find out from a frazzled lady with a clipboard the Bastards' sponsored table was up near the low stage at the far end of the room.

A tug at his arm was accompanied by a soft, "Oh hush." He recognized Crissy's voice as he turned, so wasn't surprised to find her standing next to him. "Trina, hi." He wrapped an arm around Crissy's shoulders and gave her a sideways hug. She asked with a smile, "You find your table, Retro?"

"Yeah, got a general idea where it'll be." He glanced up at the man standing behind her and felt a jarring rush of recognition that froze him in his tracks. Eyes, mouth, nose, even the tentative smile was everything he'd never expected to see again in this life. Retro stared because having a thought about something was entirely different from experiencing it in person. Knowing in an analytical way couldn't compare to the gut-punch of recognizing Clara's features on the face of a man just old enough to be her son. Which made the man Retro's son, too.

Last summer, Po'Boy had inserted himself into a situation so unexpected it couldn't have been predicted. He'd been searching for a source to tell him about cartel movements, and wound up out in the boonies on a highway in Tangipahoa Parish, sitting his bike on the gravel parking lot of a tiny gas station. Retro had been on the phone with him sorting out details of what the man needed and pairing that with what he'd be willing to pay when Retro had heard the unmistakable sound of gunfire just before the line went dead.

He'd had a general location, and quickly gotten Mudd working on trying to find out more from the slim line of info they had when the local Louisiana news stations started playing breaking news about a robbery gone bad at a tiny little gas station down Tangipahoa way, far enough off the beaten path to be a sure match with whatever Po'Boy had gotten himself tangled up into. Eight people dead, no talk of a big, black leather-wearing biker, though, so when Retro had called Twisted, he'd been able to offer that info at least.

One of the dead had been a woman. Bystanders talked about the shooters taking a child from her still warm arms, leaving after loading the little girl into a van the spectators collectively described as white, tan, black, cargo, passenger, rental, with plates from Texas and Louisiana. In other words, their eyewitness reports weren't worth a lick of salt, no matter they'd been standing not fifty yards away from the action. Retro could still dredge up the anger in his gut at the idea of a tiny child, a little girl named Abigail, being caught up in that kind of carnage, taken from everything she knew and thrust into a world where people wouldn't be nice, wouldn't care if she was afraid, wouldn't give that first shit about her.

Then his phone had lit up again with Po'Boy on the other end, asking for help, his voice so raw and stripped bare that Retro nearly didn't recognize him. He'd followed and killed the kidnappers, retrieving the girl but even in the midst of everything, having enough wherewithal to know he couldn't just return her back to the scene. He'd asked and Retro had delivered, linking him up with a woman Retro trusted to do the right thing for enough money, and he'd supplied that piece of the picture, never telling Po'Boy how much it had cost to buy his continued freedom and the child's safety.

Baby Abigail's father had been waiting at the hospital, having been called there to identify his wife's body, staying in place, thankfully, so it hadn't been hard to get the child back into his hands.

About a month later, Retro had looked up the father, hoping to find only good things in Abigail's life. The shock from what he discovered had been a tipping point for so much of the recent changes in his world, because even from the grainy distance shots he'd been able to acquire, the stamp of Clara's features on the man's face had been unmistakable.

He'd set aside the hurt and surprise, and done what he always did— started looking for more info. The man's last name tracked back to Clara's sister, her married name was his surname, and he was listed as her only child. A lone heir to his grandfather's fortune and significant holdings, and suddenly everything had made perfect sense.

So many things had fallen into place. Petr Volkov's words, so odd at the time, perfectly making sense when put into context. No wonder he hadn't wanted to terminate Clara's care, if he'd known she was pregnant. If Retro had known too, his choices would have been different. The proof of that standing here, not five feet away when Retro had expected to go his whole life without meeting this piece of Clara and his lives.

The ring under his shirt, something that Trina had turned back into a sweet memorial for the only other woman he'd ever loved, burned against his skin, hotter and hotter until Retro glanced down, surprised to find only unmarked fabric, having expected to see a charred circle in the material, baring everything.

"Retro?" From the look on Crissy's face, it wasn't the first time she'd said his name and he blinked, looking again at the son he'd never expected, had put aside even after learning of him, because what could Retro tell him at this point? Nothing good, and he wouldn't be the reason for any bad happening to this man. He'd already lost his mother and wife to his grandfather's business, nearly his daughter—*my granddaughter*— because when Retro and Mudd looked deeper, they'd found distinct trails that led straight back to the past. Bile rose in Retro's throat and he swallowed hard, desperate to keep from showing so much. Crissy frowned. "Retro, is everything okay?"

"Yeah." He swallowed again, Trina's fingers moving in his grip. She was rubbing his hand between both hers, and he knew it was because he had gone cold at the way the past could stalk into the current day, just waltzing in like nothing was amiss, leaving everything turned on its head. "Yeah, I'm fine. What's up?"

Crissy studied him, and he was struck for a moment at how much she complimented Penny in that way, hers a shrewd observation that never boded well for anyone. "I wanted to introduce you to one of my firm's clients, Mr. Pierre Landry. Pierre runs a youth outreach shelter in Ponchatoula, and they're one of the beneficiaries of the fundraiser tonight. I designed the banners." She pointed past him and he twisted to look, but Trina's eyes captured his instead, concerned and caring, and so very not Clara's, would never be Clara's and right now that killed in a way that felt like something inside him was dying.

"Pleased to meet 'cha." He rushed out the greeting, not breaking Trina's gaze. "I gotta go back outside, baby." She lifted her chin slightly, still not looking away. "I'll be back in when I'm back, yeah?" That was as unsubtle an order to not come looking for him as he could issue without laying it out for her and Trina didn't mistake him. The color fled her face and she looked like he'd slapped her. Behind him Crissy was murmuring something, telling the man standing beside her a tidbit about Retro and he found himself straining to hear Landry's response, pissed as fuck when they walked away and he was standing there holding Trina's hand. "I'll be back, okay?" He licked his lips, suddenly unsure of himself in a way he'd never been. "I'll be back."

"Can you tell me what that was?" Pitched soft and low, her voice didn't carry past his ears, but still felt like an unwelcome bullhorn calling him to task.

"Trina—" He cut himself off before he could say anything he couldn't take back. Pain still had his gut in a rolling knot, but she'd done nothing to deserve the rough side of his tongue. "Can I tell you later? I will, swear. Just later." *Please, give me this.*

She nodded, fingers tightening on his. "Thank you." Breathed out softer than a whisper, he read her lips as much as heard what sounded like a prayer.

Clara wouldn't have questioned him, wouldn't have stopped him from doing whatever he'd wanted.

She ain't Clara.

Her fingers loosened and suddenly he was the one holding on in desperation, surprising her, because she was about to step away, step back and give him that space he'd begged for. He was holding on because he suddenly didn't want her to give it, wouldn't take it if she handed it over, wanted to keep his place at her side because what they had together mattered so much more than any shadows from the past.

She firmed her jaw and he thought in that moment that she'd never been more beautiful, and he'd never loved her as much.

She ain't anyone but herself.

"I thought you were headed outside." She'd stopped retreating, the rebound from her failed escape bringing her closer to him until she put up a hand to steady herself against his arm. Heat flicked under her touch and his cock woke up, fattening against his hip. "Retro?"

The question in her voice made her sound unsure of herself, and he'd done that. *God, I'm a fucking asshole.* Taken the confident woman he'd been watching claw her way out of the well where she'd been shoved by men who didn't give a shit about her feelings, the same one who'd answered his question outside with such a sense of rightness, and turned her into the girl he'd first met, who believed her lot in life was to take whatever shit someone dumped on her because that was the best she could expect. Someone who was now questioning him and his devotion to her, hell, questioning herself, because he'd seen a ghost from his past and had reacted badly.

"Changed my mind." His voice was rough and scraped up his throat, a bitter coat of regret stinging with every word. "I'm stayin' right here, with you."

***

Trina

"Okay." She dipped her chin, but he captured it between thumb and finger, lifting and holding it so he could stare into her eyes. Even with that she tried to avoid, looking down and to the side.

"That man, that Landry fella?" Her gaze flicked back to his, and she trembled under his touch, because whatever this was, she knew instinctively that this was big. So big. Bigger than meeting his kids and friends, because this had been unexpected and he'd reacted to being blindsided. Not something a man like him would ever appreciate, but it had thrown him even more off-stride. "I told you about Clara." Without care for whatever audience they had, he was going to tell her now, instead of waiting.

He'd been about to flee, she'd known it in her gut, the fear and anger and pain swapping places on his expression demanding an outlet he wouldn't find here. He'd been about to flee and for an instant, she'd wondered if he'd come back for her, if she were worth it, whatever this was costing him.

"You want to wait, I can listen later, Retro. I'm good."

"Well, I'm not. I'm not good, and I want you to know because you asked what that was, and I got answers. They aren't good answers, but I got 'em." He squared up to her, shoulders and hips in alignment as he prepared for the pain whatever he was going to tell her would cost him. The ring and chain under his shirt moved and she couldn't tear her eyes away from that, knowing this had to do with her, somehow. The woman he'd loved, and lost, because he'd told her everything. Told her about their love, and that had nearly been too hard to listen through, but she'd done it because he'd needed her to know. Walked her through Clara's final days and hours, his argument with her father, and through the years between that and meeting Wanda's father, making an agreement that would forever change his life. Clara had been in this room tonight, in some fashion, and it had wounded him.

Trina copied his movements, crowding close to him. Thighs to thigh, belly to belly, she linked her fingers through his belt loops to hold him against her. "Okay. Tell me." Eyes closed, she waited, unprepared for the gentle caress of his lips against her forehead.

"God, I don't deserve you." That would likely be the only acknowledgment of what had been on the line a moment ago, but it didn't matter so she let it slide away without remarking that she felt the same, only opposite. "Pierre Landry is the spittin' image of Clara. He's the right age, and Landry was her sister's husband, but that man, that Pierre, he don't look nothin' like Clara's sister. He's Clara made flesh again. His wife was killed in a botched cartel move last year, daughter kidnapped from where she'd fallen, dying. He got his girl back but lost his wife. Baby, I did the math when I saw a picture of him then. He's my kid, I know it. Mine, but not, because all the paperwork makes it so he wouldn't know. I decided I couldn't tell him. Couldn't tear apart that family built on the loss of Clara. And so I didn't. I kept my distance, didn't come around to catch sight of him, figuring out of sight out of mind would work. But knowing that he was out there, that his little girl was out there, that part of me and Clara walked the earth didn't stop tearing me up inside."

"Then you met me."

He nodded. "Then we met, and I fell for you. Fell hard, and found that the teenie-bopper love I'd felt for Clara weren't nothing when held up against the real thing. Met and was consumed in a fast minute, and didn't have another thought about Landry or baby Abigail. And just now?" He laughed, but the sound was filled with broken shards of hurt, tough to listen to and she suspected more difficult to voice.

"You didn't expect to see him, have him shoved in your face, not being able to tell him who you were." He stared at her, the crinkles around his eyes taut with pain. "So you were going to go off and lick your wounds." The longer she thought about it, the angrier she became. "Didn't think to ask for help or for someone to talk to. You were going to just shut me out and go out there, and maybe get on the bike and ride, let the wind blow it out of your head." He didn't argue, just stared at her, looking lost. "You don't get to do that anymore. You and me"—she poked his chest—"we're in this together. You told me so, and you told me you don't lie to people you love." She poked his chest again and he lifted a hand to capture her finger. "Do you love me?" He stood there staring at her, his steady breathing speeding up, chest rising and falling faster. "Well, do you? Because if you don't, then everything you've said to me is suspect, and if I *know* that, I can deal." Mouth dry, she repeated her words, because he needed to understand. Out of everything, he needed to know this. "If you don't love me, then I can deal. But if you love me, and you were still going to just try to leave, because that was less painful than standing beside me, then I can't deal. I can't deal, Retro. I'm so deep in this now. If you aren't with me, then I need to get out. If you aren't in this, then I'm the one who needs to run away. So, do you love me?"

He sighed heavily, then bent and put his forehead against hers, eyes closed. Another slow, bottomless exhalation and he took the hand in his grip and flattened it against his chest, over his heart, and she felt it pounding crazily inside him, a direct contradiction to his steady breathing. "I love you so fucking much."

"Were you going to leave?"

"Not after I looked at you. I couldn't, baby. I saw you and saw where I want to be. Not after I looked at you." His eyes opened and blinked, so close she could see the way his pupils changed, contracting as he focused on her. "You're it for me."

"That's the right answer," she whispered, and his mouth curved lopsidedly, the pain not quite gone yet. "You matter so much to me." She remembered his words about wanting to know, needing to know, because he hadn't felt treasured in a long time. "Jerry Rogers, how I love you." The smile faded away, and in its place came an expression she knew she'd do anything to have him keep giving her. Adoration and peace and hope and relief. A bone-shattering relief that told her how deep it ran for him.

***

Retro

"How the fuck did I get so goddamned lucky?"

He didn't expect an answer to his muttered question, so the laughter took him off-guard. Retro looked around to where Twisted and Ace stood, Wrench to the side, Po'Boy standing behind him.

"What?"

"Some men have shit luck all their lives, and never dig outta that ditch." Twisted shook his head and pointed to where Retro had been looking, where Nelda sat beside Trina, both sets of eyes wide as they listened to whatever story Penny was spinning. While he watched, Nelda reached out and gripped Trina's hand, clutching tight and Trina slipped an arm around his girl's shoulders, neither taking their gaze off Penny who was now laughing so hard she was cradling her belly in both arms.

"And some men get shit luck and then figure out how to turn that around, and make it good again." Po'Boy laughed and then huffed out a grunt when Wrench hit him in the ribs with an elbow. "What? I was talkin' about myself, baby."

Retro rolled his eyes. "I have a question for you all."

"Oh, man. The famed Retro's askin' for insight and wisdom from someone outside his inner circle? Say it ain't so." Wildman had walked up to stand beside him and Retro wasn't alone when he twisted to stare at the man. "Yeah, that's right. I'm offering up my wisdom on demand. You tell me what you wanna know, and I'll get it for ya."

"Wildman, you do understand you don't bear my colors, right?" Retro shook his head. "And I wasn't asking business. I have a personal question."

"IMC stands with the Bastards." Wildman stared at him. "And you got a personal question? Like does it burn when you pee?"

"Are you fuckin' kidding me?"

"Yes, I am." Wildman gave him a smile and he stared at him. "But I'm also a good set of ears if you have questions I can answer."

He turned to glare at Twisted who held up both hands, already rejecting whatever Retro had been about to say. He huffed out a chuckle and shook his head, laughing louder. "You are ridiculous."

"Dude, I've been called worse," Po'Boy put in. "I think ridiculous isn't half bad, patch. You're doin' a little bit of all right for yourself." He held up a fist and Wildman reached across Retro to give him a bump, the two of them doing some complicated tween-move blowup at the end.

"Do they ever stop?" he asked Twisted, but Ace laughed and answered.

"Not to my knowledge. I've watched for a while now, and they just play off each other, getting more and more torqued up."

"Ridiculous."

"What'd you want to know?" Wrench tipped his head to the side and waited.

"If you knew something about a person, and you knew it could possibly damage their lives if you informed them, and there was no danger in leaving it a secret...would you sit on the information and keep it close, or tell them and hope the fallout didn't break them?" He looked from face to face around the circle of men. "If you would change their lives without knowing it would be better or worse, should you?"

"No."

"Yes."

He looked back and forth between Po'Boy and Twisted, not surprised they were the first to jump into the breach. "Yeah, that solves everything."

"No," Po'Boy shook his head adamantly. "You don't have the right to impact somebody like that. Just because you can, doesn't mean you should. Didn't anyone else watch that dinosaur movie?"

"I'm on the opposite side from you this time, brother." Twisted stared at Po'Boy for a moment, then turned to Retro. "Does not saying something have a price?" Retro drew his mouth to the side and Twisted understood. "Then I'm changing my answer. If there's no cost, then there's no clear benefit, either. That's not a win-win, that's a losing proposition. Better off keeping your yap shut and letting it go."

"And if I cain't let it go?"

"Then we'll back your play, no matter what." Twisted reached out and grabbed his forearm, gripping tight as he said loudly, uncaring of the ears listening, "Incoherent stands with the Bastards, until the earthball stops circlin' the sun. You need us, you got us."

Wrench elbowed Po'Boy again, then took a step forwards. "I didn't answer, because I think I know what you're considering. There's no gain, brother. No gain, and once you open that door, you can't close it again. Look over at that table and see what you'd risk. Look at her and then you decide. But, like IMC, if you need us, the CoBos have your back. Count on it."

"I'm so fuckin' blessed."

He'd forgotten about Wildman until that moment, startled when a heavy hand fell on his shoulder, and a rumbling voice in his ear told him exactly what he'd needed to know. "You're blessed, that's true. Because you see your woman and your girl, you heard your son's voice last night, and that was something to witness, that look of joy you wore. If in your hypothetical situation sayin' something puts one iota of that at risk, then don't do it, brother. Don't do it. You hold onto what you've got, hold on and hold tight, because you are blessed."

Chapter Ten

Retro

"New business?" Twisted sat positioned at the middle of the table, an intentional placement, and Retro knew what it meant. His grandfather had been the club's founder, and the chair still used by the president had supported that man for decades, taking up the same slot all that time. Neither at the head nor the foot, Jimbo had ruled from alongside his men, the same trait Twisted shared, and a memory of that grandfather he continued to honor.

"Ayeap." Po'Boy pushed back from the table slowly, climbing to his feet with effort. Every movement was laced through with sorrow, and Retro understood. "I have something to bring to the floor."

Twisted stared at Po'Boy for so long Retro felt uncomfortable, the air in the room growing heavier with each breath, each blink of an eye, each ticking of the clock on the wall. Twisted's fingers tightened around the baseball bat used as a gavel in this clubhouse, fat end wrapped with a bicycle chain stained red with something Retro felt strongly wasn't rust, but did not dare ask. Didn't dare ask about the symbolism of the bat, either, even if he knew it would eat at him until he knew. Of all the outside people on the clubhouse compound property this morning, Retro and only Retro had been invited into the closed-door officers-only church they'd all known was coming.

What he'd told his men still stood—he believed this to be a political decision by Twisted to have an independent observer at a historic event. Only now, it looked to be stalled because the national president was not acknowledging the request from the national VP, a child's ploy of "if I ignore it long enough it will go away" that Retro knew wouldn't work.

Finally, fucking finally, after what felt like two lifetimes of Retro holding his breath out of fear of tipping some unseen scales out of balance, Twisted shifted in his chair and without dropping his gaze, nodded once, then a second time. Then he spoke, his voice somehow sounding like a youthful version of himself while still holding the vibrating timbre of age.

"Granted. Just—" He shoved his chair away from the table and stood with such violence the chair nearly toppled over, righting itself finally, four legs rattling on the floor. He lifted the bat, moving with intent and Retro found himself holding his breath again, because this wasn't how this was supposed to go.

Retro wasn't the only one who moved involuntarily to stop Twisted, to impede his progress, to protect Po'Boy from what was coming, all while Po'Boy stood tall, unflinching, gaze locked on the man who'd been his ride-or-die for decades.

Twisted made it to the end of the table, where Catfish had pushed his chair back and looked prepared to stand, to interfere, to somehow stop this train of reaction no one had expected—and turned the other direction, towards a corner where he hung the bat on a rack specific for the purpose, the wood below where the handle affixed was scraped and torn from the chain dragging against it. He turned back and Retro pulled in a breath, hearing movement throughout the room as men settled.

Seat reclaimed, he didn't push back under the table, keeping his distance as he stared at Po'Boy for another moment, then growled out a painful-sounding, "Granted, brother."

What transpired next seemed almost anticlimactic after that, the fading drop from such a huge adrenaline rush giving Retro cottonmouth as he listened to Po'Boy's reasoning on patching out, the focus completely on the impact to the Incoherent club, as it should be. Care of the CoBos would happen later, and on a different timeline, in a different clubhouse, one where Po'Boy would never have a place of power such as he had here. Po'Boy was eloquent and wise, and that alone reinforced what the IMC would be losing in his move, and Retro hoped Ace knew what he'd gained today.

At the end of the meeting, Po'Boy's vest was locked away, folded with respect and placed in a cabinet with other former members' cuts, patches left intact in a move so weighed down with unspoken hope of a someday return that Retro shook his head to witness it. But witness it he did, showing utmost deference for the changes begun at this table where he had no voice, but could bear the truth of how it went down out into the world, changing the direction of worldwide reaction ripples with his words.

Retro was the first to exit the room, as was proper, last in first out, and normally that would fall to the lowest ranking member or officer in the meeting. Today that person was him, which meant he had a prime position to witness the rank and file reaction to Po'Boy walking out naked, not even a vest to cover his back. He understood, and knew Po'Boy did, too, the why of what Twisted had chosen to do. Still, he wondered how the resolve would hold when he had to shoulder stiff new leather along with a bright and shiny patch, both shouting to anyone with eyes to see that he'd made a life shift along the way.

Wrench stood across the room, Crissy at his side, and Retro wondered at the wisdom of having the two partners at an event where Po'Boy would always remember with grief. Then he felt fingers at his belt and lifted an arm, letting Trina snuggle up close, cheek to his chest, and he understood. Even if Po'Boy didn't traverse the space towards where they stood immediately, when he needed them—and he would eventually— they'd be there to catch him.

"Kids excited about heading home?" The rough, unused tenor of his voice was a surprise, but then he realized he'd just sat through a four-hour meeting in strict silence, these the first words he'd spoken since he'd left her in bed at Twisted and Penny's this morning, a kiss to her shoulder waking her for a quick goodbye. "You get somethin' to eat, baby?"

"Yes, and yes," she responded, and he looked down to see her studying his face. "Are you okay? You sound...subdued."

"Historic shit going down here today. Something to be writ in the annals for generations years from now to read about. It's heady, being asked to be here, and gut-wrenching at the same time, because there stands a man I've mentored, who I love like a brother, and I'm watching him cut away a big part of himself to do this thing." He lifted his head and looked out across the room to where Po'Boy stood at the bar, wallet out and money in hand to buy a round of drinks for every IMC member. Now a privilege of a trusted friend, not the right of a club officer or member to have the cost put on his tab to settle up at the end of the month. "A lot of changes happening right before my eyes." Cash on the barrelhead for Po'Boy here, and a non-voting membership in store for him at the CoBos house, keeping him suspended in a limbo he suspected wouldn't sit well with the man for long. "Just a lot to take in, you know?"

"Oh, I think I can relate." She had laughter in her voice and he glanced back down to see her smiling up at him. "As someone who has turned her entire life over, tumbling all the known things around and discarding a lot of it in favor of taking on new challenges, I think I can safely say I know a little bit of what you're saying."

Fuck, she's right. "I'll make it worth it to you." He liked how her eyes softened at his words. "Fuckin' promise you now, you'll never regret a bit of it, Trina. I'll make it worth everything."

"It already is." Trina reached up, wrapped her fingers around the back of his neck and pulled his mouth down to meet hers and Retro let her, giving way to her determination and need to reassure him in her own way. He let her control the kiss for a moment, but the instant she sucked on his tongue, it was on, and he ravaged her, biting and sucking, stroking and fucking her mouth, eating down every groan and sigh she gave him, currency to salve his worries, because she gave him everything. *As she always does.* When he'd worked them both up nearly to the point of no return, body pressed tight to the wall, hands pinned over her head, he slowed things down, ignoring the pounding of blood through his rigid cock.

"Retro," she whispered, and he heard it in her voice. That need and trust he stirred in her, all mixed through with love, and that settled him even more.

"Right there with you, baby." He mouthed along her jaw and then the sleek skin of her neck called him, so he kissed and licked until her flesh was reddened in response to his unshaven face. "Fuck, you're gorgeous." He pulled back and stared into her kiss-addled face, bending to press his lips to the tip of her nose. "Probably shouldn't fuck you up against the wall of this place."

"You keep talking about wall sex." She pretended to pout and he laughed softly. "Just sayin', you're gonna have to pay up again someday."

"Y'all about done with the PDA of the year?" Twisted's amused voice whipped through the air and for a brief moment, Retro considered telling him about the things he'd missed happening by not being a Bama Bastard and gaining entry to the closed, club-only nights at the Birmingham clubhouse, but Trina got there before him.

"Not half the show we put on the other night, but sure, Twisted, if you need my man, I can give him to you for a few." He loved how she owned the kink she'd discovered, knew part of that was his acceptance and enjoyment of it, and part was that Rhonda, a woman she liked and respected, shared the same excitement.

"Oh, Lord." Wrench coughed and choked from behind him and when Retro turned to look, the man's face was bright red. "I'm not sure I wanna know." He cleared his throat. "You must be Trina."

Retro made sure she was steady on her feet before he moved to the side and Trina offered a bright smile through rouged and puffy lips. *Jesus, she's something else.* "I am. And you have got to be Wrench. I wanted to meet you last night, but the tables were too far apart. Crissy's got lots of stories about you, though, so I feel like I already know you." Wrench's neck turned even redder and Retro laughed. "So many stories." Trina pushed a knowing smirk into her words that had the man dropping his head and muttering a soft, "Fuck me."

"Wrench, well met, brother." Retro offered his hand as he shifted away from Trina, smiling as he felt her fingers drift down his back, tracing muscles through his shirt until she got to his belt where she latched on. "Good to see you."

Wrench pulled him in for a one-armed clinch, and Retro grunted at the power behind the pounding fist on his back. "I'm glad you were here for this, brother." Wrench left a hand on Retro's shoulder when they pulled back. "I didn't get a chance to say it last night, but congratulations on ridding yourself and your club of a poison apple. Good riddance, I say."

"Interesting how many of my friends have the same words in their mouth these days, but never once offered that advice through the years." He lifted his chin, shaking his hair back. "Makes a man wonder how many other bits of wisdom they hold close to the vest, not sharin' until after the fact."

"You know as well as I do that a man's woman is his problem to solve. Not sayin' something about the person warmin' his bed is just keepin' the peace." Twisted lifted one shoulder and finished, "Bein' a good brother is bein' there to listen if it's needed, support when the shit hits the fan, and then commiseratin' when it's in the past."

"And we were all prayin' for the day when that particular fit hit the shan, that's for sure certain." Po'Boy walked up behind Wrench, Crissy under his arm. She transferred seamlessly to Wrench, and Po'Boy fit himself to their backs, draping an arm over either shoulder. "And the fact you picked a goddamned good woman for yourself, because we know the she-bitch weren't no pick of yours, means we don't have to bite our tongues no more. I can say right out that she's sexy as fuck, and I do appreciate a fine piece of ass, so I like her for you. Keep her, and keep bringin' her around." He jumped slightly and frowned down at Wrench. "The fuck you doin' pinchin' me, motherfucker?"

"Some things you don't say when the lady is present, babe." Retro watched Po'Boy's face as the endearment rolled off Wrench's tongue, saw the flash of private pleasure and grinned.

"See? Everybody's got something good to say about you." Retro pulled free from Twisted's grip and brought Trina up beside him. "Told you there wasn't anything to worry about. You won them over with your beauty alone."

"And she's smart and funny," Crissy put in with a grin. "Plus gorgeous as hell, because my man's not wrong."

"True that, she's not hard on the eyes." Wildman joined their circle and Retro dropped his chin, glancing at Trina to find her smiling broadly, laughing.

Perfect for me.

***

Trina

Retro tensed under her hands as they turned into the driveway, and Trina leaned forwards to tell him, "They're going to love it." She knew he was anxious for the kids to settle into the house quickly, wanting to give them a home like they'd never had before, carrying over the good feelings of their time spent on vacation with friends to the house they'd be living in going forwards.

She had been astonished at how easily his children had accepted her. Not just accepted, but folded her into their family as if she'd always been there, Nelda casually passing her a brush and asking for help putting her hair into a ponytail, Jimmy flopping onto the couch next to where she'd been talking to Penny so he could get her opinion on some kind of sporting equipment she'd had no idea about, and Saya seeking her out to crawl into whatever chair or seat she occupied, squeezing himself into space that didn't exist until he was wedged in beside her.

Each time it happened, every instance Retro witnessed, she'd fallen a little more in love with him because of the way his face softened, his eyes brightened, and that deep and boundless love for his kids shone straight out of him.

She had a feeling she'd passed some kind of test with his friends, too, because after the big meeting at Twisted's clubhouse, everyone, including the BBMC men, had been more deferential to her than before. And that was saying something with Retro's men, because they'd already treated her as if she mattered.

Everything was settling into place, pieces sweetly slotting into position as their lives tangled more and more every day. She couldn't imagine anything else that would give her such pleasure and satisfaction than seeing Retro smile at her like he had last night, still inside her, intimately connected. And the expression on his face told her he felt it too, soul-deep and strong. *Fast doesn't mean shallow.* She remembered the story

Penny had told her about meeting Twisted, and in the space of a single night, they'd fallen for the other. It might have taken weeks for them to come together, but she'd said once their souls had touched, they'd known there wouldn't ever be another.

That's how I feel.

They rounded the corner of the house and Retro lifted a fist into the air, their speed slackening. A car sat sideways in front of the garage, a recent model of an expensive sedan. Behind the wheel sat a woman, and from the descriptions and shared genetics of the kids, she knew this had to be Wanda. Retro was even tenser under her hands and she leaned up, crouching on the pegs of the bike to get her head next to his helmet. Retro's features were taut, strained.

He motioned the other bikes to pull to a stop along the edges of the driveway, then idled up to park in front of the back door, away from the car. As if there was nothing different about this stop than any other, he heeled down the kickstand and then climbed off the bike before turning to Trina and fussing with the strap of her helmet, loosening and then removing it to hang from the handlebars. His own dangled from the opposite side, and then he was all she could see, eyes staring at her.

"I'm going to deal with her. You don't have to." He kissed her, fast, hard, his caress holding back the anger she felt rolling off him. "She doesn't touch you."

"I love you." She gave him the only thing she could think of and, for an instant, his eyes warmed, then the car door slammed behind him.

"What the hell, Jerry? What the hell?" Retro's eyes closed and he breathed deeply before he turned to face Wanda. "What the actual hell?"

"You want to see the kids, you call me and set it up. I'll work with your schedule, but it will be when it suits the kids and me." Feet firmly planted, he stood in front of the bike, arms folded over his chest. Trina glanced around to see the bikes the kids rode on were staged farther down the driveway than she'd expected, giving her some hope they might be spared hearing the argument Wanda was clearly thirsting for. Then that hope was thrown aside when Nelda bailed off Mudd's bike, helmet tossed to the grass as she came storming up to the house. "What you don't do is show up here uninvited." Trina swung her leg over the bike and stood, earning only a haughty glance from Wanda.

"You sent the papers to Daddy's house, knowing how much it would embarrass him. You even used Gaetano as your delivery boy, knowing how much that would embarrass me." She tossed her head. "That's a new low, even for you. I would think I've earned a few moments of your precious time."

Nelda had made it past the line of idling bikes, and the look on her face was filled with such rage Trina flinched. She took several fast steps angled away from the bike, intending to intercept the girl before she did whatever it was she had in her head to do, because no matter if it was wrong or right, nothing that happened in this moment would end well.

Retro spoke, his voice intense and pitched to carry. "You'd think wrong, then. I'm done with you outside of arranging visitation, so my kids can see their mother." Trina took her eyes off Nelda for a moment to look at him, seeing every muscle in his back was bunched, flexing as he moved. He must have heard Nelda running because he turned and stretched out an arm just in time, pulling her to a stop in front of him just as Trina reached for her, too. "Nelda, no, honey."

"Why are you here?" Nelda's shout was louder than Wanda's had been, voice filled with pain. "Why are you here now, huh?"

"Nelda," Retro warned, but Wanda spoke over him.

Wanda sneered as she said, "It's none of your business, Nelda. Go get your brother and get into the car. Go get Jimmy."

"They ain't goin' anywhere with you right now." Adamant and clipped, Retro's words dropped into the space between them just as Nelda's shout barreled over anything Wanda might have been going to say.

"I'm never going with you. Neither are Jimmy and Saya." Nelda scoffed. "Not that you'd want Saya, anyway, but you can't do this, Mom. You can't show up out of nowhere and decide you want to be a mother again. That's not how any of this works."

"Nelda, get in the car." It was as if Wanda hadn't heard anything said so far and Trina could see Retro winding up to deliver what would no doubt be a blistering set-down to the woman. Of course, as far as she could see, Wanda would deserve every word, but she couldn't let him do that with his kids within earshot. Couldn't let Wanda ruin the homecoming and have this taint the kids' view of the house.

"You don't know me." She stepped forwards, shifting to stand slightly in front of Retro and Nelda. "But I'm Katrina."

"Don't want to know you." Wanda flipped her hand, fingers waggling. "Go back and crawl under whatever rock you climbed out from under, honey. This is for the grownups to deal with."

Years of dealing with her mother's irrational behavior, balanced by Dolph's brash and rough exterior had Trina uniquely positioned to handle Wanda and she smiled inside, knowing Retro was about to see something he hadn't expected.

"No, this does impact me, because when you drive away in your pretty car, it'll be me who helps pick up the pieces. I've heard about you, your antics, the way you treat people." Trina propped her fists on both hips, lifted her chin and used her most critical expression to look down her nose at Wanda. "Heard my fill from the women in the club you treated badly. I've also seen how sweet Retro is when I do something, anything for him. That tells me that you weren't part of a partnership, because that would have implied an equal investment in making things work. So he's right, you don't get to roll up here and make any demands at all. That's just not going to happen. You're a terrible person, Wanda. Such a terrible person, your ex couldn't wait to be rid of you. The women and men in the club were glad you were gone, with no reason to come back. Heck, word of the divorce made it as far as Louisiana, and I got to listen to a dozen people telling me one Wanda the Witch story after another, and let me tell you, not a single one of them was flattering. Look at your daughter, Wanda. Is this really the image you want her to have of her mother?"

"You're divorced now?" Nelda twisted in place to stare up at Retro. "Custody and everything?" He looked down at her for a moment, then nodded quickly, as if get it over with. "So we really don't have to go with her?"

"No, baby, you don't." Nelda shifted and he loosened his grip, stepping back as she turned fully, expression hopeful and looking so young and innocent it made Trina's heart skip a beat. *She's her daddy's girl.* "Not if you don't want to."

It took a moment, a long breath where all three of them ignored Wanda sputtering in the background, father and daughter communing in silence, and Trina taking it all in, knowing that if she and Retro had children, they would get this, too. Finally, unspoken communication done, Nelda asked, "In that case, can I have the keys? I want to take Saya in and let him see his room."

Voice sharp, still visibly angry at his ex, Retro asked, "Where are the boys?"

"Still on bikes out front. I told Mudd to keep them running, so they wouldn't hear anything." *She's so smart.* "I'll take them in the front door, and we'll go from there." Retro dug in his pocket and handed her a set of keys he must have prepared before they even left for Louisiana, because they were on a gaudy unicorn keychain, covered in sparkles. "Oh. My. Gawd. Daddy, have I told you I love you?"

"Not lately, but I'll remind you the next time you're complainin' about me." He reached out and gripped her shoulders and gave her a tiny shake.

"I love you, Nelda girl. So fuckin' much." She stretched up and kissed his cheek, then stepped around him and without looking back at her mother even once, dashed away to the drive, and around the house.

Trina looked up to see Wanda approaching Retro, and the anger that had been simmering inside her about the woman who'd dared to do this, who didn't care about her kids enough to call them even once while they were away—and she knew because she'd overheard Retro asking each child individually, getting a negative response each time—but thought she was entitled to come here and create a scene just to ruin what Retro was building, boiled over.

"No. No you don't. You get your butt back in your car and you leave." Trina got in Wanda's face, staring her down. Up close it wasn't a pretty picture, years of anger and frustration had left their trace, deep lines bracketed the woman's mouth, and her brows were drawn together in a scowl that rivaled any of the grizzled bikers Trina had met this weekend.

"You don't have a place here. Never will if you keep this up. Because if you think those kids haven't already remarked on how nice it is to not have daily stress bubbling around them, you'd be wrong. My job as his ole lady"—she flung an arm out towards where Retro stood—"is to make his life easier. And as much as he didn't want your mess to touch me, making his life easier right now means I deal with you, so he doesn't have to. So you get your butt back into your car and you drive away. This isn't your place." An arm stretched around her shoulders and tugged her against his hard body, and she went with it, giving easily. "This has never been your place, not really. You had a chance at something so unbelievably beautiful with this man, and thank God for me you passed it up, picking anger and lies instead. Thank you for doing that, because that gave me this." She wrapped an arm around his belly, eyes on Wanda. His hand threaded through Trina's hair and cradled the back of her skull with care, holding her close.

"But your time of making his life, or the lives of his kids, or the lives of anyone around him miserable? That's over, Wanda. That's over, and you need to understand this is the only thing you'll ever take from us. This moment in time. He gave it, and Nelda gave it, and now I'm giving it. Here's your clue, go be happy. Life's a lot better that way."

"Jerry." Wanda looked beyond Trina at Retro, and screwed her face up as if she'd try crying next.

"Oh, stop it. You're being a cow. Just get back in your car and go." Trina tried to step away, but Retro's arms were bands of steel, firmly holding her in place. Wanda opened her mouth again and Trina shook her head. "No. Go. Just go."

"Jerry?" A tone of incredulity in her voice, Wanda made a final plea.

"You heard my ole lady. She wants you off her property." Humor laced his voice and Trina yanked her head around to look at him. He was smiling down at her. "And what my ole lady wants, my ole lady gets."

Heels clacked away and Trina was reminded of the real estate lady. She checked. Sure enough, Wanda's shoes were sky-high and complicated. And noisy. She glanced down at her functional black leather boots, knowing her sneakers were tucked inside her bag. Wanda slammed the car door and a moment later, the engine roared.

Trina and Retro backed up towards the bike to give the woman ample room to pull out, then she turned and watched with heart in her throat as Wanda sped down the drive, beside all the motorcycles with men seated on them.

"Well, that was interesting." Trina hadn't meant to speak, but a moment later was glad she'd blurted it out, because Retro's whole body was shaking as he laughed loud and long.

***

Retro

"Uh huh. Well, isn't that something. Thanks, Todd. What would I do without you?" Nelda's voice drifted into the kitchen where Retro stood, stirring the hash browns he was frying for breakfast. "See you when school starts." She sounded perky and entirely unlike herself, and he smiled down at the pan of potatoes. "Hey, Daddy." Her normal voice preceded a squeeze around his waist and then she was past him, headed for the refrigerator. "Smells good."

"Who's Todd?" He didn't look around, didn't have to in order to know she'd frozen in front of the fridge. The cool air swirling around his feet told him that much. "Close the fridge, honey, lettin' the chill out."

"You already know." The door closed so abruptly the jars inside rattled together. "How do you already know?"

"Don't try to con a con man, honey." He picked up tongs and used them to turn the bacon frying in a second skillet. "I've been at this game a long time."

"If you're so smart, tell me what I learned."

He smiled again, not turning around as he said. "Cheerleading tryouts are tomorrow. The senior girls, of which there are ten, want the squad to be upperclassmen—or upperclasswomen, in this case—and they've been working with a cheer coach who won several competitions with her team last year." He grabbed a loaf of bread and took four slices out, put them in the toaster and pushed the lever down.

"Your girls got a tip a couple of weeks ago that a college cheer coach was looking for a younger squad to work with, and they applied for and gained the position. So they've been working with a woman who coaches at the national level, and has a couple of world wins under her belt. I'd say your girls are going to upset the applecart when it comes to what the seniors wanted, because the woman they've been working with is good. Real good." He worked to remove the bacon from the skillet, placing them in a paper-lined plate sitting nearby.

"You just told your boy Todd—and I know he's not your boy, but whatever—that the seniors are so much better, there's no way they can't win, because he's got a bet on the side with his boys. Means he's going to lose his high school-sized shirt when he reneges on the bet, because he ain't got the cash to back his roll, and he's going to be persona-non-grata for the year. And the why of all this?" He started cracking eggs into a bowl, salted them, added a splash of milk, and beat them frothy, the clack of the metal whisk competing with the soft sizzling sound of the frying potatoes.

"He bragged he bagged your gal last year, started rumors and got her all upset, when in fact, she'd cut him down cold. Now she'll be on the varsity cheer squad, and he's gonna be circling the fringes of his friend group, flip-flopping the social dynamics." He glanced at her as he poured the scrambled egg mix into the bacon skillet, taking in the stunned expression on her face. "How'd I do?"

"I hate you sometimes."

He grinned at her then looked back down at the eggs, poking at the edges with his spatula. "I love you, too, baby girl."

"Do I even want to ask how?" He shook his head. "Or why?" He shook his head again. "You..." She had an accusing tone in her voice. "You're the one who fed the coach info to Michael, and he told Darlene who told me."

"And you ran with it. You were on the right track, looking to see who they were working with and where. All I did was give the info a push your direction. You got it, put together everything you needed to, and ran with it." He pulled out four more slices of bread, swapping out the toast with the untoasted when it popped up a second later. "That's pretty damned impressive, if you ask me."

Arms around his waist then, Nelda pressed a kiss between his shoulder blades. "I love you, Daddy mine."

He repeated his words from a moment ago, because they were still, and would ever be true. "Love you too, baby girl."

A few moments later it sounded like a herd of buffalo was traipsing down the stairs and he smiled at the noise and racket. This was what he'd wanted when he first saw the house. His family here, making it a home, and knowing it came with mess and arguments, with tears and laughter, with trust and love—made everything worth it.

Chapter Eleven
Retro

"Boss." Mudd yelled through the clubhouse for him, so Retro stuck his head in the back door and paused, because his second was as rattled as he'd ever seen him.

"'Sup, brother?"

Mudd changed trajectories and pointed to the closed office, then underscored that with a jerk of his head. Retro set his beer down and followed.

It had been three weeks since they'd returned from Louisiana, the kids had started back to school Monday, and tomorrow morning, Saturday, he'd planned on taking his family on the promised camping trip. Trina couldn't wait, and he'd laughed at her excitement. According to her, she'd never been camping before, not really, and he couldn't wait to introduce her to fucking au naturale.

When the door closed behind him, he frowned as Mudd reached to a shelf and took down a device they seldom had to use. There was a brief high-pitched hum and then silence. He pulled out his phone and checked, seeing the No Service message at the top of the display.

"What the fuck is so wrong we need to use the blocker?"

"Cartel's on the move."

"So." He shrugged. "That's Louisiana. We gather info and feed it to our allies there, and help out if needed. It's not dire news. That's just another Friday around here.'

"No, boss. They're transporting from Mobile to Nashville."

Retro froze. "The fuck they are not."

The cartel had been putting the squeeze on him for years, rolling forays into his territory that he responded to with force, driving them back to other places with less possessive dominants. He hated the drug trade, hated everything about it, hated it because it had taken Clara from him, took so much from so many. *Fuckers ridin' in on the backs of people who can't afford to pay rent, let alone buy smack.* It had become a personal mission to derail any and all attempts on the cartel's part to make a place for themselves within what he considered his. *Goddammit.* With other clubs facing the same issues, maybe it was time to do more than talk about the problem.

Mudd stepped to one of the screens and woke it, then navigated to a folder they had on a private cloud server. He clicked a link Retro recognized as one of the government feeds they'd used in the past, then toggled through a series of windows entering passphrases as he went, until he got to another folder. "This is from an hour ago." He opened up a sequence of images, and Retro took a moment to study them.

"Son of a *bitch*."

The images were of three sections of highway leading out of Mobile and up to Birmingham, and in them were shots of rental straight trucks with less-than-discrete escorts. He didn't have to see the drivers to know they'd be packing, and he didn't have to hear the communication between the groups to understand the strategy.

"Backtrack to the offload site?" He stared at one image, showing the top of a truck which had been painted with a middle finger emblem. *Fuck, it's almost like they knew we'd find these.* "Actually, nix that. What if you look over towards Meridian? There's some fucked-up shit happens there."

Mudd stared at him a moment, then nodded and used the mouse to manipulate folders again, backing out of where they were to a different directory, then diving deep until he found the right location. He opened and closed several folders, then changed the view to show thumbnails. Retro leaned in closer to the screen, scanning along line by line.

"There." He pointed. "And there." Another image. "Fucking hell, and there."

Mudd opened the images he'd indicated, and the screen was filled with pictures of more straight trucks, these with discrete escorts. Different names on the trucks, all coastal businesses, probably bought at auction to fit in better than the rentals.

"There. Now, see if we can backtrack to the offload site. These are the real transports, and this is what we'll hit. You do your thing." He motioned to the door. "I'm gonna make some calls, get help lined up for what we're gonna do."

"What are we gonna do, boss?" Mudd didn't look up, already working his way back through images and folders, layering them into a tracking software they used to map information like this. When Retro didn't respond right away, he looked up, gaze intense as it met Retro's.

"Gonna go to war."

***

"You rang?" Greg sauntered across the parking lot towards where Retro and his men had pulled to a stop. This was the first contact, and if things went the way Retro planned, Greg would handle the rest of the notifications going forwards. *I got my own shit to deal with*.

"Pooka." It didn't hurt to lead with the tidbit most likely to gain the man's full attention, and by the way his gaze jerked to where Retro was climbing off his bike, he'd done that. "Wanted to let you know what's about to go down." It had taken hours, but Mudd had found the place the cartel had docked their ship, and it was north of Mobile, way up in the farthest tendrils of Mobile Bay. "Courtesy call and all that."

"What is it you think I need to know, friend?" Retro nodded when Greg acknowledged their long association, and hoped it would stick. "You call out of the blue, after I haven't heard from you in weeks, and ask for a meet."

Retro let his mouth twist in a wry smile, because it had been less asking and more dictating when and where, but he'd give Greg that in the name of peace. "Found some unwelcome guests all up in our territory, thought I'd give you a heads-up before I do some evictin'." There was always the chance that the local mob family had joined forces with the Mexican cartel currently trucking millions of dollars of drugs through his territory, but he hoped for Greg's sake that wasn't in play. "So this is your notification. As of now, there are no routes through Bastards' territory. Zero, and that ain't likely to change, so if you know anyone in the market for one, they might as well set-up elsewhere."

"What routes you lookin' to shut down?" Greg's jaw ground back and forth, and Retro watched for a moment, tracking the red racing up the man's neck and into his face, cheeks blazing. "You wantin' a partner for this li'l project?"

Retro nodded at the loose confirmation there wasn't any collaboration between Greg's arm of the local mob and whoever the main drug lord was from Chihuahua. He'd rather have it in uncertain terms, so he asked, "So nothing to do with you?" Greg shook his head.

"Gonna need words, there, big boy. This ain't anything I'm willin' to fuck around with."

"No, if there's cartel routing through this region, it's not with our knowledge or permission." Greg propped one foot on the curb in front of Retro's bike. "That clear enough for you, friend?"

With what he knew to be a humorless smile on his face, Retro nodded. "Yeah, it is. Good." He stretched out a hand, accepting Greg's shake. "Well met, and I got a plan. You know I got a plan."

***

Trina

"Hey." Gary was out of the kitchen and standing behind the counter. "You got a call." He was holding out a cell phone, but it wasn't one she recognized, not the one Retro had given her all those weeks ago.

Tentatively she took the device, then lifted it to her ear. "Hello?" Her soft greeting was definitely a question, because the few people she'd talked to on the phone all knew not to call during her shift. Even if this would be one of the last she worked here at the diner, because she was set to start at the shop on Monday, something she still had a hard time believing because it sounded so fun. "This is Trina."

"Sweetkins." Only one person called her that, and Trina relaxed, blowing out her sudden anxiety on a long sigh.

"Dolph." Then she regained all that unease as sudden fear struck her. "What's happened to Mom?"

"Nothing, sweetkins. Your mama is fine. I've called you to talk about a different matter." As ever, his speech patterns were slightly stilted, illustrating that English wasn't his first language, but this sentence held more formality than he normally gave her. She'd heard him with his friends often enough to recognize this as his "serious" voice.

"What's wrong?" It couldn't be anything good, not if Dolph had somehow tracked down Gary's phone number to contact her. "I'm at work." Something he already knew, but she wanted to make a point. "You could have called the diner."

"I need you to take the phone and go out the back door."

"What?" Trina shook her head and turned to see Gary traipsing down towards her few occupied tables with a coffee carafe in hand. "I can't, I'm working."

"Gary will cover for you. He has already called in another waitress. Go out the back door, sweetkins. Please." His voice made her uneasy; it was tense, harsh and grave in a way she'd never heard it before and she instinctively followed his instructions, pushing through the pass-door into the kitchen.

"Dolph, what's wrong?" She opened her locker and took out the bag with her jeans and boots, slinging the strap over her shoulder. Him calling her sweetkins and then saying please was enough to make her trust whatever he was doing was for her best interests. Somehow, someway, what he was asking her to do would keep her safe. He'd done similar things when she still lived in Atlanta, and later she'd find she'd been out of harm's way when something violent happened.

Through the door and into the back lot, she stopped when she saw him leaning up against a large, black car. She disconnected the call and leaned back inside to place Gary's phone on the counter, then made her way to Dolph who had his arms out, waiting.

"What's wrong?" She mumbled this against his chest, because as he had all her life, Dolph greeted her with a tight hug that felt like it could right all wrongs. "Why are you here? Not that I'm not happy to see you, because it's been too long, but what's going on?"

"Your man—" She stiffened and he laughed dryly. "Yes, I know much about many things, and one of those is always my sweetkins. But this is more important than me knowing something you kept secret for your own reasons." None of her calls home to her mother had talked about the changes. It felt too new, too fragile, and she'd wanted to keep it close for a while. "Your man has put things into motion that makes you a target. He doesn't know this, but I do. So I will keep you safe."

"What do you mean?" She pulled away and put distance between them, knowing she'd displeased him by the frown, but for once not caring. All her life, Dolph had always been like family to her, and as an honorary uncle and her mother's best friend, she trusted him completely, but his words right now didn't make sense.

"He has enemies. You must know this." A statement not a question, because Dolph knew she was smart. And Trina had figured it out just by Retro's lifestyle, her first stumbling attempts to address the biker part of the equation had been abandoned as unnecessary, because everything Retro did said he expected something at any time. He was always armed, sometimes with more than one gun. He always traveled with at least two other men, surveyed his surroundings constantly, and ducked off into closed rooms for conversations. She knew him, knew the man, and knew his morals—so she trusted that whatever he was into, whatever the club did that had him always on edge, wasn't something that would make her run if she knew. She'd hoped he'd trust her with time, and had been waiting it out. So yes, she knew he had to have enemies, just by his actions. Having it confirmed didn't give her any satisfaction right now, because it was Dolph and not Retro telling her.

When she didn't answer, Dolph continued as he reached to open the vehicle's back door. "He has initiated a plan to push those enemies from his territory. This will have consequences. I will make certain you are not one of those, because his enemies know you matter to him." He gestured impatiently. "Get in the car, Trina." Then he paused and when she didn't move, added softly, "Please."

"I'll get in, but you'll tell me everything." He nodded. "And I'm calling Retro first, so he knows where I am." He nodded again and she dug around in her bag until she unearthed her phone.

The ringing in her ear stopped and she heard Retro's voice. "Hey."

She'd opened her mouth to respond, but when it clicked and beeped she realized she'd be speaking to his voice mail. "Hi. I'm leaving the diner early. My mom's friend," a pained expression swept over Dolph's face at that, but she didn't have time to think about it right now, "Dolph is here and he's picking me up. He said something's happening, and it's to keep me safe. I'll call again soon, but whatever's going on, *I'm safe*." She emphasized those last two words, and repeated them as surety. "I'm safe, and I love you."

Dolph's head lifted abruptly and for an instant she was reminded of Retro when something was happening just out of sight and he wanted to be sure what it was. "Get in the car." A vehicle backfired somewhere nearby and he barked, "Now, Katrina."

She scrambled for the door, lunging inside with her bag, phone in hand, and he slammed it shut behind her. A moment later had him in the driver seat, and she suddenly realized they weren't alone in the car. There were two men she didn't recognize, one in the front seat, and one in the back beside her. "Dolph?" She hated the way her voice shook. "What's going on?"

"These are friends, and they will help me keep you safe, and hopefully keep your man alive."

***

Retro

He looked to where Mudd stood and got a nod in response. His phone buzzed and he glanced down to see a voice mail notification. Someone must have called while he was talking to Twisted and Wrench, coordinating final details for the joint operation about to get underway. Mudd had been on the horn with Greg, and that single nod meant things were beginning to play out.

The plan was simple and complex all in the same breath. Under Greg's direction, the mob would intercept the trucks already north of the city. They'd been able to track and trace all routes used over the past week, so Retro could say with confidence what the best play was there. Greg agreed, and they'd be en route now to confiscate the trucks and their contents, with all necessary force.

Retro and his men would do the same with the trucks that hadn't yet hit the city. Ignoring what he felt were lures, the trap trucks, they'd been able to do the same course tracing for the Meridian to Birmingham path. He and his men were positioned close to the truckstop the cartel used to change drivers, every time. *Shouldn't have been so predictable.*

Twisted and Wrench would hit the boat location, collecting all information they could on where the initial shipping had happened, because that was outside of the Bama Bastards' normal information network. Then they'd torch the boat and any product left inside. The rough estimates for the cartel losses from today's work would be in the ten million area, and would be a big enough setback that everyone agreed there would be a pause in activity, then the cartel would probably find a different distribution route in the future. *In one fell swoop, we'll clean it up for my kids' lives, please, God.*

Mudd called, "We ready, boss?"

Shoving the phone deep into his pocket, Retro reached up to tie the bandana over the bottom of his face, helmet going on next. A moment later he nodded. "Fuck yeah, we're rollin'." On his bike, he took a moment to gaze around, marking every man who rode alongside him. There was every chance one or more wouldn't be going home to family tonight, and he thought of Trina and his kids. *Do my fuckin' best.* He nodded and pulled out, knowing without watching that his men followed him.

In less than fifteen minutes, just as they approached the turnoff for the truck stop, he spotted a dozen cop cars or more, wailing as they turned into the drive, lights and sirens blowing any pretense of stealth apart. *What the fuck?* Instead of following them in, he changed lanes quickly and whipped his line of bikes into the parking lot of the convenience store across the highway. They ranged along the edge of the lot, facing the truck stop and without a word passing among them watched as the police fell onto the trucks the club was there to commandeer. *Fucking son of a bitch.*

Then Retro's blood ran cold as the backs of the trucks opened, men spilling out in unexpected numbers. His breath came short as he heard shouts, bursts of orders yelled over screaming responses, and then the men from the trucks opened fire. In a few moments it was over, no chance for him or his men to ride to the rescue before the cops came out from behind their cars and stood over the motionless bodies lying on the tarmac.

One of the escorts tried to get away by driving over the curb and out into a field, where the vehicle promptly sunk to the frame. From the way the men crawled out of the windows under the watchful eyes of officers with weapons drawn, it looked like the doors were unable to open, held closed by the soft dirt. Sucked in by the promise of solid ground, only to find treacherous footing instead.

Cuffed and no doubt divested of their weaponry, the remaining dark-haired men from the trucks and escort vehicles were placed in rows, lined up in full view of where Retro sat.

"Intel was wrong." He pushed the words out, feeling like his chest had caved in on itself. If they hadn't been cut off by the police, he would have lost more than one or two men. The quick head count he'd done told him they would have been outnumbered three to one, faced with a deadly surprise of disposable soldiers hiding in the back of the trucks, when they'd expected drugs instead. He turned his head to look at Mudd over the bandana, seeing he was as pale as Retro felt. "That's some shit."

"That's some good luck shit."

Retro nodded. "It is, but not sure we need to sit around and watch them get bagged. In fact, I'm gonna vote no, and say let's roll back to the house. Mudd, go ahead and get on the horn to your folks, make sure they aren't fucked like this. I'll tag mine." Mudd nodded and the two men dug their phones out. It took Retro three attempts, but he finally connected with someone who had a clue about what was going on down by Mobile Bay, and knew it was all favorable to report at the moment. "Leveled" was the word used when he asked about the shipping compound. He hung up feeling better.

Mudd looked relieved, lines around his eyes less pronounced. "Other arm of things went as planned. No surprises there. Makes a body wonder what the fuck happened here, don't it?"

He huffed out a breath and opened his mouth to respond then remembered the voice mail waiting, and held up a finger. There were two now, the first Trina, and her words left him breathless with fear, like he'd been punched in the gut. "She's safe? What the fuck does that mean, she's safe? Mudd, who the hell is this Dolph character? Did we get any intel on anyone with that name?" He remembered now. Trina had mentioned him in passing before, but Retro had misplaced the info until now. "A friend of Trina's family, that's all I got." Before Mudd answered, the second message started playing and now his blood wasn't ice, it was boiling.

"Retro, you do not know me, but we have a common interest in keeping Katrina safe. I have her at your home, with your kids, and you should come have a conversation with me." A pause before the deep, accented voice continued with, "Soon."

He held the phone, listening to the automated prompts to delete, or save, or change greetings, and when it started the third round of the same toneless voice saying the same toneless words, he disconnected the call and stared at the phone. This didn't happen, a new player in town that he didn't know about. Someone pulling strings around him, without his knowledge.

"If it's to do with Trina, that's got to be Dolph Chulpayev. Boss, he's big-time Russian mafia. He *is* Atlanta when it comes to their operations. Big cheese in the region. What's going on? We've had too many surprises today already."

"I do not disagree." He looked at Mudd. "Man is at my house, with my woman and kids."

"*Fuuucck*." That came from Crazy Mike, who sat his bike just past Mudd, listening in as he stayed focused on the proceedings across the highway.

"Yep." Pulling the bandana down below his chin, he turned to Marlin on his other side. "I find it suspect that we were being set up, and then were saved from the setup, and now there's this big toad in the system sittin' at my house. How about you?" He got a slow nod in response. "Fucking hell." Blowing out another breath, he told them through gritted teeth, "Everything in me wants to go racing in and deal with it, because that's my woman and kids, but I cain't have this, man. What I do can't follow me home, I've seen that...had that before. I cain't have my kids living with the fear of that. Gonna call Trina, test the waters." He looked back at Mudd. "You call Greg. Ask him straight out about this man—what he's capable of. Fuck, they're probably cousins or some shit." Hands shaking, insides shaking, voice shaking, he confessed to his brothers. "I cain't sit here much longer, cain't keep it together, man. Cain't."

"Call Trina, talk to her, talk to the kids, and we'll ride, boss. We'll follow you into hell if needed." Agreement from the line of men had Retro bowing his head. "Call her, Jerry. Make the call."

Her phone scarcely rang before Trina's voice filled his ear and Retro had to stifle a gasp of tiny relief. He'd been afraid the man Dolph would answer, would hold information hostage as he was holding Retro's family.

Afraid of the answer to the questions burning in his gut: Is she safe? Were they unharmed?

"Retro, are you okay? Is everything okay?" Terror made her voice tremble and he had to swallow hard to get words past the immediate lump in his throat.

"I'm okay. Baby, what's going on? Are you okay? My kids? Are you safe?" Eyes closed, he listened to her breathe, rasping contrast against the calm sounds in the background, and somewhere not too far away he heard Nelda laugh, the sound light and free. "What's going on?"

"Yes, we're fine. Nelda's making Dolph and his men"—*his men*—"something to eat. The boys are in the pool, and there are two men outside, making sure they are okay." *Dolph plus two, how many more?* "Please, Retro, please. Are you okay? He is being annoyingly tightlipped about whatever the danger was, so I've been terrified for you. I knew since we were all here, it had to be you."

"How many men does he have there? What did he tell you?" He forced himself to pull in a breath. "Trina, are you really okay? What's happened?"

She sounded puzzled, whether at his continued questions or the tone of his voice, but she gave him enough to ease his heart, at least. "Only two men, Alex and Tony. The kids were home when we got here, so there's been no disruption to their day. I'm okay. There was apparently a shooting at the diner right after we left, and Dolph assumes it was aimed at me, for some reason. He said you have enemies, and had set a clock ticking, and was moving me out of the way. I don't know what any of that means, Retro, but I trust Dolph. I've known him my entire life, and he's never let me down." Her voice was shaking now, and Retro squeezed his eyes shut.

"I'm coming home now, Trina. I'll be there in minutes, and I want to meet this Dolph. Be safe until I get there, yeah?" He waited but she didn't respond; instead, he heard Nelda laugh again, followed by a deep rumbling sound of a man's voice. "Answer me, honey. Tell me you'll be safe."

"I'll be here, and safe. Of course, of course." She blew a kiss into the phone and then was gone without a goodbye.

"This Dolph has Trina and my kids at home. He got her out of the diner just before there was a shooting, which seems about the same kind of coincidence as that"—he gestured across the road where the mass of police cars had doubled, a barred-window bus pulling in now—"does, which is to say not at all. I'm riding home. You boys—" He swung to look at the line on either side. "—should do the same. Check on your folks. If word of what we were doing leaked out somehow, and they went after my family…" He paused to swallow down the curse words that wanted to leap out. "No reason for them to go after family at all, but just go home, hold your hearts in your hands tonight. I'll call if I need you."

"Fuck that noise." Crazy Mike started his bike and Retro stared at him. "Following you, Prez." His shout was echoed by the men around them.

Retro bowed his head, humbled by the depths of loyalty in his men. "No, brother. I appreciate it, but you should go home." Mike shook his head, followed by Mudd's head swinging back and forth. "Dammit. Do as you're told." Another set of headshakes, and he dipped his chin, gut churning to already be in the wind. "Then let's get this over with, so you can be with your family."

"Boss," Einstein called from Marlin's other side and Retro turned to look at him. "In case you missed the goddamned memo, you *are* our family."

Chapter Twelve

Trina

She stood at the doors leading from the kitchen to the patio and watched Nelda try to flirt with one of the men standing near the pool. From his stance she wasn't making any headway, and Trina wanted to smile at her antics. Wanted to, but failed. Nelda didn't have any clue what had happened, and that was as it should be. Retro hadn't answered any of her questions, but she had an idea from the breaking news coverage on the wall-mounted TV behind her.

"Katrina." Dolph stood behind and slightly to the side, and instead of turning as she knew he'd prefer, she watched his reflection in the glass doors. "Everything is fine. You know that. I would do anything to keep you safe." This was his non-answer to her repeated question of what he'd done. She'd gone over and over his words to her at the diner, not finding anything of substance she could hang her fears on.

"You speak of enemies as if it's a given. What kind of life do you think Retro lives to have enemies?"

"He is not without influence in the region."

"But what happened today—" She paused and angled her head, listening, but what had sounded encouragingly like bikes in the distance had faded away. "What happened to cause you to decide to make the drive to Birmingham without calling, and then come and whisk me away from work?" She gestured towards the TV. "Is the shooting at the diner connected with that?" There was drone footage of a massive police sting currently underway. Truckloads of illegal weapons confiscated at a local truck stop, dozens of people arrested on drug and weapons charges, mention made of suspected trafficking of another kind making the too-polite news anchors mince words into tiny pieces.

When they'd rounded the corner from the back of the diner, Trina had realized what she'd thought were muffler backfires had actually been gunfire. Two men had been lying on the parking lot in front of the building, the windows spiderwebbed with cracks from ballistic impacts. The news called it an altercation, suggesting the two dead men had been arguing. That seemed too tidy, and she didn't trust the news to report on anything more than was fed to them. Dolph had been on the phone nonstop in the car, his conversations muffled by the acoustics inside the vehicle, but she imagined him conducting some kind of coverup. It was just too much to believe he felt her in danger, came miles and miles to rescue her, just when two men shot each other in front of where she worked. Had worked, because she knew even if she'd wanted to keep up with a shift or two, Retro would veto it now.

"Your man—"

"Retro." She interrupted him, letting her irritation show in her voice. It wasn't the first time she'd firmly corrected him and asked him to use Retro's name. Saying "your man" like it was a position and not a person riled up her possessive instincts. "His name is Retro, or Jerry if you aren't comfortable with the club version."

"Retro should be the one to explain." Dolph stepped up beside her and looked out at the pool. "This is a good life, Katrina. Why haven't you said anything to your mama?"

She lifted her chin. "I told her about him. Once. The next time I called she'd forgotten already." She shrugged. "Until she meets him, until she comes to visit, it wouldn't be real to her and would make her anxious."

"You're a good daughter." He stroked the back of her head then gripped her neck and pulled her close so he could kiss her temple.

"She's a good mother." She shrugged and stepped sideways, uncomfortable around him for the first time in her life. "Why are you here, Dolph?"

"I have family in the area." That was it, the sum total of his explanation and she shook her head.

"Not good enough."

"No, it's not." Retro's voice came from behind her and she whirled with a cry. He didn't look at her as she ran to him, gaze fixed firmly on the man she'd left standing by the door. "Not nearly good enough." He caught her and swayed back and forth, arms wrapped around her, and whispered beside her ear, "Scared the fuck outta me, gettin' that message like I did. You sure you're okay, baby?"

"Yes." She pushed certainty into her voice. "We're all okay." Footsteps behind him had her head up and she stared at the mass of men crowding into the short hallway that led from the living room to the kitchen. "Mudd, Mike, Marlin, Einstein..." She nodded at the rest of them. "Is everyone okay?"

Mudd offered her a wry smile, his eyes like Retro's, not moving away from Dolph.

"Yeah, everyone's okay. Everyone." She turned in Retro's arms to look at Dolph. He'd pulled himself up tall, broad shoulders filling the glass of the doors. He looked *more* than she'd ever seen him, larger and extra commanding somehow. "Pooka sends his regards, Uncle Dolph. He'll be here in a few."

With a twisted smile, Dolph nodded. "Well met, Jeremiah Rogers." He stepped towards them, hand out, "I am Dolph—"

"Chulpayev, yeah I know. What I don't know and would give your left testicle to know, is what the fuck you're doin' in *my* town, in my *house*, with *my* woman and kids." Retro shifted, legs in a wide stance as he released her, moving her behind him where Mudd gripped her arm and put her behind him, then another man, until suddenly, there were half a dozen men between her and where Retro stood. Over the shoulders of the men, she saw black leather through the windows, saw a dozen or more men approach the pool, watched as Dolph's men lifted their hands shoulder-high, heads swiveling towards the house. Tension vibrated through everyone, and she realized there was a very real danger here today, and it wasn't Dolph and his men.

This is what Retro is, she reminded herself. *This is what he does. Whatever's needed to take care of his own, and I'm his.* Before she could think of anything to defuse the situation, Dolph spoke, and the rug was yanked out from under her.

* * *

Retro

He watched the man in front of him stiffen at the sounds outside, but Dolph didn't turn to see. Didn't look away from this stare down they had going on, and that was fine by him. The longer the man stalled, the safer his family would be, the meeting now controlled by BBMC and not some nameless, faceless muscles standing around his goddamned kitchen and pool.

"You know who I am?" More of a statement than a question, but Retro still nodded. "Then you know why I'm here."

"Not sure that's a true statement, my friend." He noted the slight jolt at the word and wondered if Dolph expected anything else. "Might wanna lay it out for me, simple like, given I'm just a poor country boy from Alabama. Not a high roller from Georgia." Dolph's lips twitched at that and Retro nodded. *Yeah, that's right, I know more than I'm saying.* His call to Greg had given him more info than he could process at the time, but he'd had the whole ride home to think and consider, and plan. Which got him here in his house, with the upper hand in all ways, and Dolph probably knew it.

"This is not how I wanted things to be told." Dolph's quiet complaint didn't matter, and Retro shook his head.

"Might shoulda said something before now, in that case. You left it decades late, man."

"Things are...complicated." Eyes narrowed, Dolph lifted one shoulder. "You're going to ask when are they ever not, and I know. I *know*. But I liked being who I was with them." Retro didn't respond, just stared until Dolph sighed heavily. "I'm Katrina's father, as you no doubt already know." The tiniest gasp from behind him said Trina was still within earshot, as he'd intended. *She deserves to know everything.* "Her mother is my light, my love. And she was targeted by people who wanted to hurt me, much as these men today intended to strip you of your love. Deloris lived, but was changed, so very changed...and yet life went on."

"You let her think they were alone." Not an accusation, but an echo of the pain he'd heard in Trina's voice as she'd talked about her life with her mother. "Played the part of family friend, without telling her the pedigree of her blood. Without telling her the truth of what might someday happen." Part of the play today had been to eliminate Trina, knowing it would enrage Dolph and cripple Retro. That was a piece of what Greg had gleaned from his enthusiastic questioning of the men he'd taken captive. "Today wasn't on me, and yet you told her it was my enemies who were targeting her. Put me out there as the bad guy, all while you set yourself up to save the day. That's a jackass move, man. Not a fan of jackasses."

"Yes." Nothing more, just the bald declaration and that pissed Retro off.

"Yes? Fuckin' *yes*? Like there's not a world of explanations owed this woman behind me? Like there's not years upon years of lies you need to make up for? Goddamn, man, you're fucked in the head if you think I'll let you be around my woman if you're not willing to man the fuck up and sort your shit right here and now." He lifted a fist and pounded his chest, keeping tempo with his heart.

"You got to watch your girl grow up into a woman, and I want to do that with my own daughter. By being here today, you've set a larger target on this house than I could ever manage on my own. My contacts"—after talking to Greg, he'd called a couple more folks, picking their brains and had found a surprising connection he would never have guessed at—"tell me that you know Petr Volkov. And that means you probably know my place in his saga. Man saw *his* daughter killed, dying in the prime of her life, cut down by his enemies, who have moved on and are now your enemies. And now, by putting yourself into my goddamned fuckin' business, they will probably be mine, too. I got a woman, a girl, two boys, and please God, more kids to come, and from where I stand, you've put all that at risk." Retro shook his head. "Well, fuck that. Fuck that goddamned *hard*, man. I do not abide someone who doesn't consider the consequences of their motherfuckin' actions. I do not abide someone who doesn't own up to their own bullshit. And, Dolph, I cannot find it in my gut to abide you. So take your partners, and get the fuck off my place."

"I saved you today." Dolph lifted his lip. "With a single call, I saved your men so they go home to their families tonight. Are you throwing that away?"

"Someone set us up in the first place, and I got nothing that tells me that wasn't you." Retro shrugged. "Easy to stop a play when you're the origin." He inclined forwards slightly, chin thrust out as he gritted from clenched teeth. "I do not abide. Get the fuck out."

Dolph stared at him for a long minute. Retro could nearly see him considering and rejecting ideas or things to say, and was surprised when after everything he'd said, the man admitted something that could damn him in even Trina's eyes.

"My family is dangerous. Enemies go back generations, slights and insults festering over time to become deadly feuds. And now our business is under attack from abroad, and not our normal competition within the brotherhood of the bratva. Your reputation is considerable, and I knew you would work with your friends across state lines to eradicate the threat. It was no mistake those images found their way to your hands. It was no mistake that Pooka, as you call him, has cultivated a true friendship with you. It pays to befriend those who fight on the same side as oneself, and he's always been a smart boy." Retro didn't bother to smother the low rumble of disgust that rolled out of him. "Yes, I know how it feels to find your strings have been pulled. Not nice, not good, but as much as you may vow it will never again happen, it will. It happens to me. My mistake was not talking frequently enough to Katrina. Not following the line of inquiry after I heard you had a new woman in your life. My mistake was in knowing too much about one thing, and not enough about another."

"Would it have changed what you did?" Shuffling feet behind him marked Trina's passage through his men until she again stood at his shoulder. "If you had known, how would that have changed things?"

"I would have…" Dolph trailed off and shook his head. "It would have been handled differently."

"You're my father?" Her voice wavered and Retro slipped an arm around her shoulders, keeping silent because this was Trina's to discover. He'd already played a larger part than he'd like in the reveal, but as when he'd seen Landry's pictures and known, the gut punch felt when he'd caught sight of Dolph, the male version of Trina's features, there'd been no question in his mind the information had to be laid bare. *She's suffered enough, thinking her mother abandoned.* This was Dolph's chance to lay a foundation, if Trina would allow it. "Really?"

"Yes, sweetkins."

Sounds fractured through the middle with pain, she breathed a wispy echo of his word. "Sweetkins." Trina leaned hard against Retro's side. "I need a bit to come to grips with that." Honest and bold in her words, she shook in Retro's grip and his heart broke for what she must be thinking. He could almost feel the effort it took her to say, "If you're done here. I'd like you to go." *She needs steady.* Retro brought her in front of him, wrapping his arms around her protectively. *I can give her that.* "I'll call, Dolph."

"Do you promise me?" Now Dolph's voice was the one shaking and Trina nodded.

"Yes. I promise."

***

"Well, that was a fuckin' story and a half." Twisted's words didn't convey the anger his face did and Retro winced. "Woulda been nice to know you were fuckin' tied to the fuckin' mob, brother."

He sighed and lifted his hand, middle-finger first as he flipped the camera off. "Pages within books within libraries, you know?" He shrugged. "I didn't know Clara's father was mob until right about the time she got shot. I didn't know I had a kid that was practically neighbors with you. And—" He snorted a laugh at Twisted's eye-roll. "Fuck off, man. I didn't know Trina was tied up with mob, either. They seem to haunt me, yeah?"

"Yeah, it's practically a funhouse all up in your life there, brother. Fun fuckin' house." That was Wrench from off camera on Twisted's end of the call, where he'd stalked out of range while Retro was explaining what'd happened back in Alabama while they'd been taking down the boat dock and trucking company.

"There's gonna be more." Po'Boy thumped the table hard enough to shake the camera on their end as he shook his head. "This won't be the end of it."

"Prolly not." Retro looked around him at each man in the room. "We'll stand." He nodded. "We will fuckin' stand."

"We always do," Einstein grinned at him.

"Yeah, we do."

***

Einstein

He pulled into the driveway in front of his house, making quick work of the three-point turnaround needed to back in beside his wife's car. It was dark in the house, not surprising since it was later than he'd expected to get home. *Least I'm home.* He sighed as he parked and climbed off, placing his helmet upside down on the short passenger backrest.

A sound from down the street made him pause and listen, but whatever it was didn't repeat, so he used his key to enter the house. A dim light over the sink lit the kitchen, and he smiled to see the carefully covered plate waiting for him on top of the stovetop. They'd been together nearly seven years, and this was something he would never get used to, the way Lauren wanted to take care of him. A warm sense of approval and desire swept over him. *God, I love her.*

The TV was on in the other room, sound low so to not wake their daughter. He thought for a moment about Retro's speech earlier, and how it had resonated with him. The reason he'd left Philly and come back to his wife's roots was exactly that. Wanting better for his daughter than he could offer her there.

Now if they'll just leave me the fuck alone.

He grabbed a can of beer from the fridge, and was still seeing stars from the bright light when he walked into the living room. That didn't keep him from seeing his wife, terrified eyes trained on him over the gag that kept her quiet. On the couch next to her sat his old president, the man who had singlehandedly run him out of his previous club, not taking his patches easily, but requiring a brutal beatout, all of which had paved the way for where he was now.

"Hello, motherfucker." Heavily accented, the words grated through the air, slicing through parts of a good life he had believed safe from this. "You might wanna rethink that." The man pointed to the hand Einstein had hovering over the gun on his hip. "Hella welcome for an old friend. We're still friends, right? It's always good to keep men like me close, don't you think? Make sure you have the right people at your back, ones not afraid to do what it takes to handle problems?" The man grinned, gap-toothed and arrogant as ever. "Yano. Dangerous people?"

He was wrong, the most dangerous man in the room wasn't him.

It was Einstein.

FINI

THANK YOU FOR READING *TRAPPED BY FATE ON RECKLESS ROADS*!

In this story, Penny and Twisted play host to Retro's kids for a few weeks in the summer. They had more than one cookout, but here are Jimmy and Saya's favorites from those evenings that happened off-screen.

Penny's Cajun Barbeque Shrimp

- 1 cup unsalted butter
- 4-5 cloves garlic, chipped
- 1 medium tomato, thin skinned works best
- 1 lemon, juiced and quartered
- 2 tablespoons Worcestershire sauce
- 1 bay leaf
- 3 tablespoons Creole spices *
- 1 1/2 pounds shrimp, peeled and deveined
- 1 baguette, sliced

- This recipe is enough for a family of four. Of course, if you're making enough to feed the clubhouse, you gonna have to double it, but be careful to make batches about that size to ensure the butter is done right.
- In a medium cast-iron pan over low heat, melt butter with the garlic, lemon juice, tomato, Cajun seasonings, Worcestershire sauce, and bay leaf. Keep at a slow simmer until the tomato cooks down to just pulp and juice. Remove skins as desired. Remove the bay leaf before adding shrimp.
- Increase heat and immediately add shrimp, cooking a couple minutes each side. Stir frequently.
- Add lemon wedges last minute or two, stir well.
- Serve over sliced bread, or other base preferred like rice or fried potatoes.

Twisted's Slow Cooker Red Beans and Sausage

- 1 pound dried red beans
- 1 pound andouille sausage, sliced and cooked
- 1 tablespoon oil
- 1 large onion, diced
- 1 green pepper, seeded and diced
- 1 cup celery, diced
- 3 tablespoons Creole spices*
- 6 cups chicken broth
- 6 cups cooked rice

- Soak beans, rinsing and changing water a couple of times.
- Brown the sausage over medium heat with the oil. Add onion, green pepper, and celery. Stir frequently, cook until the onion is translucent.
- Combine beans, sausage mix, and seasonings in a large slow cooker. Add broth and stir. Cook covered, 8-10 hours on low, or until beans are tender.
- For a thicker dish, mash up a couple cups of the cooked mix and return to the slow cooker and stir.
- Serve over rice.

Nelda's Bread Pudding with Whisky Sauce

Pudding
- 6 cups cubed bread pieces
- 1 quart full-fat milk
- 3 large eggs
- 2 cups white sugar
- 2 tablespoons vanilla
- 3 tablespoons melted butter

Sauce
- 1 cup sugar
- 1/2 cup butter

- 1 egg, beaten
- 2 oz whisky to taste

- Soak bread in milk until soggy. 5 minutes or so is usually ample.
- Add eggs, sugar, vanilla, and stir well.
- Drizzle butter in baking dish, spread evenly.
- Add bread and bake about 45 minutes, until puffed and firm to the touch.

While that's cooking, start your sauce.

- Combine sugar and butter in top of a double boiler and bring to a slow, rolling boil until sugar is completely dissolved.
- Drop tablespoon of sugar mix into beaten egg and whisk, then add egg mix to the pan and cook, stirring constantly until thick.
- Remove from heat and allow to cool slightly.
- Stir in whisky to taste.
- Remove pudding from oven and cool, then spoon into serving dishes.
- Top pudding with sauce and serve immediately.

Creole Spices

Want to make your own creole spices? Easy 'nuff:

- Combine a quarter teaspoon each of onion powder and garlic powder. Add a dash or more of oregano, basil, thyme, black pepper, white pepper, cayenne pepper, and paprika. Salt to taste.

Enjoy!

RETRO'S PLAYLIST

Retro's music surprised me in many ways, because it was more country than I expected, but of course, includes many old school selections:

Retro's playlist: bit.ly/ntnt-recklessroads-playlist

ABOUT THE AUTHOR

Raised in the south, MariaLisa learned about the magic of books at an early age. Every summer, she would spend hours in the local library, devouring books of every genre. Self-described as a book-a-holic, she says "I've always loved to read, but then I discovered writing, and found I adored that, too. For reading...if nothing else is available, I've been known to read the back of the cereal box."

Also by MariaLisa deMora

Alace Sweets

A dark thriller, this book is not a light read. Filled with edge-of-your-seat suspense, this intense story commands the reader's attention as it drives towards the explosive ending. Alace Sweets is a vigilante serial killer, with everything that implies and is sure to trip all your triggers. Be ready.

At seventeen, Alace Sweets turned a corner in her life, taking the wrong shortcut home from school.

Resisting the harsh knowledge her attackers will never be made to pay for their actions, Alace takes a stand. Justice must be served, and if fate's scales are out of balance, she's determined to set things right as best she can.

When the laws of men fail, the rules of Alace prevail.

5-Star Reviews for Alace Sweets

"deMora has a superb story-line and exceptional character development. All of her characters have such depth that will intrigue the reader..."
~Turning Another Page

"Hot, sweet, dark thriller."
~Beth D

"It will keep you on the edge of your seat and give you chills."
~Escape Reality Book Blog

"Disturbing, haunting, sickly; yet hot, sexy and heart racing!"
~Amanda L

"From the first page [deMora] pulls you into the world she has created and you do not even try to escape..."
~Little Shop of Readers Blog

"A must read for all those dark, gritty romance fans out there."
~Sweet & Spicy Reads

"You will find yourself so drawn into the story that the outside world is blocked out and your locking the doors and turning on all the lights."
~Danena F

"Don't judge me for bonding with a vigilante serial killer, she's more than what she does."
~iScream Books

"Thrilling...chilling...full of suspense, nail biting edge of your seat excitement."
~Tracey H

"Every time MariaLisa deMora picks up her pen (or opens her computer), she creates characters you want to believe in."
~Gail S

"Intriguing dark storyline, beautiful love story and nail-biting conclusion, what more could a reader ask for?"
~Manda M

"This book takes you a dark and twisted ride that is gripping..."
~Renee Entress' Blog

"This book is dark and gritty and I literally had to take a day off from reading it because it's that intense."
~My Girlfriend's Couch

"This is my favourite book so far from this author ... I recommend this book if you enjoy dark romantic thrillers."
~Cheekypee Reads and Reviews

"There's not enough stars to give this book and 5 just doesn't really do it justice!"

~DeLane C

"I couldn't put this book down from page one! Tried to stop and go to bed but couldn't sleep thinking about Alace, and got up and finished the book."
~Debbie M

"MariaLisa DeMora, wordsmith that she is, made this a story of the enlightenment of a woman and finding love in a life where she has had none."
~Kat W

"Whatever deep dark trench [deMora] pulled a character like Alace from should be revisited again and often."
~Confessions of a Serial Reader

ADDITIONAL SERIES AND BOOKS

Please note that books in a series frequently feature characters from additional books within that series. If those books are read out of order, readers will twig to spoilers for the other stories, so going back to read the skipped titles won't have the same angsty reveals.

Rebel Wayfarers MC series:

Mica, #1
A Sweet & Merry Christmas, #1.5
Slate, #2
Bear, #3
Jase, #4
Gunny, #5
Mason, #6
Hoss, #7
Harddrive Holidays, #7.5
Duck, #8
Biker Chick Campout, #8.5
Watcher, #9
A Kiss to Keep You, #9.25

More information available at mldemora.com.

www.ingramcontent.com/pod-product-compliance
Lightning Source LLC
Chambersburg PA
CBHW070046030726
47506CB00002B/370